D0982510

Books by Richard Condon

The Oldest Confession
The Manchurian Candidate
Some Angry Angel
A Talent for Loving
An Infinity of Mirrors
Any God Will Do

Any God Will Do

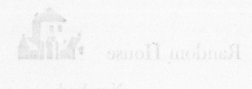

Random House
New York

Random House

New York

Any God Will Do

Richard Condon

First Printing

Typography and binding design by Victoria Dudley

For Harold Matson

Any God Will Do

Interest is the key to life,
Interest in the clue,
Interest is the drum and fife
And any God will do.

—The Keeners' Manual

Chapter 1

When he heard the shot in Mr. Hibbert's office, Francis Vollmer saw his future flash before his eyes. It was an indistinct vision, as the outline of a lovely body might be seen under fur, but he understood its encouragement and agreed with its meaning. His yellow eyes flickered in his bony face. He sat motionless while he confirmed the sound.

Outside the bank, at 6:05 P.M. on a rainy Saturday afternoon, Broad Street was deserted. Aside from the watchmen, Francis and Mr. Hibbert had been the only two people in the building. Francis' office was directly next to Mr. Hibbert's, facing Broad Street. It was an angular, narrow office, with many burglar-proof files and steel furniture. Mr. Hibbert had permitted no one to share the office with Francis; his secretary, Miss Emmaline Mechanic, worked across the corridor in the open bull pen.

There had been no warning for the shot. As ungraceful as it might seem for a bank president to shoot himself in his own bank, Francis knew that Mr. Hibbert, the son, grandson and great-grandson of bankers, had taken it as his right, as a Pharaoh or a Viking chief would have done, to die at the crest of his mountain of money.

Francis' thoughts wandered onward, brushing veils aside, to the significance to himself of Mr. Hibbert's death. At last the time had come for him to learn the secret of his identity. He and Mr. Hibbert had understood mutually that Mr. Hibbert's lips must remain sealed in life, but death brought truth. Very soon, somewhere in Europe, most likely in England, they would learn that Mr. Hibbert was dead and therefore had revealed the secret of Francis' birth, as it had been intended he do. Very soon, knowing that he knew, They would summon him to them. It made Francis' mind tilt, almost buckle.

Motionless in his chair for seconds after the shot, Francis reminded himself that he too was a banker who had spent most of his life seated at the right hand of the president of a great bank whose total resources exceeded $775,493,531, as of its annual statement which had been published two days before, on December 31st, 1918; with deposits on the same date totaling $583,786,091; and, in comparison to the annual statement of the previous year, showed increases in resources of $114,758,235 and in total deposits of $49,504,116.

Every night since Mr. Hibbert had taken him out of the orphanage, from the age of fourteen until twenty-one, Francis had written fifty times: "I am a banker." Though Mr. Hibbert had sponsored him, he had not been able to adopt him for reasons which they both fully understood without ever once discussing it. Mr. Hibbert had made Francis his personal office boy with the intention of creating a perfect banker.

Francis' respect for Mr. Hibbert overcame him. He had been one of the men who had led his nation through a victorious war from a post behind his desk, using the powers of his signature as a mighty weapon. And what a war it had been, Francis exulted. In England one field marshal, one admiral and six generals had been elevated to the peerage because of it. What a way to begin the New Year! Haig and Beatty had become earls at the touch of a sword. Earls! If the United States had known how to honor its heroes, Mr. Hibbert would have been at least a duke. A banker's honor was the greatest honor; it was higher than the healer's because money healed; higher than the teacher's because money taught. A banker was exalted above all priests because money was the truest religion; more powerful than the captains and the kings because money survived them—as it had now survived Mr. Hibbert. A banker was the steward of all things to which men turned.

Francis stood up. He was a tall, modishly slender man in a dark suit. He checked the position of the knot in his tie, then walked into Mr. Hibbert's room.

It was a glorious room for dying. A Gainsborough, two Sisleys, a Turner, four poignant Degas', and one of history's greatest tapestries hung on the walls. Forty feet square, the room preened with bibelots, velvets and masterpieces from prehistory and history. Arranged in lighted groups were the aboriginal sculptures of pregnancy from Dolni Věstonice, Lespugue, Willendorf and Savignano. The room was two stories high and mysteriously illuminated. On its south wall hung the high-loom, gold-worked tapestry called "Examination Before Trial in the Courts of Love." Reflecting Mr. Hibbert's interest in the law, it showed eighteen figures of men and women in dalliance over scrolls which had amorous inscriptions in Catalan. The furniture of the room was late Italian Gothic and extremely uncomfortable, except for the great sofas and Mr. Hibbert's own chair. The vaulted ceiling had been painted by Michelangelo for Cosimo I; Mr. Hibbert had had it removed from Florence. The enormous desk he was now slumped over had come from Renaissance Florence, as well.

A small pistol rested on the desk under Mr. Hibbert's hand. The suicide had been executed with characteristic efficiency. Francis walked slowly behind his patron's chair and noted that the well-polished shoes were still placed neatly together; a small-caliber pistol had been chosen because a large one would have knocked the body into an awkward position. Mr. Hibbert had always looked before leaping.

A rivulet of blood had stained the white carnation always

worn in the right buttonhole. An envelope addressed in saucy green ink to Mrs. Hibbert was propped against the vase of red and white carnations from which the right buttonhole had been filled every morning. Francis lifted the envelope eagerly, certain that beneath it he would find another envelope addressed to him. It was not there. But it existed. He knew. It would be found.

Francis began to think that the message might have been in the letter to Mrs. Hibbert. He wanted to open the letter to ease his terrible tension, but Mr. Hibbert's profile stopped him. Resting on the desk, it had not yet relaxed in death. Its expression showed distaste for what it had been about to do; the face had objected but the hand had won.

Francis stared reverently. This was the man who had been invited by three Presidents of the United States to become U.S. Secretary of the Treasury. This was the man who had been honored and decorated by eleven foreign governments; by the 4H Clubs and the De Molay and the Boy Scouts of America; who had been the founding force in the great community sings of his country. This was a man who had lived almost entirely by numbers, and through his unflagging sponsorship of pasigraphy as the universal language, he had hastened the day when mankind could communicate solely by numbers.

But it was appalling that such a man could destroy himself in his own bank. The press could panic. There could be a run on the bank. Francis was so appalled that he almost blamed Mr. Hibbert. But understanding intervened. He saw that he had been chosen to stop such disaster. He felt pride. Mr. Hibbert had killed himself with full confidence that Francis would manage to keep the entire tragedy from becoming public property.

Numbly, Francis took out his pocket notebook and wrote the word "Organ" on the opening page. The notebook had been a gift from Mrs. Hibbert nine Fourth of July's before. Being reminded of Mrs. Hibbert caused Francis to think of his own wife and of her peculiar relationship with Mr. Hibbert. Francis had never doubted any of her charges. It had happened; she never lied. The upsetting thing was that it had happened twice, and that he had been forced to profit from it each time as though he'd had his wife out for hire, all because he had kept two pictures of her on his desk and Mr. Hibbert had seen them.

In actual fact, Francis felt that there was little to censure. What Mr. Hibbert had done was something as old as the history of men and women. An elderly man had seen photographs of a young, very beautiful woman and by some combination of psychological imagery had turned Stacie into some object from his distant past—as though his past were a battlefield, with perhaps a breast lying under mist on this hummock of time to be matched to another breast far ahead in the future. That was why Mr. Hibbert had exposed himself before Stacie. He had looked at the two photographs, had left the office, had taken a taxi to Francis' apartment far uptown, had rung the doorbell and introduced himself to Stacie, then had exposed himself.

It didn't prove anything, Francis felt. It had made Stacie very angry and Francis very sad, but it hadn't proved anything except that Mr. Hibbert had been a very human banker.

Francis stared down at his benefactor's ruined head and tried to feel dismay. He concentrated, and it came to him at last. It was not the dismay he had sought, but rather dismay at the envy he felt for Mr. Hibbert in achieving death. Death had the permanence and stillness and dignity which a true banker must have. No matter where it took Mr. Hibbert, it had conferred the final banker's adjustment upon him: the ultimately desirable posture of silent, rigid integrity. Mr. Hibbert had foreclosed on himself, and now it was over between them. They had come to the end of twenty-four years. On April 27th, 1895, Mr. Hibbert had taken Francis out of the orphanage, ignoring every other boy as he walked along the line, then leaving without seeming to choose. Hours later, when they had all been asleep, Sister Mary Rita had prodded him awake in total darkness and had pulled him along behind her out of the dormitory. He had been kissed goodbye by the nuns, then handed into a horse-drawn carriage which took him to the Y.M.C.A., where he had lived until his wedding day.

Francis' wife wore a genuine diamond ring which had cost

three hundred and twelve dollars. Its payment had been made possible by a twelve-dollar weekly raise in salary which had been conferred after Mr. Hibbert had visited Stacie. After the second exposure Francis had been named assistant to the president. Furthermore, Francis drove a Pierce-Arrow landaulet because Mrs. Hibbert had tired of it and Mr. Hibbert had wanted Francis to be able to take his wife for healthful drives into the country. The price had been most reasonable and no interest had been charged for the necessary loan—something in itself which was against Mr. Hibbert's entire training.

Francis leaned over the body and opened the note to Mrs. Hibbert. It read:

January 2nd, 1919

Dearest Bertha:

I have just returned from a final consultation with Dr. Abraham Weiler, who, those other medical men have informed me, is the leading alienist of our country. All physicians have reached identical conclusions: that I should retire from the bank and permit myself to be committed to an institution before I can do any more "damage," and so that long-range "treatment" may be undertaken.

I am too old for long-range treatment and in no way interested in their "cure." I submitted myself to their examinations only as a gesture of good faith to the parents of the Givvens children, but I feel no guilt and will not allow myself to be confined in an insane asylum.

There are, however, the complications attending the arrest which Dr. Givvens has so grimly promised me, as well as all the attendant public defamation if I do not accept Dr. Weiler's prognosis. Therefore, I will kill myself.

Everything is in absolute order.

This is not the first time I have shocked you and so, lacking the novelty which tragedy feeds upon, my action will be easier to accept. We both deserved another chance. A fresh start.

Edward

Francis put the letter and the envelope into his side pocket and picked up Mr. Hibbert's private telephone. He gave the operator the number of James Maitland, executive vice-president and legal counsel of the bank, who lived in Great Neck, Long Island. It developed that Mr. Maitland was in New York, and in a few minutes Francis reached him at the Yale Club. He spoke very briefly. "There has been an accident, Mr. Maitland," he said. "Please come to Mr. Hibbert's office as soon as you can." He disconnected before he could be questioned.

Next Francis called the head watchman on the inside telephone and asked him to please send Mr. Maitland along to Mr. Hibbert's office as soon as he arrived. Returning to the private telephone again, he called Police Headquarters, and when connected, asked for the Police Commissioner. There was a quiet argument about how inconvenient it would be for the Commissioner to go to Mr. Hibbert's office, until Francis said it would then be necessary for him to invite the Mayor instead. The Commissioner agreed to come to the bank alone.

Francis hurried across the room to his office, where he took three large manila envelopes from his supply cabinet. He left his office, walked rapidly along the aisle which paralleled the secretarial pen. He unlocked a steel doorway, using three keys, and descended a spiral staircase. Two floors down, he worked the multiple combinations on the currency safe, pulled open the vault door, entered and walked slowly along the rows of steel bins. Using his keys, he chose currency from nine of the compartments and took out nine packets, each containing fifty one-thousand-dollar bills. He slid three of the packets into each of the manila envelopes, then sealed them. He left the vault, locked it and returned unhurriedly to his office. There, still as painfully conscious of the correctness of his handwriting as he had been at the orphanage, he addressed each envelope to himself. His script was tiny, ornamental and excessively orderly and it addressed each envelope clearly to Post Office Box 318 at General Delivery, which Francis had rented for the past few years to receive certain correspondence he felt to be of no interest to his wife. At P.O.B. 318 he received correspondence courses in etiquette, charm and short cuts to a better knowledge of English. His copy of the Social Register came there, and Francis pursued his studies of all mail while eating contentedly his lunch of jelly sandwiches among the headstones in Trinity churchyard. He also received certain personal letteres at 318, sent by unknown, excited ladies who had advertised for pen pals in the three sweetheart magazines to which he subscribed.

Francis weighed the manila envelopes, affixed the correct amount of postage out of the stamp supply he had personally paid for, and then put them in the Outgoing basket on Miss Emmaline Mechanic's desk. They would be picked up and mailed at eight o'clock that night by the night watchman on his rounds.

Then Francis telephoned James Monahan, a private citizen who was active in state and municipal politics. He introduced himself as Mr. Hibbert's assistant, and Mr. Monahan was extremely cordial. Francis explained that the Police Commissioner was on his way—alone—to Mr. Hibbert's office for a meeting with James Maitland, whom Mr. Monahan probably knew, and he wondered if Mr. Monahan would do the bank the really exceptional service of stopping by—alone—just as soon as he could that evening. Mr. Monahan accepted with pleasure.

Next Francis slid the telephone directory across his desk and searched for the number of Harold Schaefer, who, as famous as he was now, would never forget that it was Mr. Hibbert who had made his European studies possible. Mr. Schaefer had played the giant organ for the first eight years after it had been installed as a truly radical banking innovation by Mr. Hibbert. He had left the bank because, to show his appreciation, Mr. Hibbert had created a special grant with which Mr. Schaefer had been able to go to Holland to study the teaching techniques of Jan Sweelinck.

"Mr. Schaefer? This is Francis Vollmer at the bank."

"Mr. Vollmer. How nice. How is Mr. Hibbert?"

"We would like you to come to the bank."

"On Monday morning?"

"Now, Mr. Schaefer. It is so important that I cannot discuss it on the phone."

"But I am due at a dinner! In my honor."

"This is the last request that will ever be made in Mr. Hibbert's name, Mr. Schaefer," Francis said stiffly and hung up. He rose from his desk and walked slowly into Mr. Hibbert's room. He sat down facing the body, with his back to the door. He could not understand why Mr. Hibbert had not left The Message. There had not been so much as a cryptic sentence for him in that letter. Perhaps The Message had been enclosed with the will. That would be formal and proper recognition of the duty Mr. Hibbert owed not only to Francis but to the people in Europe who had persuaded him to sponsor Francis twenty-four years ago.

Mr. Hibbert had said nothing whatever, either about his intended suicide or about Francis' true identity in their last conversation twelve minutes before the shot, when he had strolled past the door to Francis' office under a straw sailor with a Yacht Club band.

"Read the *Times* this morning, Francis?"

"Yes, sir."

"See the story about the goddam inequalities in that pending income tax bill?"

"No, sir."

"They want twenty per cent on corporate income sliding up to forty on the net in excess of twenty of invested capital. You finish those merger schedules yet?"

"They'll be ready for you Monday morning, Mr. Hibbert."

That had been the farewell. Not one clue to The Message; not a word of affection.

Harold Schaefer arrived first. Mr. Mooney, the head watchman, brought him to the anteroom of Mr. Hibbert's office. Francis explained to Mr. Mooney that Police Commissioner Klarnet was also expected at any moment; then he pulled Mr. Schaefer into the anteroom and shut the door. Mr. Schaefer's cloth fedora matched his mustache exactly.

"I have terrible news, Mr. Schaefer."

"Oh, my God."

"Mr. Hibbert passed away from a heart attack about a half hour ago—"

"Oh, my *God!*"

". . . here amid these surroundings which he loved so well."

"What a tragedy! What a loss! Oh, my God."

"I have asked you here because this bank needs you to evoke Mr. Hibbert's spirit on the keys of the great organ as he is taken out tonight."

"What a beautiful, beautiful thought."

"God bless you."

"I—I just don't know what to say." Mr. Schaefer gripped his forehead. "The—uh—Central Canadian Organists' League is giving a dinner in my honor tonight. It's even being covered by *Musical America*. The delegates came all the way from Indian Head, Saskatchewan."

"I see."

"But please believe me, Mr. Vollmer—I am the first to acknowledge the great debt I owe to Edward Hibbert."

"Then go to Edward Hibbert's organ now and begin by playing 'Jesu, Joy of Man's Desiring.' Then, because it is what he would have wanted, some ricercare and some capriccios in the style of Frescobaldi—dignified and vivacious in contrasting pairs."

"How long do you think it will take?"

"Why not program for one hour?"

"Mr. Vollmer, I—"

"You must be in that organ loft when we take the body out! I will send a uniformed officer to your dinner to say that you have been unavoidably delayed. Then, when you arrive just a bit late, you will have the bank's permission to tell them all what happened. They know Mr. Hibbert as a great patron. Well, the whole effect will be very dramatic—particularly for *Musical America*."

"Yes! I see. I agree. Wonderful!"

"As we take him out, what would you think of playing the Buxtehude arrangement of the Christmas melody from 'In Dulce Jubilo'? Even though it is January 2nd."

"I half agree. That is, 'In Dulce Jubilo' by all means, but Mr. Hibbert was a Bach man and the Bach transcription is far more varied and decorated. After all, he starts against a running counterpoint, but almost instantly the other voices enter in double canon for a full twenty-four bars. A rather amazing achievement, I think you will agree."

The organ music began almost instantly. Francis sat staring at the body as the great sounds rolled like gun caissons through the marble halls. He found himself weeping at the beauty of dying in one's own bank, with a loyal friend nearby who had arranged for magnificent music to be played. Who could possibly believe any irresponsible suicide stories when it was established that the bank had sent for such a distinguished musician as Harold Schaefer to commemorate the death of its leader, struck down with his hand on the helm?

Someone began to bang on the locked door. His cheeks scalded, Francis admitted James Maitland.

Maitland dashed across the forty feet to Mr. Hibbert's desk and stared at the body as Francis relocked the door. Then he wheeled and cried, as though it were he who was breaking the news, "Ed killed himself!" Then, questioning his own statement, he said, "Why did he kill himself?"

Maitland was a short, bulky man, very tense. He was too dramatic to be a financial lawyer, but too rich not to be one. He was wearing a cartoon banker's coat with a deep fur collar, and it had climbed up under the brim of his homburg, which had been pulled down, in grief or in the anticipation of the need for anonymity, over his ears.

"Maybe it isn't suicide," he said wildly. "It could have been made to look like that. The Bolshies are everywhere. They blew up that judge's house in Pennsylvania."

"It was suicide."

"How do you know?"

"I was in the next room."

"Didn't he leave a note? They always leave notes."

"No, sir."

"You must have talked with him before he did it. What did he say?"

"Well, he walked past my door with his hat on and said he

was against the income tax law mentioned in the *Times* this morning. He also asked me about the merger schedules. Then he walked right in here and shot himself."

"This is terrible."

"Yes. Terrible."

"The bank can be ruined. Has misuse of the bank's funds crossed your mind?"

"It is out of the question, sir." Francis said the sentence slowly and very distinctly. He stood taller and glared at Maitland.

"Oh, no, it isn't. There were one or two things you don't know, Vollmer. Blackmail was very much in the cards for Hibbert, and I am not revealing privileged information. I am a principal officer of this bank, first and foremost."

"You are *the* principal officer now, Mr. Maitland."

"But what are we going to do?" Maitland wailed. He cracked his knuckles, made fists and rapped upon his temples with them. His chin bobbled. His voice broke. "I have to think. I have been trained to think, and I cannot think."

"The newspapers will never get this story the way it happened, sir. Not like this."

"Why not? How can we stop it?"

Francis was red-eyed from weeping and this made him more convincing amid the morbid setting and the sound of the mighty organ music. He put his long bony hands on Maitland's shoulders and pushed him back into a chair.

"I've had time to think, Jim," Francis said. It was Jim now and soon it would be Jim and Francis, Francis and Jim. "The most vital decision was the interval between the time of death and the police record of when the death was reported. I called the Police Commissioner. He's on his way here now."

Maitland stared at him in horror. "But that's policy," he said, almost choking. "That's a decision for the board."

"Please bear one thing in mind, Jim. Mr. Hibbert died of a heart attack. Keep saying that to yourself. I'll handle everything. Don't panic. Just take it easy."

"A heart attack?"

"Yes."

"But that's a gun in his hand. And it made a hole in his head."

There was an insistent knocking at the door. Facing Maitland, Francis edged toward it. "Now don't panic," he repeated. "Just sit quietly and let me handle everything."

Francis unlocked the door, and pulling Police Commissioner Klarnet through, he waved to Mooney and slammed the door, but left it unlocked. He greeted the Commissioner as he steered him toward Maitland, but the Commissioner ignored Maitland's extended hand. He stared at the body, walked to the desk, then part way round it, never taking his eyes off the pistol.

"What the hell is this?" he inquired in a high-pitched voice.

"Mr. Hibbert shot himself," Francis answered ingratiatingly.

"But, Vollmer—" Maitland protested.

"What are you trying to pull off here?"

"You are the senior police officer of this city," Francis answered, "and we have come to you for protection."

"Are you asking me to cover up the suicide of a man like Hibbert? A man who makes the news Hibbert makes? If it is a suicide."

Maitland sat with his face in his hands.

"It is suicide," Francis said blandly.

"Not me, mister," Klarnet said. He walked to the telephone. "This is for Homicide. This is routine. This is just another case."

Maitland moaned into his fingers.

"Don't telephone, Commissioner," Francis said. "Give things a chance to happen."

"What to happen? What else, fahcrissakes, can happen?" Klarnet turned to glare at Francis, but suddenly his eyes flicked over Francis' shoulder to the open doorway; there stood a tall, fat man with a network of ruptured blood vessels across each cheek.

"The lad is right, Phil," the big man said. A diamond and ruby stickpin in the shape of a bathing girl blazed in his necktie. "Which one is Mr. Vollmer?"

"I'm Vollmer. Mr. Monahan?" Francis crossed the room as though on wheels and shook Monahan's hand warmly, then guided him toward James Maitland. "And this is James Maitland, our senior vice-president and legal counsel. Mr. Maitland is the principal stockholder in our bank. Jim—do you know Big Tim Monahan?"

Maitland stood up weakly and smiled as shyly as a sleepy child.

"How about a cigar?" Francis asked as he leaped to open the mahogany chest just west of Mr. Hibbert's head. Everyone took a cigar and the rich smell of the smoke mingled with the heavy smell of the flowers in the overheated room.

As the muscular organ music pealed, they all sat down in a semicircle around the desk. Maitland looked much brighter. Francis looked more crafty. The Commissioner looked dreadful.

"I've heard a lot about you from Ed, Mr. Monahan," Maitland said. "He always enjoyed the happy game of politics."

"Yes, he did. He was a good citizen."

"And a friend of the party."

"Yes, he was. Charley Moolens wouldn't be in the Senate today if it wasn't for Ed's generous support."

"He dined with the Mayor not four nights ago," Maitland said.

"I read that Governor Smith will boom the Mayor for the White House," Francis added.

"The Governor being exactly one day in his new office, it would be a little soon for him to start a boom for himself," Monahan answered happily.

"He was a good friend of Ed's," Maitland said.

"I suppose an accident like this could make the bank a lot of trouble, couldn't it, Mr. Maitland?" Monahan asked.

Maitland nodded unhappily.

"Could cost a fortune, I guess. Even ruin the bank, maybe."

Maitland nodded grimly.

Francis said, "Has the party formed any ideas as to who our next mayor will be, Mr. Monahan?"

"It's a wide field and wide open, Mr. Vollmer."

"Our bank would certainly like to make a suggestion in that regard," Francis said earnestly. "If that were absolutely proper and aboveboard."

Maitland stared at Francis with alarm, but Monahan listened with deep professional interest. "Of course it's aboveboard and proper, Mr. Vollmer. You speak for the leading bank of our city. Who has a better right?"

Monahan and Francis spoke to each other diagonally across the corpse. Commissioner Klarnet sat at Monahan's left and Maitland sat at Francis' right. Francis made a steeple with his fingers and tapped the fingertips together. "As Mr. Hibbert's assistant and close associate—and speaking for Mr. Maitland, of course—I'd like to say that the resources of this bank, if given the chance, would be solidly behind Police Commissioner Philip Klarnet for Mayor."

The Commissioner took the big cigar out of his scowl. His face went blank. He pursed his lips into a snout to keep from saying anything at all.

"Yes," Monahan said, "I think I get your drift. But it would be an expensive campaign, you know. Phil isn't all that widely known and that means hard campaigning." He puffed comfortably on his cigar. "Don't you think so, Mr. Maitland?"

"Cost must not stand in the way," Maitland said slowly and clearly. "If we begin to put price tags on securing good government and electing the great leaders, we'd deserve what we would get."

"And Mr. Maitland speaks as the principal officer of the Hibbert First National Bank—now that Mr. Hibbert has suffered this fatal heart attack," Francis added.

"Well, Phil," Monahan addressed the Commissioner. "Would you like to make the run?"

Klarnet nodded vigorously.

Monahan stood up and stared at the dead man. "A heart attack is the way to go." He reached over and slipped the pistol out from under Mr. Hibbert's hand and put it in his coat pocket.

"Phil, d'ye know Doc Reyes in the medical examiner's office?"

Klarnet nodded so vigorously that he shook the ashes off his cigar.

"He's a heart man," Monahan said, "so I think he'd be better than some police surgeon. We need a specialist here and Doc Reyes knows the human heart in all its malfunctions. He's the one I think you should call, Phil, and when you do, have him call me about the death certificate. Just tell him to call me, then you get out of here. Are you free for lunch Friday, Phil?" The Commissioner nodded. "All right. One o'clock at Delmonico's then."

Monahan shook hands with Maitland and then with Francis as he guided him out of the office.

When Francis turned around, the Commissioner was talking into the telephone. "Doc Reyes?" He waited for the answer. "This is Phil Klarnet. What's Tim Monahan's private telephone number?" He waited. "Okay. Please get over here as fast as you can to Mr. Edward Hibbert's office at the Hibbert First National in Broad Street, and come alone." He disconnected and sat down with a thud, then pressed his features into grotesque shapes with his right hand. At last he spoke. "For the twenty-three years I know him, Doc Reyes wants to be State Boxing Commissioner. How about that for an ambition, fahcrissakes?"

The medical examiner came in on the balls of his feet like an armory fighter springing out of his corner, hoping to pick up a few points on sheer form. He was an olive-skinned man with cheekbones like the beams of a Mexican *fonda* and teeth like a whitewashed garden wall, and he wore a high-crowned Alpinist's hat with no more brim than a chamber bowl. He charged at the body, looked above and below the desk, nodded to the Commissioner and said, "Where's the murder weapon?"

"Call Monahan," Klarnet said. "I done my part." He left the room.

Reyes' voice came charging out of his throat as if over hot sand. "What kind of a police answer was that supposed to be?" But Klarnet was gone.

Francis approached the medical examiner with his hand extended like a greeter in a drummers' hotel. "I'm Francis Vollmer, Doctor," he said sociably, "and I am quite certain Mr. Monahan wants you to call him before you reach any conclusions."

"Ho, ho!" the doctor said. He turned away from Francis and picked up the phone.

Maitland was gripping the chair tightly with both hands, as if afraid he might fall off. Francis patted him lightly on the shoulder. "Never forget you for this, Francis," Maitland mumbled. Francis walked to the window and stared at the shining-wet street while he listened to Dr. Reyes get his instructions.

"I got it, Tim. We can go over the fine points later—except for one thing. Who'll be the undertaker? Important? It's the most important leak we could have. Sure, Jim Nolan is a good mortician. No question about it. Beautiful work. I seen three of his railroad-wreck cases and a drunk who's been in the river for nearly five weeks. But he doesn't really know me and I don't really know him, if you get what I mean. Well, here's a man obviously dead of a heart attack, but with the wrong undertaker—right? Yes. Yes, I know a fella. My own brother-in-law, Frank Heller. He works uptown, but what the hell. He knows his job, and you know I'm not just saying that to get the contract for him. I mean, this is a silver casket job. Okay, then. Okay and all clear with me. Another big man drops dead with heart failure and another State Boxing Commissioner is appointed." Reyes turned to Francis. "He wants to speak to you."

Francis took the phone. "Yes, Tim?" It was Tim now and forever.

"Francis, the good doctor thought of something we had overlooked. I'm afraid Mr. Hibbert is going to have to be buried from Harlem."

"Well, I—" Francis looked helplessly at Maitland, but Maitland looked even more helpless. "I am sure the board will want Mr. Hibbert to be laid out right here at the bank."

"Good thinking. Now, it will have to be a silver casket. That's the undertaker's part of the contract."

As Dr. Reyes completed the death certificate he said, "Heart disease is our biggest killer."

"Will you be waiting for the undertaker?" Francis asked.

"Yes. But he won't be long."

"Then—if you don't mind—we have so many things to attend to under these extraordinary—"

"Perfectly all right. I'll be fine here. I'll do the inventory of his pockets. Want to witness that?"

"Mr. Hibbert never carried anything in his pocket. In fact, he had his trousers made without pockets and those are just flaps on the jacket. Just the breast pocket for the handkerchief, that's all."

"I'll be damned."

When Francis and Maitland got into Francis' office, the lawyer suddenly took charge. "I'm all right now and we're safe, thanks to you. There is nothing, and I mean absolutely nothing, that this bank will not do for you. We'll go into the details of that statement with the board. Right now get Ferguson and a picked team of auditors in here. I want the cash vault checked because that's the first thing the board will ask me. We'll split the work. I'll begin to call the board members. You find Ferguson and send him to me, then you take care of the undertaker and the newspapers and stay right with Ed until that casket is sealed. Make the statement to the press short. 'Edward Groves Hibbert, sixty-three, president of the Hibbert First National Bank, succumbed to a heart attack at his desk in the bank at such-and-such a time today.'"

"Mrs. Hibbert?"

"I'll handle her." Maitland hurried off to his own office.

Francis called Stacie and told her he would be at the bank all night and that he would explain when he saw her. It took him fifty minutes to organize the team of auditors. No one asked irrelevant questions. The president of the bank was dead and this was the first of many audits.

Francis began to write the eulogy which he would ask Big Tim Monahan to ask Senator Moolens to deliver. Theme: Was death's only meaning to make a space on earth for another life? Resolved: No. Argument: Witness the long, honorable and exemplary career of our departed brother, Edward Groves Hibbert.

A lot of the significance—maybe all of it—of Mr. Hibbert's life took money. But that way of life should have a meaning; if there was no meaning, grief and hopelessness would rack the land. Francis had denied himself many things. Here he was thirty-eight years old, and he had never gone to bed with a woman other than his wife. He had never eaten in a good restaurant—why use the money?

But Francis knew how to live well. He had studied Mr. Hibbert to the last detail and he had always known that some day he'd have enough money to do all those things. Beyond that he'd had to save in order to be ready when The Message came, and now he was proud of himself for all the things he had made himself do without, because the time had come. He would be told soon. He would join Them soon, and he would have enough money to go to Them in proper style and to be accepted by Them with pride. After saving and scraping all his life, ten minutes in the cash vault with three manila envelopes had made his acceptance sure, no matter how exalted their standards were. What was money but the world's approval?

Dr. Reyes put his head into Francis' office. "Franklin has him in the basket as neat as a pie," he said. "He's ready to go uptown."

Francis telephoned to Mr. Mooney to come with as many men as he could spare. He put his hat on, then entered Mr. Hibbert's office and was introduced to Dr. Reyes' brother-in-law, whose eyebags were so dark that he resembled a tremendous raccoon. They had begun to discuss the silver casket when Mr. Mooney knocked to say that he would be able to spare three uniformed men and that he would get into uniform if there was time.

"No time," Francis said. "You heard the news?"

"The Commissioner told me."

"We've lost a good friend."

"God rest his soul. Who'll be his successor?"

"It's up to the board."

"There's an anti-pension faction on that board, Mr. Vollmer."

"I wouldn't say that."

"Mr. Hibbert favored the pension but he told me they block it."

"How long have you been with the bank?"

"Fifty-one years. I come here when Mr. Hibbert's grandfather was here."

"Do you—uh—feel you are ready to retire?"

"I been ready for fifteen years. Mr. Hibbert's dying is a serious thing to me, Mr. Vollmer."

"What do you think should be the minimum term of service?"

"Well, I'd say fifty years."

"Line your men up. Mr. Hibbert is leaving the bank for the last time."

From the organ loft, Mr. Schaefer could see the procession starting out under the shadows of the Gothic arches, and he began to play the "Lux aeterna" and the responsory "Libera me" from the *Manzoni Requiem* of Verdi because he remembered that Mr. Hibbert's only joke had been to refer to Giuseppe Verdi as Joe Green. Francis led the solemn procession: a tall figure, hat held reverentially over his chest, his lean, bony face a mask of sorrow, his yellow eyes overbrimming with tears. Two bank policemen, including Mr. Mooney, walked on either side of the casket. Dr. Reyes and Frank Heller brought up the rear. The undertaker pushed the wheeled stretcher and the medical examiner chatted happily beside him. They were respectfully muted as was fitting in a great bank, but they chuckled and made many self-congratulatory gestures. Only once did Dr. Reyes lift his voice, ever so slightly but loudly enough for Mr. Mooney to hear him say to his brother-in-law, ". . . free tickets for every championship fight for the rest of our lives. Free baseball passes, football passes—season tickets, I mean—because if they give to me, I give to them." The undertaker rolled his black-pouched eyes and gave a kick in the manner of Pat Rooney.

Francis marched and conveyed almost imperial sadness, imagining as he went that he was in the second line of a cortege of royalty following the coffin of the late Queen Victoria, marching behind the man who, perhaps, was his father; pacing between the King of Norway and the King of Greece. As he crossed the marble floors of the bank he placed his feet down in such a manner that though they were concealed by shoes and trousers, any spectator would know instantly that his insteps were pigeon-breasted, the toes long and healthily pink, and the toenails impeccably cut. His face was pale from the talcum powder he had applied in the washroom at intervals during the long evening. His eyes were bloodshot from the weeping. He walked in semi-stooping despair, his chin thrust toward the floor over which was about to pass all that remained of his boyhood and youth.

But within this envelope of grief Francis' mind whirred and clicked, as he thought of how soon he might be able to take safe possession of the money so that he could invest it properly and allow it to increase itself; how soon he could safely leave the bank when The Message came from his parents; and whether he should learn French, since it was the language of the aristocracy.

The sad procession left the bank and grouped itself around the back of the black hearse, as vivid as Heller's eyebags against the snow now covering the street. The hearse was the only vehicle in sight, and they were the only people in Broad Street, although there were many lights in the windows of the tall office buildings.

Dr. Reyes bid them all a cheery goodnight, saying that he was off for a bowl of Belgian mussels. Francis shook hands with the bank's policemen and then he and Heller got into the hearse, as Mr. Mooney crossed himself. The hearse moved uptown at a stately speed as a reminder of death for all who looked. No one did.

Heller was euphoric. He hummed snatches from Palestrina, whistled "The Night Maloney Landed in New York" and drummed his fingers gaily on the steering wheel. "Been backstage at a funeral parlor before, Mr. Vollmer?" he asked at 14th Street.

"No."

"You'll enjoy the novelty, believe me."

Just before they reached 72nd Street in Central Park, Francis remembered he had not called the newspapers, so Heller turned the hearse across the park to a saloon under the El on Ninth Avenue, which had a telephone. Francis wanted Heller to wait in the hearse because he felt a sudden panic that someone might kidnap Mr. Hibbert's body, but Heller said it was too cold to sit in a hearse and that he had a good lock on the door to protect the merchandise.

If Francis thought the news would cause consternation at the Associated Press office, it did not. The man who took the story was so laconic that Francis felt compelled to ask if he knew who Mr. Hibbert was. Shaken, he called the *New York Times* and was received much more respectfully. The *Tribune* was neutral but sympathetic. The *Wall Street Journal* took the news as though it were a six-alarm fire. They all wanted the name of an officer of the bank with whom they could check the story, so Francis referred them to Maitland.

By the time the job was done, Heller was on his second rock-and-rye and was in a discussion with the bartender about Lady Constance Stewart-Richardson, who was currently appearing at the Palace, billed as "Patrician, Grande Dame, Aristocrat of Aristocrats, granddaughter of the Duke of Sutherland and daughter of the Earl of Cromartie" as the bartender read it from the newspaper.

There was more. " 'A supoibly comely figger,' " he read, " 'interpretin' delicious music, exquisite and inspirational. She is stoppin' ovuh at duh Palace in route to Siberia for duh Russian War Orphans Relief Fund.' " He looked up. "How about dat?"

Francis was thrilled to the ends of his hair. He had to see this woman. He had to contrive to get backstage for a chat with her. It was within the realm of possibility that she was his sister or at least a close friend of his family.

"She has to be a lousy dancer," Heller said.

They arrived at the funeral parlor at five to twelve. Heller rolled the stretcher across the icy streets with the skill of a father with a baby carriage and unlocked the side door. He motioned Francis in first, pushed Mr. Hibbert in, then closed the door. "I'll just check with my night man," he said and hurried out of the room. Francis kept his eyes to the floor until the mortician returned.

"Okay, no calls. My kind of people don't die till early Sunday morning. We can work on your friend all night if we have to." Heller pushed the stretcher into the embalming room and Francis followed him.

"Take a chair and get an education—except by the time the information is useful to you, you don't care any more." Heller skillfully unloaded and unwrapped Mr. Hibbert's body and undressed him quickly. They were both startled to see the long welted scars across Mr. Hibbert's back and chest, some of them new and raw. Francis was shocked. "Mr. Hibbert was a very religious man," he said tersely.

"Why not?" Heller replied. He made the first incision high and inside on the thigh, then clamped off an artery and a vein. "It's a funny thing how the mind works," he said. "Whenever I used to dream about having a sky's-the-limit case like Mr. Hibbert here, I always wished I could send him off the way they did it in Washington, D.C., about fifty years ago. They used to electroplate the cadaver—beautiful effect. Gave it a wonderful outside finish, just like a shiny metal statue. Never a smell. The decay was all inside the statue like in a tooth. I wish I could get somebody to do that for me. I mean, lay an electroplated cadaver in the dark velvet cavity of a full couch casket, and you'd produce an effect which would be talked about and envied. But who has the equipment nowadays?"

The mortician slipped the rubber half-circles under Mr.

Hibbert's eyelids. "I know no one would see them if they did pop open, because this is a sealed-casket job if ever there was one, but I'm a perfectionist." He began to wire the jaws shut. "My folks had this fear of being buried alive. I mean, who doesn't? I mean, that's probably why I was first in my class back at the Hohenschuh-Carpenter College of Embalming, back in Des Moines." He held up a glass vial filled with colored fluid which had a foot-long needle with a hollow point. He placed the needle on Mr. Hibbert just above the navel and pushed it in. He worked hard and silently for ten minutes, then filled in the bullet hole in Mr. Hibbert's temple with plastic wood.

"Some heart attack," Heller chuckled. "Popped out the side of his head."

"It's been a long day for me, Mr. Heller," Francis said, "and I'm not sure I feel exactly great." He felt cheated but he didn't want to hurt Heller's feelings. A man who has more money than any ten thousand people put together, who knows exactly the right wine for each dish and who can call nobility by their first names, has to have this happen to him: 115th Street and Manhattan Avenue, naked and worked over by a man whose only reason for being in such a business was that he was absolutely positive he had survived one more person who had died in the world, and that made him relaxed and happy. The depression didn't last. Mr. Hibbert won. Francis began to think about the majesty of what must be happening to Mr. Hibbert now as he marched slowly up a golden ramp to marvelous organ music and took his place among some of the biggest families in all history.

Heller wanted to talk about the silver casket. Working upside down, he was tying Mr. Hibbert's tie. "What this man will be buried in is a solid-silver cruciform casket just like the winners they used to make in Oswego. You can't touch it. I mean that. Silver is one thing, but a cruciform in silver! I mean, this man will be buried with arms outstretched to receive the Lord, in the same position that His son was sacrificed by man. The one I happen to have on hand was custom-made for one of our big bookmakers uptown here. He was the biggest man in the colored community and he picked it out when he was in the pink of health. Then he disappeared before he could pay for it. That's show biz. I couldn't send the casket back because the firm had gone out of business. I mean, wholesale I'd be ashamed to tell you what this casket costs. What an effect for the papers! What an inspiration for readers! It could start up the whole silver fad again, because a really big man being buried inside a silver cross just can't die out in a deeply religious nation like ours."

Francis pretended to listen as he pondered over all the different religions he had discovered in the past few hours. There were more gods than there were men, for it was beginning to seem to him that any man worships an assortment of invisible deities. Francis thought he had even caught a fleeting glimpse of his own god in the moment he had heard Mr. Hibbert fire the shot. Now he hastened forward to make obeisance to it.

Chapter 2

 Francis got back to the bank at ten minutes after two o'clock on Sunday morning, to find a note on his desk instructing him to telephone Maitland at the Yale Club as soon as the cash-vault audit had been completed.

Francis passed the word to Mr. Ferguson, through Mr. Mooney, that he would be asleep on one of the sofas in the board room, and would Mr. Ferguson please bring him the results there.

At 9:21 A.M. Ferguson shook him awake. Francis came out of sleep fast, and was sitting up instantly. "Did everything balance, Mr. Ferguson?"

"No."

"A shortage?"

"Four hundred and fifty thousand dollars."

"There could have been a mistake."

"I don't think so."

Francis kept his face expressionless to convey the impression that he was stunned. He got up and walked to a straight-backed chair against another wall and sat down staring straight ahead, as though he were tabulating all of the horrendous consequences of the news. As he stared he counted silently and slowly to one hundred.

At the count of one hundred he looked up at Ferguson. "You understand that this was not an official audit, Mr. Ferguson?"

Ferguson nodded.

"I'll report to Mr. Maitland now, and I'll be happy to have you come with me if you deem it necessary."

"Unnecessary."

"Please ask the men to stand by to carry out another audit. I mean an official audit, to begin at the close of business tomorrow afternoon."

"That's good, Mr. Vollmer. We wouldn't want to put it off any longer, but we could have made a mistake. I can't believe a shortage like that either. We'll start at three-thirty tomorrow afternoon."

Francis opened his mouth wider than usual as though to say something very important, but Mr. Ferguson interrupted him. "Don't worry about my men talking about this," he said. "Remember, it could be their mistake."

Francis reached the Yale Club twenty-five minutes later. He announced himself at the door, then found a Sunday *Times* and sat down to read the obituary notices. He was chagrined to discover that Mr. Hibbert had taken hardly anyone else even remotely important with him. The other obituaries were small, but the *Times* had written a long and fitting obituary for Mr. Hibbert which was amazingly complete, including as it did the charming little anecdote about Mr. Hibbert and the King of Italy. He was just finishing the piece when Maitland appeared. Francis leaped to his feet, almost upsetting the papers on the floor. James Maitland represented a part of his future. Not a great part because Francis would be called to his parents' side soon, but until then it would be wise to serve Mr. Maitland well.

At seven years of age, Mr. Maitland had been the only family survivor of a train wreck on his father's railroad. His father's executor had been Edward Hibbert's father, who had gradually consolidated the considerable Maitland fortune into banking. At seven, James Maitland had inherited one hundred and seven million dollars. At fifty, he was worth one hundred and fifty-six million dollars. He was in a high order of American nobility.

They went into the bar, where Maitland ordered a pitcher of orange juice and a half bottle of champagne. Francis asked for coffee.

"Was there a shortage?" Maitland asked. His voice had such a tremolo that it seemed to come out of him on the half shell, each quaver separate and distinct.

"Yes, sir. There is a shortage of four hundred and fifty thousand dollars, but I have persuaded Ferguson that this could be a mistake and that the audit was unofficial. He has agreed to run another beginning at three-thirty tomorrow afternoon."

"Thank God." Maitland put his hand out and touched Francis' sleeve. "And thank God for you, Francis. You've saved us in more ways than one, and the bank will never forget it. Never. Never, never."

"Thank you, sir. Whatever I was able to do I did out of a sense of duty which Mr. Hibbert instilled in me."

"Ed must have been crazy at the end. Totally deranged." A large tear started down Maitland's cheek. He brushed it aside with the back of his hand. "How much should we tell the board?"

"Sir?"

"The board will meet at two o'clock tomorrow afternoon. There is no need to drag the breadth and depth of Ed's disgrace along that table. Mrs. Hibbert and I will replace the shortage, for one thing. The audit will balance. Is it unthinkable to withhold such information from a board of directors?"

"No, sir!"

"And I don't see why they should know Ed shot himself. Their concern is the bank, not Ed now that he's gone and nothing has been harmed. That many men couldn't keep a secret like that, and if it got out that Ed shot himself it could only hurt the bank. Isn't that true? Isn't that sound business logic? You're a better banker than all of us, Francis. Give me an objective answer."

"You are absolutely right, Jim." Francis stared at the forthright effect of Maitland's nose. "And since no theft occurred, as Mr. Ferguson's audit will show, you only need to read the board the death certificate to certify the heart attack they have already accepted because of the newspapers and from your calls to them. No invidious question of your lying even comes into it. That's how I see it."

"What magnificent obituaries!"

"I haven't had a chance yet to—"

"You must order them to be specially bound in leather, and I would like all of them—particularly the *Times*, the *Tribune* and the *Wall Street Journal*—read into the minutes of tomorrow's board meeting."

"Yes, sir."

"And I would very much appreciate it if you would come in and tell the board exactly how everything happened— substituting the heart attack for the shot, of course. Everyone enjoys hearing those kinds of stories."

"Yes, sir."

"As for you and me—we are ethical men, and whatever we do we do rationally—we have to take the position that Ed was unbalanced. Which is almost precisely accurate. The last heinous business of his which I know about involved twelve-year-old twins, and although it seems impossible for a man of sixty-three who had never had a child of his own, one of the twins became pregnant as though she were some goddam Peruvian Indian in a Sunday supplement. She had to be whisked off to Switzerland for an abortion. Can you imagine the difficulties I had in making the arrangements for that? Her father was a minister in the church Ed's grandfather had established, where Ed is—was—an elder. When the swollen little girl told her father the name of the man who had been tickling them—and I defy you to find a more revolting terminology—the minister had a complete collapse. I had to put a deaf and dumb male nurse on him. It was terrible. He swung like a pendulum between the vengeance of God and the Police Department for almost a week, praying in the foulest language. For two days he wanted a gun. Then he decided to solve everything by starting a vast public scandal. But his wife, God bless her, convinced him how bad it would be for the little girls for the rest of their lives. Then finally he was able to understand that Ed was a very sick man. And he stuck with that idea. That was the condition he imposed for his silence. Ed had to be committed. It would have ruined the bank, you know. But Ed became outraged, then stubborn about that. Oh, he submitted to mental examinations to buy time, but he insisted that he was as normal as anyone else, that it was just a matter of living in the wrong time, that if it had been two hundred years earlier and he had been a feudal lord, no one would have thought anything about it—beyond the father feeling extremely lucky."

"Do you think he gave the minister the four hundred and fifty thousand?" Francis felt no disloyalty about planting firmly in Maitland's mind the idea that his benefactor had stolen the money from his own bank.

"No. The father was honest enough for a clergyman. I'm fairly certain he couldn't be bought off. I tried, and he became hysterical. Of course the twins weren't the only case by any means. There were many incidents which could have involved blackmail, but my guess is that he took the money to set up some sort of trust fund for the little girls." Maitland shrugged. "Wherever it is, we'll never find it."

Francis couldn't help smiling, but he erased it quickly, then gave his bony head a rueful shake and looked as puzzled as he could. All of this was lost on Maitland, who was pouring champagne into orange juice.

"It was all my fault," Maitland said suddenly.

"You mustn't even think such a thing."

In Maitland's sudden anguish his hand began to push his lips into droll shapes while his chin bobbled and he fought back a sob. His voice paid out words jaggedly. "Ed was a straightforward, upright man until sixteen years ago, when he made me and Mrs. Hibbert take an oath that we'd never be alone together again. We were in bed together, naked, when we took the oath. All too banal. Best friend, his wife, so on and so forth. But our families were all entangled in the bank's finances."

Francis did not wish to hear any more of this. In a few days, when the weeping and the acting had stopped, Maitland would remember telling him all this rot, and Francis would have made a deadly enemy out of a man who was rich and powerful and without question was becoming his friend. "Don't go into that, sir," he said in such haste that the sentence tumbled out of him in one word. "I have no right to know that. Regret is hopeless and useless. Regret is only worry about the past." He patted Maitland's forearm to keep their friendly relationship from being exorcised.

"Do you know Mrs. Hibbert, Francis?"

"No, sir. I've seen her pictures, of course. A very beautiful lady."

"You wouldn't believe she had a religious bone in her body. We sat on top of that bed—"

Oh, Jesus, Francis thought. He can't be stopped, he can't be stopped.

"—me with the beginnings of a paunch and the endings of an erection and she clutching a bedspread to her chest incongruously so as not to expose herself to her husband, who was breathing like a bellows. But she took that oath to heart and she was never alone with me again." Maitland downed the drink and filled the glass with champagne. "And I loved her." He managed to disguise his sob with a cough. "You'll have to come with me this morning. If you don't—"

"I'll be proud and happy to come, Jim."

"You won't be happy, son. It'll be pretty bad." Maitland took a deep breath and exhaled slowly. "Ed was about fifteen years older than Bertha, and after he found us out he seemed to have calculated how to take sly advantage of it. He began to do things he may always have wanted to do at the back of his head, but now he could do them and behave as though he were forced to it as a sort of vengeance for what we'd done to him. About a year to the day after he caught us, they caught him molesting a child in a public school in Queens. The desk sergeant had enough sense not to book him. The final adjustment cost about eighteen thousand dollars. Ed made no explanations, simply said he had no intention of paying anybody anything. So Bertha and I shared the costs. And we've been paying ever since. Sometimes once a year, mostly twice a year, but once six times in one year. If it was revenge, then it was the most vulgar revenge a man has ever taken."

Maitland drummed on the table top and thought about something. Francis resigned himself to listening.

"Bertha escaped it all by drinking. She has just enough strength left to sign checks. This is the last one and we need a witness. What the hell, Francis. You're elected."

The snow was heavy and a rude wind blustered across the Sound. It was one of Francis' great ambitions realized to be inside the Hibbert home and at long last to be meeting Mrs. Hibbert. Francis followed Maitland up the broad staircase. Mrs. Hibbert, drunk in bed, was a ruin. She looked nothing at all like any of her glorious pictures in the rotogravure taken not so very long before. She looked directly at Francis but evidently did not see him, for she did not comment. She seemed to recognize Maitland by sound rather than by sight.

Maitland opened the drawer of the table beside her bed and drew out a large checkbook. He sat on the edge of the bed and filled in a check.

"We aren't alone, Jim?" she wheezed.

"No, Bertha."

"Have whoever it is make a sound."

Maitland turned to Francis, who said, "Good afternoon, Mrs. Hibbert." She did not respond.

"Edward is dead," Maitland told her.

"So they said. Did he do something terrible before he died?"

"Yes."

"Did he have a heart attack?"

"He shot himself."

"Poor Edward."

"Sign here, Bertha. This is a check for two hundred and twenty-five thousand dollars. It is the last time."

Mrs. Hibbert signed shakily and slowly. Maitland tore the check from the book and handed it to Francis. "Please confirm the amount, Francis."

" 'Two hundred and twenty-five thousand dollars,' " Francis read.

"Are we now free from the oath we swore, Jim?"

"We're free."

"Are you laughing?"

"No."

Maitland got up and started out of the room. Francis walked closely behind him. Mrs. Hibbert began to laugh, and by the time they had reached the door the noise had built into tall, excited screams and a nurse came hurrying past them into the room.

Chapter 3

 Francis came out of the subway station at 168th Street and Broadway at a quarter to six on Sunday evening. He felt greatly confused but he had been able to convince himself that he must not judge the lives of the very rich or doubt the happiness in which they lived by what he had seen in the past twenty-four hours.

It was raining hard and three small boys stood at the subway exit, yelling, "Um-buh-rella!" Francis signaled and one boy fell in beside him, holding the umbrella over both their heads. They did not speak as they walked past the Audubon Theatre and walked down the slope of 165th Street toward Amsterdam Avenue. At the Belleclair Apartments on Edgecombe Avenue, Francis paid the boy fifteen cents and the boy walked back through the rain.

Obie Beadle, the night switchboard and elevator operator, had come on duty an hour early. He was wearing a pink, tightly fitting stocking cap. The switchboard and the ele-

vator signaled the high status of the building. East of Broadway it was the only building within miles which had either,
and Francis felt it matched his Pierce-Arrow landaulet and
his wife's diamond ring.

Obie got into carpet slippers as he heard Francis enter the
elevator. He greeted Francis informally, and they ascended
at the rate of a chloroform addict trying to get up off the
floor, the elevator car swaying heavily.

"How is my wife doing?" Francis asked. He was extremely
loyal to Negroes. He considered them the rightful American
servant class and was prepared to defend their rights hotly if
the management ever tried to replace them with German
help.

"You got to practice to play an instrument, Mr. Vollmer. I
don' say she won' practice, but she say she cain practice
because she ain' got a instrument, but I cain leave mine up
there 'cause she fingers so hard she tilts the pads."

"Do you think it is worthwhile to continue the lessons?"

"Well, I mean. I can use the money."

"Ah."

"I mean. It come in handy."

"Let me put it this way. Do you think Mrs. Vollmer will
ever be a superb saxophonist?"

"Huh?"

"Things like 'La Valse Vanité'?"

"We been on 'Ole MacDonald Hadda Farm' for two anna
half months." The car reached the fourth floor and Obie slid
the door open. The smell of olive oil cooking smote both of
them.

"Do they ever stop cooking?" Francis asked rhetorically as
he stepped out of the car.

"When they ain' cookin' wid olive oil," Obie said, "they
washes socks in it." He slammed the door shut and the car
began its infinitesimally slow descent. Mumbling, Francis
unlocked his apartment door.

Stacie's voice called out. "Who is it?"

"Who else has a key?"

His wife came flying out. "Honey, what happened?"

"Mr. Hibbert died last night."

"I know. I saw the paper. Ellie Lewis called twice for the inside story. But what happened after that?"

"You can imagine what happens at a bank when the president drops dead at his desk. We had the police and a medical examiner and I called Jim Maitland downtown and he wanted a routine audit run and a board of directors meeting set for Monday. Then we had to tell Mrs. Hibbert."

"Did you meet her?"

"I had to go out to the Hibbert house. It took most of the afternoon."

"Was it gorgeous?"

"The epitome of gracious living."

"How was she?"

"She was extremely gracious."

"Francis, guess what? I met a woman who knows Chevalier Furtado's nephew."

"Who?"

"The Chevalier was the inventor of the copophone."

"What's that?"

"A musical instrument. Glass tumblers on a sounding board. Chevalier Furtado gave a fabulous concert in London. It was in the papers."

"A concert? But what the hell—"

"You play it by moving wet fingers along the edges of the tumblers. The nephew told this woman he could play Berlioz' *Requiem* on them, and he gives lessons."

"What would you want to play a thing like that for?" Francis was vexed. "It's even sillier than the saxophone."

"Honey, I decided I don't want a sax."

"Stage fright? Carnegie Hall a little scary?"

"The fingering is getting very tricky."

Francis tilted her chin and kissed her. "Stacie, make me a cup of coffee, please?"

"Is it all right if I stop taking sax lessons?"

Francis sighed. "You studied violin when Gerald Washington was on the day elevator. Then banjo with Big Fats Munchy, who gave me permission to call him Fats instead of Leroy. Then the saxophone."

"Honey, I live for my music!"

"But can you play a violin? Can you play a banjo? And could there be anything more ridiculous than a housewife playing a saxophone?"

"What can I do? My instrument is the piano, but we've never had an elevator man who could teach piano. And, anyway, we don't have one."

Francis kissed her again and folded her into his chest. "Tomorrow morning," he said, "I want you to go out and buy a piano."

Stacie pushed him away and stared at him with astonishment and utter adoration. "Francis!"

"And we'll hire a real piano teacher to come twice a week. I don't care what it costs."

"Oh, Francis! I heard of a man who can teach how to play by ear. No scales!" She reached up, took his face in her hands and pulled it down to her lovely mouth.

Francis awoke at six-twenty on Monday morning overcome with fear that he was about to be arrested. To banish the fear he thought about the $450,000 waiting for him at his post-office box. He knew that for the rest of his life he would never again awake in the old way. No more nagging, worrying need that he had not done enough to pull himself ahead. He had to invest that money as soon as possible. It might be years before he could take the chance of using it, but it could not be allowed to rest; it must work and earn. Why, Mr. Hibbert would whirl in his silver casket if he knew that Francis had four hundred and fifty thousand dollars in cash and had not invested it.

He slid out of bed silently, gathered up his clothing and slithered into the bathroom. When he was bathed, shaved, dressed and the top had been screwed upon the toothpaste with care, he went into the living room and wrote a note in large block letters. It said: DARLING STACIE, WHEN I RETURN AT SIX-FIFTEEN THIS EVENING I HAVE EVERY REASON TO BELIEVE THAT I WILL HAVE BEEN MADE AN OFFICER OF THE BANK. TO CELE-

BRATE WE WILL GO DOWNTOWN TO DINNER
(*NOT* TO MINK'S) THEN TO THE PALACE THEATRE
TO SEE LADY CONSTANCE STEWART-RICHARDSON
GRANDDAUGHTER OF THE DUKE OF SUTHERLAND
AND DAUGHTER OF THE EARL OF CROMARTIE. I
AM TOLD SHE IS SUPERB. DO NOT TELL ELLIE
LEWIS UNTIL TOMORROW ABOUT THE PROMO-
TION WHEN WE ARE SURE.

LOVE, FRANCIS

When Francis left the building, it was a flawless winter
morning. When he reached Amsterdam Avenue, the black
teeth of its hundreds of fire escapes grinning down at him, it
was half past seven and Boehm's ice cream parlor was open.
He sauntered in, savoring the smells, and sat at a high stool
at the counter. He told Mrs. Boehm that he had never eaten
ice cream for breakfast, and at twenty minutes to eight in a
winter morning he ordered a banana split. It was a dish he
had denied himself since his boyhood except on Stacie's
birthdays. As he ate it he realized that all the things he had
ever dreamed about were real. He knew he would be told
who his parents were very soon, and that they would call
him to them with pride.

Francis left the subway at Wall Street and went directly
to his post-office box. The three manila envelopes were there.
He could feel the money through the stiff brown-paper
parcels under his arm as he entered the bank and bade Mr.
Mooney good morning. Walking directly to his office, he
locked the envelopes scarred with canceled stamps in the
second right-hand drawer of his desk. He double-locked the
drawer.

For a moment Francis allowed himself to slip into a
reverie. One day, through Big Tim Monahan's political
power and through the two senators and every representative from the State of New York, he would arrange to pass a
law creating a titled American aristocracy. Francis knew
business leaders very well. They would support the bill
secretly from the day it was announced, by saying it was
something their wives wanted, but would urge all senators

and congressmen to oppose it until the day of voting. They would contribute hundreds and hundreds of thousands of dollars to help the campaign with public opinion. It would become a law by a landslide vote. Francis would get a peerage; that would be the condition for his conception of the law. If it could be done soon it would mean that he would go to his parents with a peerage—not equal to theirs, perhaps, but in keeping with the family.

He began to work on the draft of the eulogy to be delivered by Senator Moolens. Then he made a note about finalizing the merger agreements. Then he prepared an agenda for Jim Maitland for the board meeting, as he had done so many times before for Mr. Hibbert. He decided that the bank should close all day on Tuesday, in official mourning; on that day Mr. Hibbert would lie in state in the bank in his magnificent cruciform casket. Emergency banking conditions must be arranged for clients in need that day.

Francis composed a full-page advertisement to announce the closing. He wrote:

THE DIRECTORS OF THE HIBBERT FIRST NATIONAL BANK AN-
NOUNCE WITH SORROW THAT THOSE WISHING TO PAY FINAL
RESPECTS TO EDWARD STOKES HIBBERT MAY DO SO ON THE MAIN
BANKING FLOOR IN BROAD STREET ON TUESDAY, JANUARY 7TH,
1919, WHEN THE BANK WILL BE CLOSED IN RESPECT FOR MR.
HIBBERT'S CONTRIBUTION TO AMERICAN FINANCE AND BANKING.
EMERGENCY BUSINESS MAY BE CONDUCTED BY TELEPHONING
EXT. 318.
THE FUNERAL WILL BE HELD AT ST. THOMAS CHURCH, FIFTH
AVENUE AT 53RD STREET, ON WEDNESDAY MORNING AT 11 A.M.
THE INTERMENT WILL BE PRIVATE.

Giving the emergency business extension the same number as his own post-office box was a sentimental indulgence on Francis' part. In the upper right-hand corner of the sheet Francis wrote "18 copies please," then buzzed for Miss Mechanic, dictated covering notes to the advertising managers of the metropolitan newspapers and had the copy sent off by messengers.

Next, Francis placed a copy of *Who's Who in America* on

his desk, opened it to "Hibbert, Edward Stokes," took a freshly sharpened pencil from a tumbler filled with sharpened pencils and began to compose the eulogy:

> An American hero has passed away, leaving a stricken family, saddened associates, a mourning America and a diminished world behind him . . .

In thirty-five minutes he was able to write in the upper right-hand corner of the first page "18 copies please— urgent" just as Miss Mechanic came into the room with a basket of yellow telegrams, followed by three messengers also carrying baskets of yellow telegrams.

"What should we do with these, Mr. Vollmer?" Miss Mechanic asked somberly.

"Please put them in Mr. Hibbert's office. No, better in the board room," Francis ordered. As the first basket passed his desk he took a telegram at random off the top and read it:

> BOSTON, MASS. 4 JAN DIRECTORS HIBBERT FIRST NATIONAL BANK, BROAD STREET, NEW YORK.
> THE INTERNATIONAL COMMUNITY OF MEN AND WOMEN AND THE CHILDREN WHO ARE OUR CITIZENS OF TOMORROW STAND WITH HEADS BARED UNDER GOD'S SUNLIGHT AS THE SPIRIT OF A GREAT LEADER AND PATRIOT TAKES ITS PLACE AMONG THE IMMORTALS SIGNED LOUIS B. MAYER

Francis felt the thrill of contact with the aristocracy of the world. Perhaps he should cancel the formal celebration with Stacie planned for that evening and instead invite her downtown to read the messages which would be pouring into the bank all day from the peerage of America.

"*Gentlemen,*" James Maitland said with sure authority, "I have asked Mr. Francis Vollmer, who has been Mr. Hibbert's closest associate for the past twenty-four years, who was the last man to see Mr. Hibbert alive and to speak to him, to tell you his very nearly eyewitness account of the passing of the greatest leader and finest gentleman this bank has ever known. Bearing the welfare of this bank and its stockholders in my mind, I cannot stress too gratefully how extraordinary—extraordinary beyond the call of duty—were

Mr. Vollmer's self-initiated services from the moment he realized that Mr. Hibbert had passed away. He deserves to be recognized for the mature decisions he made while he was alone, with no possible chance of turning to this board for direction."

James Maitland was elected president of the bank. Francis was made a vice-president and was asked to continue as assistant to the president. Francis' salary was raised from $107.12 per week to $133.25 per week and he was voted a bonus of $500. The short agenda that followed established minimum service requirements of fifty years to entitle such an employee to a pension to be determined by the executive committee. The board was advised that a routine audit would begin at three-thirty that afternoon. The next day they were notified by telegram that the audit had been completed and had balanced.

When Mr. Hibbert's will was read, it was learned that he had left Francis $10,000 for "loyalty, honesty and fullest achievement of promise," but although the lawyers for the estate were questioned closely by Francis, they stated that Mr. Hibbert had given them no letters for him. Francis was totally bewildered as to where he was to turn, who he was and where he belonged.

Chapter 4

 The spring of 1919 was a pleasant one. Russia was in chaos, Pétain was made a Marshal of France, Churchill was appointed Secretary for War, and Generals Pershing and Wood seemed to be the likeliest possibilities for the Republican presidential nomination. Kangaroo shoes had caught on, thirty-six states had ratified the Prohibition amendment, while a Soviet decree ordered death for any high officials who were caught drunk.

Professionally, Francis was content. Working with Jim Maitland was quite unlike working for Mr. Hibbert, but an aura from the immediate past seemed to protect them. Francis called Mr. Maitland Jim only when they were alone.

Their shared danger made Maitland admire Francis tremendously, and he was restive when his assistant was out of his sight. Francis had fewer and fewer lunches of jelly sandwiches in Trinity churchyard; Maitland would insist that they lunch together at Eberlin's or the Bankers' Club or

India House. On these occasions, though conversation usually opened with references to Maitland's early days with Mr. Hibbert, it usually degenerated into expositions by Maitland concerning the number of husbands he had cuckolded on the North American and European continents. If the claims he made were true, Francis reasoned indignantly, there would have to be very few virtuous women left among the aristocracies.

Francis soon got damned sick and tired of these endless sagas, even though Maitland paid for the lunches and was introducing his assistant, even if only casually, to some very important men. But Stacie was keener about hearing Francis' Maitland stories three times a week than any Londoner had ever been about keeping up with Little Nell. She would shriek with laughter and hold her breasts tightly with each hand as she leaned forward to hear every word. She longed to meet Maitland "just to see him" or sometimes "just to hear him."

Maitland was grooming Francis for bigger things at the bank far faster than Mr. Hibbert had, but he felt it necessary to talk constantly about sex to keep them from talking about the manner of Edward Hibbert's death and how they had concealed it. Francis didn't sense this, and out of boredom and disapproval took to avoiding the lunches whenever possible—which was how the invitations to dinner came about and how Stacie met Maitland.

At some time Francis had mentioned to his new chief that his wife lived for music. Throughout his life Maitland had been quite civic-minded in a non-political way. He gave money to the arts; he aided city planning; he assisted in the direction of principal charities. But his strongest interest was music, and he was a dedicated, active sponsor of the most prominent musical organizations and societies in the city. Ten days before the opening of the Philharmonic season he invited Francis and Stacie to a dinner party before the concert. Josef Stransky was to be the conductor and Percy Grainger the soloist. "Grainger was a pupil of Busoni!" Stacie told Francis excitedly. "He was a friend of Grieg!"

Music had been Stacie's life ever since she was born. The

first job her father, a prototype mechanic, had executed while in the employ of Thomas Alva Edison, the Wizard of Menlo Park, had been to build the first working model of what was to be known as the phonograph. Young Bert "Black Jack" Mayers had gone home that evening flushed and excited, and had poured out all the musically revolutionary significance of the device to his young wife. For the first years they were among the few people in the world to possess such phonographs, and to have available all the tubular test recordings of voice, song and instrumentation which were made. Music became their fixation. Stacie was born on January 12th, 1897, and was soon seated in a high chair in the kitchen of the cold-water flat on West 67th Street, facing her singing father, who played record after record to her, solemnly keeping time with the index fingers of both hands.

Stacie's father was called "Black Jack" because he chewed such quantities of Black Jack chewing gum. He was a man who had satisfied his need to participate in music by taking up handbell ringing. He and three male friends, all equally hairy and equally possessed with a desire for harmonic clamor, had formed a handbell band and had become the stellar attraction among the church societies and sodalities of the neighborhood. "Black Jack" was the leader of the band, and the sweat would glisten on him as he chewed his gum and stared at the air four feet above the heads of the audience and performed his handbell solo with wildly swinging arms.

By the time Stacie was five her father had placed a phonograph in every room of the four-room flat in order to make changes of tempo and tone all the more vivid to her. "Old MacDonald Had a Farm" was one of the first musical pieces Stacie ever heard. Her father also taught her an incredible amount of musical information. At six she knew such esoterica as that the German tenor Max Alvary (Maximilian Achenbach) was the first singer to play Wagnerian roles without a beard. She absorbed the libretto and score of every known opera, the works of every composer since Filippo di Monte, and the techniques and indiosyncrasies of every contemporary musician. However, her father was so intent on pulling her into the world of music, that her ability to retain tonal pitch or to make music herself became hopelessly confused. It might have driven a weaker girl mad. Her father would have one phonograph playing "The Shepherd's Complaint" in the kitchen; then he would draw her by her adorable, fat little wrist into another room to hear Smetana's tone pictures of the River Moldau. In the next bedroom Francis A. O'Connell might be singing "Tolentine's Just Down the Way." Then, in the parlor overlooking the gas house, she would be told to taste Sir George Martin and Lady Judith performing on the glockenspiels in the *Davidsbundler* dances. The music would change with the quarter hour in all four rooms of the flat on every Saturday afternoon, on most of Sundays, and for forty-five minutes just before Stacie's bedtime.

Stacie adored it and she would imagine herself chatting with the great men of music. But though she knew the keys in which the individual pieces had been written, her ear had been unbalanced and her sense of rhythm impaired. Although she could hear all the great music of the world in her head, she was never to be able to carry a tune by voice or with an instrument. By the time she married Francis Vollmer, when she was nineteen and he was thirty-five, her discouraged father had given up expecting melody from his black rose whom he had transformed into one of the great musical repositories of the West.

Francis had come to take all that for granted. Furthermore, he had seen the guest list for Maitland's dinner and he was dazed with awe. There would be people at that dinner who though he had never seen them were as familiar as saints to a hagiophile. Made somber by the cost but determined to be correct, he made the decision to buy, not rent, a suit of full-dress clothes and he graciously approved Stacie's petition for a new dress.

Stacie was the star of the dinner. He gaped. She held Percy Grainger, himself, in conversation about the piano for over twenty minutes in the presence of two delighted and wholly impressed women who were respectively the social leaders of Philadelphia and New Haven. Everyone in the room sought her out after that. She sat at Maitland's left, next to a renowned flutist, and discussed music and musicians with such wit and style that within two days they had other invitations from thrillingly distinguished people to attend every sort of a musical gathering. It was more difficult for Francis, who although he could fall back on banking, knew nothing about music beyond the organ programs he had kept for Mr. Hibbert. So, at Stacie's urging, he took instruction night after night from her in various easily assimilated conversational gambits about music. She insisted that this was all that most of the other guests would ever know, and because she was so knowledgeable she was almost able to make him a musically fascinating man.

Maitland was delighted with the Vollmers. Three months later, when an opening occurred on the committee for the Chamber Music League, he insisted that Stacie accept the appointment. Then, in rapid succession, he asked her to serve on the boards of the City Parks Music Muster, The Confraternity of American Opera Associations and, finally, on a programing committee of the Philharmonic Society. Because they insisted on it, Stacie began to call people by their first names, people whom Francis had worshiped from afar for many years. Francis began to feel a certain amount of awe as he listened to Stacie speak authoritatively to famous conductors and musicians and heard them answer with passionate interest. "Beethoven and his individualism were so complete," she said to Richard Starkey, "that he prevented any German descent into mere subjectivism. Don't forget that he and Goethe were the heavenly twins of that society, in an era when music still had universal significance."

While discussing music Stacie was mature and profound. When she was not talking music she was a sweet, dear, extremely pretty twenty-one-year-old girl. What she had coached him to say to musical society taught Francis that education meant power. He began to think of the many other things he should learn so that he could rise, as his wife was rising, to a position of dominance over the biggest people in America. That alone was a good enough reason, but if he mastered all the things he should know he would be worthy of being the true son of his parents, and when this mysterious waiting period was over and he received The Message, he would be fully qualified for the world of command.

The extent of their social success settled one thing for Francis. He would have to spend some of his savings. Living at the Belleclair Apartments on Washington Heights was now out of the question. Within six weeks after the first glorious dinner party, fifteen weeks after Mr. Hibbert's death, Francis rented an apartment at the Apthorpe, one of the city's most prestigious dwellings, on West 79th Street. The building occupied one square block between Broadway and West End Avenue. One entered a great *cour d'honneur* past a uniformed private policeman. R. H. Macy & Company maintained a special department to service the occupants of the building. The apartment had six rooms, two baths, its own refrigeration system—a feature unequaled by any other apartment building in the city—plus mail chutes. It had a maid's room at which Stacie looked wistfully, but Francis felt that, all expenses considered, the room could be better used as a combination sewing room and pantry.

The $450,000 remained locked in Francis' second drawer, but the responsibility of its possession never stopped gnawing at him. Out of duty he had to find a way to invest it, but by necessity he had to move very slowly. This built enormous pressure inside him. To ease the tension he began to study other essential conversational strengths in the way he had studied musical conversation. First and foremost he felt compelled to learn restaurant-French for four dollars per hour, including food and wine, from a teacher whom he had located through the French Consulate. Monsieur Grondet, a French national who had been a restaurateur in Dijon, Lyon and Marseille, consented to undertake to teach Francis, provided he agreed to follow his methods diligently.

M. Grondet lived in a rambling flat on the Lower West

Side of Manhattan, near many of the best food markets. He was a very stout, dark man of about sixty, with shining hair and skin, with eyes as green as pistachios, with an avidly worldly manner and with an agitated gout condition in the large toe of his left foot. He accepted three pupils daily.

During their first interview Francis explained that he sought to understand any menu written or spoken in French, to be able to order food in French, to know which wines to order and how to pronounce them without the assistance of a headwaiter or wine steward. M. Grondet did not explain that he taught only the complete French language; he was a good teacher who knew the pupil would learn best when reached through his interest. He said that Francis must learn how to prepare food to be able to order it correctly and well, and that by tasting and discussing wines in French, he would learn their qualities and how they enhanced food.

M. Grondet ate fully at each lesson. Because of his gout he was unable to move about, but he could give minute instructions from his rocking chair, and because he spoke so little English most of the instructions had to be in French. Thus, he was paid four dollars an hour by three pupils to cook two meals for him every day except Sunday, when his gout had to rest. In a very short time they learned to speak basic French and to cook simple dishes very well.

At first Francis had no interest in cooking, but he accepted M. Grondet's pedagogical theory because he could see that it was working. It also occurred to him that when he had access to his money it would be quite useful to know how to prepare little dishes for hasty midnight suppers with beautiful dancers, or perhaps a duchess. By teaching Francis how to cook "aphrodisiacal little suppers" M. Grondet taught Francis how to speak French.

The Grondet kitchen was larger than most of the Vollmers' old flat at the Belleclair Apartments. It had a six-burner coal stove, earthenware pots, heavy iron frying pans, copper saucepans and an enormous larder, and it was brilliantly lit. Slowly, Francis was taught the basic details of the culinary arts, and while he diced vegetables or prepared puff paste, they would sit around a circular table with a heavy wooden top as thick as a butcher's block and M. Grondet would talk about the chemistry of cooking, the effect of asparagus on wine, the tyranny and the mockery of champagne or, even more frequently, about gout.

"Is gout a curse? Well, is civilization a curse? Because gout was surely one of the first diseases which came when man began to taste the luxuries of civilized life. And why have medical historians been studying gout since ancient Greece? Because of gout's constant preference for the great and wealthy and because before doctors are healers they are snobs."

This jocular representation of the sort of people preferred by gout insured Francis' irrational interest in the preparation of food—which, in turn, required that he understand the French language. As the months went by, he learned the names and varieties of all kinds of French food, while at the same time, almost without knowing it, he learned French grammar. He learned French wine while he learned French irregular verbs. Seated at the table, M. Grondet would play the part of a haughty maître d'hôtel—"Like Luigi, the monster of snobbism who runs the service at the Embassy Club in London, may you never meet him"—who was gradually forced into admiration as Francis ordered an imaginary dinner for two.

Francis' skill as a cook amazed and gratified M. Grondet. In time his pupil began to improvise with instinctive brilliance. Grondet called him a natural cook with the makings of a *great* cook. And Grondet knew how to reach Francis. "Do you know what *Punch* wrote in 1900?" he asked. " 'In keeping with the spirit of a more democratic time gout is becoming less upper class and is now open to all. It is not fair that a man should be barred from enjoying gout because he went to the wrong school.' " Francis produced such a dismayed look that M. Grondet was able to laugh in spite of his pain.

M. Grondet's niece, Denise Hillairet, appeared at the flat infrequently. She was a handsome woman of about thirty-five who spoke only French; she would eat the food Francis prepared, analyze it critically and speak to Francis with appreciation but polite detachment about his skills as a cook. She was a widow who owned a barbershop on Lexington Avenue; she had not learned English because from the time she had arrived in America from the South of France twelve years before, her husband had told her that eventually they would be going home. Now that she knew she would never be going home, she had no interest in learning English because not having to listen to it and try to understand what she heard gave her more time to think.

But mostly Francis was alone with M. Grondet, concentrating on learning how to cook and unable to avoid learning French. Francis took lessons on Monday and Wednesday from noon to one-thirty P.M., and on Saturday from eleven A.M. to five P.M., during which time he prepared all of M. Grondet's meals for the weekend. After many weeks of this Francis found it impossible to keep his new knowledge to himself, and since it would be some time before he was able to use the skills around midnight in a bachelor apartment, he could not keep from showing off to Stacie at home. At the end of May he arrived at his own doorstep, staggering behind paper bags filled with food. Stacie asked with amazement, "Where did you find all that stuff? Did someone leave it on the subway?"

"No, no. It's a very big surprise."

"But I hate surprises."

Francis emptied the bags on the kitchen table. "You have no idea how enlightened the bank is getting."

"But what about all this food?"

"That's it. They're giving the executive echelon a chance to study French. A sensational new system—and very necessary, of course. We'll be doing a big foreign business now that the war is over."

"But, Francis, why did you get the food?"

"That's the method. They teach you to cook, and while you concentrate on cooking, the teacher speaks in French—and believe it or not, you learn French."

"You may learn French but you can get awfully fat. Say something in French."

"Je t'aime."

"What's that?"

"I love you."

"The bank taught you that?"

"As you know, we are the friendly bank. But please don't ever mention this to Jim Maitland. He thinks it's a crazy idea, and you know how men are about admitting their mistakes." Maitland was the only bank executive Stacie had met. "Please promise never to mention it to Jim."

"I promise, but tell me more."

"When the meals are cooked, we have customers in to lunch in the executive dining room. It's good for business."

The mussels took two hours to prepare, the *daube* one hour. They ate at nine-twenty, and Stacie said it was the greatest meal she'd ever had in her life and that he had to show her how to do it.

While Stacie taught him musical conversation, he taught her cooking and the beginnings of French. She wasn't a very good cook, but soon she enrolled in an extension course in French at Columbia and rapidly overtook him in the language. Francis now saw every new knowledge leading to another; if he persevered, by the time he was able to claim his fortune and his family, he could be a cultivated, accomplished man.

Six weeks after he began with M. Grondet, Francis had begun to study in the reading room of the main public library. He started by making himself familiar with the principal foreign cities, poring over street maps and guide-books and making his way, in imagination, from the best hotels to the best restaurants and to the leading theaters and museums. While on the subject of museums, he saw that he would have to learn about painting and sculpture in the way that Stacie had taught him musical conversation and M. Grondet had taught him cooking. And as he learned the whereabouts of the principal flower shops in Paris and London, he decided he must be able to converse on varieties of flowers so that he could order them with sophistication. Then he had to know about precious stones and their settings, and to be informed on silversmiths and furs and perfumes and standards of fashion so that he could buy or discuss them with authority. Francis began to bring books home, and Stacie, who was interested in everything that interested him, was fascinated by the reasons why he had to know all these things. He told her that the managing director's job in the London branch might be open in a year, that it was considered one of the best stepping stones in the banking business, and that he wanted them to be well informed on such matters so that they would be welcome everywhere, just as music had made them welcome among Jim Maitland's friends in New York.

Stacie accepted the explanation completely and enthusiastically. Just as she had taught him to absorb information on music, she gave Francis an organized drill every evening they were at home. After he had cooked and served a meal, they would leave the dishes and pots and pans for Stacie to clean up the next morning and would settle down opposite each other at the dining-room table to study books on painting, ranks and titles, jewels, architecture, furniture, capsule literature, porcelain, comparative religion, rules of gambling, high fashion, poetry and English politics. They would quiz each other, one holding the book while the other took over a "conversation" on a chosen topic.

For example, Stacie would begin with, "I see that Knoedler is having a Sickert exhibition."

"Uh—Sickert? The one who worked in—uh—Whistler's studio? Did he?" She nodded. His yellow eyes stared at her deeply.

"Well—uh—isn't that interesting? Degas had a strong influence on Sickert."

"Where did he work?"

"Which one?"

"Sickert."

"Uh—in London and, well, in Madrid."

"No, darling. London was right, but Venice, not Madrid. And you aren't making *conversation*. You're saying it as though it were a test in a schoolroom."

"Well, can you give me an example of what you mean?"

"Just let it flow. I mean, no one at a dinner party is going to be exactly desperate for this sort of information. Say it like this: 'Sickert? Good, I must stop by at Knoedler's. If one can't afford Degas, Sickert is the next best thing.' Or maybe: 'Sickert may be one of the few painters who ever met Whistler's mother socially. He worked at Whistler's after he left the Slade, you know.'"

"What's the Slade?"

She shrugged. "Some English shire, I suppose. I mean, what's the difference when it's just talk at a dinner party?"

"I like to be accurate. I like to be ready."

"I'll look it up."

"Maybe it's 'after he left the slate'—like a blackboard—in some school."

"Now you try it with pottery," she urged him. She searched for the book, but not finding it immediately, she started without it. The long years of memorizing musical facts to please her father had given Stacie an amazing memory. "Heavens," she said, "what outlandish words Wedgwood uses to describe pottery colors. What on earth does 'rosso antico' mean?"

"Anything from dark red to chocolate. They have more obscure names than that—how about 'cane buff'?"

"A cane buff is someone who is wild about walking sticks."

"How about 'drab ware'?"

"What's that?"

"It seems to me a rather negative way of saying 'olive gray.'"

"Oh, Francis! That was perfect!"

Francis beamed and blushed. Then he said, "Do you think it's wrong to be as ambitious as I am, Stacie?"

"Why should that be?"

"Sometimes I think I live in the future all the time."

"I don't think it's wrong for *you.*"

"Why just me?"

"Well, the orphanage, for one thing. Then when Mr. Hibbert took you out but didn't adopt you. I guess it made you want to have to be somebody just to show him that he'd been right to pick you. Anyway, none of us know who we are until we realize our dream."

"Yes," Francis said very quietly. "I do have to find out who I am."

In the summer of 1919 Stacie was twenty-two years old. She was a voluptuous miniature of a woman whose presence was reminiscent of the old folk song about "black cherries and the darkness of fire, the snapping of twigs and the sound of a lyre." She smiled when she slept, and she was gifted with life in abundance. She never had to peer around the corner of the calendar to long for tomorrow; she was perpetually pleased with what she had.

Stacie had met Francis because her father had taken the stand that since New York City had been good enough for his father, it was good enough for him, and had chosen to make the long, daily journey between New York and New Jersey. Because Black Jack lived in New York, he was asked one day to stop at the Hibbert First National Bank to pick up an envelope and deliver it to Mr. Edison the following morning. But since that evening was the occasion of a rehearsal of the Handbell Band for a post–bar mitzvah performance to be attended by the Cardinal himself, Black Jack asked Stacie to pick up the envelope.

The Edison envelope was waiting on Francis' desk at the bank. When the reception desk called to have it sent out for Miss Mayers, who was calling on behalf of her father, Bertram Mayers, Francis' built-in aristocracy-detector clanged wildly. His step to meet this beautiful young heiress was quick and light as he carried the envelope to the reception room. When he saw Stacie he almost lost his balance.

"Good afternoon, Miss Mayers. I am Francis Vollmer, Mr. Hibbert's assistant."

"How do you do, Mr. Vollmer. The organ music is wonderful."

"Mr. Hibbert's idea."

"Isn't that Pachelbel's *Durch Adams Fall?*"

Her words impaled Francis. Culture meant breeding, and breeding meant money, and money was the American aristocracy. "I do believe it is," he said.

"May I have the envelope?"

"Oh. Yes." She thanked him and turned and walked away.

"Miss Mayers!"

When she turned he took three rapid steps toward her. "I have tickets for a musicale at the end of the week," he said. "At Carnegie Hall." Surely something would be playing at Carnegie Hall. "Will you join me? On Friday? Perhaps we might have an early dinner, then—"

Though Stacie's father had discouraged every beau she had brought home, she knew that he knew it was a losing game. When she explained that the invitation was for Carnegie Hall in the company of the assistant to the president of the Hibbert First National Bank, her father would have to surrender. "I think I would enjoy that very much, Mr. Vollmer," Stacie said.

By the time Francis discovered that Stacie was not an heiress and knew nothing beyond music and basic reading, writing and arithmetic, it was too late, no matter how he struggled with himself. And struggle he did, for weeks and weeks, for he was betraying his lifelong plan. How could he present to his parents when they sent for him a wife who was the daughter of a mechanic? He loved her far beyond his own belief in his capacity to love at all, beyond his love for his family. Stacie solved his indecision as a billion unschooled but intuitive women before her had solved it: suddenly, from a rock-solid position of strait-laced shock at his slightest suggestion of erotic valor, she gave herself over to carnal abandonment with Francis, and within the following lunar month, managed to convince herself that she was pregnant. The pregnancy had not ensued but the marriage had, at City Hall on July 17th, 1915.

The Vollmers went to the Hotel Glenmore, Big Moose, New York, for their honeymoon.

Chapter 5

 On July 15th, 1919, the Vollmers left New York on Francis' annual two-week vacation, for the Hotel Glenmore at Big Moose. They made love in a noisy bed at the highest point in the central Adirondacks. The shrieking bedsprings were no accident. The manager's wife was an *écouteuse* who prowled the halls around the clock. They rested by gliding across the lake in canoes, walking up the sides of small mountains and drinking beer. The bank seemed far away.

On the day Francis was to leave for Canada, on bank business as he had explained to Stacie some time before, they went out on the lake in a guide boat with a basket lunch. The graduated growth of the pine trees on the shores and hills around them was as kempt as an Edwardian beard. Stacie lay on cushions at the bottom of the golden-ribbed boat, one pink finger trailing in the water.

"I wonder where we'll be ten years from now," she said in her sweet, endearing voice.

It was such an unexpected question, and so mirrored the

thoughts which had obsessed him since Mr. Hibbert had died, that Francis was startled into answering honestly. "I think about that most of the time," he said.

"Tell me."

"I mean, that's the way my mind has worked since the orphanage."

"The same dreams?"

"They *were* dreams. I call them plans now." Francis rowed steadily, smiling at her, convinced that she was the most pleasing woman in the hemisphere.

"What were they when they were just dreams?"

"Most of us at the orphanage dreamed about the same thing, I guess. Who our real parents were and why they abandoned us. After a while I knew my real parents could never come for me and that they sent Mr. Hibbert instead."

"Did you really think that? Or is that what you wanted to think?"

"I think it now."

"Did Mr. Hibbert leave any clue?"

"Nothing. It . . . it upset me very much. As you yourself said the other day, he was careful not to adopt me—under orders, you may be sure. He was to sponsor me, give me a start, so that They could test me and see if breeding would tell."

"You didn't think you might have been Mr. Hibbert's son by another woman?"

"Well, at first, yes. Frankly, yes. But I soon figured out that in that case there would have been no need to send me to an orphanage in the first place. I would have been sent to nursery school, then to boarding school, then to prep school, then to college for the first twenty years of my life. No, it's fairly clear now. My mother is—or was—a high-born person who fell in love. It also seems clear that my father must have been a truly important figure in a very important family. Perhaps he was married. Or it could have been a matter of state—either politics or a religious difference with a political twist. Whatever, it made the presence of a son very dangerous business. The family obviously banked with Mr. Hibbert and I had to be put aside as long as the peril existed."

"Like Moses in the bulrushes." Stacie grinned at him, enjoying the game.

"Yes." Why was she smiling?

"What a lovely game for a little boy."

"It is not a game!" Francis pronounced each word loudly, each word separate from the others.

Stacie looked puzzled, then quickly made her face expressionless. She knew she had made a mistake.

"Three times Edward Stokes Hibbert was asked to be the Secretary of the Treasury of the United States of America. He was a man so trusted with the confidential affairs of the finances of the governments of Europe that he was decorated with the highest honors they could award," Francis said coldly.

Stacie had never seen his widely staring eyes look like this. He had slipped away from her. "Why should a man like that suddenly show up at an orphanage? A whim? Not likely. And why that particular orphanage? There were sixty-four boys, and he never stopped as he walked down the line to inspect us. We were all lined up against the thick yellow-brick wall, and he walked slowly while Sister Mary Rita recited each boy's name. I remember distinctly that he hesitated, almost stopped, when he was abreast of me and she said my name. He seemed to want to put his hand out and touch me on the shoulder. Then he moved on. But I had seen what was in his eyes. I knew. I knew."

"Why did he come?"

"The most famous banker in the United States was sent to bring me out into the world so that I could be watched and tested."

"Tested for what, darling?"

"I don't know." He stopped his slow rowing and stared at her helplessly. "I am waiting to be told. Perhaps a throne, perhaps something less, but They have to make sure that I can behave like an aristocrat of strong character and utter loyalty. A man who knows where to place his devotion."

"You are those things, dearest. You've done what you set out to do, with character and loyalty and true devotion. You've made your own way, and you are a very valuable and important man. All because you believed in that boy's dream."

"It was not, is not—repeat *not*—a dream!" He shipped the oars and sat looking at her distantly until he gained control of himself. "I suppose it is a rather difficult story to understand," he said tightly and looked away from her.

"It isn't difficult to understand at all. Darling, please don't be angry. Please don't be upset." But Francis' eyes remained fixed upon some point above her head, looking far beyond the horizon.

Francis took the night train to Montreal that evening. He would return in two days. In the compartment on the train he went over his correspondence with Carr's Bank of Canada Limited, which had begun the previous April. His first letter on the stationery engraved with "Office of the President" said:

April 15th, 1919

Mr. C. N. Carr, President
Carr's Bank of Canada Limited
440, Matsner Street
Montreal, Canada

Dear Mr. Carr:

Our valued client, Mr. Francis Vollmer, has informed me that he will be in Montreal on July 18th in conjunction with the settlement of an estate. He has asked me to refer him to a bank in Montreal to serve his needs for the transfer of assets abroad.

Mr. Vollmer's substantial account has been handled by this bank for many years. You may be sure that any services you may extend to him will be most warmly appreciated by our bank and by me personally.

Very truly yours,
James Maitland

All mail addressed to Maitland had to cross Francis' desk, so the risk was small, and had anything gone amiss, Francis would have explained that he planned to invest Mr. Hibbert's legacy in foreign currency speculation. The written reference to the president of Carr's Bank was essential.

He knew that no bank would undertake the transaction he had in mind without such an introduction, either from another bank or from a responsible customer, because Francis intended to open a number account in Zurich, a new development in international banking which the Swiss had innovated in 1912. The Swiss bank, in its turn, would insist upon a reference from the Canadian bank, so Mr. Carr's needs had to be anticipated inasmuch as the only address either of them would have for Francis personally would be c/o P.O.B. 318, New York.

In the letter to which he had forged Maitland's name, Francis enclosed six specimens of his own signature, to be forwarded to Zurich after he had independently submitted his own specimen signatures to Zurich at the request of the Swiss bank. The Swiss would resubmit these to Mr. Carr for checking, and the number account would be opened and the money hidden forever.

Francis had considered forming a company in Lichtenstein in which he, as beneficiary, would remain nameless in the Articles of Association, and two local administrators would be employed to carry out the beneficiary's wishes. The only advantage of this system was that the money could then be deposited in different cities of the world. But the running expenses, taxes and other charges on such accounts were high, and in the end he had decided that a Swiss bank was the most sensible repository.

At last his money would be available for sensible, responsible investment. He would ask the Swiss bankers to make their recommendations for investment to him by mail to 318. Then he would check these recommendations against the virtually limitless facilities of the Hibbert bank, which had offices in eleven principal cities of the world. He would have access to the latest, most expert investment information, and when he had made his decisions he would return the list to Zurich with his buy orders. In time he and his bank would understand each other, and with such pooled information he should be able to do very well indeed. He meant to double his money in eight years—let the less conservative chance-takers double theirs in five—and to keep doubling it after that.

Two weeks later a letter addressed to Jim Maitland from Carr's Bank of Canada Limited had come across Francis' desk.

2nd May 1919

Dear Mr. Maitland:

I have been out of the city, but on my return I read with great pleasure your letter of the 15th April. We are prepared to extend to Mr. Francis Vollmer any banking services he may require.

Be assured that I regard your referral of Mr. Vollmer to this bank as a compliment of the highest order. Your comments on the activities of Mr. Vollmer and his wishes will have our best attention, and we wish to thank you very much for taking the trouble to write to us.

With kindest regards and reiterated thanks we remain,

Very truly yours,
Carr's Bank of Canada Limited
C. N. Carr

Francis read the letter twice before he burned it.

Mr. Carr showed no surprise when Francis opened the shiny black attaché case and disclosed $450,000 in cash. He did ask a few sly questions about Mr. Maitland, but this was reflexive and his heart wasn't in it. When Francis casually dropped the name of Mr. Maitland's tennis professional, which Mr. Carr did not know himself, and when he heard Francis repeat Maitland's pet catchwords as a banker, he accepted Francis completely and merely asked for his passport for identification and for confirmation of the specimen signatures.

Carr's Bank of Canada Limited agreed to remit $450,000 to the Bank Graubunden-Zug in the Bahnhoffstrasse, Zurich, with instructions that it communicate its recommendations for investment to P.O.B. 318, Wall Street Branch, New York, N.Y. The whole transaction took thirty-five minutes, and Francis found himself in Montreal with most of the day to kill at twenty minutes to ten in the morning. Although it was the first time Francis had ever been outside the United States, he decided to use the time before lunch in sharpening his conversational gambits in the city's public library.

It was an excellent library. They had many books on London which he had not seen before and there were some interesting volumes on the local cuisine. Francis browsed through the shelves until he came upon a book called *The Eternal Courtesan*. He decided that reading this would be a pleasant way to spend the morning; it was the sort of thing which could add raciness to a conversation without making it vulgar. As he took a chair at the long walnut table near a window he began to imagine the elderly English gentleman with whom he would be chatting sometime in the near future. The Edwardian survivors of the nineties had been through quite a number of these women: Cora Pearl, The Comtesse de Loynes, Liane de Pougy and La Belle Otero. He memorized the words of Sir Kenneth Digby as he had gazed upon the naked, sleeping body of Venetia Stanley: "Out of that darkness did glisten a few drops of sweat like diamond sparks, and had a more fragrant odor than violets or primroses." He absorbed brief accounts of the lives of St. Mary the Egyptian and Ninon de Lenclos.

But as Francis began to read about The Gypsy a sense of prescience came over him; he felt the same sort of inner exultation as when he had realized the secret of his own life and inevitable destination. His daemon, Francis knew, was showing him what he must do to release himself from Stacie. He could not hurt her directly because he loved her more than almost anything else in the world, but he couldn't possibly take her with him. But here was a way he could separate himself from Stacie without a scandal being attached to him, and which therefore could not be a source of anxiety or alarm on the part of his parents. He stared at the page as though it were a manual of arms or a locksmith's handbook. He read it again, then set out to memorize it.

"I knew," said The Elector, narrator of the account, "a famous courtesan in Rome who was named The Gypsy. She was the mistress, for a considerable time, of an English lord. After they parted, The Gypsy had a desire to visit England and, being come there, made discreet inquiry to learn whether or not the Lord's wife had remained faithful to him. 'How could you have known that she had not remained

faithful to him?' The Gypsy was asked. 'I trained her husband so well,' she boasted, 'and taught him so much of
amorous knowledge that he could not help but improve
upon the amorous knowledge of his wife, and it is impossible
that she could withhold from showing others what she knew.
Our trade is so ardent when you know it well that there is a
hundred times more pleasure in instructing and practicing
with separate persons than there is to be got exercising it
with one alone.' "

Francis grinned with delight. It could be done. When the
time came to extricate himself from the bank and his marriage he would investigate where and how he could be
taught sex, just as he had been taught cooking, French and
specialized conversations. When he had mastered sex and all
of its stimulations he would instruct Stacie, putting his back
into it, as the saying went, until she was unable to think
about anything else. Then he would sit back and wait for her
to indulge in flagrant sexual dalliance with another man. No
one would be able to blame him for what followed, least of
all Stacie. By causing her to sin against him, he would only
be more beloved by her and she would yearn for their past
together because she had hurt him. Thank heaven for the
gift of patience, Francis thought. At last he had discovered
a way to disappear.

As he rode the evening train back to Big Moose, Francis
examined all his motives and intentions. Was he moving too
fast? He must tread very carefully. Though now the money
could never be traced to him, he must not succumb to the
temptations of using it before the time had come. Timing
was all-important. He had not been sleeping well for some
time, but perhaps now that the money was out of the
country he could relax. Perhaps the constant and tedious
anxiety he lived with was why They hadn't sent him The
Message. Long ago he had given up trying to understand
why Mr. Hibbert had failed him. Perhaps Mrs. Hibbert had
come upon the letter and had destroyed it, just as he had
destroyed Mr. Hibbert's letter to her.

He had to get back to Stacie. She gave him peace. He
began to wish that he could have been like other people, but

the disloyalty of the thought shocked him. He had been born to the nobility and, for better or for worse, that was where and how he must live his life. He must train himself not to think about Stacie. After he had left her he must concentrate on forgetting her, literally on putting her out of his mind forever, or he knew he would not be able to carry on.

Chapter 6

 In December, 1920, only twenty-three months after Mr. Hibbert's death and seventeen months after Francis had moved his money to Zurich, the Vollmers had acquired a player piano which played Albéniz' "Triana" by Artur Rubinstein as well as Isham Jones and "Whisperin'." D'Annunzio had declared war on Italy. Harding was President, the automobile industry expected sales of over 700,000 cars for the next year, and Shanley's, at 43rd and Broadway, offered a seven-course luncheon for $1.25. Prohibition was eleven months old and the five thousand cases of champagne then en route from France were for medicinal purposes only.

Also in December, 1920, Francis Vollmer decided that the time had come to begin his sexual studies. It had been a busy twenty-three months. His French was superb and he had become a better cook—M. Grondet astonished himself by saying it—than ninety per cent of the professional cooks of France. His constant and extended studies at home of fashionable conversational topics must have helped him, he felt, because Jim Maitland had said that Stacie had grown into one of the most brilliant conversationalists in New York.

Francis had begun a scrapbook of his wife. He was inordinately proud of the fact that she had appeared three times in the rotogravure sections of the Sunday papers, and in her growing aura of personal glamour. Music committees, charity luncheons, balls, her flawless French and her picture three times in the rotogravure sections made him dread, in a certain human way, what he was going to have to do. He had been able to calculate everything else rather well, but he still could not understand how he was going to live without her. Unconsciously, this gave his attentions to her a deeper sweetness which kept her radiantly happy. Often when he was alone Francis wept bitterly, and he had not been sleeping well at all. But Stacie had to stay behind when he was called. He had prolonged, painful headaches, but he would not permit himself to falter. His parents probably already had chosen a wife for him; this could be of infinite importance to them politically, and he must present himself to them unencumbered. Responsibility had to be faced; noblesse had to oblige. He began to have to keep his hands clasped over his stomach or in his pockets because they trembled unaccountably. His eyes burned all the time. Stacie read to him when he could not sleep—for entertainment, not to learn anything. And she massaged him or fed him hot milk or held him close to her.

Francis realized he had to find an accomplished mistress, a skilled, prodigiously well-schooled woman with a good body and basic vitality. But he wasn't sure where to look for one. He knew one would be found eventually and that his studies with her would take him away from home for short intervals, so he prepared the ground by telling Stacie that the bank was thinking of sending him to Washington for one day and two nights each week to co-ordinate international financial matters which were too complicated for him to try to explain.

One of Francis' active accounts at the bank was that of Joseph M. Fox, the producer of two of the most fabulously successful musical comedies of the twentieth century and a man who obviously had an inherent understanding of sexual matters because he had made an important investment in brood mares. Fox, who had quit the theater while he was ahead, he said, and had become a sober man of finance, checked with Francis six or eight times a week because his account was extremely active. He would either telephone or appear suddenly in person in one of the tiny suits which he had had cut in London by the tailors to Arthur J. Balfour, a former prime minister of Britain whose style Mr. Fox had come to admire. As Mr. Fox never tired of telling Francis, Balfour had framed the Balfour Declaration which had established a place for the Jews in Palestine, and the least he could do in tribute was to patronize Balfour's tailor.

Mr. Fox invited Francis to lunch and dinner many times, and with the invitations to dinner had gone the implication that there would be no reason for anybody to yell *ouch* if he happened to bring a couple of beautiful janes along. Mr. Fox liked Francis even though he didn't need him. Francis liked Mr. Fox, but it was a hopeless situation. Where could it lead except to a lot of ragtime cabarets or restaurants such as Jack's? As for that sort of woman—well, Francis was no snob but the only definition for such women, in a social sense, was impossible.

However, when Francis decided that he had to learn advanced sexual accomplishment, the only source he could think of was Mr. Fox. As soon as he had made up his mind he began to wait impatiently for Mr. Fox to telephone or visit the bank, but over ten days went by and he heard nothing. His impatience drove him to calling Mr. Fox at home in his mansion on East 51st Street. A servant answered the telephone, and then there was a very long wait before a small voice said, "Is that you, Francis?"

"Mr. Fox?"

"Did the market crash?"

"The market?"

"Francis, why are you calling me at my house for the first time in my life?"

"Well, I hadn't heard from you. You hadn't been in."

"You were worried, Francis?"

"Well, you see—"

"Don't be ashamed. It's killing me to stand in a draft and talk on the phone, but thank you, Francis."

"Have you been sick?"

"Take a tip. Don't ask. Nobody in the world has time enough for the answer, that's how sick I've been. You're a good man and I thank you for this call, but also you might be killing me, so I'll see you later."

It was another eight days before Mr. Fox showed up at the bank. He never looked better, Francis said, but Mr. Fox said that personally he thought he had looked much better while he had been reading the notices for *Bubblebath*, which had closed after one performance. He sat at Francis' desk, switched some holdings, bought some stock, shuffled a few municipal bond options around, manipulated some foreign currency, then said, "How's about we'll take a sannawitch?"

"I'm afraid lunch is out, Mr. Fox," Francis said slowly. "But—uh—inasmuch as my wife will be away for a few days—uh—how about—uh—dinner?"

"Frails?"

"Pardon?"

"You mean you are looking to climb some gorgeous chorus girl who I just might happen to know and bring along to this here dinner?"

Francis blushed.

"Listen, don't be embarrassed. If it's dinner, chorus girls have to eat like everybody else—right? What kind of a jane do you like, Francis? Not so frail? Blonde? American Indian? Short? Tall? Maybe a singer?"

"Well, to tell the truth, Mr. Fox—if you know someone who is really learned in a sexual way—"

"What?"

"You know—a woman who really knows—uh—various, different—uh—a girl who has really made a study of—"

Mr. Fox guffawed with growing amazement. "I had you figured wrong, I swear, Francis. For years I saw you as one of the world's great straights and all the time you are deadpanning me. Sexually learned? What's to learn? You get tired doing it one way, you do it some other way." He stopped laughing suddenly. "Say, what kind of a kidder are you?"

The dinner was a failure. The girls were strikingly beautiful and looked quite clean, but their speech was loud, their accents shocking, and most of the time they told dirty jokes in some incomprehensible show-business jargon. Francis pretended he had a sick headache and contrived to make it an early evening.

The next night, in his locked office, Francis went through the files of the various women with whom he had corresponded as a pen pal. Many had enclosed photographs with their letters and some of them were quite attractive women —though the one woman who had submitted her picture in the nude had not been facially pretty. Of the thirty-six pen pals with whom he had corresponded at least once, one lived in Jersey City, two in Manhattan and one in Staten Island. One of the four seemed to signal sexual experience; that is to say, she had mastered a way of implying things without actually saying them. Her name was Frieda Thesselson, and it had been almost two years since he had corresponded with her. She might be a starting point. He didn't expect anything sexually spectacular; after all, a woman who had to pay to place an advertisement in a sweetheart magazine might have the appetites of a Messalina but it followed that she had not been given the opportunities for much practice.

Francis pulled up the typewriter, inserted a sheet of white, unmarked paper and wrote:

December 20th, 1920

Dear Miss Thesselson:

It has been some time since we corresponded inasmuch as my company sent me to Canada on an interesting assignment, but I have been thinking about you a lot and wishing to meet you. This letter is to ask if you would be free for dinner next Tuesday evening. I work in the Wall Street area but could meet you wherever you say or pick you up at home. I would suggest the main entrance to the Aquarium. I am six feet one inch tall, have yellow eyes, high cheekbones, and will be wearing a flower in the buttonhole of a heavy black overcoat. May I hear from you at P.O.B. 318, Wall Street Branch, Manhattan? Please enclose a recent picture for ready identification.

Sincerely,
Leonard Shannon

Miss Thesselson's reply came two days later. The photograph she enclosed bore no resemblance to the one she had sent him two years before, and the handwriting of the second letter didn't remotely resemble the handwriting of the first. Could a group of such girls be sharing advertising costs?

Miss Thesselson was at the Aquarium when he walked toward the entrance at exactly six o'clock. It was dreadfully cold. She came running out of the shadow beside the doorway, saying, "Leonard—or do they call you Lennie?" She was much better-looking than either of the photographs, but resembled neither. They shook hands briskly.

Miss Thesselson was a thin woman in her early thirties with an enormous bust. They were not just breasts which might have been appreciated as being unusually large; they formed a promontory on which he could have rested his hat and gloves. It was as though all her growth had gone into her chest, and that it was still demanding an insatiable tribute in flesh from the rest of her almost emaciated body. She wore a bottle-green suit with a jacket trimmed with old fur. Her hat was an exaggerated artist's beret in green velour which slouched so alarmingly down the right side of her head that it could have been filled with walnuts. She wore rimless eyeglasses behind which, Francis could see, were avid eyes. She talked steadily about baseball as they walked to the small Italian restaurant he had chosen, using a deep voice to talk about the weather now and then, and clinging to his arm with a dead weight as though to keep him from drawing a sword against those who might rush up to claim kisses from her.

"In all fairness," Francis interrupted, "I think it is only proper to tell you that this restaurant at which I have booked a table is a speakeasy. If you have any compunction about flouting federal laws, or any fears about arrest, I will of course understand and we will go elsewhere."

"Oh, Lennie!" she cried and gave him a painful push with her bony hip.

Francis did not believe he had heard Frieda correctly when he thought she had said, "Have you bought your burial plot yet, Leonard?" as they sat down in the restaurant. But the waiter came at that moment, and though Francis ordered all the food in French she didn't seem to be at all aware of it. This irritated Francis.

"You were saying about a Murray Hill boite?" he inquired politely when the waiter had gone.

"No. I asked you if you had a burial plot."

"No."

"You are part of a family plot?"

"No. Not yet, that is."

Frieda pouted, placing her lips in the form of a plumber's plunger. "Why not?"

"Well, I'm an orphan."

Frieda grasped his hands across the table. "But you're not afraid of death?"

"I don't think so."

"Don't ever be afraid. Never, never. I used to be terribly afraid."

The waiter trundled up the antipasto wagon.

Although Francis was somewhat mystified, he was encouraged. Frieda had opened the way to their mutual transaction. She was overdoing the novelty approach, true, but she was obviously absorbed in sex. He chose crostini de mare, some fagiòli Toscani col tonno and insalata di funghi, though absent-mindedly. Despite her many interrupted lines of face and body and the unaccountable shards of her emotion which seemed to have been strewn in a trail from the Aquarium to the restaurant, he was able to convince himself that he could be sufficiently attracted to her to undertake the sexual studies and drills with her.

As Frieda ate spaghettini and veal marsala she offered him further little aphrodisiacs while the scratchy phonograph in the back of the room played "Ora e sèmpre addio" very loudly. "It's really hard to determine which is more for-bidden, sex or death," she said vivaciously. "People allude to sex all the time, of course, but everyone claims they're against it. Death doesn't even get that much of a break—they just pretend it isn't there. They treat it like a fairy tale."

"Sometimes they believe in it," Francis pontificated. They both stayed within the security of the third person because it was a touchy subject. "I mean they see it happen or they—"

"Oh, bereavement! But bereavement is when someone else dies. We may mourn our loss but we aren't capable of mourning the loss to death of ourselves. What I am trying to say is—I have a wonderfully responsive body and it loves me, it truly does—but when I die, I lose that body. I lose the only important thing I have, the only thing that loves me. Other people—"

"I don't think I get—"

"I'm just about to say it. Other people live for twisting their bodies into all the fantastic attitudes of joy. I can tell that you do; I can see the way your eyes open like flowers, the round part gets wider and wider when I talk to you about doing it. But when I talk to you about death your eyes get all tiny in the center, so I know that you don't under-stand death and don't appreciate it."

"You mean religiously?"

"I mean simply that if you avoid celebrating death every chance you get, you'll pay for that dishonesty not only with a fear of death but with a definite callousness about your life."

"But—just how do you go about celebrating death?"

"Well, look at a bullfighter. Look at steeplejacks. Look at some of your top criminals."

"It's kind of late for me to think of getting into that kind of work."

"Never mind." Frieda smiled at him so sexily that he could feel it deep in his stomach, as though a live chicken were trying to escape down there. "There are other ways," she said. "You'll see." She seemed to be breathing differently.

"How?"

"Once you see, you'll never want it any other way." She lodged her tongue between her open teeth to keep herself from talking while the waiter cleared the table. Francis ordered some espresso coffee and some grappa, but in English, and Frieda played with his long, bony fingers until the waiter returned. As they sipped coffee and grappa she whispered, "Where shall we go now?"

"Did—uh—you have anything in mind?"

Her head lowered, she leaned far across the table and he could feel the weight of her breasts on the backs of his hands. "Would you like to make love to death so that you'll never be afraid of it again?" Her lips were trembling and her eyes were hot. She slithered back into her seat, moving her breasts slowly across his knuckles.

"What?"

"We can take a subway to Woodlawn," Frieda said huskily. "No taxis—I don't want you to touch me until we get there."

"Get where?"

"No one is in the cemetery at night. Not in winter. I have a key to a certain vault and—oh, Leonard, it can be so wonderful!" She closed her eyes convulsively and gripped his hands tightly in a long spasm.

Francis got up as soon as he could get free. Frieda's eyes remained shut as he moved away from her. When he got to the coat rack the waiter appeared beside him. He paid the bill, including an ample tip, hurried out of the restaurant, then walked rapidly toward the South Ferry subway station. There must be some other way to disengage himself from Stacie painlessly. He decided to go back to the bank and try to think things through in a more orderly manner. There had certainly not been anything orderly about tonight. It had been absurd of that madwoman to think she could have gotten him into a freezing mausoleum to make love in the dead of winter. Granted he was interested in learning, but that didn't include erotic studies while dressed in overcoat, muffler, woolen mittens, galoshes and a fedora hat jammed down over his ears. And how in the world could he have passed such exotica on to Stacie, the entire purpose of the project?

Before he reached the bank, Francis felt hungry despite the meal he had just eaten. Anyway, he wanted to cook so that he could think more clearly. He needed to talk the problem over with someone. Although he had lived in New York ever since he had left the orphanage, he could think of only one person who would be willing to listen to him sympathetically. He called M. Grondet from a drug store near Wall Street.

"Monsieur Grondet? This is Francis Vollmer."

"Ah, Mr. Vollmer."

"How are you, Monsieur Grondet?"

"Gout."

"Bad?"

"Yes."

"Then I'm sure you won't want me there jabbering away at you."

"On the contrary, I should be very grateful. Were you thinking of visiting me?"

"Yes. I wanted to—"

"Good. Please bring the following: I feel the need of a ballottine de volaille. A nice fat chicken—please ask Les Rois for a hen—about five pounds. Four eggs. A pint of cream. That will do for the quenelles. Then a half pound of cooked tongue and some truffles. Also, a veal bone. I have onions and nutmeg, the cloves, the carrots and the garlic. Oh, yes. You must bring some mushroom caps and green olives."

"But it is almost eight o'clock, M. Grondet."

"So?"

"Everything is closed."

"No, no. Go to the kitchens of the Waldorf. Ask for the *souschef*, Benoit Les Rois. Ten dollars for the steward will cover everything. He will have it wrapped and ready for you because I will call him right now." M. Grondet groaned. "And hurry. A good ballottine is the only way I can fight this gout."

Francis appeared at the Grondet kitchen forty minutes

later. He had been delayed by his fascination with the flawless hotel kitchen, and he had persuaded M. Les Rois to take him through every department, talking all the while more animatedly than he ever had at the bank. M. Les Rois had treated him as a fellow professional, and the food had only cost six dollars "for a bottle of good wine for the steward."

"Split the chicken," M. Grondet said by way of greeting. "Put one half in boiling water, then strip the raw meat off the other half for the quenelles. Were you able to get the truffles?"

"Oh, yes."

"Benoit said he might find two hearts of artichoke as well."

"I have them. Is he a good cook?"

"Very professional. Very steady. But not as good as you. I mean it. Now get to work."

Blushing, Francis took off his overcoat and jacket, put on an apron, checked his knives, unpacked the food and washed his hands.

"I am lucky the gout stays in that one toe," Grondet said. "By now I should have it in both large toes and in both ear lobes. Hippocrates had three aphorisms which pertain to gout, but when all is said and done, it is only a chalky excrescence which looks like crabs' eyes."

"What were the aphorisms?" Francis was washing the chicken.

"First, eunuchs do not get gout or become bald. Second, a woman does not get gout unless her menses are stopped—although Galen and Seneca did not agree with him on that."

Francis worked skillfully while he committed to memory what M. Grondet was saying. Already he could envisage it as part of a civilized conversation over port in his father's London club.

"The nature of women does not alter, but their manner of living does, and Seneca knew that gout is the rosy daughter of the ancient family of Bacchus and Venus. Hippocrates' third aphorism was: 'A young man does not get gout until he indulges in coitus,' which in those days meant after puberty."

Francis had split the chicken and cleaned it; now he put one half into a pot of simmering stock and began to remove the meat from the other half.

"There seems to be such a strong correlation between the sexual powers of men and their gout that they were proposing castration as a cure as late as the eighteenth century. At my age maybe I should try it."

Francis was grinding the half of raw chicken and pounding it in a mortar. "Uh—speaking of sexual powers," he said, "I—uh—realize that you dislike discussing anything except gout or cooking, but as a matter of orientation—after all, you are a worldly man—I wanted to ask if I could—uh—consult you on a personal matter."

"Of course. State the matter."

Francis added salt and pepper and nutmeg to the chicken and continued to pound it into a paste. "I am," he said, "almost forty years old. But the customs of one country are seldom the customs of another."

"The customs of one country are the prejudices of another."

"The fact is that I have been married for some years, and now I—uh—feel that the time has come when I should—uh—find a mistress. But despite the fact that this is the biggest city in the Western Hemisphere, despite my age and position—the truth is, Monsieur Grondet, I don't seem to know where to begin to look to find a mistress."

M. Grondet regarded him steadily, nodding with a kindly expression. "That is serious," he replied.

"Yes, it is." Francis added the whites of two eggs gradually, then began to rub the forcemeat through a sieve while M. Grondet pondered.

"I may be able to help you," Grondet said after many minutes of silence. "That is, if you are not too rigid in what you seek to find in a mistress."

Francis shrugged. "I don't ask for a lot. A healthy woman. Handsome, perhaps. Not too young, but younger than I am. The coloring doesn't matter. In fact, it doesn't matter if she is intelligent, but a good disposition would be essential, I think." He looked up from his work for a moment to see if he had gone too far.

"But intelligent women are to be preferred to stupid women."

"Yes. However, the only really essential requirement— well, Monsieur Grondet, I'll be frank. It is vital that this woman know considerably more than I do about sexual matters."

"*Pardon?*"

"I say it is very important that she know much, *much* more about sexual matters than I do."

"Are you a sexual moron? I am not sure that I understand."

"Well, I'm no virgin, of course, but I am not an exotic either. That is, the only woman I have ever been with is my wife and—"

"Then of course any mistress would know more about sexual matters than you do. That is her métier!"

"It may be that I lack an imagination."

"Do you lack vigor? Can you uphold your part of the arrangement?"

"Oh, yes, I have an excess of vigor, but what I seek is a woman who understands the—well, the *art* of sexual practice rather than its content, if I make myself clear."

"You are a thoughtful man."

"Well—"

"I have no wish to pry," M. Grondet said carefully while Francis placed the sieved meat in a saucepan over cracked ice and began slowly to pour heavy cream into it, "but are you equipped financially to undertake to support a woman of value in the proper manner?"

"Is it very expensive?"

"It is a matter of qualifications," M. Grondet said, leaning back and forgetting his gout momentarily. "My only requirement for a mistress, *au fond,* is that she have but one interest in life: herself. Her profession makes her so entirely dependent upon her protector that the more she lives for him the more she will be helping herself. Such women deliver the best value and rarely deceive. Women often do have interests other than themselves, you know. Oh, yes! Causes, old mothers, young children, et cetera. I once knew a woman who was suspiciously interested in sports. It was unnatural, and in time her interest proved to be in athletes themselves, including a grotesque lady wrestler in Hamburg. Disregard women with other interests. They have short spans of attention. Support only those whose interest is in their mirrors and you will find the perfect mistress."

"Uh, you were saying about the cost?"

"That depends much upon your management of a woman. The expense should be just slightly more than the cost of a wife; men are usually consistent about how they allow others to spend their money. Old fools not included, of course. Nor idiots. The cost should be slightly higher because there is more romance involved with a mistress. After all, such arrangements are not intended to last forever, and the economic law of the short season applies. You will have to maintain a second flat, and to pay for her clothing, food, wine and telephone bill. As to clothing, her professional ethics will demand that she ask for an entirely new wardrobe because you are a new man. But unless you plan to take her to restaurants—or out in public generally—I would refuse this request. Only when a comparison to the generosity of a former lover is made are these things meaningful, and only a man who likes to show his women off in public cares about them. From what you have told me about your plans, your mistress will hardly have any time to get dressed anyway.

"Now, there is an unwritten agreement in such relationships that the woman must be allowed to telephone whomever she chooses, no matter what the telephone bill—*but for local calls only*. It is fair. Very happy arrangements have been shattered by the denial of telephone rights. It is lonely work for them. Next, you will have the increased cost of taxis between your two establishments. That mounts up. A healthy woman requires little medical expense, but they do have time on their hands and they will eat soft candies, so the dental costs are usually higher than with a wife. You will have no insurance charges, however. They must bury themselves—a basic rule.

"Some like to have little dogs for company. Some even paint, but avoid them; they will be moody. As an interest, painting is too subjective and it only adds to their self-importance. Some read, and reading is to be encouraged because the libraries are free and that diminishes the entertainment costs. Allow ten dollars a week for pocket money. She will want more, but give ten and be firm. Always remember that there isn't a woman alive who will not do everything a man demands, *providing*—and this is very important—that the man knows what he wants. The trouble that most men have with women can be traced to the fact that most men do not know what they want; this forces women to think, and they resent that.

"I have always offered a bonus to the women who will make their own clothes; it is not only a saving but a pastime. Not that they should make their own furs, of course, but I do not recommend that you think in terms of furs unless you are really wealthy, because the word gets around and when the next mistress comes she will want furs immediately, even if it is midsummer. Establish a fur policy straight off. From the beginning it must be understood that the furs belong to you, and that when you decide to take a new mistress the furs will go with you.

"It is important to keep them busy whether you are there or not; in idleness the stupid ones always fall in love with you, or else they become unnaturally committed to cheating on you. Lesbians are the worst types in this regard. They are excessively possessive women, whether with a man or a canary or a rubber plant. With the more or less normal women it depends upon how they were treated by the men immediately before you. A stingy predecessor creates a spending woman with his successor. An impotent man will pass on an avid woman. An impotent and unkind man will produce a woman predisposed to fall in love instantly with her succeeding patron, whether he is kind or potent. Allow all of them a shakedown period for that reason.

"On the whole, I think kindness is the best policy with them. The stupid ones don't understand kindness or else seek to misunderstand it, but then they are unruly anyway. Always face them when you hit them; always look directly into their eyes as you strike, and they will learn quickly. Personally, I have an extreme distaste for the moody ones—and, worse luck, such neurotic women are beginning to become fashionable. Twenty years ago things were different, you know. It is the damned newspapers and magazines and films which form the dispositions of these people. It may be pleasant if a woman is handsome, yes, but it is hardly the vital factor the damned magazines and films would have us believe. Far better a sensible, sweet-tempered ugly woman. There's much more endurance in them, and their gratitude can be touching.

"Always chat with a prospect and dine with her before making a commitment; it is worth finding out whether they are sensible. *Pourquoi?* Think of a heart attack. Or a severe stomach seizure which might or might not require hospitalization. The stupid mistress—that is, the unsensible one— always wants to show the wife that she is more worthy, because otherwise the husband would not have been with her when it happened. Really a most arrogant and unacceptable conceit. But the sensible mistress! She will know the name of one's personal physician, and when the blow falls she will see that you are hospitalized by your doctor and will have a sound, believable story ready, one which leaves herself entirely out of it, so that the distraught family will be accorded all comforts.

"Sensibility, good health and a good disposition—these things combined with utter selfishness. That is what makes a great mistress."

During this monologue Francis had stripped the boiled chicken, covered its flesh with a layer of the farce à quenelles à la panade and sprinkled truffles on top. He kneaded it into a firm lengthwise roll, having packed it with filets of tongue, chopped truffles and another layer of quenelles.

"You said you might be able to help me with this—uh— mistress thing."

"I have been helping you. My God, to give advice at my age! What a clown I have become."

"Please, Monsieur Grondet. I've memorized nearly every word you've said, and I shall never forget it. What I meant was, can you help me find the right woman?"

"Hm. Now if you wish to save money—"

"Yes?" Francis was alert as he tied the cloth around the ballottine.

"I know an engaging and really extraordinarily talented young woman who happens to be married, but who gets restless. However, she must get home to prepare a light supper for her husband and to make breakfast. She is available only in the afternoons, and she would teach you all you seek to know for an apple—"

"I'm never free in the afternoons."

"Ah."

"And I would rather not have a married woman anyway."

"Well, there is a contortionist I know from a fine old European circus family. But they are habit-forming, those women; that sort of high specialization spoils other women for you, and she has to travel a great deal in her work."

In a pan partially filled with water Francis was surrounding the ballottine with a veal bone, onions, the bones from the chicken, cloves and garlic. "I might learn a great deal more with a contortionist than with another mistress, but I couldn't really pass the information on and, frankly, I'd rather not become sexually dependent."

"I am in accord."

"Also, if this arrangement cannot be made tonight or tomorrow night, I will have to wait until a week from tonight."

"I see. All right, I will think. I will inhale the wonderful smells of your glorious cooking and I will think."

Four minutes before Francis served the meal, M. Grondet's niece, Denise Hillairet, walked in, saying that the cooking smelled so wonderful that she had imagined she could smell it across the city. They sat down to eat. Nodding, beaming, shoveling, chewing but rarely talking, they sipped and nodded and smacked. Grave professional chewers at their anointed task, they bit, swallowed, savored and burped. They closed eyes to encapsulate a taste. They mewed occasionally, served themselves again and again, and finally mopped up everything with crusty bread. In a sudden silence they sighed. As senior chewer, Grondet spoke first. "You are a master, Mr. Vollmer."

"You are a great artist," Denise said.

"You do me too much honor."

"You have gained some weight since I saw you last. Is that not so?" Denise asked.

"Twenty-one pounds."

"But you are tall. It is nothing on you."

M. Grondet coughed lightly, as though to get their total attention. They both turned to face him. "You are my finest pupil," he said, "and not only that, but you know instinctively things about the cuisine that very few people—French or foreigners—ever learn."

Francis shrugged, "Cooking makes me happy."

"You should be happy. Yes." He turned to his niece. "Denise, I learned this evening that our friend, Mr. Vollmer, is seeking a true and good friend."

Francis turned slowly and looked at Denise as though he were seeing her for the first time. He was astonished to discover that she was looking at him in exactly the same way. She was a surprisingly appetizing woman, he saw. She could, he knew, eat, drink and sweat gracefully, and she had never failed to volunteer to do the scullery work. As far as he had noticed, she was a woman with a sweet disposition. She was handsome, undoubtedly healthy and certainly sensible. How could he not have thought of her before?

Denise also seemed to like what she saw. "My husband has been dead for three years," she said slowly. "I parted with my own last friend ten days ago. Not that I was sad. He was not a kind man, and he was able to give much less of himself than he imagined he was giving."

M. Grondet sipped his wine. "Perhaps we have helped each other," he said. "I sincerely hope so. You two must do the washing-up now, and then you must have a good, long chat."

The riddle had been solved; the impenetrable had been penetrated; Francis' advanced sexual instruction began. He was greatly relieved to discover that sex was not something he could have learned by himself—not in a lifetime. Denise

Hillairet—as soon as she understood what was wanted—was a patient, thorough teacher, and though at first Francis was impulsive and in that way slow to catch on to the wealth of techniques at her command, when he did grasp them he brought everything he had to the task—as he had to the bank, to his conversational absorptions and to his cooking.

Denise lived in the three-story building which she owned, which was over her barbershop on the corner of 31st Street and Lexington Avenue. Her apartment was on the top floor and she rented the one below to the master barber and his family.

When she brought Francis home with her that first night after the triumph with the ballottine, Denise undressed him as though he were a child in her charge, then examined his flat body minutely for rashes or blemishes. She gave him a pair of white cotton pajamas, explaining that the first time she had experienced orgasm at the age of fourteen in a field "on the other side of Toulon," her lover had worn a white shirt as he hovered over her. It was her talisman for a good beginning, she explained.

Denise asked Francis to undress her slowly. He became greatly excited as he did so, but she talked to him softly, stroking him the way a groom pacifies a horse. She lay in his arms for some time before she would allow him to move, talking to him slowly and telling him in a muted voice, which gradually became huskier, that everything depended upon an absence of haste. She taught Francis that this was possibly the greatest advantage of being human; a gibbon can make twenty-two separate sounds of speech, a dog can laugh, elephants have memories, birds can migrate and dolphins can think, but if he could master himself to do exactly as she told him, then they had one golden advantage over all living things. No more hand-wringing over clocks and calendars: what they could know together was compensation beyond price for having been born with the knowledge that they would die.

It took time, quite a long time, really, but Denise drilled him demandingly and he trained himself to learn his lessons. He learned, at last, the infinitesimally subtle movements that produced the cries which came to him from some other dimension, and when he did learn it he learned it forever, executing with his characteristic bloodlessness all the splendid moves as though he were a learned horologer and she a priceless watch.

Each time Francis left Denise he would try to relive their experiences in his mind. He knew this to be the woman's role, but by remembering it minute by minute he understood better. He did so not with nostalgia or lust, but as a drill sergeant goes over the movements of a crack drill team being rehearsed to win the division championship. He would recall her gasped gratitude, her feebly passionate certitude that he had proved himself a great artist in still another field, and each time he passed one of her demanding tests he would pass the knowledge along to Stacie, working with thorough objectivity toward the goal of exploiting her ecstasy and propelling her into the arms of some other man.

Stacie was bewildered by the unfathomably sophisticated and powerful pleasures of their new sex life; it was all so overwhelming that it was some weeks before she began to wonder how it had suddenly happened to them after years of marriage. She was certain that the bank could not be providing the instructions, as with cooking and French. It was as though a straightforward mechanic who had proved that he could fix any Model T Ford had suddenly begun to manufacture transports of flying carpets woven out of purest hashish, or great, soaring, saddled swans sculpted out of mist.

Francis was relentless. He conferred the new mysteries so militantly, so efficiently, so inexorably—night after night after night—that sex became all Stacie could think about during the days and nights when he was away.

On Tuesday and Wednesday nights Francis studied under, over and around Denise, and on Saturday afternoons he cooked for her and M. Grondet. Sometimes, when they were alone, Denise wanted him to read to her or to explain some of the things going on in the world outside, but he wanted only to talk about food, wine and sex. Mostly it was sex: theory, practice, anticipated responses and the erogenous reasons thereof, the effects of clumsiness, and every kind of psychological and physiological aspect of the subject. Denise discovered that she knew far more than she had thought she knew, but to her dismay she saw that she knew nothing about Francis. He was male, but that had never been an enigma to her before. He was dispassionately insatiable in sex; by any logic he should have seemed possessed by the subject, but he was not. They might have been squirrels talking about an autumn's yield of acorns, or wrestlers on the same Olympic team testing each other's flaws, then discussing them dispassionately so as to gauge their possible effect upon some future opponent.

The financial part of the relationship was established easily. Francis opened an account for Denise in a savings bank on 34th Street; he never gave her money directly. She kept the passbook in a drawer in the main hall table, and he would take it with him every Wednesday morning, make the deposit and return the replenished passbook to the drawer each Wednesday night. She never urged him to stay when he said he could not stay. She did not fall in love with him. She told him that he was the best cook and the best lover, in that order, she had ever had, but she was too sensible to allow herself to fall in love with him for these reasons.

One morning, a few months after the lessons had started, Francis was awake, as usual, while Denise slept on. He wandered with random interest around the apartment. He had dressed and was waiting to leave for the bank. Under a table he found an old family Bible which contained family pictures. He admired the pictures of Denise as a bride, fourteen years before. Then he noticed that her husband had been an American, born in New York, as had his father and mother before him. This odd fact pressed upon his mind all day; somehow he had the conviction that it held a solution to his long and so far insoluble problem of how to use his money and how to disappear on his search for Them. That night he began to talk to Denise about it to see if he could discover the reason her husband's ancestry fascinated him.

"One time you told me you hadn't bothered to learn English because your husband was always saying that he would be taking you back to France."

"He liked to say that. He was delighted that I could speak only French."

"But early this morning I was going through the family Bible, and it says that both your husband and his parents were born in New York."

"That is so."

"Then how could he say he wanted to take you home to France?"

Denise shrugged. "The French and the Irish use the Old Country they never saw to protect them from the frustrations of the country in which they live. It was a harmless game."

"How did you meet?"

"What has come over you tonight, Francis? Are you falling in love with me?"

"I love you," he said simply. "I don't fall in love."

"You love me?" Her eyes went wide with a dozen questions she knew she would never ask. "That is touching, the way you say it. So unexpected, I suppose. I detest weeping women, but I cannot help these few startled tears." She brushed at her eyes. "I love you, too. It is sad, because we don't mean the same things when we say it, but that is quite beside the point."

Francis appreciated her detachment. "How did you meet your husband?" he continued.

"It was amusing because it was so old-fashioned, and because it shows how little we have to say about our destinations. I was born in France. I am in New York today, not greatly changed, but I never knew how until well after it happened. His parents were what you might call professional French, and they wanted a French bride for their son. They were frugal and had worked hard; his papa owned three barbershops. So they wrote to the mayor of the town from which their own parents had come. Maybe it was their grandparents. They had never seen the town, or even been to France. They were explicit and generous. They waived the dowry. They would transport the bride to New York, and they enclosed a picture of François. To me, he seemed a beautiful man.

"But a droll thing had happened thirty years before they wrote that letter. There had been a slight industrial shift, and the only people left in the town were my father, my mother and my six sisters. So it was quite proper for my father to open the letter addressed to the mayor. Somehow the poor man had gotten the first four girls married. I was the fifth. Marrying us off properly was a thing very much on his mind, I can assure you. He told me nothing. First he took me to Marseille and bought me two new dresses, a hat, new shoes and a trunk. Then we came home, and my mother, my youngest sister and myself sewed and sewed to fill the rest of the trunk. Then he called all my married sisters in. We had a wonderful family dinner, and at the end of it he read the letter and his reply to it. The next thing I knew I was married in America and living in this flat."

The next day, using bank stationery marked "Office of the President" and signing James Maitland's name, Francis wrote to the New York City Bureau of Records. He enclosed one dollar and asked for a copy of the birth certificate of François Hillairet, born to Arlette and Jean-Claude Hillairet on September 26th, 1877, at 322 Lexington Avenue, Borough of Manhattan. Then he looked up ATTORNEYS in the Classified Telephone Directory; he selected Max Braude because it was the same last name as the palmist Stacie's friend, Ellie Lewis, went to. The man's office was in the St. Paul Building on Lower Broadway. He telephoned Mr. Braude and made an appointment for three o'clock that day, stating that the purpose of the meeting was to ask him to set in motion a change-of-name proceeding.

The meeting was perfunctory. Francis took away with him a petition stating his name, address and date and place of birth. As reason for the change of name, Francis petitioned that he wished to honor his dead benefactor, François Hillairet, the man who had done so much for him as an orphan boy. The petition recorded the date of his marriage and the birthday of his wife, and stated that they were residents in the household of the Hillairet widow, Denise. Francis forged Stacie's signature and returned the papers to the attorney the following day. Braude submitted the form for the signature of the judge who was qualified to make the ruling, and who happened to be his brother-in-law. On May 15th, 1921, the order was signed by Judge George Ornstein of General Sessions, and Braude turned over to Francis certified copies of the order. Thus did Francis Vollmer become François Hillairet.

With the Hillairet birth certificate in hand, Francis went to the Customs House and applied for a passport, submitting his own photograph, as required. The completed passport was delivered to Denise Hillairet's brass mailbox six days later, and Francis was able to pick it up on his way to work while Denise slept. He was confident that Stacie would soon commit her sexual indiscretion and he was now completely prepared for everything that would follow.

Chapter 7

 Over a period of weeks Francis accumulated two thousand dollars of traveler's checks from the American Express office nearby on Broadway and felt a twinge of conscience because he had taken the business away from his own bank. He was very pleased to sign "François Hillairet" over and over again. Then he drew a certified cashier's check for eight thousand dollars; this, with the traveler's checks, represented a little less than one half of his savings. The remaining eleven thousand four hundred and twenty dollars he transferred to a savings account in Stacie's name.

The checks were kept in Francis' locked second drawer, along with several letters. One letter, addressed to Stacie, enclosing the savings bank passbook, was written in the tone of a heartbroken husband betrayed by the sexual appetites of the woman he loved. To express the love which had been so cruelly sullied, he was herewith turning over to her one half of their life's savings, with the advice that it be invested

carefully. Without ever actually saying it, the letter closed
with the implication that Francis had gone off to join the
French Foreign Legion.

In the same drawer there was an affectionate letter addressed to M. Grondet, saying that next to Mr. Hibbert he
had been the best friend Francis had ever had and begging
the indulgence of being permitted to send M. Grondet the
farewell gift of a case of Romanée Conti '06.

There was also an extremely cold letter of resignation
addressed to James Maitland. Francis had already decided
that by now Maitland must have made his move in Stacie's
direction, and that Stacie must have been inflamed enough
to reciprocate.

Almost as much as the letter to Stacie—which had made
him weep—Francis mourned the impending change in his
life which would take him away from Denise Hillairet. She
was an adorable woman, a model mistress. Often he had
worried that the people who served Them might be having
him watched, but though he was horrified by the thought of
Them reading a report stating that he was dallying with a
common barber's widow, he had decided that such liaisons
could always be forgiven if they remained frivolous. "You
have given so much to me" he said in the letter, while he
realized that she would never know that through him her
late husband's spirit would at last see the shores of France.
He had enclosed a check for two hundred and fifty dollars,
and he sent another check to Charles & Co. with instructions
to send Madame Hillairet a Pont Levecque cheese each
week while it was in season.

Though he hated to see it go, he destroyed the sweetheart
letter file.

When he felt that his affairs were entirely in order Francis
began to plan the changes he would need to make upon his
face and figure in order to eradicate his old identity as
Francis Vollmer. He would do nothing drastic. They would
be subtle changes. His hair would have to be longer and he
would wash it daily to make it bulkier. He would grow a
moustache and reshape his eyebrows. He would wear horn-
rimmed glasses and he would have suits made for him in
Paris of exaggerated Continental cut.

When Francis could no longer live with his headaches and insomnia he consulted Dr. Peters, who was the bank's doctor. It was frugality which led him to this almost fatal mistake. Peters gave him a long, silent examination and then prescribed some pills. But the very next afternoon, after Maitland had signed some papers which Francis had brought to him, Francis was asked to sit down and chat for a moment.

It was the same room Mr. Hibbert had occupied, but Maitland had replaced the extraordinarily lavish Florentine Renaissance décor with an antique reproduction of the main room in a Vermont country farmhouse. There was a roll-top desk with several dozen small pigeonholes, a large barrel marked *Crackers* in black paint, and a large kerosene chandelier hung from the ceiling.

"I have a note from A. D. He's worried about you."

"Who, sir?"

"Peters."

"Oh."

"He's worried about you."

"Worried?"

"He thinks you need a rest."

"I get more rest than anyone I know."

"Just once let's admit that a doctor as good as Peters knows more than you do."

"But I feel fine."

"If you feel fine, why did you go to Peters?"

"I have these headaches and they probably keep me from sleeping."

"Then why not lose the headaches. Take a month off—two months. Take Stacie and get on a boat and relax."

Francis watched and listened to Maitland carefully. There was tension in this effort to persuade him to take a vacation that made him sure that Maitland and Stacie were already having assignations. Maitland the wife chaser, the veteran of a hundred boudoir skirmishes, was probably ready to move on to another woman, and if he could trick her husband into taking Stacie away for two months, the whole thing could be broken off gracefully. For a minute Francis thought about pretending to go away for three days and then slipping back and catching them in bed together. But he was too tired.

"Thanks, Jim, but I'm all right."

"Francis, I think you're the best young banker I've ever known. Ed Hibbert, who knew you better, went even further than that. He hoped—and I hope too—that some day you'll be president of this bank."

"That's about the nicest thing anyone ever said to me."

"Take a year off, if you have to. If a change will help, then take any overseas branch you're attracted to and run it for a year. London, Paris, Rome—you decide."

Francis learned many things from this short talk. It was obvious that the affair of Maitland and Stacie had involved the banker more deeply than he had intended. Or perhaps Stacie would not let go, and now Maitland had to get rid of her even at the price of banishing Francis. That was how much all that talk about his being the best little old banker meant. Mr. Hibbert could have said it, but it would only have been as a tribute which he might hope would get back to Francis' parents. President of the bank some day—what a cruel thing to say. Francis was surprised to notice suddenly that he was sobbing. He seemed unable to stop.

It was Thursday, and when Francis got home it was understood that he had returned from Washington. Stacie asked him how everything had been, and he told her that everything had gone very well, that Washington had been hot but that he was enjoying the work.

"I talked to Jim Maitland at the Oratorio Society meeting today," Stacie said quietly.

"A chat about my health?"

"Yes. A little of that. I also complimented him on his idea of giving the executives French lessons and cooking lessons." She took a deep breath.

"I specifically told you never to mention those lessons to Jim."

She ignored his words. "At first he thought I was joking; then he was mystified. Finally he said that the bank hadn't done any such thing."

"And what else did you talk about?"

"Why did you tell me such a silly lie?"

"I had to learn French and there was no way to explain it to you. I had to learn about food and wines so that I could be at ease in my family's world, but you have never believed in my family. I'm being watched all the time. I have to measure up."

Stacie put her arms around Francis, but he shook her off. "We have to get this settled," she said.

"Neither of us has the power to settle anything. We'll wait, and when They're ready I'll be told."

"We will not wait! We'll go to the orphanage. We'll ask for a records search. We'll find out who your parents were."

"No!"

"Dearest, you're doing terrible things to yourself."

"Don't you ever again so much as speak of going near the orphanage. If you do—this marriage is finished."

"Francis, darling—" But he pushed her away.

"No one knows anything about me at that orphanage. Mr. Hibbert knew—no one else. I was left on the doorstep of that orphanage in accordance with a deliberate plan." He was speaking brokenly as he backed away from her, and then he turned and ran out the front door, slamming it behind him.

*C*hapter 8

 Francis had chosen the detective agency two months before, but he entered it for the first time on Friday morning. Its shingle on Beaver Street was a huge eye around which there had been printed the legend WE NEVER SLEEP. The agency was one flight up rickety stairs, and the outer office was guarded indifferently by a young, very fat girl who was puffing heavily from the exertion of typing a letter. She didn't ask Francis his name or business, but waved him on into the only other room. A lump of a man with green teeth and straw-colored hair took down all the details of the assignment with somber interest. Francis produced the names, addresses and photographs of Stacie and James Maitland and said he wanted a full report on when and how they met, how long they were together and where, and haggled bitterly over the suggested fee of twenty-five dollars a day plus expenses. Francis refused even to consider the price. The man said he'd need an off-sider and that extra men cost money. He asked Francis to state what he considered

would be a fair price; they settled at last for twenty-two fifty
a day and no expenses. The man said that in cases like this
bribes were frequently necessary; Francis said that if the
need arose he would do the bribing. They agreed that a
weekly report would be filed unless the two people were
alone together at any time in closed premises, at which time
Francis was to be notified by telephone.

In two weeks there were no results. The subjects had met
twice in that time, in the company of from fifteen to sixty
other people, respectively, at meetings of musical societies.
Although Mr. Maitland had had carnal relations with several other women during this period, Mrs. Vollmer had not
been alone with any other man or woman. Distraught, Francis canceled the surveillance. He was being forced to
abandon the theory on which he had placed so much depen-
dence. Between Denise Hillairet and the detective he had
spent an extraordinary amount of money, and he had fool-
ishly devoted hundreds of hours to sex instruction, time
which could have been devoted to improving himself cultur-
ally. He could not shake the conviction that somehow he
had taken the wrong turning despite all of the care and
thought and caution he had given the task. He even had the
nagging suspicion that he had somehow made a fool of
himself.

For two days at the bank he brooded; once he even
shouted at Miss Mechanic. At home Stacie made him take
the pills which Dr. Peters had prescribed and he was put to
bed almost as soon as he came home each day. He did not
visit Denise nor M. Grondet nor explain his absence.

In the middle of the third week the detective telephoned
Francis at the bank and asked him to come to the agency at
noon. Francis assumed that the detective had been chagrined about accepting money without any results and had
persisted with the investigation on his own time.

The very fat young lady was still puffing over her typewriter. The detective was truculent, and as soon as Francis
sat down he began to talk in a tone so nasty that he must
have been working himself up to it long before his client
arrived.

"You're vice-president of that bank, right?" Francis nodded. "And this here James Maitland is the president, right?"

Francis looked at the detective as though he smelled bad. "Get to the point, man. What happened? Where did they go? What did they do?"

"Go? Do? Where do you think you'll go, my snotty friend, if I tell your boss you had a tail on him for no reason whatsoever for two weeks?"

"Whaaaaat?" Francis was unable to believe what he heard.

"Start getting used to one thing, Vollmer. You are gunna pay me one hunnert bucks evvey week from now on, because if you don't, I go to Maitland and you are through."

To Francis it was as though a serf on his father's estates had tried to pull him off a horse. He picked up an imitation marble ash tray on the desk and drove the flat side of it with all his force into the man's face, knocking him head over heels in the swivel chair. Then he rushed around the desk, picked up the bleeding man and knocked him backward through the flimsy closed door into the anteroom. The very fat girl squealed like an armadillo caught under a descending elevator. The dazed detective tried to stagger to his feet, his nose mashed, his eyes swelling rapidly, but Francis was upon him again, grabbing him by the front of his clothing and dragging him out to the corridor. At the top of the stairs to the street he bundled the man into a neater package and flung him down the steep steps. At the bottom the detective rolled to a stop at the feet of a city policeman, whom Francis did not see as he sprang wildly down the steps two at a time and began to kick the unconscious body. The policeman had to use force on Francis to stop. When he came to consciousness he was in an ancient cell at the Old Slip Police Station.

When he became aware of his surroundings Francis demanded attention violently. Two detectives talked to him. He admitted the assault but asked for a lawyer. He told them that he was a vice-president of the Hibbert First National Bank and assistant to the president, and he insisted that the police ask James Maitland to send a lawyer to arrange his bail. He threatened dire consequences if the matter leaked to the newspapers, and as soon as the policemen left his cell he fell asleep.

The police called Maitland; Maitland called Tim Monahan and a bank lawyer; Monahan called the precinct captain, who came out of his office to greet Maitland when he arrived. The bank lawyer, a wise man, called a criminal lawyer and told him to meet them at the Old Slip station house. The police captain told the three of them that the man who had been assaulted intended to bring charges of mayhem, assault with intent to kill and attempted manslaughter, so the criminal lawyer asked if he could talk to the fellow, and while Francis slept on, they were taken to Bellevue Hospital in a police car. The private detective was suffering from a broken nose, a fractured femur, a concussion, six broken ribs, a broken jaw and severe facial contusions. He said he would only speak to Maitland, and alone. Then he told Maitland that he had tried to blackmail Francis, and why, but said that he would deny it. Maitland was flabbergasted by the detective's story, but he promised results, and when he left he sent the two lawyers to the bedside, where they worked out a settlement of twenty-five hundred dollars in return for dropping the charges against Francis. The criminal lawyer then arranged for bail while Maitland returned to the bank, telephoned Stacie and asked her to come directly to his office.

Stacie took her husband home in Maitland's limousine just before five o'clock on Friday afternoon. Francis explained everything to her in the car. The private detective from whom he had defended himself had been an employee of the bank whom he had discharged five months before. The man was deranged; he had called Francis and threatened to shoot him. Francis had been forced to strike the man, who unfortunately had fallen down a flight of stairs.

When they got home Francis repeated the story again as though he had forgotten he had told it. Then he went to bed and slept until twelve forty-five the next afternoon. When he got up Stacie was waiting for him in the living room. She asked him to get dressed.

"I'm very tired, Stacie. I think I'll just have something to eat and go back to bed."

"We are going to the orphanage."

"Why?"

"Because I went there yesterday. They have a certified record of who your parents were, and I want you to hear it from them."

"No! It's a lie!"

"It is not a lie. It is an official file—a whole set of documents, Francis. Affidavits, with city seals attached to them. You are going to know who your parents were so that you can get well and live a normal life."

"I won't listen! I won't go with you! If papers like that exist they are forgeries to cover up the truth!" He was screaming.

"Francis!" She struck him hard across the face. He stared into her eyes, breathing with enormous difficulty, as frightened as a horse in a fire.

"Your mother was forty-seven years old when you were born. She died at your birth and is buried in Calvary Cemetery in Queens. Her death was caused in part by the sudden death of your father two days before. He died in a circus fire. He was a dwarf. A dwarf clown."

"*No!*"

Francis shut out of his mind what Stacie had just said, and to keep it out of his mind he shut her out forever. She vanished. She had never ever existed. There had never been any such woman in his life. A dazed but peaceful look came over his frightened eyes. Stacie began to weep. He turned away from her; she said nothing because she understood he would not be able to see her or hear her.

Francis returned to his bed, locking the door to the room. He got up quietly at a quarter to five the following morning, dressed carefully and packed two suitcases. Stacie's door was shut, but he would not have remembered who she was even if he had seen her. He was leaving to find his parents.

Francis sat in Central Park until nine o'clock, then took a

cab to the Cunard Line in lower Manhattan and booked passage on the *Aquitania*. He presented his new passport and asked the booking office to procure a French and Swiss visa. Then he left the suitcases to be transferred to the ship and took a taxi to the bank. He was there just long enough to empty his second drawer. At the pier he mailed the letters.

Francis Hillairet sailed for Europe on the afternoon tide.

Chapter 9

 After settling in his
double stateroom on the
main deck, Francis sum-
moned the ship's barber. The barber's name was Marcus
Reuben. He was from New Forest, Hampshire, and he was
all apple cheeks and belly butter.

The ship was foaming with people who were exuberant
because they were leaving Prohibition behind; they were
laughing like macaws and the sharp shots of champagne
corks went off like firecrackers. In his stateroom Francis
explained to the barber that he intended to grow a mustache
and wished to consult him professionally about it; in effect,
to take mustache lessons. Reuben was flattered. "Personally,
sir," he said, "considering the interesting shape of your face,
I would most earnestly recommend the Giacomo Puccini."

"Why?"

"Because it has a sense of bristlin' emotion, sir. It symbol-
izes Puccini's constant melodic invention. A man is his mustache and its meaning, isn't he, sir?"

"But I mean—an *Italian* mustache."

"I admit, sir, that had the war gone the other way, men might right now be settling their sights on a mustache like Field Marshal von Hindenburg's—which might just be one of the finest examples of mustache architecture of our times, sir, if you care for that sort of thing. Out of the question now, of course."

"I am sorry," Francis said simply. "I cannot agree."

"No reason why you should, sir. A mustache is as personal as—"

"Can you imagine the mustache of the late Edward VII with the beard removed?" Drugged by his dream, which was coming true at last, Francis felt sentimental. After all, it was not beyond the bounds of reason that Edward VII, a most wide-ranging man in his attraction to ladies, was his natural father.

At that point Reuben took over. They agreed that the Edwardian mustache without beard could have been designed for Francis. Reuben took Francis' headline backward on either side of his head, which changed his position considerably. His hair was brushed back and made to stand up, which made him seem even taller. Two months before he had secretly acquired the heavy black-rimmed eyeglasses; now he wore them with the heavy authority that other people sought to acquire by smoking a pipe. Reuben indicated the point to which his sideburns should be permitted to grow during the voyage, lowering them about three eighths of an inch. Reuben was a master pogonotrophist. He outlined the desired shape lightly with eyebrow pencil, and the mustache assumed its shape by the third day. Reuben looked in on it every morning and evening. "The word mustache comes from the Greek word *mastic,* sir," Reuben said as he measured and balanced the outline, "meaning the upper lip. Because you have planned your mustache so carefully, you will find that any barber in the world will be able to follow the trimming pattern which we have so inexorably set down."

It was a rough crossing. The seas were so heavy that most of the passengers kept to their staterooms, and four fractures

were reported among those who did not. Day and night the
great ship seemed to be deserted, but a somnambulistic
Francis created his own activities. The terrible anxieties
which he had managed to submerge beneath the surface still
plagued his unconscious mind and interfered with his sleep.
But it had been so long since he had slept well that he had
convinced himself he no longer needed it.

During the first two nights he walked around and around
the promenade deck. During the day he remained in his
stateroom to avoid his enemies. Though he knew it was
grotesque, he had become more and more certain that the
passenger complement consisted mainly of dwarfs. They
would kill him if they could, and somewhere deep within a
mist he could recall hearing another plan they had for him
which was even worse. He refused to remember it, but he
knew he feared it more than dying.

He felt safer at night, and he felt safest of all near dawn,
when he could sit in a chair in the main salon while the
stewards cleaned the room around him. It helped him to
think of the ship as one of his father's palaces.

The Palladian lounge of the ship had a ceiling like a
placid pond reflecting views of Paradise. These were separated by plaster scrolls, making it into an upside-down
formal garden where the flowers took the form of sleeping
cherubs. The chairs of the lounge were heavily brocaded
with designs which whirled and retreated into immeasurable
distances. The carpet was blue and red and white, and it
whirlpooled. The solid furniture seemed to stand placidly
upon a writhing mass of colored snakes. After the second
night Francis avoided the Palladian lounge because its
movement was frightening. He could rest in the main salon.
It offered orderly self-regulation, columned Georgian white-
nesses. He could sit there and stare at the five large seashells
above the round globe of light over his chair until he
became dangerously drowsy and fell into nightmares of
dwarfs, which would bring him to his feet running, to begin
his turns around the outer decks again.

He tried to remember to eat when he was in his cabin; he
could not go into the dining salon. He could not sleep

because he always dreamed. The ship's library had Haydn's *Dictionary of Dates,* containing the history of the world to the summer of 1885. He started to read it, beginning with AA, and it so soothed him that he stopped walking the decks altogether. It was an exulting pastime; not only was he helping his problems but he was also memorizing some amazingly useful information. He was able to forget the enemy again. Something nearby was dangerous, but he no longer feared it so much. He was able to spend two nights in blessed numbness and blankness, until he came to the page marked DW.

It was just after two o'clock in the morning when it happened. He was reading under a small circle of light, with a four-day growth of pepper and salt stubble sprinkled on his upper lip. When he came to the entry on DWARF he turned pale; his blank yellow eyes seemed made of clay. He could feel the fur of his fear inside him as it wriggled and slithered out of his control.

. . . or Philetas of Cos, distinguished about 330 B.C. as a poet and grammarian, was said to have carried weights in his pockets to prevent his being blown away . . . Julia, niece of Augustus, had a dwarf named Coropas who was two feet and a hand's breadth high . . . Alypius of Alexandria, a logician and philosopher, was one and a half feet high and seemed to be consumed by his satanic nature.

Beyond the reading light Francis could see nothing. If he moved, their teeth would sink into him. They were waiting out there for him to break and run.

. . . Jeffery Bocca, an English dwarf, when a youth of eighteen inches high, was served up to the table of the King and Queen of England in a cold pie by the Duchess of Boult in 1626. In 1653 he challenged a Mr. Johannus Starr to fight a duel and shot his antagonist dead . . . Dame Maria Van Slyke, height twenty inches, weight four and one quarter pounds and a woman of exemplary beauty, married General Francis Vollmer, height twenty-two inches, weight nine pounds, in New York State on December 6th, 1879. Their marriage was re-enacted more then 1800 times in circuses throughout North America.

Francis screamed, the chilling hopeless screams of a man being pulled into quicksand in a forgotten forest. He knew again what he feared—the dwarfs were his false parents. If they were allowed to, they would drag him off the ship and hide him from his true parents while their surgeons used all their skills to shrink him to their size. They had been drugging his food to make him weak. They would overpower him by force of numbers. He snatched his feet up from the floor just in time and flung his legs over the arm of the chair. For almost three hours he protected himself that way, listening intently and swiveling his head, until dawn came up and the stewards came in to clean. Not until light filled the room and the stewards were at work did he place his benumbed legs on the deck again.

That evening Francis went to the purser's office and withdrew one hundred dollars from his money in the safe. At seven o'clock he appeared in the office of the chief steward. He made a fan of twenty dollar bills and placed it on the desk between them. "I suffer from insomnia," he said. "I am a trained amateur cook, acceptable by professional standards, and I wish to ask you to find me night work in the galley between now and when we reach Cherbourg."

"Very unusual," the chief said, looking at the money. "However, we exist for passenger accommodation." Drawing the fan toward himself, he allowed it to fall into the top drawer of his desk. "I will accept this only on the condition that it go into the Fund."

"Of course."

"The night shift begins at four bells—ten o'clock tonight. If you would report to me at nine-thirty?"

Francis' terror gradually turned to elation; he had beaten them. He could barricade himself in his cabin during the days, eating nothing. He would pay the night steward to walk with him to the ship's galley and would spend the hours until daylight in the company of tall men.

Francis worked in the galley with enormous pleasure, ate

well and was able to sleep during the days. He made good friends with Smadja, the night chef, who openly admired Francis' work in the predawn hours when Francis insisted that he sit, rest and enjoy, and allow his new assistant to prepare the short orders after the principal work of the watch had passed. Given his head, Francis made sandwiches with cod's roe and chopped parsley and shallots fried in butter, or boiled beef paste and shredded boiled beef mixed with pickled cabbage, or bearded oysters pounded in a mortar in their own liquor with butter which had been mixed with cayenne pepper and lemon juice. The night chef began to eat and gain weight as though he were a first-class passenger, and he stared with amazement when envelopes addressed to *The Chef* containing large tips began to come down with amazed and grateful notes from the passengers.

For light delicious suppers which would permit heavy copulating almost immediately afterward in the hundreds of cabins over his head, Francis offered creamed beef with prunes, or chartreuse of hare, or breasts of pigeons cooked with diced bacon and chopped veal and walnuts. All these dishes were good with champagne, and they fortified the male passengers while the females primped and sluiced in the lavatories. Smadja beamed with pride while carefully pocketing all tips. The little notes which came in from every cranny of the ship were touching. The night cabin stewards were like gamblers to whom the same tout keeps giving winning tips on horses. Francis was the most popular passenger the line had ever carried.

When the night's short orders were executed, Francis' heavy work of preparing the ship's breakfast got under way. There was bacon cooked three ways; link sausages, and coiled glistening Wiltshire rings, or served in patty cakes; kippers, bloaters and ptarmigan pies; gallons of porridge and frumenty; fried potatoes and small game; skuets, those memorable sweetbreads wrapped in bacon and breadcrumbs; kidneys and deviled bones; kedgeree, fish cakes and finnan haddie; braised meat and game pies; and fourteen ways of preparing eggs. The Cunard Line believed in English breakfasts. It was a steady, rhythmical work and it soothed Francis. He learned a great deal about preparing food in quantity which he yearned to write to M. Grondet.

The activity kept him safe until the last dawn had come up and Cherbourg could almost be seen beyond the bow. When the strangely shaped French tugs made themselves fast to the great ship, the fear came over him again and he had to leave the kitchen to vomit. He asked for permission to return to his cabin. When his cabin steward, by now an admiring friend, came in to collect his luggage, Francis was sitting jammed into a corner of the room to protect himself, still in his pajamas, his bags not yet packed. He told the steward he would not be going ashore.

"You've decided on Southampton, sir?"

"I may return to New York."

"Very good, sir."

Francis was suspicious of the steward's instant agreement. The dwarfs could have gotten to him. Stewards thought in terms of tips, and tips could buy the man's silence while the enemies poured into his cabin and captured him. He would have to be cunning. "I tell you what," he said. "If you'll just see to all the other passengers' luggage and then return, I will have decided what to do."

Francis thought furiously. Since his false parents were American dwarfs, a return to New York was out of the question; they would have far more confederates in the United States. Haydn's Dictionary had stated that they were circus people, so there wouldn't be a hamlet in America to which he could flee where they would not have their spies. A small number of them were aboard now and ready. But if he let the cabin steward tell them he planned to return to New York, they would relax their vigilance. In the meantime, he would call Smadja to awaken two of the huskiest night stewards; with their help he'd make a dash for it. His enemies would be caught by surprise. He must leave at once, while his steward was busy with the other baggage. But his legs could not stand, he could not dress himself. With enormous effort he was able to pick up the telephone and call the galley. The night watch was still at work and he was able to persuade the puzzled night chef to send him two very strong men at once. He specified the knock they were to give at the very top of the door to his stateroom.

Francis leaned back and laughed. He brayed triumph and contempt. General Francis Vollmer. Dame Maria Van Slyke. Bah! Dwarfs with delusions of grandeur! What pitiable, hopeless and ludicrous pretensions they had. But size and weight had little to do with lust for power. By God! He was suddenly able to see their plan! Pretending to be his false parents, they would have him cut down to eighteen inches because they knew who his true parents were, and after announcing his rank and position they would place him on the dwarf throne with themselves as regents. But he did not want any throne which was not his by birth and divine right; he came from a line long accustomed to thrones. He would rather be a simple peer of England then the false king of all the dwarfs in the world. Proudly he pulled himself to his feet.

The two off-duty night stewards earned five pounds each in addition to the twenty-three-odd pounds which had come their way because of Francis' cooking. They dressed him with tender regard, packed his bags and asked no questions. They took him off the crew plank the moment the ship was fast to the dock, and at his urging hired a burly Thomas Cook representative to accompany him by hired automobile to Paris. There Francis wished to be put aboard the first train to Switzerland in a locked compartment. In Geneva the first Cook's man would have arranged for a second to take him to a hotel, from the safety of which Francis could place himself under the protection of the bank.

On the dock Francis hastily scribbled out a telegram and handed it with a five-pound note to one of the night stewards, with the instructions that it be sent off immediately. The message to the main banking office in Zurich announced that he would present himself at their Geneva branch the following day. Francis smiled sardonically as he wrote it, knowing that no dwarf alive could overcome the client of a mighty Swiss bank. A few minutes later he was driven rapidly away from the quay before a single other passenger had come down the gangplank.

Once in the car, Francis overpaid the Cook's man so that the man would not feel a need to chat. They reached Paris only one hour and fifty-five minutes later than the boat train, rolling stealthily around the outer ring of the city, west to east, and screeched to a halt at the Gare de Lyon five minutes before the departure of the Geneva train. The second Cook's man was waiting for them, and Francis and his luggage were bundled aboard. After instructing the Cook's man to lock the compartment and to keep a close watch for small men, he fell asleep instantly and did not awake until their arrival in Geneva.

Francis was registered at the Metropole Hotel on the Grand Quai, facing the lake and the English Gardens. He felt certain that he had not been followed. He bathed and dressed slowly because he felt so strange, and then asked the operator to please find out the name of the director of the Bank Graubunden-Zug in Geneva.

As he buttoned his waistcoat and adjusted his jacket, he chanced to look out the window. His blood ran cold; in the shrubbery of the English gardens he saw a whey-faced dwarf staring up at him.

Francis leaped backward, knocking over a small table. Sweating, he headed with tiny crablike steps around a chair to the far side of the window curtains and peered from behind them. The dwarf had vanished. Obviously, having spotted his prey, he had hurried off to report. Now his enemies would attack before help could be summoned. Francis rushed across the room and pushed a large highboy in front of the door. It was brutally hard work. The sound of the telephone ringing almost struck him down, but he took his courage in his hands and answered it. It was the operator, who said that the name of the bank's director was Jacques Crouch. He asked her to connect him with M. Crouch at once, and then fell into a chair to try to decide what he must do. There would be blood; at least it would be the blood of battle, not the blood their surgeons intended to extract from him. The telephone rang again and Francis picked it up with trembling hands.

"How good of you to call me, Monsieur Hillairet," M.

Crouch said. "I have had a telegram early this morning to expect you. Before me lies the duplicate of your portfolio, and—"

"Monsieur Crouch, please listen carefully," Francis whispered hoarsely. "I had hoped we would lunch, but I cannot leave this hotel."

"Perfectly all right, Monsieur Hillairet."

"A bank the size of yours must have private security agents. City police must not be involved."

"Involved?"

"I must have protection. Total protection."

"Protection from whom, sir?"

"A band of dwarfs is trying to kidnap me to keep me from my parents. Vitally important European politics are involved, and if my enemies can get to me they will operate and reduce me to eighteen inches. They want me as their king. But we cannot go on talking like this, because they are listening. I have blocked the room. When you arrive, signal me with four knocks, two short and two rapid. Do not enter the hotel through the entrance on the lake side: they have men there. How quickly can you be here?"

"I will come at once," M. Crouch said sadly. He disconnected, then telephoned Zurich for instructions. A few minutes later he was telephoning Dr. K. P. Boscawen, whose mental clinic overlooked the lake at Anieres. Dr. Boscawen said that she would send two very tall attendants and that neither he nor the bank was to worry. Everything would be all right.

Chapter 10

 "Dear Dr. Boscawen," Mrs. Recknell's letter read, "I spoke aloud yesterday while walking with Francis Hillairet. The effort tired me, but I felt no guilt or remorse. Perhaps this means I may go home soon." The psychiatrist filed the letter and locked the cabinet. She was wearing white hospital dress, but on her bosom she wore three fine brown diamonds. There was also a large green diamond on the third finger of each hand. She was a tall, exceptionally handsome woman with puzzled eyes.

Dr. Boscawen left the sunny office, climbed a flight of stairs and walked along a glistening, silent corridor which was as introspective as a snail. She knocked at the door of Room 46 and was invited to enter.

Francis was sitting at a table in the sun, wearing white cotton pajamas and an ivory wool robe piped with French blue. With a large illustrated book propped in front of him, to which he occasionally referred, he was engaged in carving a bust of Marie Antoinette from a large white radish. An exquisitely carved bust of Louis XVI in a tiny vegetable frame against a background of a block of walnut butter rested upon a rectangle of ice standing in a white enamel basin. Francis stood up to greet the doctor.

"How beautiful," she said, "and how unbanal of you not to have placed their majesties' heads in tiny guillotine baskets."

"They are for Professor Nolan's farewell lunch."

"How pleased he will be. I hope he is cured this time, but he does love to come back here." She sighed. "Why French royals?"

"He teaches French history in New Hope, Pennsylvania."

"Ah, so he does. And with new hope, if I may say so, although what Professor Nolan keeps hoping for anew at his age will never cease to surprise me."

She sat down as Francis busied himself making tea. "Mandarin tea with lotus blossoms," he said. "Less tannic acids, but with a definite taste and a superb bouquet."

"Mr. Hillairet, how did it happen that Lady Sian spoke to you yesterday?"

Francis blinked like a drunk rabbit. He could feel his face grow plush red. "Lady Sian?" he asked in disbelief. He was stunned that a titled personage could exist somewhere nearby.

"Mrs. Recknell is the Marchioness of Shattock. She uses her husband's family name here."

"Her husband?"

"She is a widow."

"Mrs. Recknell is a marchioness?" Francis was incredulous. "A marchioness is only one rank below a duchess." He turned toward the window as though in hope that he could observe Mrs. Recknell, to see if she looked any different passing by, then he poured the tea with absent-minded anxiety.

"Marchioness is second of the five descending grades of the peerage," he murmured, walking to the red-bound volume of De Brett which he kept on the table beside his bed for casual reading. He turned its pages. "Well! 'Dowager Marchioness of Shattock. Sian Evelyn Deborah Recknell, née Lady Sian Manderson, only daughter of the Earl of Donen. Born, April 15th, 1881, married Colin Kenneth Recknell, 14th Marquis of Shattock, January 14th, 1900; educated at,' et cetera, et cetera . . . 'marquisate established in 1501 by Henry Recknell, K.G.'—think of that, they have a garter! —'one of the most accomplished gentlemen of his time . . .' What a thrilling, distinguished family!"

"Mr. Hillairet, what made Mrs. Recknell speak to you?"

"Forgive me, Doctor, but please listen to the courtesy titles of her family. Earl of Winikus, Viscount Schute and—look here!—the baronetcy descends through the female line. Luckily they do have a daughter: Celia Fiona Hilary, born 1901, the Baroness Keys." He closed the book reluctantly and turned to the doctor. "But why has Lady Sian never spoken before?"

"The war, indirectly. She lost everyone—husband, brothers, cousins, and her father died in 1917."

"What was her husband's regiment?"

"I have no idea."

"It could have been The Rifle Brigade. Second Battalion perhaps. That's what I would have chosen. There was a *corps d'élite!*"

"Why did she speak?"

"I really don't know. I was speaking French. She interrupted me. Her French has a strong British accent, with a voice as precise as a croupier's. It is harsh and insistent, too. She said, 'Your are an American, Mr. Hillairet,' which had nothing to do with what I'd been saying. I'd been telling her about a painter called Sickert who may have been one of the few painters to have met Whistler's mother socially—which is a joke based on Sickert having been a student of Whistler's, you see, and therefore theoretically could have been in the studio while Whistler painted his mother's portrait."

Dr. Boscawen sighed.

"Mrs. Recknell—Lady Sian, that is—laughed before she spoke. I must say she laughs exactly the way I've always imagined a marchioness would laugh."

"How is that?"

"Like the horn of Rolande. Then she said I had mastered

more useless information than she had imagined existed, and that she had the distinct impression that I didn't understand the meaning of any of it. Which was an odd observation, considering that I have taken her on daily walks for over two months and that she has never spoken to me before."

Francis was a new man. The mixture of gaiety under a surface of dread gave him a romantic, mature, mysterious air. His hair had become gray and his Edward VII mustache, now full and stately, was quite silvery. His glasses were severe, and in the evenings he wore them on a black ribbon.

The clinic, overlooking the snow-fed lake and the Jura Mountains, lazed on a butte at the top of a noble hill behind the village of Anieres, eleven kilometers from Geneva. Francis had been there for a little over three months and was making faster progress than any other patient. Mrs. Recknell had been there for nearly three years.

It had been a gently warm, luminous summer. Francis often just stared out at the lake for hours; sometimes it was veiled in white mist, and at others it ruffled itself under a *bise* which raised whitecaps. At midday the sun fell on grapes which would be dry white wine in the autumn, and there were extravagant flower farms beyond the broad lawns of the hospital grounds.

Dr. Boscawen allowed Francis to cook one meal a week. Mrs. Recknell had been invited to one of these dinners because the doctor had asked Francis to invite her. Mrs. Recknell had enjoyed the first meal so much and had written such deft, complimentary thanks on a small square card that it became traditional for Francis to include Mrs. Recknell in all his dinner plans.

His life at the clinic seemed ideal to him. His bankers were nearby and came to consult him once a month about his investments. His tailors came all the way from Paris. Armand, the master shirtmaker of Geneva, made his shirts, pajamas and regal dressing gowns, while Francis pondered whether he should continue to wear ready-made underwear. He spent time on his vegetable and butter sculpture, on planning menus and in continuing his studies of books mailed from London and Paris. Each week his laundry was sent to a widow in Vienna who had done the laundry of the late Archduke Franz Josef and for Dr. Sigmund Freud. He was continually engaged in the reconstruction of his biography, not for publication, but to remind himself of who he had been and of how the past had shaped his future. He was firm about his birthplace and date because that was set down in his passport. He knew that his permanent address was care of the bank in Zurich. Each day he worked to create one more little fact about his past and to insert it gracefully into the chain with the others. His parents had been forced to abandon him into the charge of the president of the Bank Graubunden-Zug, who in due course had sent him to the best boys' school in Switzerland, where he had roomed with the second son of the King of the Belgians and, later, the third son of the King of Spain; wonderful fellows. Later he had attended the Sorbonne and Harvard. It was understood that his parents were of extremely high station, but because their families had taken opposite sides in a vital political struggle, they could keep in touch with his welfare and security only through the bank.

When he had been admitted to the clinic Francis had struggled continuously in restraining sheets for thirty-six hours. In his delirium he had recited whole pages of *Burke's Peerage* and the *Almanach de Gotha,* and in a wildly cracked voice had sung choruses of "Colonel Coote-Manningham," the regimental song of the Brigade of Rifles.

But gradually sedation had soothed him, hypnosis had convinced him, and layers and more layers of his past had been submerged by the slow growth of his new belief that he was a Franco-Swiss-American gentleman on his way to possessing one million dollars because of shrewd investments, whose amusing hobby was *haute cuisine,* and who was an impressively informed conversationalist. He had never married, out of devotion to his parents.

He was encouraged to glide out of his simple breakdown from the overwork caused by the responsibilities of his distinguished international banking career, and to reconstruct his life to the point where he was endowed with an unrelenting, ingratiating viewpoint which was the result of a perfect past.

Dr. Boscawen and Mrs. Recknell sat on a small private porch overlooking the lake. The doctor did not refer to Mrs. Recknell's letter, nor did she seek to prod her into speaking. Silently they watched the long white side-wheeling lake steamer and the surrounding small boats with puffed sails. Then, for the first time since they had met almost three years before, Mrs. Recknell spoke.

"Today the lake makes me think of the transparent water tanks above the urinals in the men's public toilets in Holborn," she said slowly in her harsh voice. "My husband was so delighted with them that he paid the attendant to let me go in to see them. The tanks had large copper ball taps and nearly emptied themselves each time a urinal was flushed. The attendant kept brightly colored fish in them. Quite surprised fish they must have been. They could never have grown accustomed to their element emptying, then replenishing. Red and golden fish with undulating fins in each tank."

"I would like to see that," Dr. Boscawen said. "My mother kept fish." She beamed at Mrs. Recknell for having spoken to her. "What else have you been thinking about?"

"So many things."

"Tell me two."

"My husband playing billiards in a pub called the Crown at the edge of St. John's Wood. The seats were horsehair. It was the summer of 1911, and no one knew where to find us."

"It was a lovely summer. Oddly, I remember it well." She sipped tea. "And now another thought of yours."

"My father. Well, not really my father, but something my father once told me. When he was dying he explained that his sight was fading, diopter by diopter, and that everything was slowly turning to different shades of brown. 'The browns are becoming darker and darker, so brown must be the color of death,' he said, and then he died." Mrs. Recknell

smiled. "Morbid, ain't I?" she said. It was a smile which
exploded out of her dark-skinned face the way lightning
flashes: bursting and white and hot and fleeting. Her voice
seemed raw from overuse; it sounded like an old pol's voice
after a long day at the hustings, rather than one which had
been laid away for three years as carefully as old silver.

"Does your throat feel strain? Do you have to force your
voice?"

"No. It wasn't there and then it came back. I knew it was
there again and I used it."

"What made you use it?"

"I don't know."

"Mr. Hillairet?"

"Do you mean did I feel an attraction to Mr. Hillairet
which had to be sustained through speech?"

"Something like that."

"No."

"Was it something he said?"

"It was everything he had been saying interminably for
three months. He is the most accomplished bore I have ever
heard, and he has no humor whatever to leaven that endless
lecture of facts. Were he not so deeply impressed with what
he says and how he says it, I would suspect him of being a
paid entertainer who has memorized everything he says."

"That's not very kind, is it?"

"I'm not kind. Oh, perhaps I am to horses."

Mrs. Recknell was a long-legged, short-waisted woman
with red hair and splendid carriage. Her eyes were hooded
to conceal the pain she cherished. They glistened under her
straight brow, over round cheekbones which rose like dove's
breasts in her heart-shaped face. She looked thirty-two but
was thirty-nine years old. The disguise of time which made
this possible was her eyes, her carriage and her unoiled-
millstone voice, but it was her nose which made her memorable. It was flaunted, and it should have been part of a long
and narrow face in which it would have appeared cruel and
ascetic. In that rounded face with its sweetly pointed chin,
the nose was eloquent and passionate; it was a nose well
suited to the mistress of a satyr or to someone bent upon
vengeance.

"Just why is Hillairet here?" Mrs. Recknell coughed lightly. "Or is it gauche to ask?"

"He is a banker. He had a nervous collapse. You can help him."

"Really?"

"Delusions are quite usual in these cases."

"In all cases, inside and outside this place."

"It would make him very happy if you permitted him to call you by your title, and if you insisted that he accompany you into Geneva. He believes kidnappers await him there."

"He is so entertaining in a perverse way! And it must be that he has helped me. I am talking to you, but I did talk to him first. At any rate, a cook as good as Hillairet is worth saving. I shall invite him to take me to Geneva tomorrow."

The following morning, while Francis was working under his tall white hat in the kitchen, Mrs. Recknell paid him a visit. She could see a reverent expression in his eyes as he looked at her which was very different from his patronizing manner during the previous weeks.

"Now that I am able to speak," Mrs. Recknell said, "I shall introduce myself. I am the Dowager Marchioness of Shattock. You may address me as Lady Sian. Not Shawn, *Shon*. Can you say that, Hillairet?" She could have sworn he was debating whether or not to curtsy. "I wish to go into Geneva this morning," she added with an imperiousness enhanced by her nose, "and I want you to escort me."

Francis' attitude changed before her eyes. Suddenly he seemed to be trying to swallow his laundry. "Uh, thank you, Lady Sian—"

"*Shon*."

"Lady Shon." He seemed terrified, and she remembered his conviction that he would be kidnapped. "I will be greatly honored," he said hoarsely.

They left before noon in a Renault touring car provided by the clinic. Francis was perspiring and he gripped the wheel tightly. They drove along the Route d'Hermance, through the ancient village of Collonges, then into Vesenaz, where Lady Sian made him turn up the hill to the Route de la Capite so that they could drive through Cologny and see the house where Lord Byron had lived.

The diversion helped to take Francis' mind off the dangers of Geneva. "Byron's father was a profligate who died in France, you know," he said.

"Have to die somewhere."

"Do you recall the name of the man with whom Byron departed London, almost directly from the House of Lords, to embark on his famous Mediterannean tour in 1809?"

"No."

"J. C. Hobhouse."

Mrs. Recknell stared at him, blinking softly, but he was gesturing toward the nether slope. "Percy Shelley and his seriously compromised ménage lived right down there."

"Good enough. Now we must push on to Geneva."

As they drove toward the city she could feel Francis trembling beside her. This wasn't a man trying to call attention to himself with grandiose tales of kidnapping. "Are you sure you're all right, Hillairet?" she asked. He did not hear her; he was staring at the road ahead, and trying to look around each bend of the road before the car reached it. Mrs. Recknell began to admire Hillairet; though almost paralyzed with fear, he was not faltering for the gallant reason that she had asked him to escort her to Geneva. She started to prattle about the weather and how well he drove and whether they might be able to rent a boat for a row on the lake, but as they came to the Route de Frontenex leading directly into the city, she had to stop speaking. The tension was so palpable that she began to wonder whether what Dr. Boscawen had dismissed as a delusion might have basis in shocking fact.

Francis' eyes were bulging like those of a carousel horse, but as they passed the Salle de Reformation he said in a shaking voice and with a chivalric effort of will to entertain and inform her, "In that hall for the first time in history, only eighteen months ago, the representatives of forty-one nations sat down together in common council and formed the League of Nations, which has abolished war from the world."

"I had read about that, I think."

"Where may I take you?"

"Shall we have an ice in the English Gardens?"

Francis braked the car involuntarily. "I should prefer it if we had an ice indoors somewhere. I am told there is an excellent *glacier* near my bank."

"But indoors on such a day! And with such a view of the lake as we would have from the English Gardens?"

"There is the balcony of the Hotel des Bergues just across the bridge."

"But it has been so long since I've been in anything even *called* English that I yearn to have an ice in the English Gardens."

Francis stopped the car. "Please," he said. "I . . . I . . ."

"Hillairet, are you all right? You seem ill. I don't like your color at all."

"Forgive me, my dear Marchioness, but I will have to confide in you."

"Please do so, Hilliaret, if it will help in any way."

"They know I am in Switzerland," he said. "They know who my parents are, and they are waiting for me in the English Gardens."

"Who are they?"

"They are . . . they . . ." His wild eyes wandered frantically from her to the buildings around him. Faintly he said, "I cannot remember who they are."

"Then you must not remember. I don't much understand the treatments at the clinic but I do know that we must not remember."

"What they are scheming to do to me is . . ." Francis' mind went blank again, and he fell back on surer ground. "I have to find my parents. If you could help me, in your position in the peerage . . ."

The man needs! Mrs. Recknell thought passionately. He has need! He is not just a stick and an almanac. There is no one to whom he can turn and I can help him. Her head and her heart had become bleak stones because she had despaired of ever finding again a man who needed her. But his need had melted the stone. This immeasurably boring, pathetic, beautifully dressed, exquisitely mannered handsome man had filled himself with terror—which was far worse than bleakness—and in time it would turn him not to stone but into a crawling animal.

He had caused her to talk again. But that was worthless by itself unless it could be used to help a man. His therapy, into which generosity had never entered, put her in his debt. But she owed him a further debt for providing incontrovertible proof that she could once again feel the thrill of being needed by a man. She would use the speech he had returned to her to coax him out of his caves of terror. What he felt might be delusion, but she had grown to understand that delusion was the only reality, a reality of deserts and fires and impenetrable forests. She would use her voice to help him across those terrible dangers, and if he really believed that beyond his delusion there was a promised land, then she must try to lead him there.

"Are your parents of the British peerage?" she asked blandly.

"I have reason to believe so."

"Well, I know most of them, and among them they know all the rest, and if this is of any help to you, I am at your disposal."

Francis expression changed to one of beatitude. He clasped her hand and made tiny nods, encouraging her to repeat what she had just said.

"Furthermore," said the Dowager Marchioness of Shattock, "as for those who would conspire to prevent a meeting with your parents, may I remind you that it is the *English* Gardens to which we are now going to enjoy our ices. No one would *dare* to affront a British subject in those grounds."

Francis put the car into gear and turned into the Grand Quai. In a trembling voice he said, "When the French Revolution drove Brillat-Savarin to the United States, he spent his two years of exile introducing ices and—of all things—Swiss fondues to that newly independent country. We must try a fondue in Geneva one of these days. I am so happy that you are fond of ices. I enjoy preparing iced pineapple à la Chantilly, and I shall see that you have it for dinner tomorrow night." He parked the car across from the

English Gardens, then ran around to open the door for her. "Oh, Hillairet," she said. "What an amusing man you are."

"When may we leave?" Sian asked Dr. Boscawen.

"We?"

"Hillairet and I have made a pact. He is going to inform me about everything at great length and I am going to tell him what it means."

"Which is how the male and female have always co-existed," Dr. Boscawen said, smiling.

"Is it? Was I that way with Colin?" Sian ran her thin hand across her eyes. "I suppose it was like that. They search and we explain, I suppose, but I don't want to talk about it."

"Then talk about it."

"What?"

"If at no other time, it's when you are in a mental clinic with your favorite doctor that you should discuss the things you wish to avoid. Am I right? At least you should find out why you don't want to talk about them."

"You probably have some idea that I feel unfaithful to Colin because I have become a friend to Hillairet. Bosh! I don't want to remember Colin because he isn't there any more and I have honored him enough. I honored him so well that I became insane. That should suffice. I am out of that now. Life will be so much less murky with Hillairet. He searches with his prayer-wheel of a voice, and I will try not to mock him. I suppose that has been going on between male and female since the beginning, as well."

"There is one other thing."

"Hm?"

"You must not blame Mr. Hillairet for not being Colin Recknell."

"That is good advice." Lady Sian smiled her brilliant smile, which was as sudden as a beanbag thrown without warning. "How useless that would be, confusing Hillairet and Colin. But it isn't possible; it is I who have changed and whose position has become so different."

"Never *so* different," Dr. Boscawen murmured.

"Still, it will suit me to keep Hillairet safe, and that *is* so different from the woman I once was. He will call me Lady Sian and dear Marchioness—so grossly incorrect, you know —until the genius of his snobbery leads him into calling me Mrs. Recknell again. I shall call him François, I think, though Hillairet, simply Hillairet, comes more naturally because he is such a vulgar man. I will see that he meets a princess or two, a duke here, a Grand Elector there. I will find him a flat in London and decorate it for him while he explains the motivations of Peranesi and Hoppenhaupt and regales me with useless information he has acquired that very morning."

"Is he such a bore?"

"Worse. He's crashingly unilateral. Everything flows toward self. Empathy is not given to the unilateral, nor to infants, is it, Doctor?"

"Have you just discovered empathy or are you rediscovering it?" the doctor asked slyly.

"We were discussing Hillairet's empathy," Sian replied tartly. "You know I'm not ready to find myself even if I could, but I will never forget there is the inner secret. As for Hillairet, he must learn to feel something other than terror. I am convinced that somewhere under those layers of acquired banality there must be a lode of sensuality. I shall dig for it, and if I ever strike it I will force him to trade with me—a sensation for a fact, an emotion for a statistic. But I will probably never find it. Hillairet is touched by titles. He yearns for the extinct. The people to whom he has dedicated spending his life are dead on their feet and the way they lived is dead. And quivering, arrogant, exultant me is reduced to the meaninglessness—no, the uselessness—of guiding poor Hillairet through that scarified park called England, which for me is filled with the ghosts of merry souls who died at Passchendaele and Ypres."

"My husband was killed at Verdun."

"I didn't know that."

"It wouldn't have helped you to know, would it? But you are leaving now. I simply meant that all the world is filled with such ghosts and that I understand what you feel."

"I am ashamed."

"You are silly for the first time since I have known you. Please go on about you and Mr. Hillairet."

"To pay me for my trouble—and I shall take great trouble for him—Hillairet will teach me his art, for he is a master of a great art which thrives in all times of ugliness—the art of self-delusion. Great countries have it; they need it because in acquiring greatness they have lost beauty and found ugliness. People sometimes have it because they live in those countries. Hillairet's snobbism—his belief in the superiority of his delusory nobility—is a very American form of the art, which was perhaps exquisitely refined by the convenient presence of the Negro."

"What is the English form?"

"Our delusion? It is even more pathetic. We think we are the master race. Pitiable, really, but when self-delusion becomes an art as England and Hillairet have made it, then it can sustain one. I am not mocking Hillairet, believe me, Doctor. I have faith that if I, not as an Englishwoman but as an individual, can learn this art from him, I will be able to see what no longer exists. Yes! Perhaps I will be able to make myself believe that we are all together again. I could be happy for the rest of my life—may it be short, please God—by seeing my husband and my brothers and my father walking rapidly to meet me at some beautiful house only a few streets away. He will teach me how to stalk all my exhausted dreams. And perhaps—since nothing is impossible really to a great artist of self-delusion—I can try to teach him how to feel. He will delude himself that he has reconstructed a vanished world, and I that I have found a man who needs me. It is the only way we can save each other."

"And if you find that he has no knack for feeling, and you no knack for self-delusion," the doctor asked with sadness, "what then?"

"Oh, my God, what then?" Sian said, and she covered her face with her bony hands.

C hapter 11

 Sian's mother had been a sweetly vacillating woman, given to forgiving and to loving gentleness. As a girl and afterward, Sian had remembered the forgiving fondly and the loving gentleness with awe, but she had felt contempt for the vacillation. She determined to emulate what she considered her father, Lord Donen, to be: forthright, decisive, always sure. This had served her well enough at schools, but it had melted almost instantly before the resolution of her husband, from the moment he had arrived in her life. As she looked back now, she realized that she too had become vacillating, which made her wonder if her mother had been forthright and definite before her father had stormed on the scene. Perhaps her own daughter was presently making promises to herself about vacillation, also in vain.

But now Colin was gone, deep into French mud—whatever had been left of his body by the unspeakable war. The night before she left the clinic at Anieres, Sian resolved to set forth and regain the self she had been before she had known the man who had broken her heart by dying. As an uncertain start, she held one of her irregular meetings with the past, not deluded at all that she was being heard by her late husband but speaking directly to her memory of him. She lay back upon the pillows in the silent darkness and concentrated upon a plot of ground in France which she had made herself visit twice since the war. It was the last place he had lived, and it was to this aliveness that she spoke.

"I make no apologies to you, Colin," she said fiercely. "I point out that life must go on, et cetera. I have no sentimental or sensual designs on Hillairet. He needs me to feed his delusions, and I must have a companion, no matter how eccentric. I must study his artistry if I am ever to find you again. Poor Hillairet has a lumpy psyche, but he is quite a handsome man, though in a different way from you. More feral. And you have never heard such an accent when speaking French! Yet he delivers everything with the air of one who has taught diction to the Rochefoucaulds. Everything he has sought to learn has the quality of 'personality.' He can chat about building a bridge, for instance, with statistics and anecdotes about bridges, engineers, steel, rivers and the bridge in literature, dentistry, billiards, and symbolism, but one is at the same time certain that he would not know a bridge if he were crossing one.

"If Hillairet ever took me to bed—alas, impossible for both of us—I feel instinctively that he would bring the same sort of expertise to the act, the sort of cleverness in sex possessed by Casanova. I say that because he seems to have no *feeling* for anything. I know one thing: that respect is the only successful aphrodisiac. While I cannot respect him for not feeling, that does not mean that he is not to be respected—if you follow me, darling.

"He is kind in an abject sort of way. He is a gifted cook. He is wealthy. He has surprising good taste for such a driven snob. The fact that he happens to be insane doesn't come into it at all. In the first place, it would hardly be a fitting judgment coming from me. Secondly, madness is much more prevalent since the war, and many of my co-inmates in this peaceful place seem far more sane than many of my friends outside. The pace toward insanity is quickening, and I daresay it is not merely a fad. Besides, poor Hillairet has an endearing sort of paranoia. He suffers from snobbism carried to its ultimate degree, far beyond the we-are-better-than-anyone-on-earth-so-let-us-help-you-or-we-will-have-to-kill-you sort of thing which other rich Americans try so hard to project.

"Hillairet has been a banker, he says. Well . . . possibly. His clothing suggests the manic conservatism which is the confidence trick of the banker. He says he is here for a rest cure after 'too damned much hard work,' and he is trying to locate his parents, who presumably are Kaiser Wilhelm and Queen Mary. Evidently they had to abandon him on the desk of a bank president soon after birth because of cruel politics. Does he sound harmless? Dr. Boscawen thinks he may be entirely harmless. So you see, Colin, I am not being faithless. If we are to weigh faithlessness, examine your own death, please, and Arthur's and Pa's and Tim's and Cecil's and Henry's."

Sian's eyes held the vision of that muddy plot of ground, and she covered her face with her arms.

C hapter 12

 Francis cooked a farewell dinner for Sian, Dr. Boscawen and his banker, Jacques Crouch. For a centerpiece he had carved the Bear of the Canton and Republic of Geneva out of *beurre noir*, and for the first course had prepared a distant relative of the trout called omble-chevalier in wine sauce in the style of Zug. There followed a saddle of lamb and a purée of string beans. After the entree, Francis rose from the table and gave an emotionally charged speech, which could be heard by all the patients in the dining room, on the subject of Reblochon cheese. "Reblochon," he said, "is a semi-hard cheese made from cow's milk in the upland pastures of Thomes and the Great St. Bernard in our neighboring Haute-Savoie, and it is a tangible association I shall always cherish with this place I have come to love so well. Reblochon's fat content is only forty-five per cent of its dry matter, and that dry matter is not less than forty-five per cent of its total weight. Whenever I taste this king of the cheeses of France, no matter where I am, I shall think of all of you."

He leaned forward and stared at each of his guests, then over their heads to all the patients in the dining room, his eyes soft and his head tilted sentimentally. "Reblochon is of the type of Port Salut, but everything about it exceeds Port Salut. It is shaped like a Camembert, but no Camembert ever made offers its immaculate goodness. Indeed, no lover of cheese could find it in his heart to cut away the rind of the Reblochon. It has given me some of the great moments of my life"—his voice quavered, then broke. "I will always be grateful to our home here in Anieres, and to the wonderful people who order our food, for the privilege of being invited, for the first but certainly not the last time in my life, to bite into, chew and savor a genuine Reblochon cheese."

Exhausted by his emotion, Francis' head fell to his chest at the end of this peroration. The patients applauded him wildly, and not a few of them rose to their feet, crying "Bravo!" and "*Bis!*" Then a few began to climb upon the tables and chairs. He had overexcited them, but he had reached them. When they began to throw little things at the light fixtures, Dr. Boscawen motioned the attendants into action and she suggested to Francis' guests that they take their coffee on the terrace.

Sian found herself deeply moved by Francis' speech; it was the first time she had ever seen Francis express any emotion about anything. Though her forearms began to ache and her hands to hurt, she could not stop applauding until Dr. Boscawen gently stayed her arms. All at once she saw that the outsider, M. Crouch, was painfully embarrassed, and she did not know which way to look because Francis had not moved since he had finished his speech. He stood like the statue of a hero, head down on his chest, eyes closed, arms limp at his sides. How disappointing it would have been, Sian thought, if the first time Hillairet had revealed that he truly did have feelings it had been about something like kittens, or broken-winged birds or people.

They left from the Cornavin station late the next day. Sian sent Francis into the station ahead to oversee the luggage, while she looked back at the lovely lake and at Mont Blanc, drawing the last sigh of serenity from the scene. She had been safe for almost three years, but as she began to feel the terror of the chaos to which she was returning, she wheeled briskly and strode purposefully into the station, humming loudly and tunelessly to drive all thought from her mind. She wore a beige traveling suit. The waistline was below her hips, and she wore a "flattener" to compress her unfashionably full breasts. Her black satin hat resembled a picador's beaver, and the heavy tweed skirt which dropped to her ankles had four large buttons descending below her knees.

When she reached the train she could see that Francis must have told everyone within earshot that he was traveling with the Dowager Marchioness of Shattock; he was preening bashfully and the porters and guards were staring at her as though she were a heavyweight champion. She attempted a caricature of imperious royalty, and because of her wonderful nose she brought it off quite well. "Be sure they haven't lost the case with the jeweled snuffboxes, my dear," she said in French as she was assisted aboard the train by two guards.

Francis had so much luggage that he'd had to take a separate compartment. Sian had only one case, but she said she would match him trunk for trunk, and then some, when they left Paris for London. They sat in her compartment and for a long while sat silently listening to the foreign sounds of the outside world.

After Lausanne, Francis opened the picnic basket and they had cucumber caprices and lobster nips with champagne. Sian took his hands.

"Your hands are freezing," she said.

"Yours seem colder."

"So they should. I have been almost three years away from the noises."

"Are you frightened?"

"Of course I'm frightened. But I must take you into the world. I've seen it, but I didn't think I'd ever look at it again."

"You are very kind."

"You must not be frightened, Hillairet. You will get everything you desire and all your enemies will be defeated."

"What I desire is that you call me Francis."

"I'm perfectly willing to call you Francis if you'll stop calling me dear Marchioness and Lady Sian."

"What may I call you?"

"What in hell do you think you should call me? Dear Dowager Marchioness? Call me Sian. Not Shawn. Its pronounced Shon."

"Shon."

"How clever of you."

"Will we stay in Paris long?"

"Who knows? I have to go to the dressmakers, and I've been on the telephone to friends. Prince Christopher, brother of the King of Greece and a darling man, has just married an American widow, and that brought the Grand Duchess Xenia and the Grand Duke Michailovitch back to the city."

Francis swallowed heavily and decided to open another bottle of champagne.

"Biscuit is the color this autumn. Very large sleeves. Jonesco, the Rumanian Foreign Minister, is in town; he always brings hordes of incredibly beautiful women with him. If we can all manage to be at the same place at the same time I'll introduce you to Charlie Chaplin."

"The actor?" Francis suspected she was making fun of him.

"The artist. Have you ever been to Paris?"

"I've passed through it."

"They are racing at Enghien, and if it will amuse you, I will bring two or three horses over from Ireland so that you may have inside information before you place your losing bet."

"You own race horses?"

"I did once; I suppose I still do."

"I can recite every winner and every winning jockey of the Derby, St. Léger and Ascot, going back to 1875."

"If you do, I shan't send for the horses."

"There is a trick to it, of course,"

"Please don't teach it to me. The Autumn Painting Salon opens on October 13th, and we must stay for that. Then there's the Automobile Show, and Lucien Guitry is starring

himself in three plays at the Edward VII. I may even find
you a little princess—Italian or Belgian, we'll see—and of
course you'll be wallowing in countesses, even a few English
ones."

"It sounds very exciting," Francis said as he chewed at his
mustache in an effort to control himself.

"Here comes the world again," Sian sighed. "And I can't
take my hiding places with me."

"I am with you, Sian. And there is nothing I wouldn't do
for you."

She laughed harshly. "Can you protect me from ghosts?"

Francis smiled patronizingly. "There are no ghosts. Have
some champagne."

"No ghosts, Francis? You will find them. It takes living.
You will turn in to a street and they'll be waiting for you,
but you cannot join them. I could die. I told myself—there's
nothing to that. But how could I do it? I would shame them
if I did, because they died bravely and patiently, each
awaiting his turn. One very dear man has left thousands of
ghosts behind him and I have been in love with every one of
them."

On the morning of October 6th, 1921, Sian and Francis
were installed in the Hotel Bergquist in the rue du Faubourg
St. Honoré, a thoroughfare which had been there since the
Middle Ages. It was the street of generals, great bankers, the
caricaturist Monnier, Madame de Pompadour, the author of
"La Marseillaise," the hairdresser of the Empress Eugénie,
one emperor and all the presidents of France. The Hotel
Bergquist was acutely conscious of the tradition of the street
and maintained at all times a policy which exceeded mere
decorum. To be admitted to the Hotel Bergquist was not
unlike gaining admittance to one of the great men's clubs—
with the additional requirement that the applicant had to be
rich.

The Dowager Marchioness took three rooms on the third
floor and Francis was given two rooms on the second floor.
The management was ecstatically happy to see her and was
not unkind to him.

In the lift, Sian shook Francis' hand and said she would

expect him to appear at her door, dressed for dinner, at eight o'clock that evening. "We have been invited to dinner. I didn't want to overexcite you on the train, but tonight you will dine with a Grand Duchess of Imperial Russia—which no longer exists, of course, but she can't just blow away, can she? You will also meet one ex-king."

Involuntarily, Francis leaned against the wall of the elevator. His legs had turned to water.

"I will tell the porter where to book you for lunch, and he will have a cab at the front entrance at one o'clock. I have sent for a car from London; it will arrive this evening. The chauffeur is Powell, the footman is Shaw."

The lift stopped at the third floor, and they stood together in the hall for a moment while the lift waited for Francis to descend.

"Take notes, please, Francis."

He took a black notebook from his pocket and the slim gold pencil which Mrs. Hibbert had given to him on a Fourth of July long past, and held them at the ready.

"Your hats are too bizarre," Sian said, "and you will need a hat for the evening. After lunch, go to Gelot in the Place Vendôme and put yourself in their hands. I will choose your ties. The French make quite good men's shirts; you will go to Boivin this morning to be measured. Have them send the shirts to 15 Queen Street, Mayfair, in my care. Plain white shirts, please; we can depend upon the London *chemisiers* to tart you up."

"Shall I order suits? My tailor is Parisian."

"Francis! You are dressed like a Serbian political assassin as it is! Your suits will be made by Poole in London. Their Mr. Gilhead saw to my husband and brothers, and he shall see to you. In the meantime, God help us, you will have to look the way you look, I suppose." She sighed, patted his cheek and went into her room.

Since the age of seven Sian had had thick, waist-long polished copper hair, but before noon it was bobbed as short as her ear lobes.

It was a painful experience, but she refused to think about it any further. At her dressmaker's she announced that she wanted all her clothes to be as deliberately progressive as Mme. Vionnet wished to make them. As she was fitted she telephoned friends in Paris, London, New York, Rome and Copenhagen.

Because she had nothing even remotely acceptable to wear to dinner, and also because she was the Marchioness of Shattock, a miracle was passed, and at seven fifty-five that evening Sian was able to put on a dress that was just a few feet in front of the current fashion. When Francis knocked at her door at one minute after eight she had become a totally different woman. She had been transformed from midwar Britain into postwar France, and the change thrilled her so that she glowed with longing to be seen by a man.

Francis stood in the doorway and stared at her glassily. Finally he closed the door; then he turned to look at her again and said in awestruck tones, "My dear Marchioness."

"Francis, I have been meaning to tell you that it is incorrect to use the 'my dear' to anyone under the rank of duchess."

Francis stored this fact instantly, but his train of thought was not to be diverted. "You can have no idea of the technical virtuosity of the cooks of this city," he said.

From above the neckline which would have brought down the wrath of her husband, from below the sensationally cropped hair, Sian stared at him and tried to believe that she had not heard what she thought she had heard.

"I went to three restaurants, tasted lightly and observed. In the third, the rush was over, so I took my courage in my hands and—"

"You clod! Damn you, Hillairet!"

"Excuse me?"

"Am I your damned scullery maid that you must tell me about your grease and garbage?"

"Lady Sian! Mrs. Recknell! My dear Marchio—you have cut your hair!"

She exhaled strongly and composed herself as best she could.

"They have cut your beautiful, beautiful hair!" he repeated.

"Cut it? I am very nearly bereft of it. Do you, uh, like it?"

"It's—it's stunning! And your dress is fantastically beautiful. Why, you are a young woman, Sian."

"*Shon,* damn you, not Shawn! What the devil did you think I was?"

"I'm sorry, Sian. Please forgive me. What I meant was—"

"I am not angry," she said angrily. "I am pleased that you like my hair and this dress."

"I simply can't believe I'm not seeing you for the first time." He walked closer. He stared at her hair, then into her deep-set green eyes; then his eyes flickered momentarily to her neckline. At last he looked away, and she was astonished to find herself wishing he had not looked away so quickly.

"How very sweet you are to say that," she answered huskily.

"You smell wonderfully," Francis said lightly, but his voice shook. "You have made everything come alive. It was just a hotel a moment or two ago, but now I am in a palace with a beautiful princess. I want to touch you." He lifted his hand slowly and allowed two of his fingers to glide down the skin of her bare arm so lightly that they almost did not touch her.

"We must not be late," Sian said. She turned away from him, and out of nowhere a lady's maid appeared holding a fur wrap. Sian slipped into it and walked to the door and flung it open. Without looking back she strode out of the room toward the lift. Francis followed her like a sleepwalker.

The dinner was being given for the Spanish Ambassador by the Grand Duchess Metrophanie. It was served at a circular table for twenty-six people, who sat within a hedge of thirteen footmen, matched for size and coloring in the apple-green livery of the house. The ceiling of the circular dining room was a white Gothic plaster vault supported by plaster columns, and the tracery of the five large windows of the room had the delicate absurdity of the best Georgian Gothic, an endearing conceit for a Russian who lived in

France. Balalaika players and singers dressed as Cossacks in authentic rented costumes roamed the room behind the hedge of footmen, and a maddened boyar was banging on a cymbeline somewhere in the background.

One hundred and four crystal glasses in four sizes shimmered on the soft rose cloth under a chandelier which had once been loot from Poland. Two hundred and eighty-six pieces of silver gleamed heavily on fretted silver place mats which had taken nineteen women in the hostess' home province six and a quarter years to complete. Though the total effect was numbing, the sounds around him distracting, the glistening teeth and jewels of the women mesmerizing, Francis remembered and recorded every detail in his diary before he slept that night. As the entire party entered the dining room, he found himself standing next to the *sommelier* as he waited for Sian to appear. "What is your name?" Francis asked in a kindly way.

"Henri Emmet, sir."

"What is your stance with regard to the service of white wine with lamb?"

"White wine, sir? With lamb?" The sommelier covered a grin with his gloved hand.

"Are you implying that spring lamb, pale and tender, is not properly accompanied by a stout Montrachet, or a Corton Charlemagne, a Clos Blanc de Vougeot or one of the better Meursaults?"

Emmet suppressed his laughter—almost. "I can say one thing, sir. You must be an American."

"Indeed I am!" Francis bridled. "I will ask you another question. Who in this room do you consider your master as an oenologist?"

"In this room, sir, tonight, sir, will dine the finest, most sensitive, most inexorable wine palate in France—the Prince de Rochemont."

"In that case, my dear fellow, I will bet you one hundred English pounds against one miserable French franc, the Prince de Rochemont, a stranger to me, to be the judge, that spring lamb is best enjoyed with white Burgundy wine."

Emmet's face froze. "I will do better than that, sir. I will accept your one hundred miserable English pounds, but if the Prince de Rochemont endorses white wine with lamb I will shoot myself."

"I couldn't ask for more than that, could I?" Francis said coldly as Sian came along and helped him to find his place at the great table.

The hostess was known internationally as "The Dragnet" because she had been to bed with so many men from so many areas of human endeavor; partial to no class or creed; favoring neither rich nor poor, man nor woman. She had just arrived in Paris after giving a party in Monte Carlo, a thrilling Prince and Pauper Ball which mixed gigolos, whores and other moneyed notables with the visiting aristocracy of the Côte d'Azur. Because hotels had refused to rent their ballrooms for such a motley affair, she had been forced to rent a large villa for five thousand francs for one night, from seven P.M. to seven A.M. But the party was such a success that in the morning the Grand Duchess could not bear to turn such wonderful people away simply because her lease was running out, so she had bought the house for a hundred and twenty thousand francs and the party and all the beautiful people were able to continue for another two days. Of course, she had not used her own house in Monte Carlo; that beautiful such people were not.

Francis had memorized each name and each title to whom he had been introduced, and preoccupied himself with guessing the names of the tailors, dressmakers, jewelers and florists who had clothed and decorated them.

At the round table he was seated on one side next to an elderly, quite-drunk Russian lady wearing the most formidable diamonds he had ever seen, to whom no one at all had spoken; in fact, the absence of an introduction had been so conspicuous, Francis surmised that her chauffeur had delivered her to the wrong party. On his other side was one of the three Italian principessas in the room, who promptly ordered him to call her Giovanna.

Sian was a third of the table away, out of earshot but clearly audible if she shouted, as most of the other guests were doing. She was placed between Don Jaime Arias, the

Spanish Ambassador, and a Danish falconer named Rifbjerg who owned six rare Arctic gyrfalcons and who, at the moment Francis looked in their direction, was reproducing the sound made by a Golden Eagle—*kewpeng, kewpeng, kewpeng*—which he followed with a curdlingly realistic scream of falcon rage—*hek, hek, hek, hek, hek*—as Sian smiled pitiably at Francis.

Giovanna was a slender woman with a snowy bosom of admirable muscle tone. Her mouth was so red and heavy that she seemed to have lost the strength to hold it in the shape of anything resembling a human feature. It spewed itself across her face, and its perpetual abandonment to pleasure was as exciting to Francis as it was incredible. He chatted away and tried to look away from it into her hot, dry eyes.

"You like woman?" the principessa inquired, the vowels struggling like lost souls to escape from her undulating rubber mouth.

"Which woman?" Francis asked, looking about alertly. They were still over the soup, a Polish *hlodnik,* whose ingredients Francis was breaking down as he chatted.

"All woman. Any woman."

"Well—uh—yes." The soup definitely contained shrimps, sour cream, beets and beet tops. The stock was chicken broth with perhaps a touch of shark's fin. "Some of my best friends are women."

"Mr. Hillairet!" Sian was shouting at him across the wide table, and both Rifbjerg and Don Jaime were staring at him intently and expectantly, though Don Jaime appeared skeptical. "To settle a little point, can you tell us when Easter celebrations began?" She smiled at him confidently.

Francis was very pleased that she had been thinking about him. "Easter began at about 68 A.D.," he bellowed to carry over the eleven other conversations. "It is called Easter in English after the Saxon goddess Eostre, whose festival was in April. Then, after altogether too much contention between the Eastern and the Western churches, the Council at Nice in 325 A.D. settled on a common day throughout the Christian world. However, as you know, the two arms of the

Catholic Church still differ, though their dates for Easter did coincide in 1882."

"*Fantástico!*" Don Jaime muttered.

"Thank you, Mr. Hillairet!" Sian yelled.

"You come wit' her?" the principessa snarled. "Who dat?"

"I escorted her here, yes. She is the Dowager Marchioness of Shattock."

"Inglese?"

"Rather."

"You Inglese?"

"American."

"You a very beautiful man. Long. Flat. Very strong. I feel-a t'ings about you."

"How very cordial of you."

"Mr. Hillairet!" Sian was shouting at him again, and she seemed to be glancing disagreeably at the principessa.

"Yes, Lady Sian?"

"We have a little wager. Can you tell us who invented roller skates? Mr. Rifbjerg and Don Jaime have bet me a thousand pounds that you cannot do it again."

"Do what again?"

"Answer such unexpected questions."

"Oh. Well, a Mr. Plimpton patented roller skates in America in 1865, but actually they were first introduced in Meyerbeer's *Prophète* in Paris in April, 1849."

"Thank you, dear Mr. Hillairet."

"*Fantástico!*" muttered Don Jaime.

"Why she keeps interrupting-a us?" the principessa hissed.

The distinct, unmistakable sound of a pistol shot was heard close by. Everyone fell silent, then the Grand Duchess yelled, "Who is shooting off guns in my house?"

There was another considerable silence. At last the major domo appeared in the great archway. "I regret to inform Your Grace," he said discreetly but clearly enough to carry across the room, "that Henri, the *sommelier*, has shot himself." Francis felt the thrill of being right and nodded his head imperceptibly.

By the time they had finished the entree, potchki V

Madeiry à la Tsarkoe Selo, Francis had accepted an invitation to lunch at the principessa's *hôtel particulier* in the Avenue de la Motte-Picquet the next day.

At one A.M. Sian and Francis rolled homeward in her newly arrived Rolls. It was a ferryboat-sized automobile with high seats and huge windows which had been designed to display British royalty. Its elderly driver, Powell, who seemed to be as much a part of it as a centaur is to a horse, wore the permanent expression of an ambitious clergyman who had been unfrocked for simony. Shaw, the footman, was a robotic device who sprang out to open doors and accept packages with the wonderfully contrived agility of a mechanism designed by Breguet.

"Did you enjoy yourself?" Sian asked.

"It was so wonderful that it will be days, perhaps months, before I sort it all out."

Francis stared out dreamily at the pretty lights across the Seine. Sighing, he said quite absent-mindedly, "Was your new hair a success? But that's a silly question."

"I think so. I surprised everyone, anyhow. Or rather I surprised them by appearing out of nowhere with a man. They'd all supposed that I was in a nunnery, I think, and some of them didn't like it at all."

"Your hair?" He was incredulous.

"No, silly, you. They think of me, then they think of Colin. They can't see me any other way."

"Who is Colin?"

"My—late husband."

"You've never mentioned his name."

"True. Did you enjoy chatting with the Princess Umbaratchini?"

"Uh, Giovanna?"

"Giovanna, is it? She's always been so democratic—even venereally democratic. Now you'll say that I'm anti-Italian, I suppose. Or opposed to tiny, slender women with dissolute mouths. Didn't you think she had a mouth like Caligula?"

"Her mouth seemed fatigued really."

"And so it must be. How exhausted all of her must be.

Most of Paris feels that she is only wasting her strength when trying to stay erect."

Francis arrived, prompt as always, at one o'clock at the principessa's many-windowed house in the 16th arrondissement. They were thrashing wildly about her huge bed at ten minutes after one, and during the next two hours, while she accepted his most thorough ministrations, he tried to convince himself over and over again that he was actually making love to a genuine princess.

Unfortunately, Princess Umbaratchini turned out to be the sort of woman who boasts about her conquests. Whatever it was she said to the two German baronesses who were sisters, they telephoned Francis at the Bergquist the next day, and in no time he found himself in bed with both of them together in a *meuble* in the rue de Ponthieu which rented luxurious rooms for elegant people by the hour. In turn, the sisters explained Francis' special effects to a Rumanian countess, a member of the party of the visiting Rumanian Foreign Minister. She waited for Francis in the lobby of the Bergquist until he returned late one afternoon from a séance with the sisters, introduced herself humbly and then invited herself into his rooms, all with a minimum of talk because she spoke French with a bilateral emission lisp. Francis found himself staring in the mirror after she had left, trying to convince himself that he had had carnal conversations with a princess, a countess and two baronesses and that it was literally impossible to say how high the whole thing would take him.

When Francis realized that his name was being bandied about a city of the reputation of Paris, he winced, but he was so naïve that it did not occur to him that his prowess might be discussed by the four ladies with many other ladies, or that such discussions would eventually reach the ears of the Marchioness. He was studying reports on securities in his apartment when Sian knocked on his door one afternoon a few days later. As he admitted her he noticed that she seemed distraught.

"How dare you!" she snarled at him in her harsh, hoarse voice as she slammed the door heavily behind herself.

"Excuse me?"

"How dare you carry on day-long orgies with four women, day in, day out, like a manure-flecked satyr, and then ride beside me from house to house in Paris at night with the decorum of a curate?" She hit him on the cheek with all her force. "You oily, smarmy, sacerdotal ooze of a sneak."

"Who could say such a thing?"

"Your four mistresses are not gentlemen, that's who could say such a thing! The Principessa Umbaratchini, for example, tells all France and, one presumes, all Italy by telephone and telegraph that you are a bull god whose spine seems to have been removed."

"Preposterous!"

"Eleven women and a creepy faggot have had the pleasure of telling me that the Raddatz sisters think of you as Siegfried returned, and that they are racking their alleged brains for a way to persuade their father to offer you a place in the family's *Wurst* cartel."

"Ridiculous on the face of it! What do I know about *Wurst?*"

"All Paris—and I can assure you that protests have been made to the Quai d'Orsay by Take Jonesco—buzzes with the gossip that your passport may be picked up because of your various disgusting turpitudes with the Countess Smornya-Bakrescu. Ha! A Rumanian countess! She has told Jonesco and a number of journalists that she may kill herself, because each time she sees you it gets better and better and she fears that some day it will have to stop and she cannot bear to live with that thought."

"I have never heard such vulgar claims."

"What a banal man you are."

"Sian! Listen to me! I swear to you I never dreamed that any of this could happen—and then it was happening."

"If you didn't know that, then perhaps you don't know that there are approximately thirty-seven women in this city at this moment who are preparing to find a way to sink you

into the feathers. Before this week is out you will have been
smothered under a mountain of them, eaten alive and melted
into a puddle of slime. And good riddance, Hillairet!" She
slammed the door as she left.

Francis ran into the corridor after her. "Sian! Please don't
leave me! You've got to help me."

She stopped but did not turn around.

"I would have done anything to have avoided all this, if
only because it has upset you." Sian wheeled, charged him
with stiff arms, pushed him backward into his room and
slammed the door shut again. "You have not upset me, you
silly bastard!" She was in an eye-popping fury. "I'm a forty-
year-old woman, not a lovesick, milk-sopping, tangle-curled
girl, you silly bastard!"

"I certainly seem to have upset you."

"Who wouldn't be upset? I have already written to friends
in London sponsoring you. You have made a fool of me in
Paris, and now it is all over the civilized world. What kind of
fool will I seem when I disavow you?"

"Disavow me?" It was a wail of agony.

"It will be all over every newspaper. And a fine figure
you'll cut with your majestic parents!"

"Sian! Oh, God."

"You didn't think of that while you were dipping your bull
god's wick, did you, you silly clot?"

"What am I going to do? I beg you. You've got to forgive
me. What can I do?"

"You must leave for London at once—within the hour. Go
directly to the channel train at the Gare du Nord. It will
mean a four- or five-hour wait at the station, but you must
disappear."

"Do you think there is a chance that—"

"A very slim chance. But you've got to move quickly.
Now, dammit. Move!"

As Francis emerged from the lift, the Countess Kaya
Smornya-Bakrescu was standing directly in his path. A
somewhat burly woman, with chutes of black hair and
smudged ballerina eye make-up, she was weeping noisily.

Her shoulders were bare, and as she shook her jeweled hands in emotional punctuation the several diamond bracelets on each wrist rattled loudly. "My dollink, my dollink," she moaned. "My prance, my prance!" She grasped his lapels, hung by them with all her weight, pressed the top of her head against his white shirt front and left a dark pomade mark when he pushed her away forcibly. A short man with long black hair and an interested expression stood discreetly beside them and took notes. "Here, here," Francis said. "What the hell are you doing?"

"Morrie Cleve, London *Evening Standard*," the man answered laconically.

The countess grasped Francis' head roughly and turned his face to hers as three photographers' flash guns went off. "They told me you were livving me, my dollink, my prance. No, no, no!" Francis could not extricate his head from her grip, but out of the corner of his eye he saw Cleve taking notes steadily. "Damn you, sir," Francis barked. "I'll thank you to remove yourself, if you please."

"Dollink, come wit' me," the countess moaned. "Now, come now. We ron. I got my car." She tugged at him with the strength of a team of oxen, but the Bergquist's deeply shocked manager and concierge were pulling his other arm. "I'm afraid we can't have this, sir," the manager said. "I must ask you to pay and leave. No photographs!" he screamed at the photographers.

The countess threw her head back, stared at the ceiling and screamed so loudly that the hotel men dropped their grip on Francis and leaped back to safety. She reached into the yoke of her gossamer dress with both hands and pulled heavily. The dress ripped downward to a point just below her dark and mossy navel. "I am ugly?" she asked at the top of her lungs. "You turn your back on these? These you don't want any more?" The cameras flashed. "You are my prance, and no one else will ever have you!" She pulled a knife from her purse and sprang at him. They grappled, with Francis gaping about him in desperate search for the sudden surrealistic touch which would assure him that this was all a gruesome nightmare. As he fought for his life he had the

impression that he saw the Dowager Marchioness of Shattock standing in a corner grinning with malice. At last the
police rushed in and dragged the countess off him, while the
hotel management on the other side pushed the mass of
bodies surrounding him toward the cashier's window.

Francis' bill was ready, and he could hear the countess'
sobbing recede as he paid it over the jabber of the journalists
hammering questions at him in French and English. In
another moment he was propelled across the pavement into
a taxi, which sped off immediately.

At the Gare du Nord, he paced up and down alongside the
train, faint with anxiety, until, three minutes before departure time, Sian appeared following a wagon filled with her
luggage. "Good evening, Francis," she said gaily. "Is this our
car?"

He nodded dumbly.

"They said you had caused a scene in the hall of the hotel.
I said that was ridiculous, that it couldn't have been you."

"There was a dreadful scene."

"Oh, Francis."

"And somehow—I tell you I don't understand anything
any more, I don't see how such things could have happened
—the press seems to have known there would be a scene. I
shall be ruined in England before I ever get there. My
parents will disown me before I ever get there." His eyes
filled with tears.

"But what happened?" she asked with detachment.

"It was that bloody Rumanian woman. She can't be a
countess. She must be neurotic. Somehow—I will never
know how—she found out I was leaving France. She tried to
kill me. The press was everywhere. Police too. She stripped
herself to the waist!"

"Whatever for?"

"There were photographers!" Bitter tears streamed down
his cheeks. "Who could have told all those people I was
leaving? Who could have made it happen? Thank heaven
there was a cab waiting. I'm afraid I overtipped the *chasseur*, but I got away."

"Well," Sian said, "as we sow, so shall we reap." She

patted his arm and smiled at him dazzlingly. "I have booked rooms for you at Brown's," she said, "and we'll have news of a flat for you in a day or two."

"Thank you. Thank you very much." He moved to assist her up the steps of the train.

Chapter 13

Francis moved slowly, as though a sudden movement might pierce the golden haze in which he floated. He was in London, the capital city of his family! Its people were like beautiful leaves of autumn who swirled gracefully about. His weightlessness, on achieving his destiny, moved him away from the other beautiful leaves, and he felt no fear. The light of London was as soft as promises. He had found his way unerringly to the exact core of the universe, and he knew that now it was centering itself on him.

He was sure he was being watched as he left the hotel. It made him stand straighter: a tall, well-kept, proudly maintained man; he hoped the reports being sent to Them would make Them proud of him. He sucked in his cheeks to give his face a hawklike, aristocratic cast because he knew that They would be having him photographed in Their setting to make sure that he qualified, even though he had kept the faith through all the years apart.

He sauntered into Albemarle Street and turned toward Piccadilly, breathing the effluvia of ancient kings and queens and the fealty required from all. At Piccadilly he turned right toward Green Park, because across it he would be able to see the outline of Buckingham Palace. At the corner of Berkeley Street a newspaper headline caught his eye: WOMAN ASSAILS MYSTERY PRINCE IN PARIS. Its crass, offensive mention of nobility impelled him to buy the newspaper, and he stood in the mild evening breeze mildly titillated as he read the account—"Last night in the main hall of the Hotel Bergquist, the most distinguished hotel in Paris—" because he had been at that very spot at about the same time and because he'd had no idea that the Bergquist was such an exclusive hotel. Leave it to Sian, he thought. She knew. Idly he read on, but the phrase "Beautiful Countess Kaya Smornya-Bakrescu, almost deranged by love" made him blink. He felt a terrible pain in his bowels and his hands trembled. " 'My prince, my prince,' the countess sobbed, a large knife in her hand, as she sought to prevent the departure of a tall, handsome mystery man." His eyes rolled across the page to a three-column photograph of the bare back of the countess and his own startled face; then, his gaze dribbling as slowly as cold ketchup, he examined another picture of the two of them in profile, showing the countess swinging like a shrieking tassel from his lapels.

Francis dropped the paper and fell back against the building wall. The newsvendor became alarmed and hastened to his side, saying, "Are you all right, sir?" Wordlessly, Francis shuffled away from him to the bar entrance of the Berkeley Hotel, while the newsvendor picked up the newspaper and dusted it off for resale. At the bar, Francis drank two double whiskies slowly, then found a telephone and called Sian.

"Sian? Have you seen the *Evening Standard?*"

"I have not yet reacquired the newspaper habit."

Francis made a gargling sound. "Hillairet! What has happened?"

"Two pictures. Front page. The Rumanian woman."

"Oh, that. Yes, I'd heard about that."

"Heard?"

"I've had almost two dozen calls."

"Why should anyone call you about it?"

"My friends read the story and they naturally called people in Paris. The people in Paris told them you had been seen constantly with me, and so they called me."

"What will this do to my parents? Oh, my God." Sian had a fleeting image of the Kaiser Wilhelm and Queen Mary raging at each other over a closed-circuit telephone.

"Just a moment, Francis. You know the rules. The newspaper did not say who you were, so there cannot be a libel action. They said you were a prince and the Hotel Bergquist will most certainly not deny that."

"Do you really think so?"

"Anyway, I should think that your parents, being the sort they are, would be quite amused. I mean, it was just harmless hi-jinks, and no one has printed your name. I'm sure they're loving the whole thing."

Sian could see that the art of self-delusion wasn't difficult at all, once one got the hang of it. Rather fun, in fact. "And quite apart from your dear mama and papa, I have been telling members of the most exalted peerage all afternoon that you are the natural son of mad Louis of Bavaria. They are all dying to meet you. Do you speak German?"

"No, actually."

"No matter. I shall change the course. I'll say that you are the natural son of the pretender to the French throne."

"What is a natural son?"

"A bastard. As a matter of fact, I remember calling you a bastard in Paris."

"May I come to see you? I am shattered. You have held me together, but I must see you." Francis had almost achieved Sian's accent to perfection; that is to say, no Englishman would have taken him for an Englishman, but a Canadian or an Australian or anyone who had attended vaudeville performances regularly would have been fooled.

"At once," Sian said.

She hung up the telephone, feeling very fond of Francis, as though she were a bride and he her perfect omelet. She felt much less brisk and objective about him, much less scientific in her interest, and she damned Umbaratchini, the German sisters and the absurd Rumanian for having been so hysterical about his particular knack. Well, not a knack, she forced herself to admit because she detested thinking like this, perhaps more genius than knack. She damned the power of suggestion and her own weak embarrassing reactions. Why must she be forced to think about sex with her body again when she was sure she had mastered the art of thinking about it only with her mind? Damn sex and damn Francis. She would inhale deeply three times and it would go away. She inhaled deeply and then observed the responses from her erogenous zones. Good. It had gone away.

Francis walked rapidly through Shepherd Market to Curzon Street and thence to Queen Street. He stood for a few respectful moments on the opposite side to admire the broadness and six-story height of Sian's imposing town house. Eighteen servants! A housekeeper, a lady's maid, upstairs and downstairs housemaids, a tweeney, a kitchen maid, upstairs and downstairs laundry maids, a dairy maid, a still-room maid, a scullion, a cook, a butler, a chauffeur, three footmen and a boots boy. In the country, Sian had a groom, a head gamekeeper and an under gamekeeper, a gardener and two assistants, land stewards, bailiffs, park keepers, whippers-in, racing grooms, jockeys, pages and seamstresses. He needed only to walk across the street, press the brightly polished bell and he would be received by the Dowager Marchioness of Shattock; what's more, she would receive him immediately. And all around him, in these orderly streets and silent buildings, there were hundreds and hundreds of other servants all waiting on duchesses, marquises, earls, viscounts, barons, knights, esquires, chieftains, lords spiritual, provosts, canons, admirals, generals, lord advocates, lord mayors, justice generals, high sheriffs, chancellors, high commissioners, ministers plenipotentiary, companions of honor, and Fellows of the Royal Colleges of Organists, Physicians, Architects, Antiquaries and Dentists. Francis felt exalted as he crossed the street in stately measure and rang the doorbell. He was taken to her ladyship's boudoir, thirty-six feet square and with ornamental plastered walls and ceilings by Thomas Clayton. It was a jolly, informal sort of room, a most relaxing place to chat.

When Sian looked up at him it occurred to her that Francis was an exceptionally handsome man, despite the French tailoring. And he was such an aristocratic-looking man—exactly as aristocrats always looked on the stage. In actual life they almost always resembled boxer dogs, chrysanthemums or clock faces, whereas Francis had the good lines of a polished billiard cue. He handed her the newspaper, and as she glanced at the pictures and story she grinned wickedly.

"I wish I could honestly say whether I am a prince or not," he said plaintively.

"You certainly are a prince of good fellows," Sian answered sweetly.

"Perhaps I should be grateful to the *Evening Standard* for bringing me to the attention of my parents."

"If they're alive."

"Well, yes. Of course."

"And if they're in this country."

"There's that, too."

"As you have said, they may be German or French royalty."

Francis laughed deprecatingly. "I hardly think they are royalty," he replied modestly, "and in any case I have a conviction that they are English. Theoretically—in a manner of conjecture, that is—you could be my sister."

Sian blushed instantly; she could feel the heat in her cheeks. Her conscience had been warning her for some time, and now it was telling her that she was straying to the very brink of what could be—theoretically, in a manner of conjecture, that is—incest.

"It is decent of you not to have said that I might—conjecturally—be your mother," she answered with the lightest sarcasm. "But then the search would be ended, wouldn't it?" She had begun to think with her body again, and she was astonished to find that she possessed so many areas of aphrodisiomania. She rose, walked to the window, opened it, took three deep breaths and exhaled fully. The moment of swinishness departed and she closed the window. It had been such a long, long time since it had been allowable to think the other way. She turned to face Francis, "I think I shall take up smoking cigars after dinner," she announced.

The telephone rang. "Hello? Gant? Is it Lord Gant, the embarrassing practical joker? Darling, how are you? Oh, indefinitely, I should think. No, not at all. He's an incognito prince who was very, *very* nice to me in his little country, so I shall be nice to him in mine." She beamed across the telephone at Francis, who got flustered hearing himself spoken of like that. "Help me, will you, Lord Gant? How delightful. Yes . . . yes we'd love to. Thank you so much." She hung up. "You see? That's what's been happening all day. You are a celebrated legend in your own time."

"Sian, is genealogy difficult?"

"To live or to read?" She wanted to bang him over the head with a book. Good God, what a bore he was. "That was Lord Gant, also a celebrated legend in his time. He imports practical jokes from America. A sadist, but a delightful man. We will shoot with him the first weekend in November."

"How nice." he paused. "I would like to learn about genealogy," he said persistently.

"I suppose some rainy day you could go through *Dugdale's Baronage* and *Collin's Peerage.* Especially the Collin's. The famous sixth edition of 1806 was edited by a man with whom you have much in common."

"I do?"

"He was the heraldic genius, Samuel Egerton Brydges." Fight them with their own weapons, she thought. If he bores, rebore.

"Really?"

"He compiled the standard work in the Georgian period. He worked it out that since 1265, at least one hundred baronies-by-writ had fallen into abeyance." It wasn't working. He wasn't bored at all.

"Abeyance?"

"When heirs vanish, titles might be claimed by just any-body. But stop panting, Francis, because that door was slammed shut forever over a hundred years ago."

"I shall begin to study genealogy at once."

"My dear, it would take you months just to learn a fretty from a hurtleberry. Doris Spriggs-Danvers has an uncle who is a genealogist, but please, Francis, don't rush. We have an exhausting season ahead of us. We must find you a flat. You've simply got to get some new clothes. This entire house will have to be redecorated, and if I am to entertain in the manner to be expected by your parents, I have at least two country houses to think about—that is, if you are to be launched at all."

"I am dazed. London, the newspapers, your incredibly kind zeal—I am numb."

"Feeling is all that matters, Francis," Sian responded gravely. "Feeling is all the art and all the learning and all the meaning that there is. It took me nearly three years of silence to realize that. Have you ever felt anything?"

"What an extrordinary question."

"What have you felt?"

"No one could answer such a question—just like that." He seemed to be racking his brains to remember. "I've kept no precise inventory."

"I am not referring to your little ecstasies with Umbarat-chini and pertaining thereto. But you are a great cook, and the feeling for food means more than the feeling for sex to many people. After all, the need for it occurs more often— with some people, that is, though of course I am not imply-ing that this applies to Umbaratchini."

"On that basis, breathing is the most sensual thing we do."

"Very sage. Allow me to hold your head under water for a minute or two and breathing will become scrumptiously sensual to you. Besides, we can't smell without breathing." She was boring him! Just as she was becoming interested in the conversation, he was bored to distraction.

"All right," Francis said. "Have I ever experienced feeling? Once I was an officer of a bank that had the biggest and best pipe organ in North America, and that bank hired the finest organist obtainable to play the best classical music every day. That makes you feel—that sticks. Have you ever heard of an organ in an English bank?"

"Francis, I wasn't attacking the United States."

"Please answer my question."

"Of course we don't have organs in English banks. We are much more religious about money than you. We hardly ever speak about the stuff, much less hum while we count it. We could not take money that lightly. An overdraft by Bach? My God."

"Well, that organ music made me feel. I was at work, yet I felt many beautiful things."

"That's very good."

"I am not made of wood, you know. And if I bore you, I apologize."

"We are friends because you bore me. It seems an odd thing to say, but your fascination is in the enormously complex variety of subjects on which you are boring."

Francis stood up at once. "Good day," he said, wondering as he turned to leave how he was going to meet other members of the peerage to help him with the search.

"You can't leave and you know it," Sian said. "I have all the keys to every door of your need. Sit down. Don't be impulsive because what I say is a compliment doesn't sound like a compliment to you."

"I'll tell you one thing which is even more of a bore," Francis said hotly, "and that is your assumption that you can go on indefinitely with this idea that you are entitled to punish me because of what happened with five women in Paris."

"Five? *Five?*"

Francis shrugged. "The hotel manager's wife let herself into my rooms with a passkey early one morning."

"You fool!" She looked away from him so that he couldn't see the tears of anger in her eyes. "And now we are having our first quarrel," she said. "You are right and I was wrong. I didn't even know that I was punishing you." She turned to face him again, and perhaps because of the light film of tears, there was a light of special pleading in her eyes. "But I do want to teach you to feel more than I think you do now. I suppose that is presumptuous, but dammit, Francis, what I am trying to say is that information for its own sake is meaningless unless it is a key which will help admit you to greater and more meaningful experience. You were able to have all of that information drilled into you. Well, I am going to drill feelings into you, and you will have to accept that as my price for launching you into your great search." Her commanding nose seemed ready to charge at him and cleave him, and her full, soft mouth formed itself into a determined line.

Chapter 14

Sian was almost forty years old. She had been married since seventeen, and before that she had been adored by her four brothers and her father. Now she suddenly felt that she could no longer bear the fact that this icy man rejected her, day after day, out of hand. Did she have to love him before she could expect him to love her as those others had loved her? Like a brutal slap, it came to her mind that she had sinned so enormously once that until the sin was washed away she would have to pay grievously to thaw the emotionless façade of this man—first to make him feel, then to make him feel a need for her, as she knew she needed him now.

From the moment she had recognized her sin, over four years before, she had been made to pay for it with the lives of her husband, her brothers and her father, and with the death of all joy and reason. Now the promise of joy had been made to her again, and if she was able to touch and hold what she sensed was about to be offered her, she must absolve her sin. It was her last chance. If she did not, she must go back to the silence, back to the contemplation of her terrible waste, back among the insane. She felt a terrible urgency to begin at once. After Francis' departure she hastened to her writing desk.

Dearest Celia:

As you may know, I have been ill for some time in a mental clinic in Switzerland. I have recovered fully and have recently returned to London. I want very much to come to Donen Hall to see you, if you will invite me. I have so many things which I must say to you. Please let me come.

Your loving Mother

Sian was driven along the graveled road two miles beyond the main gate, toward a sober baroque palace of yellow sandstone which was streaked with reddish brown veins. It balanced sixteen chimneys serenely on its crown. The driveway was enclosed by stretches of stone wall to the left and right which were embellished with archways surmounted by urns and sundials and studded with splendid lion heads with iron rings in their jaws. Nearer the house the walls flared outward and disappeared before a great expanse of velvet lawn for what seemed to be miles.

The car halted at broad stone steps which mounted to the great entrance of the house. Sian got out of the car and walked up the steps. The main door was opened just as she reached it. She greeted the butler and the housekeeper, who stood inside to welcome her, gave them her coat and gloves and walked ninety polished feet through widely spaced columns, past great pots of flowers, and through the tall French windows to the terrace. There she paused, astonished as she had always been by the incomparable view of trees, hills and great formal gardens. Beyond the gardens the lake still rippled, and on its island, exactly aligned to the main axis of house and garden, was the granite keep which had once been the prison of the first Earl of Donen.

A fair-haired, beautiful young woman with a clubfoot was seated before a canvas on an easel, holding brushes and a palette and painting a ballerina in full flight. She turned at the sound of the terrace door opening.

"Hello, Mama," she said faintly.

"Hello, Celia."

Sian crossed the stone terrace and kissed the girl on the top of her head, then sat down next to her in the pale sunshine. "Pleasant out here," she said in her harsh voice while thinking of many other things and pretending to peer intently at the landscape.

A footman appeared. "A whiskey, please, Goodson," Sian said and remembered that this would be the first drink of whiskey she'd had since the night of her collapse in Paris, three years before. She had not seen Celia for five years— since she had been fifteen years old, since Colin had been killed, since all of them had died.

"You are so pretty, Celia," she said when the footman had gone.

"Thank you, Mama. You are looking well."

"Thirty-five months of rest. I should."

"Was it pleasant there?"

"Quite." Sian moistened her lips nervously. "You look like the men in our family."

"I am told that I resemble you."

"I would like to think that."

"How long will you stay?"

"Sunday night, I think. Perhaps Monday."

"Will it be a good season?"

"Quite good, I imagine."

Sian knew that Celia knew that she did not love her—had not loved her. But like everyone else, she did not know the reason. That was Sian's sin—not that she had not loved her daughter, but for not concealing it, and beyond that for allowing Celia to believe that the reason was Celia's ugly, twisted, deformed foot. Celia was permitted to believe that her mother's otherwise flawless existence could not accept such ugliness. But the truth of Sian's sin was that she could not love Celia because her daughter, by being, had taken away part of the love Colin and her father and her brothers had had only for Sian. Once she had been the center of their world, and at eighteen it had been bitter to have to pretend that she adored her baby. They had grown up together, she and Celia, but only Celia had come to maturity. Her twisted foot had conferred maturity. Then the war had started, and Celia had been banished to Donen Hall, alone among tutors and servants, by her mother. Because of the war Sian was able to pretend Celia didn't exist except on her birthday and at Christmas. Then Colin had been killed, and in a few months all the rest had died, and she had begun to drink until she was taken away to the sunny room in Switzerland.

Now she had to explain all this to Celia. She had to tell her why she had not loved her and she had to make sure her daughter knew she loved her now—whether the child wanted her to or not. She had to be forgiven by Celia, for something was singing inside her, saying that it was safe for her to love Celia now because all their men were dead and there was no one left who could love Celia more and love Celia's mother less.

In the train she had read over and over again her daughter's reply to her letter. At first she had thought it was meant for someone else and had been slipped by mistake into an envelope addressed to her. It made her cry tears of pity for Celia and tears for her sin. The letter proved how the years of loneliness had stunted and stifled her daughter, because after reading it a few times Sian realized that nothing in the letter had ever happened to Celia, and that no one in it had ever existed.

Dear Mother [the letter said] I will be happy to see you any time you can come. Maureen C. and Charley were due back to work on Saturday. They never came. They turned up on Sunday and collected six pounds from the Post Office and spent all of it on a pig and Maureen collected all her things. Then they went up to Miss Ennis' place, broke down the door and actually left with Kate Crosby's Wellingtons, which were new, and Kate's husband had gone bail for Charley the time before.

We now suspect that yarn about the baby dying was all a louse. Hugo woke early one morning and wrote all over the walls with Sally's lipstick and emptied her Floris into her boots, and yet he thinks he can come back here on another holiday. It is still raining and I am afraid we will lose a field

of hay and the raspberries are not too happy. Kati Taylor
goes to Cork to retire with her new Singer sewing machine.
I had a nice letter from Mr. Cudihy enclosing a nice cheque
for 54s, 2d for the repair fund.

Sian had never heard of a single one of these people. It
was the first letter she had ever received from her child; the
phrasing was vaguely foreign, and the places, people and
their behavior could not remotely have been a part of Celia's
experience.

We had such a thunder downpour on Friday. Nothing could
bear up. Maisie Carnaghi nearly got struck by lightning while
she was driving the car under the Iron Bridge, and had she
been a few minutes sooner she would have been killed. It's
a metal bridge and she had the window open. Bridey phoned
to say she would be back to Granny Norton on Saturday;
then the message came saying she would not be back at all,
and all the while she had been phoning for money. Emma
Cole is not well and Fanny has died and that Will Lear has
gone to London for a holiday with his son, while Ruby was
not even asked. Wendy Bennett dreamed the other night she
did not get to play Father Christmas and it depressed her,
but she doesn't know why. Shirley Parker does nothing but
wash blankets, according to the Citrons. Your daughter,
Celia

The letter was an autistic nightmare, and Sian began to
fear that there was a hereditary taint in the illness which
had driven her to a mental clinic. Celia imagined a life of
vital, rambunctious people because she had been left alone
in a soundless park. The letter made Sian deeply ashamed,
for it focused her guilt and the effect of her desertion. But in
a different way it made her feel stronger because it showed
her how far her selfishness had taken them. She must make it
all right. Celia had to forgive her, and when she was forgiven she would be free. Celia would be the compass by
which she would find her way out of the maze of the past.

"I wanted to talk to you about your letter, Celia," she
began.

"Yes, Mama?"

"I am not sure I understood it."

Celia dropped her eyes and her voice fell. "Did you like it? I hoped so much that you would enjoy it."

"I did enjoy it. It was lively and . . . and . . . but I didn't know a person you mentioned, and it all seemed rather . . . fantastic."

"It wasn't fantastic. I mean, I hadn't imagined it."

"Do you know all those people? Do you lead such a bustling, crowded life here?"

"No."

"Darling, I don't understand. You haven't made it up but you don't know those people?"

"I wanted the letter to be jolly. It was my first letter ever to you, and I wanted it to be gay and friendly and jolly."

Sian blinked. "You did?"

"But I didn't know how. I don't have much news. So I asked Mungo if I could borrow one of the letters she'd had from her mother in Ireland, and she let me copy it."

"Darling, who is Mungo?"

"My maid. Oh, Mother, what a silly, stupid thing to have done!" Celia looked ready to burst into tears. Sian gaped. Celia loved her! Celia loved her! How could she?

Sian groped blindly and tottered out of her chair. Celia stood up and her arms went tightly around her mother. Sian held her baby's dear head and kissed her again and again, wondering if she would ever understand the miracle which Celia had made for both of them.

C hapter 15

 On the same afternoon Francis floated around the West End on a shopping expedition. While admiring neckties in Jermyn Street he came upon a nameplate on a building, advertising the services of a genealogist. O. WORTLE LINK LINEAGE INVESTIGATED, HERALDRY SECURED AND PAINTED it read. Francis decided to pursue his researches without further delay. He climbed the dark stairs to the second floor, thinking eagerly of the day when he would confront Sian with the news that the laws of primogeniture had conferred on him a peerage.

A very short girl sitting on five telephone directories in a very small office asked Francis rudely in a bass voice what he wanted. He asked to see the genealogist.

"Mr. Link?" she boomed.

"What an appropriate name."

"How do you mean?"

"Well, he has to link names with other names in the past."

"Never thought of it that way."

"Is he in?"

"Mr. Link works in the country."

"How disappointing. Must everything be done by mail?"

"By what?"

"By post."

"Not if you'll take him to lunch. That's his test. If people are serious, they'll take him to lunch."

"I suppose I'd be happy to."

"Tomorrow?"

"Splendid."

Francis met Mr. Link in a restaurant called La Bourride in Gerrard Street, where the middle crust of tarts congregated on the street outside while the upper crust waited at the south end of Bond Street and in Burlington Gardens. Francis made his way through the throng with difficulty and entered the restaurant. When he asked for Mr. Link the headwaiter led him to a table for two where a tall, light-haired man in a country jacket was seated. He did not get up as he said, "Mr. Hillairet? Good afternoon." Francis shook his hand, noticing that an opened magnum of champagne stood in an ice bucket beside the table. Although Mr. Link did not offer to share the champagne, he did ask his host kindly if he would like anything. Francis asked for a bottle of Perrier water.

"I am so happy we could meet, Mr. Link," Francis said. "You don't look at all what I had pictured. I expected to find someone yellowed with scholarship."

"I work in the country. Windows open. Very busy, very expensive and very thirsty." Link smiled broadly for the briefest instant, then snapped the smile shut and packed it away for the duration of the lunch. He refilled his glass.

"It must be difficult work," Francis said.

"How may I help you?"

"I, uh, have, uh—"

"Mr. Hillairet, there is no reason to be timid about a natural urge. The past is a matter of pride in the best sense of the word, and I can assure you that having spent my life satisfying the perfectly understandable curiosity of people about their origins, I find no reason for any hesitation concerning it whatever."

"Thank you, Mr. Link."

"Not at all."

"You see, I have reasons to believe that my parents were either of the high peerage or were part of the Royal Family."

Mr. Link's eyebrows and forehead formed themselves into something resembling the lines of a very detailed road map. "Royalty?" he asked. "You don't mean British royalty?"

Francis swallowed and nodded.

"Hm." Mr. Link perked up immediately. It had been some time since he had encountered a nut like this, and the nuttier they were the more eager, and the more eager the more grateful, and the more grateful the more generous. "Of course, Charles II was an extremely lively breeder. What are your reasons for thinking this?"

"They are, I fear, far too complex to explain. But that sounds silly."

"It is silly. I must have the whole story if you want results."

"I will explain in a moment. You see, there are somewhat insufficient data to proceed on."

"Please allow me to judge that, Mr. Hillairet. What I need are names."

"I wanted to say first that it could be an exhausting and perhaps exasperating assignment."

"You will pay cash? When due?"

Francis nodded hastily. "In advance, if necessary."

"In advance, of course."

"Of course."

"You have sufficient cash?"

"Sufficient?"

"A good question, sir. I have three research assistants. From your name I suspect that one of them may have to work in France. What was your mother's name?"

"Uh, Vollmer."

"Then another will have to delve in Germany and Holland and perhaps parts of Scandinavia—as well as England, of course. It is expensive. Your grandparents' names may take us to America."

"Under no circumstances may this genealogy be traced to the United States."

"Why?"

"It is a condition of the retainer, that's all."

"Ah . . . Precisely . . . Nonetheless."

"For the other countries I shall have all the cash you will possibly need."

"Very good, sir. In that case I can assure you that exhaustion and exasperation mean nothing to me. If needs be, I will be able to trace you back to the Merovingian kings in the fifth century, and to unearth such a great shield of your family that it may hold as many as three hundred and sixty quarterings."

"Mr. Link! That is most awfully encouraging."

"If it comes to that, I am prepared to show that there is more of Charlemagne's blood in your veins than in those of the Royal Family. Naturally, I would offer all of this documented in several hundred pedigrees on hundreds of pages. But you can have no idea how expensive all this can be, Mr. Hillairet, and in the end I may produce you nothing higher than a baronetcy. This will then have to be fought through perhaps as many as three dozen sittings of the Committee of Privileges of the House of Lords—all of them jealous men, Mr. Hillairet—which could last dozens of years. And even when all the claims are at last presented to that body, the vote can still be returned that 'Francis Hillairet has not made out his claim to said barony,' and therefore I always recommend to my clients that we be overprepared. Do you see?"

"Oh, yes. But is there a chance?"

Mr. Link shrugged involuntarily. It was all the more eloquent because it was not an English gesture. "Always."

"Have men ever gone through all that, convinced of the rightness of their claim, and then, when refused recognition, felt morally bound to call themselves by the title in spite of the ruling?"

"Not in this country. No, sir. That is, such men have, but only in South America or Alaska, I have been informed."

"Will it be necessary for me to renounce American citizenship to accept the peerage?" Mr. Link had started to speak at the same instant, to say, "Of course, the salaries and expenses of research assistants are only a part of the costs. Why, in 1912—"

They both apologized to each other, then Mr. Link graciously answered Francis' question. "As far as Britain is concerned, if you are a peer you might be a creature from the ocean depths, but it would be yours by right of birth. However, you would be required to take an oath of loyalty to the Crown, and I shouldn't think that would go down at all well with your own people."

"As a gesture of good faith, I would renounce."

"Good faith indeed, sir. A bank check will suffice."

"Indeed, yes," Francis said reaching for his checkbook.

"Initially—repeat—initially, I should think one thousand pounds." Mr. Link's respiratory system was somewhat faulty; sinuses clattered wetly like loose steel rods in a fast-moving freight car.

Francis made out the check at once, tore it out and waved it to allow it to dry. "How long do you think the job will take, Mr. Link?" he asked.

Link did not answer until the check had dried and been handed to him. Instead, he blew his burly nose into a large handkerchief, which must have been made of strong canvas because the stream of langrel which had been stored behind his face hit the cloth so hard that his hand recoiled heavily. When he had recovered he accepted the check, barely glancing at it, and dropped it into the side pocket of his jacket.

"This is a rotten climate for sinusitis," Francis observed sympathetically.

"Do you really think so?" Link replied coldly. He took a small black book from his pocket. "I have your name and your mother's name. Now, if you please, her mother's name and your father's mother's name?"

"You see, I don't know."

"You don't know?" Link stared at him so severely that Francis almost panicked.

"It's a damnably complex story," he said hurriedly. "It may be quite impossible to go on with this at all."

Link pulled the tweedy flap of the jacket over his pocket and patted it. "I think you'd better tell me the story," he said.

Chapter 16

 James Maitland called Stacie the day after Francis had disappeared to try to get some explanation for the astonishing note of resignation he had just received, and also because he was worried that Francis might be even more ill than he had believed. When Stacie told him that Francis had left the house with two suitcases, Maitland asked if Francis had mentioned anything about the man he had assaulted. Stacie said Francis had told her that he had been a deranged ex-employee.

Maitland sighed, and there was a pause. "The man was a private detective whom Francis had hired."

"Why would Francis need a detective?"

"I wondered if you knew," Maitland replied and let it rest there.

After two days Stacie called Maitland, and because she sounded distraught he told her that no man who packs suitcases to go with him intends to kill himself, and that on the day before, Francis had been to the bank before it had opened. Stacie then said she had received a very strange letter from Francis which she simply could not bring herself to believe.

"We will have to pool information," Maitland told her. He asked her to dine with him, but she refused to leave the apartment because she wanted to be near the telephone in case Francis called.

After his talk with Stacie, Maitland ordered a spot audit. He dictated a short news item about Francis' resignation for reasons of health, expressed the bank's deep regret and dispatched it to the business-news editors. He telephoned the national private detective agency which the bank retained and set a meeting in his office at one o'clock. He called Tim Monahan, gave him the bare facts, said there was no suspicion of trouble and asked him to arrange for a concealed investigation by the Missing Persons Bureau. It was decided between them that Maitland would give all the facts to Captain Ketcham, head of the private detective agency, and that the police would pool their information with the captain. Lastly he telephoned Charles & Co. to order a pound of fresh caviar delivered with a chilled magnum of Moët et Chandon '00 to his office before 5:30 P.M., and then walked to Eberlin's in New Street for a pot of coffee and some quiet thinking about whether he should make a bid for one of Gilbert Stuart's portraits of George Washington which was about to be offered for sale.

At the one o'clock meeting Captain Ketcham said that he wanted to examine Francis' office files, and Maitland agreed. Ketcham also said he would like to talk to Mrs. Vollmer, and this was arranged by a phone call to Stacie.

It was all cut and dried. "Did Vollmer have any peculiarities?"

"None at all. A most normal fellow and I've known him for over twenty-five years. Then our doctor spotted this breakdown on its way, and Francis accepted sedation. It seemed to work. He refused to take a holiday. Then three days ago I was called to the Old Slip, where Francis was being held for every sort of a charge to do with assault. We decided to talk to the man he had assaulted, a private detective—"

"What name?"

"Let's see—I knew it, but I can't remember it. Call me before five. I'll have it then. He's resting and available at Bellevue."

"Bad shape?"

"Serious but not critical. He could talk and he did. He said that Francis had attacked him because he had been unable to gather any evidence proving that Francis' wife and I were having carnal relations."

"Uh—untrue?"

"Insane."

"Embezzlement?"

"No, Francis was a born banker. I think the best I ever knew, including Edward Hibbert. He couldn't possibly even have thought of it. But as a matter of routine I've asked for an audit.

"Did he have a mistress?"

"Impossible. He was too thrifty and wouldn't risk his rest."

"Hobbies?"

"No, for the same reasons."

Ketcham accepted coffee from Stacie. Over her shoulder he could see the Palisades out the window, but he preferred to look at her. She watched him intently, as if hoping he would have all the answers, even when it became apparent that he didn't even have all the questions. Captain Ketcham's appearance gave every cause for confidence; he had wavy white hair and a pugnacious pink face and looked like a customer's man in a big gambling house. His eyes were always bland.

Ketcham asked her if she knew why Francis had retained the private detective he had assaulted. She didn't know. He asked her why she thought her husband had disappeared.

"I don't know. I can't even think in words like disappear. He's been gone for two days."

Ketcham stood up abruptly. "I'm sorry," he said stiffly. "Thank you. If that's all you can tell me I'm wasting my time."

"But it was such a deeply personal thing!"

"You don't have to tell me about it, Mrs. Vollmer. I know of no charges against your husband. Mr. Maitland called me in because we are on retainer to the bank and because he wanted to help ease your mind."

Stacie couldn't hold back the tears, and though she did not sob she wept while she talked. "My husband was—is—a brilliant man. And a good man. You cannot begin to know—"

"It's a funny world, Mrs. Vollmer."

"He was an orphan. He was taken out of the orphanage when he was fourteen years old by Edward Hibbert and raised in that bank. This made it impossible for Francis to accept the fact that he was only an orphan among other orphans. Maybe it was because he was always so near but yet so far from all that wealth that he invented the idea that he might be the son of a king and a queen. It became very, very real to him. He still believed it the day before he left—and he was forty years old."

Stacie went on to tell Ketcham about how Francis had taught himself French and cooking, and how he had pretended the bank had given him the lessons.

"Who did teach him?"

"I don't know."

Then she showed him Francis' note to her, which had arrived in the afternoon mail. He read it slowly, memorizing it.

"How much was one half of the savings account, Mrs. Vollmer?"

"I don't know. The letter came an hour before you did. I haven't asked."

"Did he have a mistress, Mrs. Vollmer?"

"A what? A mistress?" The idea made Stacie smile slightly. "No."

"Hobbies?"

"Culture. What he called 'conversational culture.' Four nights a week for two years I drilled him from encyclopedias and public library books about all sorts of topics. He wanted to be knowledgeable about almost everything; he felt his parents would expect it of him when they finally met."

"I see."

"He wanted to be ready."

"I see."

"Then he began to have terrible headaches, and he couldn't sleep. We had several arguments because he said I didn't believe in him, or that his parents were high-born people. I wanted to try to help him find his parents. I didn't know it could turn out the way it did. I went to the orphanage and they let me copy the record. His mother had been a cashier in a lunch wagon. His father had been a dwarf, a circus clown. That's what drove Francis away from me. I drove him away."

"We'll find him, Mrs. Vollmer, and we'll bring him back."

"You'll never find Francis," Stacie said, pride mixed with her despair. "You may be the best detective there is, Captain Ketcham, but you're not as smart as Francis."

The investigation took five months to get nowhere. No passport had ever been issued to Francis Vollmer; yet the purser of the *Aquitania* remembered a passenger who had resembled his photograph. Ketcham's people interviewed the pursers of all transatlantic liners, as part of routine, but they didn't talk to chief stewards or cabin stewards or night chefs. No foreign language school in the city had ever registered a Francis Vollmer, nor had any individual French teacher in the Classified Telephone Directory, nor did any of them recognize his photograph. The story was the same with all cooking schools. But after three months Ketcham began to get the knack of thinking the way Francis thought. He went to the French Consulate, because if Francis thought of himself as a royal he would go to the available top, to the representative of the foreign government whose language had captured his interest. Ketcham asked the Consulate for a list of recommended French teachers, and interviewed all those who were not listed in the Classified Directory. He knew he had to be right, but he drew a blank. He went back to the Consulate with Francis' photograph to ask if such a man had ever inquired about a cooking school. The senior clerk remembered that the man in the photograph had asked how he could expand his knowledge of French food and

wines, and that he had recommended M. Grondet to the
gentleman.

The fulfilling smell of a sauce Aioli greeted Captain
Ketcham as he rang the Grondet doorbell. He found the
maître in his rocking chair eating a Cavaillon melon. When
Ketcham introduced himself as an estate lawyer, M. Grondet's eyes widened with pleasure and his eyebrows rose. "An
intrigue?"

"Yes."

"Who?"

"Francis Vollmer."

"Francis Vollmer? An intrigue? Impossible."

"Why?"

"He is too good a cook to take chances."

"He has disappeared."

"I know. I had a letter." Grondet shook his head sadly.
"He was a great man."

"Your pupil?"

"My best pupil. I will not ask if he is in trouble because I
know he could not be in trouble."

"No trouble. There are people who cared about him, and
they want to know where he went."

"I care about him. But if he had to go"—M. Grondet
shrugged—"then I must respect his wishes. Which is how
much I care about him."

"Did you teach him to speak French?"

"Yes. Mostly. My niece helped."

"You taught him French and how to cook?"

"I have a method."

"Could I learn how to cook?"

"How well depends on you. To learn cooking and French
at the same time is pleasurable."

"What do you charge?"

"I now charge six dollars an hour."

"Do you, uh, have any open time? I'm a bachelor, and—"

"Never married?"

"Widower."

"Then you must be tired of restaurants. In that case I will

only charge you five dollars an hour, but you must provide the supplies. Individual instruction. Do you have a mistress?"

"Do you supply them too?"

"I did once. Only once."

"Francis."

Grondet nodded. Denise was very lonely these days. Perhaps she should meet this man; what happened after that was up to her. His clothes were good, his speech was refined, his eyes were clear and he looked substantial.

"I would very much like to talk to the lady."

"She speaks only French." Grondet let that sink in. "Begin your lessons. After a while she will stop in and you will meet her; it will be more natural that way. When we all talk about Francis, I will translate, and perhaps she will remember things that I've forgotten."

"When do we start?"

M. Grondet thought about that. "We will start now. You will learn to make potage paysanne, and we will think about teaching you *le français plus tard*," he said, already beginning to mix English and French and to change Captain Ketcham's life.

While Ketcham doggedly snuffed at Francis' trail, James Maitland reported his progress to Stacie. When she realized at last that Francis was not going to telephone she did agree, one time, to spend a day on his yacht in the Hudson River. He had invited her favorite musical people and she went through the motions of having a wonderful day. But she preferred to remain closed in the apartment, unable to think of anything but the terrible thing she had done to Francis and how she had lost him forever whether he was located or not. It was a wonderful thing, when a man loved you, to think he was the only man in the world for you, but it was a bleak, empty existence when he had gone and you knew that there could never be another man but him.

It was a long, wearing-down process by Maitland to persuade her to have an occasional lunch with him, and impossible to persuade her to dine. She dropped out of all

music committees. She told him she'd rather not go downtown. She hated to have to drag herself together to the point
of making the effort to have her hair dressed for the few
times she did, finally, agree to lunch with him. Because of
what she had done to Francis she didn't want anyone to look
at her.

In the fourth month following the Grondet break, an
operative of the Ketcham agency, who had been sifting
through Francis' personal correspondence which was on file
at the bank, came upon a letter to C. N. Carr that had been
signed by James Maitland. Since in all of Francis' files there
was no other letter signed by anyone but Francis, and since
Carr did business in Canada, the letter was passed along to
Ketcham for examination.

Maitland told Ketcham he had never written to Carr,
could not imagine why Francis had done so, if he had.
Ketcham telephoned Mr. Carr in Montreal and took the
afternoon train to Canada.

Mr. Carr recalled the suitcase filled with money, exactly
$450,000 worth, and explained how it had been transferred
to a number account in the Bank Graubunden-Zug of Zurich.
He revealed further that all correspondence between the
Swiss bank and Francis was to have been through Box 318 in
the Wall Street Post Office branch.

Ketcham asked Carr if he would cable the Swiss bank,
saying that he wished to locate his client Francis Vollmer,
and would they forward his address?

"It's a very long chance," Carr said. "They'll probably
refuse."

"Stay strictly within the rules, of course. Tell them that if
it is a matter of a number account, you quite understand and
withdraw your inquiry, but if the client also maintains a
petty-cash account, you would be most grateful to have his
address immediately because it is not a matter that could be
forwarded on to him by them but an urgent financial matter
which requires his instant attention."

"You think Vollmer is an embezzler?"

"I know it."

"The Swiss law states that the bank must divulge the

client's whereabouts and holdings if the funds have been criminally obtained."

"That takes a trial or an indictment. Out in public where it can't do any banking any good. Will you send the cable for the sake of $450,000 worth of good will with the Hibbert First National Bank?"

"I detest embezzlers, sir. That is why I will send the cable."

"Thank you, Mr. Carr. I will wait at the Mont Royal hotel until you get an answer."

Zurich telephoned the following morning, and Mr. Carr asked to have the overseas operator hold the call for one hour, then called Ketcham. When the second call came through, after the amenities, Mr. Carr said he would pass the phone to Mr. Vollmer's North American representative. The Swiss official asked blandly if there was any trouble. Ketcham did not mind lying in the least.

"No trouble whatsoever," he said cheerily. "Quite the contrary. We believe we've hit an oil field—not a well, a field—in western Canada—on Vollmer land—and I must reach him to get his permission to rush quite a large number of rented rigs and men into the area. It involves a considerable sum and, in the meantime, the costs are piling up and we have no idea where we can find Mr. Vollmer."

"I see," the voice in Zurich said. "Mr. Vollmer does carry an expense account with us but he has changed the name of the account to François Hillairet . . ."

"Oh, yes," Ketcham lied smoothly, but feeling the jolt as he made the missing connection, "Mr. Vollmer frequently used the Hillairet name . . ."

". . . we received certified copies of the court order signed by Judge George Ornstein of the General Sessions Court of the State of New York which authorized the name change from Vollmer to Hillairet."

"As I said, we know all about that, sir. But where may I reach him? Quite considerable amounts of money are involved here."

"Our Geneva manager put Mr. Vollmer-Hillairet into a

mental clinic in the Geneva Canton the day he arrived. He was quite ill."

"Which clinic?"

"The Boscawen Clinic in Anieres."

"Will you spell the name of the clinic and the name of the town, please?" The voice in Zurich spelled both names patiently. "Is he there now?" Ketcham asked urgently.

"No. He left five weeks ago. We have no forwarding address but I can have my Geneva manager make further inquiries if you wish."

"Thank you, sir. We wouldn't think of troubling you further. We'll get in touch with the Boscawen Clinic directly. And here is Mr. Carr." Ketcham passed the telephone to Mr. Carr, who concluded the amenities.

Before Ketcham returned to New York he wired ahead to ask Denise Hillairet to meet him at Grondet's. He went to the Frenchman's directly from the station. On being questioned, Denise said Francis had shown much interest in her late husband's family Bible. She was happy to co-operate because Grondet had already assured her that Francis was not only not in trouble but that the information could mean a great deal to him, and Ketcham now glibly reassured her it was a matter of a legacy.

The investigation was almost over. The next morning Ketcham went to the Bureau of Records, then to the Customs House; in each case he found what he needed. On returning to his office, he telephoned the clinic in Switzerland. But Dr. Boscawen would not give him any information about Francis despite the mention of Canadian oil fields, the co-operation of the bank and some frantic pressure involving splendid acting. Dr. Boscawen would not even admit that Francis had ever been a patient.

Next Ketcham called Geneva and spoke to M. Crouch, who had been informed of developments by the Zurich office. Crouch acknowledged that he had dined with M. Hillairet the night before his departure. It was his understanding that M. Hillairet had been going to visit Paris, that he was traveling with his charming co-patient, the Marchioness of Shattock, and that they planned to go on to London.

Ketcham thanked him warmly and hung up the telephone. His contract with the Hibbert Bank was due to expire in four months and he would ask for a substantial raise. He had got his man.

Maitland turned green. "The little son-of-a-bitch pinned it on Ed Hibbert," he said, then clamped his mouth shut. His eyes rolled in his head as though the whole building were afloat and he was a very bad sailor. He breathed shallowly, then stood up unsteadily and went to the double sofa which ran along the west wall of the room and stretched himself out on it.

Ketcham was confused. He had cracked the case but apparently he had brought bad news, and he hated to bring bad news. "Is anything wrong, Mr. Maitland?"

"Oh, Jesus!"

"But—"

"We took that little son-of-a-bitch out of an orphanage. He'd be a delivery boy today if it weren't for this bank. My God—a great cook yet! And a French mistress! Is she good-looking?"

Ketcham gulped. "I think she's beautiful," he said.

"The little son-of-a-bitch! François Hillairet, a number account in a Swiss bank, and travels with a marchioness. Is *she* good-looking?"

"I looked at her picture this afternoon. She is beautiful, indeed."

"The little son-of-a-bitch—$450,000! Not the bank's. Oh, no. The bank's insured against those things." He tapped his chest feebly. "I, personally, and the late Mrs. Edward Hibbert have been robbed of $450,000 by a genius. Ed was right. Francis is a genius. And I'll never tell anyone how he did it. Never, never. I paid. If anyone wants to know how he did it, it will cost them $450,000 to find out."

"Well, right now it isn't pertinent how he did it. He did it and we have him cold. He'll be arrested in London today and extradited, tried and convicted. The $450,000 plus whatever interest has accrued to it will be returned to you and to the Hibbert estate."

"No, he won't be arrested."

"Excuse me, Mr. Maitland?"

"He'd have to be convicted and sentenced in order to establish criminal behavior to the satisfaction of a Swiss bank, and if you think I'm going to get on that stand to convict him as long as it involves either Francis or me telling what we know about what happened here the night Ed Hibbert died, then, Mr. Ketcham, you are wrong."

Maitland propped himself up into a sitting position, but though his movements were weak his face was strong and hard. "You have a big business as detective agencies go, Ketcham," he said, "and you want to keep it that way. I'd like to make it a bigger business. I'd like to start by renegotiating your contract with the bank, because you did a great job on this case just as you always do. But the case is now closed, and I want every single piece of paper on it that's in your office or your London office or anywhere else. Do you hear me clear?"

"Bright and clear, Mr. Maitland."

Maitland held out his hand, and the two men sealed the bargain. A few minutes later Captain Ketcham left the bank and headed uptown for a lesson at M. Grondet's.

Maitland told the story slowly and carefully to Stacie as they dined at the Central Park Casino. He began by saying it was not a story which he could tell delicately because there was no way of cushioning the facts, but that he would do anything rather than hurt her. She did not have to hear the details of the story unless she wanted to, he said; but he knew where Francis was and he knew that he didn't intend to come back. But he realized that no one could be expected to let years of marriage end with that brief an explanation, and he supposed she would want to know everything he knew. Stacie did want to know, and after she had been told she got ill at the table and remained in the ladies' room for nearly an hour. When she returned she was very pale, and without exchanging a word they left in Maitland's car.

"Don't take me home, Jim. I don't know if I can ever enter that apartment again. Anyway, I need some air."

They drove to Riverdale, and at the Arrowhead Inn, sat silently outdoors with a bottle of real French champagne. After some time Stacie asked, "Why did Francis beat up that man?"

Maitland coughed. "Well, uh, the man was a private detective. Although it doesn't relate to the other facts of the case," he said with glum uneasiness, "Francis was angry with the man for not finding any evidence that you and I were sleeping together."

"Jim!"

Maitland shrugged. "Francis has never been as sane as he looks."

"But how could that have been a part of his plan?"

"Ketcham's theory is that he felt the time had come for him to leave, but that he had to have a reason. If he thought he could blame us . . ."

"I think that is the worst of all he did," Stacie said with a catch in her voice. "Plotting for all those years to steal that money and then run away with it safely while he lived with me and pretended to love me was so bad that when you told it all to me, I didn't think I could go on any more. But plotting in cold blood to leave the guilt for all he did, the guilt for the rest of our lives for all he did, is so cruel and terrible that now I want to go on so that some day, somewhere, I will be given the chance to repay him."

"If you say the word we'll get on a ship tomorrow and find him and make him face us—"

"Face a ghost named François Hillairet. Thank you, Jim. No. Now it is my turn to plot. I must have a plan, then we must go out and find him. Can you prove he stole that money?"

"Not any more."

Stacie covered Maitland's hand with hers. "Francis is dead, and I'm dead, too." Maitland made a startled movement of remonstrance.

"Not the way it sounds," Stacie said. "But whoever I was when I was Francis' wife is dead; what sits here is, in a way, his widow. I could have spent the rest of my life shambling about and brooding in that barn of an apartment, but you saved me. If he and I were not both dead I could weep bitterly, because what he did had nothing at all to do with me. Francis Vollmer is dead. Long live François Hillairet so that there will be time for me to get even with him."

Chapter 17

 Carnal thoughts disturbed sleep, but she could not banish them. Deep breathing in bed did not work and it was too cold to get up. She lay in darkness and slowly recited, fifty times, her father's phrase, "Conservatism is the nature of maturity; maturity is the synonym for good sense." It did drive away the carnal thoughts, but then she would be betrayed when she fell asleep and the thoughts would return as writhing actions. Sometimes she was in Colin's arms, but more and more frequently since she had been forgiven by Celia she found herself in the embrace of Francis Hillairet, a man who behaved with less warmth to her than any of her servants. Perhaps some day she would have to face the fact that he could feel nothing except deep emotion for Reblochon cheese—she giggled in the darkness—but what mattered most was that it was clear that she was alarmingly capable of feeling all too keenly. She thought with her body now. She buzzed with petty thoughts which flew annoyingly all around the center of her terror. What would she do if he did not want her? He had accepted four sluts—my God, five sluts—in Paris with the blandness of a pawnbroker, but he could wriggle away from her because he needed her only as his foreign minister to treat with the foggy, alien world of British peers. But he was a man; managed properly, it wasn't possible that he could refuse her. "Conservatism is the nature of maturity; maturity is the synonym for good sense." Over and over she said it, giving each recitation a number.

She sped back from Donen Hall on Sunday night and rushed to Brown's to find Francis. "I have missed you terribly," he said with the slightest edge of irritation as she settled herself in his sitting room.

"I needed to go to Devon on a family matter," she answered, amazed that she was offering any explanation at all.

"But I would have adored to have seen the famous English countryside."

"With the season starting, you won't be seeing much else, my dear. I hope you can shoot."

"No."

"Then we must put your hand in a sling until December. What would you do if you had a child with a clubfoot?"

"Friend of yours?"

"Indeed, yes."

"Peerage?"

"Oh, yes." She leaned forward, confident that somewhere among his masses of arcane lore there would lie the perfect solution.

Francis did not hesitate; it was not, after all, his foot. "There is only one thing to do," he pontificated. "Plunge into the study of such deformation. Hire a special doctor to investigate and pass on to you all of the latest information concerning their cure—translated into layman's language. Enroll as a lay helper at an orthopedic hospital to spend time with children who are so deformed. Listen to what professionals say about this surgeon and that one, until you are as sure as you can possibly be about which is the right man to do the job. Then pay him handsomely to think of little else while he decides if the particular foot can be helped. That's what I would do."

She found herself looking at him with awe. Awe mixed with lust but awe nonetheless. He was right. She could give Celia this great gift which should have been hers when she was a baby. She could prove to Celia how much she loved her by helping her to walk, to dance, to move with grace.

She stared up at Francis but could not speak. She rose and put her arms around his neck and stared into his yellow eyes. He would save Celia, but he had already saved her because at last she had learned the power of self-delusion from him. She knew that she must have mastered the art because she heard herself say, "I have fallen hopelessly in love with you, Francis."

"My dearest," Francis answered with a nice regard for her arms, her words and her lips. As he kissed her the feeling of terror left. Now she was truly a body. It must be the order of first things first, she thought as she kissed him again and again and felt him beginning to undress her.

Chapter 18

 By 1921 the Army
and Navy had almost
vanished, so there were
few places for the sons of the ruling class there. Some of
them were still in Parliament—those who had survived the
war—but as they conducted their political campaigns anew,
they were beginning to see that there would have to be
changes. Careers would have to combine politics and business; the political power of their class was casting a thinner
and thinner shadow, and could be influential only insofar
as it was influential in trade. Heavy taxation had begun, and
the cost of living grew like a vine reaching for the sky. The
first of the big town houses was converted into flats; un-
married daughters opened dress shops in Bond Street. The
social mix changed, though its ferment didn't cease. Restaurant life began expansively in '21, when the restrictions
in the Defense of the Realm Act were removed. Night clubs
arrived with a strident scream, and on their heels came the
gossip columnists.

Using the fulcrum of her position and the lever of her

wealth, the Dowager Marchioness of Shattock lifted and
flung the person of Mr. Francis Hillairet into the social
season of the autumn of '22. He had yearned, and so he
learned: footmen wore knee breeches if there were fourteen
or more for dinner; country houses existed, out-of-season, to
provide hothouse flowers for town houses; Cassano's orches-
tra was the most reliable for parties at home; people now
looked for cocktails before any gathering, but it was best to
serve them in a room off the hall where the guests could
drink before coming upstairs to the drawing room. Lady
Sian had her cocktails catered by Buck's: barmen in white
coats with frosted silver cocktail shakers.

Francis was with Sian one late afternoon when she had
ordered the blue service for eighteen people laid out: the
linen, candles, plates, crystal, enameled silver, flowers, chairs
all Delft blue. But when she saw Francis to the door an hour
before dinner, she had glanced into the dining room and had
ordered it all changed to an identical yellow service. When
Francis had returned for dinner the table had been reset for
the third time to the rose service, and the delphiniums
which had become chrysanthemums had been changed to
pink roses.

That night he had listened with awe and wonderment
while a peer told of a dinner four nights before which the
Prince of Wales had attended without wearing his Garter
decoration. The host, who had worn his, had written to the
Prince immediately afterward to point out that he thought
this somewhat discourteous, and had received a charming
apology in reply.

At weekends, and in the rare intervals between parties,
Sian entertained at Shattock, or they were guests at such
great houses as Hatfield and Knole. Sian had one large and
one small country house because she would not disturb
Celia by using Donen Hall. The cottage at Gornall could not
put up more than twenty-six guests and their servants, but at
Shattock, a new Palladian remodeling of a late sixteenth-
century structure with cosmetic effects applied by Wyatt in
1801, one hundred and twelve guests and servants could be
maintained in pleasant comfort.

In London they would begin the evening with cocktails,

move on to a dinner party and then end at a night club. Or they might have dinner at a place such as the Embassy which was part restaurant and part night club, where the "new" men could be demeaned and humiliated—and therefore made extremely important—by the headwaiter, Luigi. Night after night people fought each other for the last remaining tables, and the bandleader, Roland, leaned inertly against the piano, the utter weariness in his face giving way, as the hours passed, to even greater boredom and contempt. Except for when he was alone with Sian, Francis protected himself from the peers and press lords by copying the bandleader's expressions. He admired the headwaiter, of course—who didn't?—but he couldn't summon the courage to imitate him even though he was the most socially prominent man in London.

Throughout the season Francis remained mostly silent; he could not quite believe where he was or that those people were actually accepting him as an equal. The silences made him more interesting, and her friends were happy that Sian was so happy—almost as happy as she had been eight years before.

However, no matter how high Sian propelled Francis, no emissary came forward from his parents. He became more and more anxious and tense.

"I'm surprised at you, Francis," Sian said. "I should think you would understand that they might want to watch you closely throughout one whole season."

"But They've seen me comport myself socially in New York."

"New York is not London, as I should have thought you would be the first to realize." She watched him transmute her reassurance into a nourishing substance through the alchemy of self-delusion. Within a few minutes he seemed to be completely at ease again.

The Russian Ballet opened on November 2nd, and Sian arranged for Francis to invite the entire company and ninety-seven others to a delightful "typically Russian" caviar supper at the Savoy. The party cost Francis thirty-two hundred pounds, but it made him one of the hosts of the week at the top of the season. They attended the theater doggedly, and

Sian proved to him beyond question that Shaw's "parochial tragedy," *Heartbreak House,* was a hopeless failure. "Its people have brains but no souls," she added, "and their brains are the brains of Bernard Shaw. You know they cannot feel." Then, as Francis seemed to respond with interest (he was memorizing what she said for use at dinner parties), she continued, "It is, after all, a fantasy in the Russian manner, but because Shaw applied it to English themes it is ugly and commonplace."

She took him to the Rolls-Royce Company, and dealing with her favorite, Mr. Allen, had Francis order a Silver Ghost chassis for one thousand eight hundred and fifty pounds, with a seven-passenger limousine body for another eight hundred and seventy pounds. Then, since she thought he should have a small car as well, she had him buy another chassis for the same price and a sports-car, two-passenger body for six hundred and ninety-six pounds. In twenty minutes Francis jubilantly spent five thousand two hundred and sixty-six pounds at a time when the pound was selling for $3.94, though neither car could be delivered for five months.

She explained Maeterlinck's *The Betrothal* to Francis until four o'clock one morning, sitting, nicely nude in his bed, in his flat in Farm Street. She had found the flat, then had called the most brilliant and expensive decorator of the moment to see that it was decorated with flair. The flat now had an eighteenth-century Irish brocatelle and white marble chimney piece, sideboard cabinets of harewood with carved acanthus feet and panels inlaid with swags. There were eighteenth-century French *torchères* with gilt enrichments of lions' masks, and Chippendale looking glasses of rococo design. There were open Regency calamander bookcases, wall decorations by Paul Sandby and watercolors by de Wint and Gill. As a house present for his first residence in England, Sian gave him a silver tea equipage by Philip Rollos, and because he had become so excited by her description of her father's bed, she had ordered it sent from Donen Hall. The bed's overmantel stood like the great tent of a Saracen leader, fourteen feet high from floor to ceiling; its canopy had required three hundred and thirty-six yards of heavy velvet, which was embroidered in eleven colors and which enclosed the bed on all sides. Actually, as she stated at once to silence Francis' insincere protests, it was a gift for both of them.

The redecoration was a triumph of taste and financial extravagance; it cost Francis only eight thousand seven hundred and ninety pounds, or the equivalent of seven and three quarter years' salary at the Hibbert bank, but it was cozy and it placed him closer to the very center of his dream.

As Sian was first to say, it *was* a large flat for one man, but it was too wonderfully close to Queen Street and was so extremely comfortable. It was not so large as to be unwieldy; a cook, a scullion, a butler, a housemaid and a valet were all that were needed, and of course when he did entertain, extra servants could always be hired.

Sian introduced Francis to Steve Donoghue on the night he won the Derby for the third time, and she persuaded the nation's leading bookmaker, Mr. Spats O'Toole, to teach Francis the basic rules of betting and handicapping. In the learning he lost forty-six hundred pounds in four days. Sian won eighteen hundred. Gambling was one of the important things which he must learn to do well, Sian explained. Winning or losing didn't matter at all, but he must know how to do it with flair.

Through Mr. O'Toole and certain close friends of Sian's in Ireland, she was able to help Francis buy a modest racing stable of four horses for a gross amount of only twenty-three thousand pounds. Everyone concerned was determined to work like a Trojan to get the horses in shape for the spring meetings in Paris.

Sian helped Francis every day and made desperate love to him almost every night, but she managed to spend each weekend or two days in midweek at Donen Hall with Celia, and she devoted three mornings each week to working as a lay helper at the Royal Orthopaedic Hospital in Great Portland Street.

The weeks fled, taking with them approximately forty-three thousand pounds of Francis' fortune. Everything stimulated them. One morning Lord Gant invited them to help him make out hundreds of spurious bank checks, which they all threw into the wind from building tops and from automobiles all over the city just to bring sunshine into a few hundred lives. They attended every imaginable sort of fancy-dress ball, and were among the leaders of the boom for auction bridge. It certainly was a fair semblance of a season, because everything was done with all "the really right sort of people," as Francis was quick to point out, though what with the English drought, the Russian famine, the rising prices and growing unemployment, the really best people agreed that it was imperative to keep their frivolity out of print.

Sian was drunk with love and militantly unaware of anything but Francis and Celia, Celia and Francis. Francis adored Sian in his fashion, but he was also keen on being invited to join one or two clubs. Sian tried to explain that it was rather a complicated business, because the United Service was for soldiers, Boodle's was mostly Shropshire men, while Arthur's members were mostly all from Wiltshire. Francis wasn't exactly a Tory patrician either—except in spirit, she added loyally—so that took care of White's. Whig politicians of old families belonged to Brooks' and lawyers and divines went to the Athenaeum. The Turf and the Travellers' weren't all that easy to get in, and the waiting period for election to any of them was presently just over three years. Nevertheless, after reflection, Francis chose White's and Brooks' and Sian had him put up at each of them. Now they would have to wait, she said, smiling cheerfully, and worry about blackballs.

"Do they still blackball?"

"That's all they do in mens' clubs."

"But what will happen if I am blackballed?" Francis said in anguish. "It would shock my parents. How could I face our friends?"

"You would have me, darling, and I would sing, 'Now Tom would be a clubman and Maria go to sea/ And my papa's a banker and as rich as he can be/ But I, when I am stronger and can choose what I'm to do/ Oh, dearie, I'll go round at night and light the lamps with you.'"

"It's no laughing matter. What would *you* do if *you* were blackballed?"

"I'd do what the duelist Fitzgerald did when he was proposed for Brooks' by Admiral Stewart. He went to the club on election day and waited downstairs while they voted. There wasn't a single white ball, but they were afraid to tell him, so they sent a waiter to say that there had been just one blackball and that his name could be put up again if he wished."

"Could my name be put up again?"

"Oh, yes. Three or four years' wait, but you can always try again. Well! Fitzgerald flew upstairs—a flagrant breach of rules—and scattered the members like pigeons, demanding to know who had blackballed him. No one would answer, so he made the rounds of every man in the room and put the same question to each of them. 'Did you blackball me, sir?' he asked. Everyone denied it. When he had finished he addressed them all genially and said, 'You see, gentlemen, that as none of you have blackballed me, I must be elected.' He called for champagne and made them toast his election before he would leave. He never returned there again. If you are blackballed, that is exactly what you are going to do."

"If I did I'd be a social outcast!"

"But I would be with you. Wherever you went. And if you lost your fortune I would earn another for you somehow so that you might return to your high estates." She burst into song again, this time in a high, cracked voice and a fruity Cockney accent: "Underneath the gaslight's glitter/ Stands a fragile little girl/ Heedless of the night winds bitter/ As they round about her whirl/ While hundreds pass unheeding/ In the evening's waning hours/ I'll still cry with tearful pleading/ 'Won't you buy my pretty flowers?' " She laughed liltingly in delight but she stopped when she saw the morose expression on Francis' face. "You're not being yourself, Francis," she said sharply. "Stop brooding about being blackballed four years from now. Be yourself. Quick! Out with a fact! Who designed those marvelous art nouveau entrances to the Paris Métro?"

"Hector Guinaid," he said glumly.

Chapter 19

 The Dowager Marchioness of Shattock now understood with all her being why one princess, one countess, two baronesses and a hotel manager's wife had scrambled for the rooftops to announce that they had bagged Francis as a lover. At forty, she thought of herself as worldly and certainly as sexually sophisticated, but now she felt like the village milkmaid enjoying the custom of *droit de seigneur* under a liege lord who had perfected his sexual expertise at the Versailles court. Even Francis' benumbing snobbism was exciting because it chained him to her. He had transformed her into a wanton, and she greatly appreciated that. After years of abstinence she was now a haggard sex addict, and she giggled as she imagined a long queue of sex fiends outside Francis' flat in Farm Street, extending around the corner into Hays Mews and Charles Street, waiting desperately for their ration of Francis.

Once, while she lay naked as sand, after Francis had

disappeared for a business appointment with a Mr. Link in Gerrard Street, she explained their relationship to a patch of muddy ground in northern France.

"All quite different, darling. What we had was love, and with Francis I know love doesn't come into it. For me it is a bone-building, cheek-pinking lust, though not less habit-forming than love, for all that. If I lost him, as I lost you, I don't think I'd ever have another man. You were my Love; Francis is my Experience. If I lost him I suppose I would live on as flowers would survive for a short time if one took the bees and the wind away. He makes me understand why women walk the streets in sleet and go to bed with scab-scaled strangers for ten bob and accept, with all the honking joy of a seal being rewarded with a fish, their Experience on a blanket thrown over stones. I understand perversions, lying, masochism, black eyes—oh, all the seamy things women have done to hold the favor of their Experience. There is little edifying here. He is still the bore of bores and the snob of snobs, and he has as much emotion as a tenpenny nail, but I would have this cold, unfeeling clot made a duke if I could, because that is what he wants with the same power that I want him. Any title, even Esquire, if it could be secured by letters-patent, would be acceptable in settlement, and he shall have it if I must bribe the whole of the House of Lords with my body, my fortune and my honor. Please don't think me neurotic, darling, when I say that I am *happy* that he is a cold, selfish, monomaniacal clot; he never looks at other women and he never will as long as I help him pursue his delusion that waiting out there in the mist are his parents, Queen Mary and Kaiser Wilhelm. We share his preposterous dream and he believes that I have the power to lead him to their blessing, which will be followed immediately by his investiture as a Prince of the Blood Royal at Buckingham Palace—all of it to be reported by *The Times, Le Monde* and *Vanity Fair*. For this he feeds me ecstasy and strengthens my resolve."

"Francis, darling?"
"Yes?"

"Are you happy?"

"Very."

"Do you love me?"

"Very much."

"Did you enjoy playing with my mother's jewels?"

"They were very interesting. I learned a great deal. First, I bought this excellent little book about jewels, and as I examined your mother's I matched them with the illustrations and—"

"Mother's were better, I hope?"

"—I learned that—"

"They were not sent to you so that you might learn something. I sent them in order to help you feel things. Two senses should have been working for you—sight and touch. And you should have felt greedy and covetous. Who cares what they are called and how they were cut?"

"If we are going to chat, shouldn't we put the lights on?"

"No. Lights are for sex. Dark is for talk. The civilized way."

"Why is that?"

"Seeing someone's reactions while one talks increases inhibitions. Seeing someone's reactions during sex releases inhibition."

"Not for everyone."

"I have no inhibition. Touch me—here."

"Where?"

"Give me your hand." She sighed. "There."

"How lovely you are."

"Are you married, Francis?"

"No."

"Never?"

"No."

"Why?"

"I wasn't sure how my parents would receive a wife when they sent for me."

"Of course. How stupid of me."

"I would like to go to Monte Carlo sometime."

"Yes. It's time you learned casino gambling. Francis?"

"Yes?"

"Tumble me through time again, please, like a fantailed pigeon?"

Early in the morning they grew hungry. After they ordered food, Sian began to plan their trip to Monte Carlo. "It will be our last chance for some time. Of course, Monte isn't what it used to be; we may be the only people in the hotel. But Celia will be going into the hospital for that delicate operation in two weeks and I'll want to take her back to the country for Christmas. That gives us just one week—two days of travel and five days of play. Then I'll have a week with Celia to get ready."

"Is Lady Celia like you?"

"In what way?"

"Does she look like you?"

"No. She's tiny and blond and pink and white. And her mind isn't cluttered like mine. She's entirely sane. I suspect you won't understand her, but when you do meet her, talk about dancing and Degas and botany."

"Is she pretty?"

"She is beautiful."

"Then you are alike."

Sian exploded her smile. "How sweet your compliments are. They are so rare, and because they are rare I know they must be genuine."

"If that was a compliment, it was genuine."

"Do you have many facts at your fingertips about Monte Carlo, Francis?"

"Well, yes. Mata Hari was actually unmasked there. It has a room with a ceiling covered with nude women smoking cigars."

"Everyone knows that about Mata Hari, darling. Now listen to me carefully. We must invent a system for winning at roulette."

"I thought you said it didn't matter whether one lost or won."

"At horse betting, you idiot! At roulette it is compulsory that you win, because then the others envy you so and believe you have luck and they do not."

They took the two o'clock plane of the Handley air mail service to Paris. From Croydon to Le Bourget it was only two and a half hours and they were in good time to catch the Blue Train to Monte Carlo. Aboard the train they worked out the roulette system, examining it from every aspect and resolving not to deviate from it for their full five nights of play.

Sian had been born on the sixteenth, Francis had been born on the eighteenth. She remembered that they had met on the fifteenth and had gone to bed together for the first time on the fourteenth. Everyone said thirteen was unlucky, so it must be lucky for them. She had been married when she was seventeen. On entry into the casino she would sit at the high-stakes table at the left; he would sit, with his back to her if possible, at the high-stakes table at the right. They would each place ten pounds on every turn of the wheel, on the line between the street of 13, 14 and 15 and the street of 16, 17 and 18. This was a sound six-number bet, Sian felt. At each turn of the wheel they would also place a ten-pound bet on each successive number of the six-number series; considering the significance of the numbers, how could they miss? They would also place ten pounds on either red or black, depending on the color of their individual birthday number. Sian began to estimate their winnings in a small notebook. The line bet would pay odds of five to one, or fifty pounds. The individual number bet paid thirty-five to one or three hundred and fifty pounds, and the color bet would pay ten pounds at even odds. Each time they hit all three, she squealed, they would earn four hundred and ten pounds and be the envy of everyone in the casino.

"But isn't this a rather haphazard system?"

"That's its strength! Anyone can lose with the D'Alembert System or the Cancellation System—they're calculated mathematically to an extremely fine point. Millions have been lost with both of them. The advantage of our system is that it's *ours*, don't you see? Our natural good luck takes the place of all those dreary mathematics."

As Sian and Francis were being driven up the hill to the

Hotel de Paris the next morning, the detective, the engineer, the cleaner and the supervisor lifted the first roulette wheel off its pivot for its daily inspection. The bedding was examined and a few drops of oil added. The spirit level was applied to the wheel balance; since it was off by two tenths of a millimeter, it was replaced and taken to the workshop in the basement. The ivory balls were weighed upon a gold chemist's balance and measured with calipers. The croupier's rakes were hefted, scrutinized and tapped for hollowness. A thin piece of paper had been inserted into the lock of every box the night before; if the paper was torn as the box was about to be unlocked at commencement of play, an investigation would be held immediately. The connection of the cash box to its pneumatic tube was checked by both detective and engineer. At the slightest sign of trouble the croupier would press a button and the contents of the box would be whisked into the basement.

The croupiers arrived at the casino shortly before ten o'clock in the morning at the moment when Sian and Francis were making love on a beautiful rectangular bed splashed with sunlight in their terraced apartment overlooking the harbor. Each croupier spoke French and one other language. All were Monégasques and their lives and characters had been under the scrutiny of the Sûreté Publique and the Casino's Service de l'Interieur since birth. Their professional schooling had taken eight months and included a "disaster course" in which everything goes wrong. Each man was forbidden contacts with clients outside the casino and could not accept gifts other than the tips which were dropped into the *cagnotte* and shared once each month with all the personnel. When off-duty, the croupiers were watched by telescope in Monaco, and by plain-clothes surveillance outside the principality. Their suits had no pockets.

While Francis showered and Sian bathed, the croupiers filed into the rooms of the casino and took their places. The doors were opened and twenty-eight regulars shuffled inside, taking out of reticules and pockets pencils and long slips of carefully marked paper in preparation for another day of system play. The oldest regular had appeared every morning for thirty-six years for five hours of play and accepted a *mandat* from Liverpool, no message enclosed, from the postman once each month.

By ten o'clock that evening, as Sian and Francis finished dinner and strolled across the plaza to the casino, the rooms were filled with losers of seventeen nationalities who had exchanged twenty-three currencies for chips. The *chefs de parti* at each table had the alert look of fox terriers as they watched the croupiers and the play. The *chefs* were watched by the inspectors of the Service de l'Interieur; augmenting them, an additional force of fifty house detectives roamed through the crowd, watching. Watching *them* and everyone else was a super-elite group known only as "les occults" because their identity was known to only two men in Monaco.

Francis seated Sian, then took his place at the table to the right. They were certainly the handsomest couple in the room. They each drew one thousand pounds' worth of chips and began their play, and they never deviated from the system they had so carefully devised.

In three days of play Francis lost nineteen thousand, two hundred pounds, and Sian won three hundred and twelve pounds. "The gruesome part of the whole thing, darling," she said, "was that if you had taken my table and I had taken yours, it would have been me who had been plucked. It just goes to show that there is absolutely nothing faulty about our system. It is simply a matter of choosing the right table."

Chapter 20

 When they returned to London, Sian went immediately to Devon, and Francis communicated with Mr. Link, who consented to come up to town for lunch. They met at La Bourride in Gerrard Street; as usual, Mr. Link had installed the magnum of champagne before Francis arrived. "I have news of a sort, Mr. Hillairet," Link drawled.

"What is it? Is there a basis for a claim?"

"The news is that I need more money for our work. I need it because the preliminary investigations lead me to believe that though you may not be even a direct descendant of the Plantagenets, you may have very important lineage, and this lineage could guide us directly to a claim upon a *very* important title."

"Why—that's magnificent, Mr. Link!"

"It is a start."

"What sort of a title? What lineage? Will there be land and a county seat?"

"I will require two thousand five hundred pounds more. I have recalled my men from the Lowlands and shifted them into France. Two men. That costs. Travel, wages, maintenance and insurance—to say nothing of telephone and cable costs when they have to consult me."

"France?"

"It appears that there were both Hillairets and Vollmers with the French expeditionary force led by William the Conqueror."

"No!"

"In the meantime, my home team is at work at this end. It's rather like an international construction job whose workers are tunneling beneath a mountain between two countries. The home people are slightly more expensive than those in the field because they are my regulars, men and women whom I must pay the year round so that they are available for major assignments. I regret to tell you that though I shan't be charging you for their wages, because the basic overhead of my organization is my own responsibility, but for the expenses of travel, and some entertainment in the case of interviews with the heads of various families, and maintenance while outside London, *plus* various miscellaneous expenses, I'm going to have to ask you for one thousand pounds in addition to the French two thousand five hundred, making this installment three thousand five hundred pounds in all."

"The heads of which families?"

"And I would appreciate receiving your check so that we may proceed."

"This is beginning to cost far more than I imagined it would."

"I had told you it would be costly, but of course you are absolutely free to cancel our arrangement at any time. You must pay the expenses to date, yes, but there is no obligation for future expenses, I assure you. I would quite understand. Really, it is perfectly all right."

"No, no. I spoke out of surprise. I have no intention whatever of retiring from this." Francis took out his checkbook hastily, filled it out, ripped the check from the book and waved it to dry. "Which families, Mr. Link?"

"Mr. Hillairet," Link said severely, "I believe—though one must never attempt to hold me to this and, be advised, be sure, that if anyone claimed that I had confided this premature judgment to you I would be forced to deny it, it being unethical at this point of the investigations—that I do have one or two scintilla which tell me that it is perhaps *likely* that your title will emanate somewhere in the region of Shropshire, perhaps near Ludlow, that an earldom *might* be indicated, that the title *might* be Earl of Willmott-Ludlow, and that your designation in address *might* be Lord Hunt."

As Francis gaped, Mr. Link reached over and deftly caught the check which had dropped from Francis' fingers, and slipped it into his side pocket after giving it a cursory glance.

Francis said, "Lord Hunt! A belted earl! Third in descending line of the peerage! Superior to viscount, baron, knight and esquire. The peer of dukes and kings!"

Link held up his hand. "I have said nothing. Mark that well, Mr. Hillairet, I have told you nothing. I have not uttered a word. I have made no claims of success in this matter whatever."

"I understand. I am quite aware of that. But I appreciate greatly what you . . . what you have not said."

"When the ethical moment arrives, when the claim has been completed for presentation to the House of Lords in five to seven months' time—"

"Five to seven *months!*"

"Yes. Isn't it marvelous? I knew you would be impressed. But in all due modesty, I must confess that my teams got lucky at the start and were able to tie your French beginnings to the English family with a minimum of research." Link shrugged. "The average length of time required for such a search—I mean, of course, *deep search,* of the sort which advance all evidence necessary to substantiate a claim before the Committee of Privileges—is about—and I am averaging here, mind you—three years. Of course, I have had cases which have taken twelve years."

"My! As long as that?"

"Now you certainly are entitled to know what we will

have in hand when I finish," Mr. Link said, and after belting down some more champagne he began methodically to tick off each item on his fingers. "You will receive the following: your family seal, the achievement of your arms and its component parts and your pedigree."

"Really?"

"I won't bore you with the professional jargon that applies here—lozenges, fusils, fretties, roundles, and fields of goutte d'or—this is routine, and of course you shall have it. I am sure you can see all the time it takes just to sort all these things out."

"It certainly must."

"And naturally you'll want to know about your house armor: the helmet and its crest wreath and—"

"Won't I have to wear the armor at special occasions? For coronations and that sort of thing?"

"Frankly, I shouldn't think it would fit you."

"Then let's save time by forgetting about the armor. If it isn't needed to support the claim, that is."

"But of course it's needed! Do you think I would waste my time building a case in claim before the House of Lords with a lot of furbelows? Quite aside from my obligation to you as a client, Mr. Hillairet, I have my own reputation to consider. I beg you to remember that."

"Quite. I'm sorry. Will there be much of a delay between the presentation of the claim and the decision as to my right to assume the title?"

"Yes. First we must wait until the Committee decides to sit. That cannot be foreseen, but it is usually within two years."

"Two years?"

"Yes. Then they must study our claim. That could take from two to six years. They must be absolutely sure, you see, Mr. Hillairet—as both of us, I'm sure, sincerely want them to be."

Chapter 21

 An X-ray machine had been moved to Donen Hall, and the surgeon came from London to see Celia twice. The third time he brought a consultant with him. Two days before the operation, Sian took her daughter to London in a Daimler as big as a houseboat. Powell and Shaw lifted the small girl with enormous eyes into the car and Sian tucked a blanket around her though it was a beautiful sunny day. They drove off to London. After a while Sian said, "What will you do when the operation is done?"

"Dance, I think."

"What kind of dancing?"

"Any kind. I've read a good deal about it, so I know I'm too old to study ballet. One must begin to study that as a child."

"But do you mean—to dance professionally?"

"Yes."

"In the theater?"

"I don't care where. I want everyone who saw me limp—ever—to see me dancing."

They were silent after that for a few miles. Celia was not used to either talking or traveling. After a long time Sian said, "I am sure the operation is going to be a great success."

"You mustn't worry, Mama."

"No one need worry."

"You've become so pale!"

"I don't feel at all well. I've read that people get carsick."

Celia said, "We must turn back." She reached for the speaking tube.

"Turn back?" Sian grasped her daughter's free hand tightly. "No, no—this can't be cured that way—I am sick with shame, my dearest. The consultant asked me on the telephone last night why this operation hadn't been done when you were a little child."

"It probably wasn't possible then," Celia responded loyally.

"That isn't true."

"Mama, I know you. I know you couldn't bring yourself to allow anyone to operate on a little child. I know I couldn't have done it if I'd had a baby with a foot like mine."

"No. Yes. That is true. I couldn't bear to think of it." Her voice broke as she said, "It would have changed your entire life."

"Then I'm glad you didn't. I love my life. I wouldn't ever have wanted to be a dancer if it weren't for this foot. I learned to understand serenity because of it. I learned to think and paint and listen to music."

"You've been alone so much."

"I've never been lonely."

"The war made such a difference. I had to be away. Everyone had gone. I had to go. And before that—"

"But I was much better off than if I'd been a boy. Why, some boys go off to school at five and don't come home until they're twenty. I hate to think what it must be like to live in a school filled with noisy boys."

Sian didn't think of Francis until she sat alone in Celia's room at the hospital and waited for her to be brought down

from the operating theater. She telephoned him, but Bur-
bank, his butler, said he was lunching with a Mr. Link. She
must ask about Mr. Link. Francis had mentioned his name
several times.

When the doctor entered the room he was neither grave
nor jolly. He said that this was the first of three operations,
and that as far as they could tell at the moment, it was a
success.

"Oh, Mr. Winikus," Sian said. "How dreadfully painful
even one operation must be."

"We'll hurt her as little as possible. It's a complicated
problem of mechanics and engineering and sculpture."

"When is the next?"

"Just after the New Year, I think."

"Then we will stay in London."

"Very important that you do. It would be best, of course,
if Lady Celia remained in hospital."

"Christmas at home will make such a big difference to
Celia."

"I suppose it will be all right."

It had been eight years since Celia had seen the house in
Queen Street, and it had been entirely redecorated since
that time. Queen Street itself was as quiet as any Devon
village, but the effect of the looming city all around, the
interior so different from the one which she had walked
through so many times in memory, and the rapture of being
all alone with her mother from Christmas to beyond New
Year's Day so stimulated Celia that she was almost able to
forget the pain of her small foot.

Sian knew now how much she meant to Celia's joy and
peace of mind, and hence to her recovery. In coming down
from the operating theater Celia had opened her eyes to see
her mother, and she had cried out her pleasure and put her
arms quickly around her mother's neck before slipping off
into unconsciousness again. Sian felt she was on a hurtling
swing which traversed first heaven and then hell as she
alternated between wonder at her luck and sickening remorse, not so much for what she had done to her daughter

but for what she herself had missed by abandoning her. Now she was determined to keep both Celia and Francis without the jeopardy of losing either.

Sian gave instructions that she would take no calls on the first day they were home from the hospital. Celia asked if she would sleep in the same room with her, just for the first night. At last, after Celia finally dropped off to sleep drugged with the medicine Mr. Winikus had given her for the pain, Sian was able to telephone Francis.

"It's Sian."

"Is everything all right?" he asked anxiously. "Was the operation—"

"Yes, darling. Are you all right?"

"Yes, of course."

"I must stay with Celia tonight."

"Yes. Oh, yes, you must."

"Aren't you absolutely bleak with disappointment? We've never been separated this long."

"Perhaps later. Perhaps after she's asleep I can come to Queen Street and—"

"No, not tonight. She wants me in the room with her tonight."

"Tomorrow, then."

"She'll have to nap after lunch. I'll come to you. At two o'clock, or as soon as I can."

"Can't I come there? I could read to her. I'll make conversations about absolutely anything just to give you relief."

"She has great pain, darling, and right now she is so happy to have her old Mum all to herself that I want to weep. It's so beautiful and I can't explain it. And Christmas is right upon us, and that's such a family thing to a girl like Celia— she hasn't had many good Christmases—and right after the New Year she has to have another operation. So, darling, I hope you understand why this doesn't seem the right moment to explain you and how you fit into things."

"You're right. You're doing the right thing."

"Tomorrow at two, my dearest."

"Until tomorrow, Sian."

"I love you so, Francis."

"I love you, Sian."
"Tomorrow . . ."

At some time every afternoon or evening, twice in the early mornings before dawn, and once for an entire night, Sian was able to slip away to Francis' flat. It was the most joyous balance she had ever known: the reward of Celia and the wild comfortings of Francis.

Christmas Eve was tearfully sentimental, and Sian wept when Celia gave her a portrait she had painted of herself as a ballet dancer in a white tutu peering hopefully out from the wings toward a great stage. Sian gave Celia a Degas, small but breath-taking, of a tiny dancer poised upon one toe. Her other presents were an ermine bed jacket and a small diamond brooch made out of a pair of Colin's cuff links. Together they sat up in the large bed, sipped champagne and sang Christmas carols, and then, while Sian read Dickens, Celia dozed off.

When she was sure Celia was asleep, Sian set off through the snow along Queen Street to Francis' flat, laden down with an armful of packages. She was euphoric about her day with Celia, and she had decided that Francis must come to call on New Year's afternoon. She wouldn't make any ceremony out of it; he would simply be one of a group she had invited to meet Celia.

Somehow she got through the ensuing week, worrying about Celia when she was with Francis and yearning for Francis when she was with Celia. Three times during the week on the wildest of pretexts she mentioned to Celia an American friend called Mr. Hillairet, and each time she said that he might come to call on New Year's Day. The third time Celia caught her up on it.

"Oh, have I mentioned him before?"

"Twice before."

"You'll like him, I think. He knows ever so much about music and the dance. He's very nice really."

"What's he like?"

"Oh, very tall and bony. And the only man I've ever met with yellow eyes."

"Not a bit like Daddy, is he?"

"Why should Mr. Hillairet be anything like Daddy?"

"No reason at all, of course."

Sian was blushing deeply, and she talked rapidly. "And he's a mine of hopelessly useless information."

"He is?"

"Ask him anything. You'll see. It's like chatting with an encyclopedia."

"What is he like—inside?"

"Shy, I think. Aloof. Very mental and objective and that sort of thing."

"Why hasn't he come before this?"

"Well . . . as I say, he *is* shy. I suppose that's why."

By the time Francis did arrive, Sian's fluttering and worrying had made him extremely nervous, so much so that he was not thinking at all about his parents but only about the impression he must make on Lady Celia, the Baroness Keys.

Celia was dressed in a blue nightdress and her new ermine bed jacket. Her blond hair was in short braids into which her mother had entwined blue ribbons with small bows. Her astonishingly large blue eyes seemed to be studying Francis intently as he approached the bed, and her gaze made him forget to smile. To Celia he seemed long, thin, stark and solemn, and she was very impressed.

"Celia," Sian said, "I present Mr. Francis Hillairet. Mr. Hillairet, my daughter."

He bowed; she inclined her head. He said, "How do you do?" She repeated it. Sian pushed him into a chair and asked him if he would like some tea. He nodded, then played his first trump. "That rather flourishing bow I just made, Lady Celia," he said abruptly, "I gave because of your interest in dancing."

"You did? But how—"

Sian beamed at Francis over the silver tea service. At that moment she knew he had genius.

"Louis XIV's dancing master, a man named Despréaux, taught the king how to bow. Of course, until he studied dancing, the king had no reason to know how to bow. 'Your Majesty,' Despréaux said, 'respect for your partner is shown in the quickness with which one sinks to the ground and in the slowness with which one rises, rather than in the largeness of movement. The bow of an inferior consists in sinking quickly and rising slowly. Conversely, the bow of a superior consists in sinking slowly and rising quickly.'"

"I see! I see!" Celia said with delight. "Of course, only a dancer can bow correctly! What else did he teach Louis?"

"The ballet posture."

"Which is?"

"The rotating of the legs at a forty-five-degree angle to the hip—the straight leg—and the special co-ordination of the head and arms called the *port de bras.*"

"The king studied *ballet* dancing?"

"For over twenty years."

"How wonderful! What else was he taught?"

"The king sought to strive for a brilliance of footwork and elevation—to dance off the earth, as it were. And he wanted a posture based upon a straight and rigid spine, a stiffened straight knee—this is the only form of dancing in the world that uses the stiff knee—and a level hip line. The hips must not lift, thrust out or rotate. The shoulders must not ripple."

"Mr. Hillairet, what you say is utterly fascinating."

Sian smiled from ear to ear and brought Francis his tea, then said casually to Celia, as though both she and Francis had not been close to nervous collapse until that moment, "Lord Gant has telephoned to say that he will call on you with a small surprise."

Celia clapped her hands together. "I love Lord Gant's surprises," she exclaimed. Then she glanced at the card in her hand on which she had scribbled an assortment of esoterica to test Mr. Hillairet's encyclopedic knowledge. "What are the best varieties of eating apple in the United States, Mr. Hillairet?"

"Well, the Lodi, the Grimes Golden and the Astrachan are all—"

"You must ask him difficult things, Celia. Apples are no challenge to Mr. Hillairet."

Francis blinked.

Celia said, "I've always wanted to know the names of the

winds in different places. You know, like monsoon and simoom. Do you know any of those, Mr. Hillairet?"

"I am sure he knows all of them," her mother said smugly.

"I don't think I know them all," Francis said slowly. "There are quite a few. They have the bayamo in Cuba. There's a violent downslope wind in Afghanistan called the bad-sad-o-bistroz—"

"How perfectly marvelous!" Celia said.

"Bhoot is the local Indian term which describes a relatively small-scale, counterclockwise whirling of air filled with loose dust. There's the brick fielder of Australia, the brubru of Indonesia, the karaburan of the Gobi and the waff of Scotland. There's one called the elephanta which blows strong along the Malabar coast to announce the end of the monsoon and the beginning of the dry season. The Swiss have their bise."

"Is there an English wind?"

"The helm—a strong wind which blows in the Pennine Chain. The doctor wind is a term which originated with the English for the tropics and—"

A footman appeared. "Lord Gant, milady," he announced. Fighting a smirk, he withdrew and closed the door. Almost immediately it began to open slowly. They were all watching the space above the level of the doorknob, but nothing appeared. Then the door opened wider, and suddenly a dwarf, exquisitely dressed in eighteenth-century costume, leaped into the room, drew a tiny sword from a tiny scabbard and cried out in a piping voice, *"En garde!"*

Celia squealed with joy. Sian began to applaud.

Francis screamed a maniacal scream. He kept screaming as he picked up a chair and extended its legs between himself and the dwarf. "Get back, you murderous little bastard," he shrieked.

"Francis!" Sian rushed to his side to calm him, but he swept her away with a brush of his arm and knocked her sideways over the bed. He charged the dwarf, yelling, "Are they out there waiting? Let's get this done now and forever," and jammed two of the legs of the chair into the dwarf's chest, knocking him unconscious and catapulting him into a corner of the room. Then he careened out of the room, still holding the chair in front of him; it caught Lord Gant in the stomach and knocked him down the stairway, where he fell in a heap upon the landing.

"Come and get me, you dwarf swine!" Francis shouted, and leaped down the staircase two steps at a time, the chair moving ahead of him like the front of a locomotive. He raced across the large hall, and as the impeccably trained footman opened the door, fled into the snowy night.

The consequences were appalling. The dwarf had suffered a fractured skull and a broken collarbone; Lord Gant had a ruptured gall bladder, five fractured ribs and a concussion. Francis was arrested as he wandered around at the bottom of Curzon Street and taken to a prison hospital for mental observation; the two victims were removed quickly to St. George's Hospital at Hyde Park Corner, but were not pronounced to be out of danger until seven o'clock the next morning.

Sian kept telephoning Francis at Farm Street; only after an hour did she telephone the police. Almost immediately two plainclothes officers of the C.I.D. were questioning her and her daughter in Celia's room.

"Mr. Francis Hillairet is under arrest and is being held in physical restraint. At this time he is in no condition to make any statement. Can you give us information, Lady Sian?"

As best she could, Sian told them what had happened and then explained that Mr. Hillairet had recently been released from a mental clinic in Switzerland. The men thanked her and left.

Sian went to Celia's bed and lay down beside her. Celia put her arms around her mother and held her head on her shoulder. "Please don't worry, Mama. Please don't be upset."

"I won't, darling. I'm not."

"Did you meet Mr. Hillairet in Switzerland, Mama?"

"Yes."

"But he was so sane."

"It was the dwarf. And so ends the career of Lord Gant, England's most famous practical joker. And so, I pray, may end the careers of all practical jokers."

"What can we do to help Mr. Hillairet?" Celia asked. "We must help him."

"We cannot help him from being deported," she said, struggling to sit up. "But we can help to keep him out of prison." Within five minutes she was talking on the telephone to Dr. Boscawen in Anieres.

Chapter 22

The downstairs study seemed to be filled with solicitors who were making spot decisions about the sort of telephone calls each should make to the right sort of people in the right sort of places. Some went to St. George's, some went to the prison hospital, some spoke to police doctors and to magistrates. Everything was handled correctly and within the law, but the results were obtained remarkably quickly.

Lord Gant agreed to make a statement that Francis could not have attacked him knowingly because he had no way of knowing that Lord Gant had been standing behind the door. The dwarf, whose name was Major Sherry and who was twenty-six inches tall, was willing to accept a settlement of twenty-five hundred pounds for further recuperation after Francis had paid all hospital bills.

At the police inquiry, Dr. Boscawen testified that Mr. Hillairet had been her patient and that he was afflicted with an oppressive, illusory fear of dwarfs. Did the doctor diagnose Mr. Hillairet as having paranoia? Mr. Hillairet had suffered paranoiac delusions, Dr. Boscawen said, but his condition was only dangerous and violent in the presence or illusion of dwarfs. Inasmuch as Major Sherry, twenty-six inches tall, had appeared without warning, had drawn a sword and had raised his voice to challenge Mr. Hillairet, did the police alienist believe that Mr. Hillairet could be held morally or criminally responsible for his subsequent actions? The police physician stated that under such conditions Mr. Hillairet could not be held responsible.

Francis was judged to be an undesirable alien and was required to leave the country within seventy-two hours; if that was medically impossible, he must leave as soon as he was capable of travel. He was assessed with the cost of the inquiry and medical costs for Lord Gant and Major Sherry, and it was ruled that he never be permitted to return to Great Britain.

Dr. Boscawen locked the door of the study in Francis' flat in Farm Street behind her, and walked softly toward the bed in which Francis lay. His eyes were red-rimmed and the planes of his face had been broken by fatigue and dismay. "There is nothing for me to live for, Doctor," he said, and he covered his face with his hands.

"Why believe that?"

"Whatever chance I ever had of being accepted by my family, of taking my place beside my parents, has been ruined forever by the dwarfs. I would have been a match for them at any other time, but who could expect that they would come for me there? I can't believe it. I simply cannot believe that they have won."

"Mr. Hillairet, you are over forty years old. If your parents were as important as they undoubtedly must have been to put you into the orphanage for any of the many reasons you have explained to me, they must have been relatively elderly people when you were born. You have lived an exemplary life. You've done everything a son could to make them proud of you and to make them want to welcome you as their son. Therefore, and particularly since your friend Mr. Hibbert left no word for you when he died, we must reach the sad conclusion that your parents died some time ago, and that there is simply no one left to come forward to welcome you."

Within an instant Francis looked healed. "Yes," he said excitedly. "That must be why. Why couldn't I have seen that? Thank you, Doctor. Oh, thank you very much, Doctor."

"We must get ready to leave."

"They said I could never come back."

"It's a wide, wide world, Mr. Hillairet."

"But this country is my ancient home. My beautiful flat. My art objects and wonderful furniture selected with such taste and care. My stable of horses. My two Rolls-Royces which have not yet even been delivered—what about all those?"

"First you must come with me to Anieres to rest so that we may think this through clearly; there we will find solutions. After all, you can surely see that the dwarfs have no more interest in you whatsoever. They've done what they set out to do; they have—they think through their own plans—kept you from your parents."

"I can't go to Anieres. I will have to hide myself somewhere in England until Mr. Link can present his claims and win the case."

"Who is Mr. Link?"

"He is my genealogist—the best in the field—and in a very short time he will have proved my right to an earldom. They won't be able to touch me then, not when I'm accepted as a peer."

"You cannot assist Mr. Link in any way, can you?"

"No."

"Then it's best to leave the country as the police ordered. Prove that you are a God-fearing, law-abiding man. You will rest at Anieres. No sentence is forever, neither your ban from this country nor the time you will spend in Switzerland. Then, when Mr. Link has established your earldom, the lawyers will reopen your case and because of your station the ban on your entry will be removed. If you go underground you will become a criminal in the eyes of the law. You must proceed with dignity, Mr. Hillairet. *Noblesse oblige.* You must meet this misfortune as others in your family would."

"Yes. Yes, I must."

"Then you will come with me to Anieres?"

"Yes. And I am grateful to you."

"We will take the night train to Paris. Until then, you must take these two little pills for nourishment. You have not been eating at all properly."

Francis swallowed the pills and Dr. Boscawen made him lie down again. She called Sian from the other room, explained that Francis was resting under sedation and that she would return to his flat in a few hours to accompany him to Anieres.

Sian let herself into the flat with her key and went directly to Francis' bedroom, moving with a stunned sense of loss. Clichés that she couldn't silence kept going through her head: "We have come to the end of an era"; "There were giants in those days"; and "We won't see his like again"—all of them spattered against a distorted refrain of "The End of a Perfect Day." She knew these things were inside her head because she had not faced the facts of the last twenty-two hours. Something had shriveled the maundering joy which they had bred and fed and raised together. She would follow him wherever he had to go, but now she stood in the center of such emptiness that she realized something enormously important to her life had been subtracted from it. She did not know what this could be except the self-delusion that she and Francis had glorified. Now it had been smashed, though neither of them had wanted it to be smashed—and though Francis probably did not know it had been smashed.

She locked the bedroom door and undressed. Then, her face limp with sadness, she lay upon the bed beside him and touched his cheek lightly with her fingertips. Incredibly, considering the pills, he awoke.

"Sian?"

"Yes, darling?"

"You are Queen Elizabeth." As Francis paused, she clenched her lower lip between her teeth to keep from crying. "What I meant to say is, her special titles are also your titles. So I confer them on you: this Flower of Grace, this Finger of the Lord, this Jewel of the World, these Starbright Eyes, Heaven's Chief Delight, Sweet Beauty's Sun, this Mother Dear."

She kissed his cheek. "Thank you."

"You are more than all those things."

"Touch me here."

"How wonderful you are."

"You leave tonight?"

"Yes. But not for long. When Mr. Link establishes the claims I will be back and we will be married."

"Married? Oh, Francis."

"I will have the right to ask you then."

"Is Mr. Link a genealogist?"

"Yes. And a wizard."

Sian shut her eyes tightly and turned her head into his shoulder.

"I will ask you to wait for only four more months," Francis said. "I have reluctantly reached the conclusion that my parents must be dead."

"Yes. They must be dead."

"But when the House of Lords accepts the documentation and authentication of my earldom, the police will no longer be able to keep me out of my own country, will they?"

She could not answer.

"Will they, Sian?"

"No, darling."

"I am going to Anieres with Dr. Boscawen because I need rest." He stared at the ceiling and breathed slowly. "When will I see you again?"

Sian lifted her head and they stared directly into each other's eyes, an inch apart. Her magical voice skated across the sandy vowels and gravelly consonants. "Celia must have two more operations, and I must stay here for them," she said. "Every day while I am away from you will be worse. If I ever lost you I would return into the nothingness in which I was vegetating when you found me."

"You will come to me?"

"The day Celia can travel we will leave for Anieres." She began to unbutton his shirt. "Do you remember . . . can you remember . . ." she said, "the words you told me Edward III had said . . . the words you spoke to me while you held me on that first wonderful night?"

He was breathing shallowly, and when he turned to face her his eyes were glazed with his appetite for her and he was smiling faintly. " 'The joy was unspeakable,' " he said softly. " 'The comfort inestimable, the pleasure without murmuring, the hilarity without care.' "

Chapter 23

 On June 6th, 1922, Stacie was divorced on the grounds of desertion. She and James Maitland were married in St. Thomas' Church in New York on June 22nd, 1922, in the presence of the bride's parents and a few friends.

It had been decided that it would be the best thing to have as "important" a wedding as possible, so that it might be made quite clear to anyone who might have thought otherwise that Francis Vollmer's sudden disappearance had been for reasons which he had made unilaterally. On the other hand, it seemed more discreet, inasmuch as the bride's former husband once had been the groom's assistant, to have the wedding when almost everyone was away from New York and so would gossip less about it.

The stately ceremony was reported in the Saturday editions of the New York press, the day of lowest summer readership. The newspaper accounts confirmed to the employees, executives, board of directors and depositors of the

Hibbert First National Bank, as well as to Mrs. Vollmer's parents, that Francis Vollmer had deserted his wife a year before; this guaranteed sympathy for the bride, who was very sympathetic to begin with.

To composers, musical-instrument manufacturers, professional musicians, music teachers, record manufacturers and impresarios, the wedding was a cause for great rejoicing. It meant that the Maitland fortune would continue its huge financial support of the American music industry, for had not Mrs. Maitland proved herself the sort of patron because of whom contra bassoonists must smile in their sleep? In the newspaper stories Mr. Maitland was described by the press as "a leading American banker, art patron, philanthropist and sportsman"—the last referring to his financial contributions to international tennis. Possibly the wedding disturbed the tennis industry; no one seemed to know where Mrs. Maitland stood on the sport.

The press described the bride as "the social leader known for her beauty and for the fact that she is one of the best-informed women in the American aristocracy today." A glossy magazine said, in words which would have been aphrodisiacal to her first husband, that "she is an unfailingly gracious leader of American society."

The gracious aristocrat's father, Bertram "Black Jack" Mayers, who had been persuaded by his wife to abjure chewing the great wad of gum which had agitated his face for so many years, took his daughter aside at the reception. Already he'd had five glasses of champagne and so talked freely despite the tightness of his rented morning suit.

"I don't know how you did it, Stace," Black Jack said.

"Did what?"

"Married one of the richest men in America."

"You had as much to do with it as I did, Pop."

"How come?"

"The music. Everything I have came from the music—even Francis."

"Francis is a no-good son-of-a-bitch. I always said so."

"I know you always said so, Pop."

"And I said it to him."

"Well, now you can stop saying it! Pity him. How can anybody hate him? What is he? What can he ever be but somebody locked up inside the most useless, sick dream anyone ever had?" There were tears in her eyes, and her voice broke.

"You're not still sweet on him? Sweet Jesus, Stace, not on your wedding day to a man like Maitland!"

"Listen, Pop. Do you like me?"

"Stace! I love you!"

"All right. I love you too, but if you ever want to see me again, don't ever say anything like that again. You understand that, Pop? The best thing you can do is never even mention Francis to me again."

When Stacie had at last come to realize what Francis had done to her, and the cunning and craft and cold-bloodedness with which he had done it, she had taken a taxi to the Staten Island ferryboat early one morning and ridden the five miles back and forth, endlessly passing the Statue of Liberty, for the whole day. When she disembarked at South Ferry in the early evening, she had conquered Francis. She was not naïve enough to delude herself that she was rid of him forever; she knew that she would carry him with her wherever she went for the rest of her days. But she had conquered him, and she didn't hate him any more. She had reasoned out some certainties: Francis was alive somewhere in the world; he read newspapers; he was a toady to the arts and its patrons and would be aware of all the great happenings in that world; he worshiped money; he idolized status of all sorts; he licked the boots of power.

Very carefully Stacie ticked off in her mind, which for the first time in months seemed to work with clarity and precision, everything that Francis needed and wanted. By the time she stepped off the ferry she had coldly resolved how to become enormously rich and powerful, a figure of reverence in the Elysian fields of the international arts and international society. Whatever Francis did with his stolen money, she would rip his heart out by showing him how much better he could have done it with her. Wherever he rose, she would rise higher; he would live in frustration for the rest of his life, an also-ran far behind the champion. Her determination grew the way a three-hundred-foot-high sequoia tree grows from a seed. Their love had been the nourishing soil; in it the seed of betrayal had been planted; the soil and the seed had been watered with her tears. But now the great surging Goliath of a tree that was her resolve and her revenge would mount to the sky, multiplying in size and width as it soared and set its branches across the face of heaven. The roots of that tree were strong; nothing could topple Stacie's tree.

After the wedding the happy couple departed for a grand tour of the bank's branches and the great art and musical centers of Europe. The press trumpeted that a new Golden Age of music, painting, poetry and literature in America might well be in the making.

Chapter 24

 Francis and his banker, Jacques Crouch, sat on a private porch of the clinic overlooking the lake which Francis shared with the Swiss people.

"But, Monsieur Hillairet, I have my duty! I must remind you how much of your securities you have transformed into cash already. Do you know? Have you counted? Almost eighty thousand English pounds in just over ten months. Why vitiate money by converting it into cash?"

"I must have a town house in London. Real estate is not cash."

"But if you are coming into property, why buy more? You have magnificent securities."

"Not property—at least that is not certain. I am coming into a title of the British peerage."

"Very nice, I'm sure."

"Look at the Marchioness of Shattock, for example. She

has four houses. I mean, suppose I inherit a seat in Shropshire and, let us say, a shooting box in Scotland. I'll still need
a town house." Francis shrugged.

Crouch shrugged too. "Money is easily spent, monsieur,"
he said.

After locking the door to his room and lowering the side
blinds on his porch, Francis reread the letter from Mr. Link,
smiling the pursed, lunar smile of the winner who planned
his victory every step of the way.

15th March 1922

My dear Hillairet:

We have increasing reason to hope that before long the
salutation of all letters to you will read "My Lord" or "Dear
Lord Hunt." Which is to say that excellent progress is being
made and that we are ahead of schedule.

We have completed sifting through all the parish records
and registers in western England. (In 1597 the registers were
copied into parchment volumes, though earlier registers have
survived.) We have examined family wills with painful
care. As you undoubtedly know, the Prerogative Court of
Canterbury began recording wills in 1383, and I had to do
much of this digging personally because the writing in the
Act Books is usually in Latin. It appears that your family's
loyalty to the spirit of France was complete; we have learned
that they gave shelter and daughters and sons to comfort
the Huguenot waves of 1550 and 1680. We have even
picked up traces of Vollmer and Hillairet in the French
Protestant Church in Soho Square registers—helped enormously, of course, by Lewis' *Topographical Dictionary* in
thirteen volumes, the *List of the Non- Parochial Registers
and Records in the Custody of the Registrar General*. We
have also found little footsteps of your people in *Alumni
Cantabrigienses*, Crockford's *Clerical Directory*, the Navy
list and even in the records of the Barber-Surgeons Company
and the Society of Apothecaries. Confirmatory teams are now
digging and corroborating in the records of the Services,
Religions, Trades and Professions, Schools and Universities,

the Peerage, Commonwealth and Former Possessions, and among the Index Library, Harleian Society volumes, *Miscellanea Genealogica* and *The Pedigree Register*.

Nevertheless, I must insist that none of these researches have any substance whatever until I am in a position to document them fully.

Now to another matter. It is not my intention to imply that the style and manner in which a candidate for the peerage conducts his life would affect the Committee of Privileges of the House of Lords. What I am about to suggest, however, comes from the knowledge that all of us are human and that no one could say the House of Lords is inhuman. It is a human characteristic to be able to see a man clearly as one's peer if one maintains the necessities of life at a level equal to that of the viewer—who, in present circumstances, is also a judge. One of these necessities is proper clothing. You would no more think of dressing in rags at a time your claim was being considered than you would think of painting blue spots on your face. Then there is the matter of the roof over one's head. That too should correspond to what leaders of the peerage would consider minimal. By this, pray understand, I do not mean to denigrate the nature of your present lodgings; I pray also that I am not overstepping propriety's bounds. But I have seen so *many* of these cases through.

Now—if it will help—it has come to my attention that a certain house in Gilbert Street, hard by Grosvenor Square, is about to come on the market. I am also in a position to know that if it is sold before the expenses of advertising, estate agents, etc., a *really important saving* can be effected. In such a location, if you choose not to occupy this particular house after you have been awarded your peerage, you could double your money by its sale in a few years' time.

If the purchase of the house interests you, we must act fast. You will need to send to me, by return mail, made out to Cash, your cheque for twenty-one thousand pounds. The needy owner of this property is a widowed noblewoman so highly placed in Burke's and DeBrett's that if I were permitted to reveal her name you would, verily, gasp.

Trusting that you are enjoying your Swiss holiday and

that we shall be meeting soon over a glass of champagne, I remain,

Your most obedient servant, L

Francis sent a check to Mr. Link by the afternoon post, with a note of effusive thanks.

Francis seemed enormously improved. He was able to undergo hypnotic suggestion with even more facility than during his previous confinement; he had overcome his fear of dwarfs and he accepted the death of his parents with fortitude. He spent much of his time corresponding with Sian, and looked forward eagerly to April 29th, when she and Celia would at last be able to join him.

. . . cannot imagine going on living without you. Thank God for Celia's need and my past selfishness, because only these have stopped me more than a dozen times from leaving her and flying to you, darling. I'm neither nurse nor psychologist enough to carry Celia across the mountains of pain which she endures without once complaining. If she had complained, I think I am weak enough to have said that I had done everything I could, that the rest was up to her, and then to have run away. But I cannot because she is brave. The second operation was the worst. It was so bad. I kept remembering that she had not asked for it and that if I had been any sort of a mother it would have been all over fifteen years ago. I ordained this agony egotistically so that I could prove I loved her. She has paid with tangible pain, and if she comes out of it hating me—regardless of whether or not she is whole—I will have to find the character somewhere to bear it as she has borne my desertion throughout her life.

Now the third operation is over and they say everything is a wonderful success. We will spend a month at Donen Hall until Celia regains her strength. Then back to London for the breaking of the cast and physical therapy. And then—well, I have decided that you will teach her to waltz.

Two days after she walks we can travel, they say. Plane to Paris, train to Geneva and the Hotel Richmonde, unless you will have been able to find a villa for all of us on your side of the lake. These lives of ours! These thrilling, fulfilling lives of ours!

I am in your arms. Now. *Now.* Ah, my dearest Francis,
I am only yours.

Adoringly,
Sian

P.S. Already Celia is impressed with you and she doesn't
even know how you can cook!

The day this letter came, Francis was concentrating on a
cheese test. Was the Swiss sbrinz the equal of Italian Parmesan for use on farinaceous dishes? Parmesan had been used
on millions of tons of pasta, and sbrinz on perhaps only
hundreds of tons, but he had an exciting hunch that sbrinz
could bring off the effect equally well.

He read Sian's letter as soon as it came, of course, but he
could not answer it until the tests were over, and then he
was too exhausted to write. Instead, he searched through
Sian's other letters to evaluate a new system at roulette she
had recently invented while waiting at the orthopedic hospital. After memorizing it, he drove to Evian, only twenty-
eight miles along the lake, and lost twelve thousand francs.

Early the next morning he composed his reply to Sian:

. . . and I followed your instructions to the letter. However,
though it is true that the third column has eight red numbers
and only four black, which seems to be a mathematical flaw
in the layout, and even though I consistently placed one bet
on the column and one bet on black, I nevertheless lost
twelve thousand francs. We will have to go over this together
because it seems to me that the second bet should have
been on red, not black.

I have rented the most comfortable villa for all of us on
the Haut-Crêt behind Cologny about two and a half miles
from the city. It has a view of the lake and the Jura, and of
the Alps and Mont Blanc and the Saleve. Dr. Boscawen tells
me I am in excellent health and, if my house guests have no
objection, that I may leave the clinic and stay with you.
Which servants will you be sending ahead? What part of the
staff shall I engage here? The house is modest; only twelve
bedrooms, including the servants' quarters. It is partly electri-
fied. What splendid news about Celia's foot. She might like to
know, in that connection, that March 28th will be the sixty-
sixth anniversary of the death of Solomon Foot, the Ameri-

can lawyer and politician. He was a U.S. Senator from
Vermont; not a very good orator, but extremely strong as a
presiding officer due to his knowledge of parliamentary law.
Tell her also that the word for foot in German is *Fuss*, and
that little foot of hers has certainly kicked up quite a fuss,
hasn't it? (Or are jokes about such matters in bad taste? If
so, do not tell her.)

Be sure to write the arrival time of your train. I will be
at the Cornavin station, of course.

All my love to you and warm regards to Celia.

Francis

When Celia climbed the thousands of miles out of the
anesthetic and into the pain after her second and third
operations, what filled her mind was the fear and defeat
upon Francis' face just before he had rushed forward to
attack his terror on New Year's Day.

She could not understand what her emotions were whis-
pering to her about him. He was the first man in her life who
had talked to her about the things she had wanted to hear.
Through the pain, she kept from whimpering by thinking of
all the questions about the dance to which he must surely
have the answers. She made her conscious mind concentrate
toward him and away from her pain, so that soon everything
which turned her away from it became joy which burned
just as brightly and as strongly. He was so tall, so handsome,
so yellow-eyed and concentrated. He had come closer and
closer to her as he had walked across the wide room toward
her, and his body became all face until, in her delirium, she
tried to lean forward to kiss him.

Each time she became conscious, she held off the pain by
invoking the dream of him again and again until at last she
began to feel him with her whole body. Then she lay back;
she was very weak and tired, but she had built a dream
which allowed her to dominate the pain and which made her
eternally grateful to him.

To Sian, the separation from Francis was worse than
anything she had endured since she had decided to speak
again. The separation from Colin had built a moat between

her and the world, so that she could isolate herself and her loss from everything else, and being alone with it, could try to understand why this had been done to her. She knew that Francis wasn't gone in the way that Colin was gone from her, but during the second and third week of the separation she had telephoned the clinic every day. Each time Dr. Boscawen would explain to her that Francis had not yet recovered enough to be able to speak to her. Then, in the fourth week, he had telephoned. That is, it could have been him. The voice was the same stilted, self-conscious voice, but it could have been a trick of the doctor's to make her think that Francis had not left the clinic. She had called Dr. Boscawen back at once and had asked her to please have a photograph taken of herself with Francis in his very new hound's-tooth jacket, so that she could be sure it wasn't an old photograph. But when the picture arrived it had soothed her only for an instant. She needed Francis, not a photograph.

She had his letters—distant, drugged letters, even the ink of which seemed to be sedated. They were lofty, calm, serene, hospitalized letters. They explored weather phenomena: it might rain, then again it might not; it seemed to be preparing for a warm spring. He kept count of the numbers of patients; he discussed the recipe tests he was making; he reported that his blood pressure was much lower.

She wrote to him constantly. While she sat with Celia at the hospital in London, or later in Queen Street or Donen Hall, she scrawled paragraph after paragraph the way other women might add row upon row of stitches to an endless scarf. Sometimes, suddenly thinking of something vitally important which she had neglected to say, she would mail as many as three letters a day. She needed to tell everything to his distant, disembodied presence, the same way she had needed for three years to talk to the patch of mud which had been Colin. She knew that the reason for her compulsion was to gain a measure of attention for herself, and that Francis was her contact with life, as Colin once had been. The two men proved to her that she was not merely waiting to die, that she was connected to life even though her links were through death and insanity.

> . . . so please don't tell me any more about the *bise*, or how clearly you are able to see for many miles, or whether the run of food has improved or declined. What sort of man are you? Are you not the man who nearly broke me under his body the day he left? Are you as incapable of writing of love as you are of speaking of it? Do you think of it? No, don't answer me that. Are you nothing but a mechanical stallion?

Sian did not neglect Celia in writing Francis. After the second operation she sat beside Celia's bed for forty-one hours until her daughter was able to sleep without moaning. The pain of the third operation was almost as bad, and she held Celia's hand and told her stories of the lost days when they had both been very young; when Grandpapa and Papa and the uncles and cousins were alive; when the family had carts and ponies and many small, unruly boys. She told about parties and balls long forgotten by everyone but herself, all attended by people now dead and dominated by Papa, wonderful Papa. She concentrated so hard on keeping Celia's mind off pain that she found herself describing past events which had never happened; yet as the two of them lived these fantasies, the times which had not been blended with those which had, so that fantasy became as important as reality.

"What a beautiful little girl you were and how proud that made me! Why your papa and grandpapa always said that I spoiled you; they wanted me to hand you over to Nanny. But I couldn't. I had to have you with me. You had your proper bedtime and you took your meals with Nanny, but I couldn't bear it if you were away from me at every other time. Then the war came. The war."

Celia wanted to believe it had been just that way. Whenever she awoke, her foot hurting terribly, the pain was dulled only by her exultation that she now had a real foot and her mother was sitting close beside her. Her mother was so beautiful; she hadn't slept because she wanted to watch and protect and cherish her daughter whom she loved so much. But she was haggard. There were purple shadows around the deep green eyes; under the red hair and surrounded by her startlingly white skin, they were the colors of Lautrec. But Mama was ravishing even when she was ready to sink with exhaustion, let no one ever forget it; let those jabbering servants at Donen Hall take careful note that Mama was exhausted and haggard because she loved Celia so much that she would not permit anyone else to nurse her. Of course it must always have been that way. It always *had* been that way. The war had taken all of them away from each other, and only Mama who loved her so, had found the way back to Celia. Only Mama.

They talked about dancing after the first terrible days. Sian told Celia that she deserved a great reward. "What do you want more than anything else in the world?"

"I want to dance."

"Ah."

"I want to dance and dance. I want to be able to dance every dance I've ever read about. I want to dance in ways I have never read about but which I have always been able to feel inside me. Whatever it is, that dance is what my life will be. It must be like loving all the men in the world at once, Mama."

Sian laughed with delight. "What do you know about loving—and about men?"

"I have read over twelve hundred novels," Celia said shyly.

Once they talked about Francis.

"Who is Francis, Mama?"

"Just a man who was a patient with me at Anieres."

"Why was he there?"

"He went mad because of snobbism."

"Mama! Don't joke."

"I'm not joking. He had been a poor orphan boy. Without knowing it, he revealed that every time he told me that he had been a rich orphan boy. He has convinced himself that he is really the son of a great and noble family. First he had to prove to himself that he was a better man than he thought he was; then he had to prove to everyone else that he was better than them because of the accident of his exalted birth. But he had invented all of it, it never had happened, and he drove himself quite mad."

"How awful."

"Nothing drearier. I suppose we can allow a certain amount of snobbism for achievement. People who work and sacrifice and cultivate their intelligence should have certain privileges; someone has to lord it over the lazy, or they would never stir. But poor Francis decided that he was noble, and that this alone entitled him to the homage of the world."

"But why was he frightened by Major Sherry?"

"He believes that dwarfs are the enemy of his station. He told me they were conspiring to cut him down to their size, and of course that terrifies him."

"Poor man."

"Perhaps. But he is among the blessed just the same. Francis *believes*. The reason that religions have all gone to pot, Celia darling, is because the people did not have the character or the vision to believe, or the will power to obey; the ecclesiasticals have made things easier and easier, until there is nothing left to believe in that a bank check won't pay for. These cinemas we have now will make the culture easier and soon there will be nothing to believe there either. The pols have taken the wonder out of patriotism because they will not make harsh demands upon the people's innocent need to believe. As someone wrote: 'Fields are won by those who believe in the winning.' Everything is getting blander and the world is a wreck and Francis is mad, but at least he believes in something which should still exist: *noblesse,* the obligation to self, to one's own, and his belief has made him a princely man. If he had believed in God with the same fervor, he would be the Archbishop of Canterbury. Learn to believe, Celia."

"I want to learn."

"Then you must start by learning to believe in yourself. All the rest will follow."

"What is Francis to us?"

"A friend."

"Is he your lover?"

"Why, Celia!" The reproof was mild.

"I meant really that I hope someone kind has been his lover. He's so terribly wishing."

The months had seemed endless. The weather was abominable. The foot healed stubbornly and the letters from Francis grew duller and duller. February loomed, then faded into March and March into April before the two doctors said that the cast could come off. Celia walked and she and Sian wept together. Each day she was able to walk a little more, and in six days she executed an air-light run across the room. A week after that she was strong enough for them to leave England to find Francis.

They stopped in Paris for two days. Mme. Vionnet had been kind enough to send a fitter to Queen Street, but the clothes had to be adjusted and new ones ordered.

Sian could think of nothing but Francis as she lay in the darkness on the train rocketing southward. She could feel him in her arms and legs, could feel his breath warming her shoulder. Four months without Francis—it must never happen again, because she knew she could not survive it. But though the train clamored and jolted she slept through it, because she must step down from the train at Geneva rested and, if possible, slightly more beautiful than he remembered her. This was their time, at last. And if it was not their time, if he could never be well enough to understand how much he needed her, then she too would return to the clinic. There she could be sealed within a core of timelessness, a vacuum of emotion where nothing could be felt. If Francis could not learn to love her, she would not allow herself to feel ever again. Never, never again.

Chapter 25

Francis had dreamed
again about a black-
haired, young, small, vi-
vacious woman he had never seen beyond the dreams. They
were at concerts together most of the time but there were
other times when he made love to her. She was so whole, so
completely a living entity, it baffled him that she was not
only unknown to him, but being unknown could still return
unchanged in dream after dream. Dr. Boscawen explained
it at last. The black-haired woman was merely a personified
symbol of his love for music.

Powell and Shaw arrived in Geneva before Lady Sian and
Lady Celia, with the Hispano-Suiza and the Straker Squire
two-seater. Both drivers had become lost en route and had
telegraphed for additional funds: Powell from the German
frontier above Strasbourg and Shaw from Carcassonne, despite the fact that they had started out together. When they
finally arrived a day apart Powell tried to give the impression that the roads had taken wrong turnings of their own

will, substituting false signs and routes merely to make a fool of him. Shaw implied that Powell had purposely given him the wrong directions so that he could appear the superior driver by arriving earlier.

Francis baked a welcoming cake in the shape of a roulette wheel, with a model of the Hispano-Suiza on top of it and with the letters of the names S-I-A-N, C-E-L-I-A and F-R-A-N-C-I-S substituted for the numbers on the wheel. When he met Sian and Celia at the station Powell and Shaw stood behind him on the platform laden down with flowers. They all stood at attention twelve hundred feet above the smoky cities of Europe on a brilliantly sunny day. When Sian stepped down from the train Francis discovered that he was standing at the wrong end of the car, and he sprinted toward her, shouting her name. She turned in surprise and walked toward him, laughing almost drunkenly, both arms outstretched. Their hands touched briefly, and then Celia called out from the train steps. "Mr. Hillairet!" she cried. "Please watch me come down these steps alone."

Francis and Sian stared while Celia almost danced down the steps. They broke into applause, and Powell and Shaw, bunching the flowers under their arms, joined in. Francis, remembering the flowers, whirled, grasped the nearest bouquet and gave it to Sian. Grabbing another, he raced with it to Celia. As he rushed up to her she studied his face intently, staring at his mouth, her transfixed face masked from her mother's view by Francis' back. Her large blue eyes, which dominated her face like moons, pulled him as inexorably as the tides. In that shared instant she seemed to have possessed him.

He felt exhilaration as though it were a fountain of liquid gold racing up through the thin tube of his soul. Thousands of miles into the sky it mounted, then poured itself down to cover the planet. He felt himself multiply too rapidly to be counted, and all these versions of himself raced after and overtook the uncountable multiplications of her, then these myriads of shining, vibrating immortal figures fell beside each other and imploded glories within each other. Then Sian was at his left arm and Celia had looked away from him. He found himself on the station platform again, as though he had just journeyed through the stars and the music of the spheres still rang in his mind.

In the instant she had looked at him Celia knew that Francis was her mother's lover. She had never seen her mother look so happy.

While Powell and Shaw bumbled and tripped over mountains of luggage, Francis put the ladies into the Straker Squire and they raced across the Mont Blanc bridge, then along the quay to the Cologny ramp, with Sian and Celia clutching their hats and rhapsodizing about the city. As they crossed the bridge the Alps spread for a hundred square miles before them, and to the right the Saleve sat like a huge *terrine du chef* waiting to be sliced on Judgment Day. To their left the lake stretched for forty miles in another guise of the River Rhone, and the green hills of the Jura marched northward behind them.

The two women were exhilarated again by the villa: walled gardens, rolling lawns, orchards, fields and farm buildings surrounded a large rambling country house which faced the lake on one side and the Alps on the other. After an old-fashioned, long-lined welcome by the newly assembled staff, they sat down to a modest repast Francis had prepared: potage Billi-bi, paillettes dorées; turbans de lavaret cardinalisées; le canard à la façon de Gillian Renard; les fromages de Reblochon et de Saint-Marcellin. There was a Puligny-Montrachet "Clos de la Pucelle" '04 with the lavaret, a year-old Julienas with the duck, and a Chateau Ausone '00 with the cheese.

Celia ate as though she had just discovered food—as indeed she had. "What can I have been eating at Donen Hall?" she moaned. "I've never tasted anything as delicious as this food." At the end of the meal she insisted on being escorted to the kitchen to thank the cook. Sian laughed heartily and Francis did his best to look diffident.

"Why are you two laughing and grinning?"

"Because you have been dining with the cook."

"Mr. Hillairet?"

"Please call me Francis."

Celia exclaimed that merely thanking Francis for such genius was not enough; what she felt had to be made a matter of record. She dashed out of the room, saying that she would be right back. As soon as the door closed behind her, Sian slipped quickly out of her chair, ran around the table to Francis, held his face in her hands and kissed him again and again. Then she rushed back to her seat, and Powell and Shaw entered the room as she was sipping coffee daintily.

"The baggage is here, moddom," Powell nasalated in a Scot's snarl covered with guttural gorse and brackened burs.

"You know I don't want it here. Put it where it should be."

"Yes, moddom." He backed away, and the two men collided with each other as they tried to get through the door simultaneously.

"Shall we look at the porch?" Sian asked tactfully. As they walked toward the outer door she whispered, "Please go to Geneva at once and rent rooms for us. They must be ready tomorrow, when I'll be sending Celia on an automobile tour to Lausanne."

Celia came back, half-running, with two pieces of notepaper. "You must sign your certificate as well, Mama," she said, and began to read from one of the sheets: " 'Dear Mr. Hillairet: You are one of the greatest living masters of cooking, and I hope with all my heart that I may continue to enjoy the results of your gastronomic genius for many long and happy years.' "

"I'll sign that with the greatest pleasure," Sian said.

"No, no," Celia answered. "I sign that one. This one is yours."

As she handed the sheet to her mother their eyes locked over it for a moment, and then Celia looked away. Sian took the coronet embossed notepaper and read aloud: " 'Dear Mr. Hillairet: Please accept this as my fullest endorsement of your skills in all departments of endeavor.' " She looked up quickly at Celia, and then read on: " 'Particularly insofar as your cooking is concerned. For me you are the chef of chefs, the bearer of ambrosial pleasures.' " Sian's face went quite blank and then flushed before she could force it into a gay expression. "Quite a recommendation," she said, accepting the pen from Celia, "but one which is richly deserved." As she signed her name, Francis thanked her. "I am terribly moved by this, Lady Celia," he said. "And equally grateful to you, Sian. My art means a great deal to me, but this sincere appreciation means even more."

The long trip had been quite wearing, and the ladies decided to withdraw for a nap. With a glance at Sian, Francis said that he had to go to town on business but that perhaps in two or three hours they might like to drive to Evian to test the new roulette system that Sian had invented on the spot at the sight of Francis' magnificent cake.

As he drove into Geneva, Francis abandoned any thought of making any arrangements at a hotel. Too sordid. The same applied to a room in a pension, no matter how stylish. He would have to rent a flat for the summer. *Celia.* As he considered what the flat should be, that word was illuminated on and off in his mind steadily. *Celia.* As he drove he checked off various sections of the city, but his excitement at the thought of Celia, of being with Celia did not make for clear thinking. He decided that the flat, however infrequently used, must be in the best section of the city. These were not just women he would be sleeping with; they were a marchioness and a baroness. Celia. *Celia.*

Francis drove to Regie Bonet in the rue de la Corraterie. Mme. Bonet had rented him the villa. He asked for a small flat in the rue des Granges, overlooking the Place Neuve.

"That is impossible, monsieur."

"It will be a place of repose for me—a sort of hideaway for the summer. It doesn't have to be a small flat."

"But—"

"I have not specified any minimum price, have I?"

"It could be that we have perhaps one flat—but enormous —which might just now be empty—"

"One flat will be sufficient, of course."

After consulting her records, Mme. Bonet said she was not sure that she was doing the right thing, but something possibly might be arranged—people with flats traveled. In

the Straker Squire they drove to the rue des Granges and
stopped before an imposing building. At the entrance, however, Francis stopped short and refused even to enter. "Just
one moment, madame," he said sternly, glaring at her. "You
know as well or better than I that the odd numbers in the
rue des Granges are *de trop*. The odd numbers are the
Catholic side of the street; they are simply not the place to
live in the rue des Granges."

"But you said it was to be a hideaway. What difference
can the wrong side of the street mean to a hideaway?"

"I said it was for repose, and I could not find repose on the
wrong side of the street. You will have to find me a building
with an even number."

A veritable plantation of a flat with sixteen rooms was
found.

It was sunny, pleasant, furnished and impeccably correct,
and was the property of the chief of state of one of the larger
South American republics who felt that a leader should
always have a place to go, but who had not needed to use it
yet. Mme. Bonet asked Francis if he read the newspapers
with regularity. "Every morning and every evening," Francis
answered. Mme. Bonet told him the name of the republic
and made him promise that if he should read of the over-
throw of its government, he would clear all of his belong-
ings out of the apartment within twenty-four hours. Francis
took the apartment on the spot, and the *regie* agreed to send
the contracts to the villa and handed over the keys.

On the way home Francis stopped at a café on the Quai
Gustave Ador, ordered coffee and tried to understand what
had happened to him. He could not imagine how he had
navigated through the day since the moment he had looked
into Celia's eyes on the train platform, nor how he was going
to survive the days looming ahead. He had never known a
feeling like this. It was exactly as though he had never been
able to feel anything before—as Sian had insisted again and
again—and that Celia had unlocked the hidden prison from
which his emotions had been struggling to free themselves
since his birth. He could not think of a way to be alone with
her, but it had to be done. What could be done about Sian?

It was not possible. He loved Sian; he would always love Sian. She had been very, very kind to him, but this was something that had nothing to do with her.

He had to make a plan, but it must be a plan which took cognizance of all the vital goals he must achieve in the years to come. He had just endured two near-scandals in London, the last of which had supposedly gotten him barred from England for life; indeed, were it not for his peerage he undoubtedly would have been barred for life. If Sian decided to do anything drastic when he took Celia away with him . . . He moaned as he thought of the damage Sian would do his social career in England, and there could be no doubt about the outcome. He and Celia would have to withdraw to Paris, *persona non grata* in London. But though Paris was a distinguished enough old society, even though there was too much Bonaparte aristocracy for his taste, he would be settling for second place. Warsaw? Rome? Stockholm was said to be prodigiously aristocratic but he didn't care that much for fish.

This had to stop. He had to renounce Celia. But he could not. With his peerage would come the obligation to breed sons, and Sian was too old to even think of that. It had to be Celia. He must manage everything very slowly and with complete control; he must move carefully and watch his every move. Although he knew he was merely deceiving himself, he could pretend that all this surge of emotion about Celia was just a passing fancy which would eventually disappear. He decided to put down everything he felt for her as mere physical attraction; once it was consummated, it would be over. She was a young girl who had lived a sheltered life, mostly inside romantic books. She would cherish a romantic experience, and then he could return to Sian so that they could win a distinguished place for him at the center of the British peerage. Sickeningly, Francis had the fright that he might have lost the knack of deluding himself. He knew the feelings—so alien, so disturbing—which Celia had induced in him could not be anything less than what poets kept talking about. He loved her. This was what those words meant—well, for him at any rate it was what they meant. He was obsessed with her, and it would become worse and worse. He had to keep control of himself; he had to listen to everything he said before he spoke; he had to force this prodigious emotion underground and to conceal it until the time came when he could reveal all of it.

At six o'clock that evening Powell drove them to Evian to investigate the casino. They dined leisurely and well, and then played, using the system which Sian wrote out carefully for them at the dinner table. "Everyone's name becomes a number, as on Francis' beautiful cake," she said. "I will take Celia's name, Celia will take mine, and Francis will bet on his own—as a man should. Celia, you will bet on these numbers in succession, never varying the succession: nineteen for S, nine for I, one for A, and fourteen for N." After allotting other numbers to herself and Francis they entered the casino.

At midnight, the time limit Sian had set for play, Celia had won 17,446 francs, Sian had won 46,510 francs and Francis had lost 103,796 francs.

"Oh, well," Sian said, "unlucky at chance, lucky in love."

Throughout the drive to Evian and at dinner, Sian had grown more and more intense. She was almost faint with her physical desire for Francis, and this was magnified because she could not imagine how they were going to be able to be alone together frequently. Whenever her daughter spoke, Sian found herself staring at her coldly, sometimes with hostility, until suddenly she remembered herself as the terrible woman she had been when all the men in the family had been alive and Celia had seemed to threaten their adoring attention to herself. Now once again she was beginning to isolate Celia because again her daughter had become a distraction to the only man Sian had left to herself.

She must stop herself from feeling this way; she couldn't lose Celia again. She excused herself from the table, and in the powder room, ran cold water over her wrists until she felt calmer. Then she sat alone for a few minutes, sipping a Williamine and repeating to herself over and over again that no matter what happened, she and Celia must stay together. On Celia she had bestowed new life. The girl was intoxicated by a new foot, by new dresses, by new countries and by her first experience of attention by a most courteous man, the first gallant she had ever met. Celia loved her mother very much, and their relationship must not be destroyed for the foolish, selfish reason that Sian wanted Francis all to herself. She must find serenity. If these feelings grew worse she would retreat to the clinic for forty-eight hours to think sobering thoughts about the vastness of the sky, the short-ness of time on earth, and to take long deep breaths.

Before either of them had any notion that such a miracle could occur, Francis and Celia were alone together. He stared at her as he had at the station, his eyes imposing physical weight and urgency upon her. Careful to speak very correctly, alluding to nothing in the past or in the future, he talked to her a long while about dancing, because that seemed to be her greatest interest. But finally, as he paused and looked away, he lost his resolve. In a rush of words, despite himself, he said, "This morning I cannot explain what I felt as you looked up at me. I have never felt anything like the feeling of you, Celia. Not in my life."

"Mama!" Celia whispered harshly.

Composed, Sian returned to the table in time to overhear Francis saying, ". . . and I suppose the waltz came directly from the *volta* in the sixteenth century—not directly, per-haps, but the volta was the grandparent of all ballroom dancing." He looked up. "Ah, Sian. At last." He stood up and swept back her chair.

Sian sat down, smiling sweetly. "Go on. Please go on. Don't let me interrupt."

"Francis knows so much about dancing," Celia said.

"Then he must tell me, as well."

"The first *volta*," Francis said as he sat down again, "was considered indecent, even though men and women barely touched hands."

"Just so they didn't touch hands barely," Sian said.

"Mother!"

"Gradually, attitudes changed. Men were allowed to put their arms around girls' waists while dancing. Then men were even allowed to kiss their partners."

"I don't know how that could have died out," Sian said.

"Mama has told me that you will teach me to waltz," Celia said to Francis.

"Did I?"

"I talk about dancing, but I don't waltz at all well," Francis answered.

"But they say if one can count, one can waltz."

"You must learn to dance, Celia," Sian told her, "and tomorrow we shall find you the best teacher in Geneva."

"Oh, Mama!" Celia clapped her hands together.

"How does one find a dancing master, Francis?"

"I will have his name by noon tomorrow. My fencing master or my singing teacher will know."

"Fencing master?"

"Singing teacher?"

"I always feel at my best studying something. It gives me a feeling of going forward, you know. Fencing is good for bodily poise and discipline, and the singing teacher says that I don't have a bad voice at all."

"When will you sing to me?"

Both women had spoken simultaneously. They looked at each other blankly for an instant, then began to laugh heartily to cover their confusion.

"With the Dowager Marchioness of Shattock at the piano—"

"Celia plays the guitar," Sian said with false animation.

"—and the Baroness Keys at the guitar," Francis added smoothly, "we will all delight each other at a musicale tomorrow evening."

They arrived home at two o'clock, and Francis was pleased to see that the ladies' maids he'd sent from Paris were waiting. It stiffened his belief in the system to see a lady's maid waiting, no matter what the hour.

Everyone said he was quite tired and everyone retired at once. They all slept at last, but they did not sleep until much later, and then very badly.

Though she was twenty years old, Celia had never been near a man like Francis. He seemed so wise—but the way he had reacted at the station and what he had said at dinner that evening seemed not so wise. He was so beautiful, so elegant and worldly, but his impetuousness in wanting to make love to her, as love was made in all the novels at Donen Hall, and particularly in the hoarded novels of Kershaw, the butler, wasn't worldly. Worldly men did such things imperiously, wearily. She knew about men; they were revealed for what they were in all those novels. She wanted a man of her own, and Francis was breath-taking, but she knew that he belonged to her mother and not to her. It was so sordid to think of beginning one's life with men by borrowing someone else's, particularly Mama's. But perhaps Mama needn't know about it. It certainly could not be the usual practice for young women to take their first lovers from their mothers; few young girls could have gotten started that way because so few mothers had lovers. It was also true that very few mothers had lovers who were as exciting and as endearing as Francis.

She had to decide. She didn't have to decide right now, but she might just as well do so—because he would be more insistent, and considering the high pitch on which he had started, it would not be possible for him to pursue her much longer without everything ending in a dreadful scene.

She had been alone for so many years, but now that was over. That meant not only being out in the world and going to restaurants and chatting with many different people; it also meant making love and being in love and learning about men, not from books but from loving them. She had been storing up love for so long, and now she wanted to give it to someone. Mama loved her; Francis loved her; she loved Mama. If only it were possible to know how Mama really felt about Francis—whether it was deep and forever the way it had been with Papa, or whether it was just good health and commendable appetite. If only she could be sure that her mother's feeling for Francis was nothing more morbid than sensuality, she could do what she wanted to do, which was to make love to Francis and have Francis make love to her. Her first man had to be exactly like Francis—not a boy, but a cultivated, experienced, adept and beautiful man. Francis. Francis. Mama. Oh dear, what should she do?

The next morning, when Sian heard Celia stirring in her room, she bounded out of bed and rang for breakfast. Both women reached the top of the staircase, dressed for a day in the country, at the same time.

Celia was momentarily cross; her mother was usually a late riser, and she had hoped to have had time alone with Francis. "Good morning, Mama. Did you have a good rest?"

"A wonderful rest, dear."

"So did I. It must be the altitude which makes one sleep so well."

"You are very beautiful this morning, Celia."

"Not as beautiful as you, Mama."

They trooped down the stairs arm in arm—Celia tiny, rounded and fair, Sian tall with Grecian flatness below her full, high bosom. Sian's height and red hair and deep-set eyes made Celia seem young and innocent, yet not childlike; in the way her face looked out to find the world, Sian seemed more of a child.

Francis was strolling across the lawn toward the house when they walked out on the porch. Once again everyone exchanged information about how well they had slept; then Francis asked what the program for the day was.

Sian answered instantly. "I must go to the clinic to pay my respects to Dr. Boscawen."

"Oh!" Celia tried to sound disappointed.

"I have a fencing lesson," Francis said, "and I must see my voice teacher about finding a dancing class for Celia."

"May I go with you?" Celia asked.

He was almost irresistibly tempted, but he said, "Not at this stage of my development as a fencer."

"Then this is an excellent chance for Celia to see the countryside around the lake," Sian said firmly. "I'll have Cook make a basket lunch and Powell will drive you to Lausanne and back. We'll all meet here in time for the evening concert."

"Oh, Mama, not Powell," Celia moaned. "At least give me Shaw."

"Shaw it is. How pleased that silly man will be!"

Sian was overwhelmed at the magnificence of the flat in the rue des Granges. "Good heavens, it looks like the sanctuary of some South American dictator."

"As a matter of fact, I think the *regie* said it is."

"I meant a little room somewhere, Francis darling. This is an assignation lodge for a dynasty."

"She tried to stick me with an odd-numbered building, thinking I wouldn't know."

"Wouldn't know what?"

"Well, this is the rue des Granges. It is *the* street in Geneva. But the odd-numbered side is déclassé."

She stared at him. "But how are we going to copulate snobbishly?"

"What?"

This exchange and her preoccupation with the problem of Celia prevented Sian, for the first time with Francis, from having an orgasm, which depressed her and fairly exhausted Francis. She lay on her back with her eyes closed, Francis wheezing like a steam train beside her.

"It was a dreadful mistake my bringing Celia here."

"Why?" For an instant he was alarmed that she could read his thoughts.

"Because we can't have a normal life while we all live together. For a widow of forty to be made to feel that she must sneak off to bed with her lover is repellent."

"But must we?" He was taking a chance, but he felt sure he knew what her answer would be. "Celia is twenty," he said. "That makes her a woman. Surely she wouldn't be surprised if—and the odds against it are almost impossible— she found me coming out of your room at five o'clock in the morning. She's fast asleep at that hour."

"It would be too sordid if it did happen."

"It couldn't happen!"

"Furthermore, Celia is not a woman—neither by worldly standards nor emotionally. She has had no chance to learn any of these things, and they would only confuse her terribly. For all I know she may believe in the stork."

"If she believes in the stork we are thoroughly safe, because then would she question it if I visited you in the night? I would say I had brought you a hot-water bottle."

"Oh, dammit, Francis, don't be so dense! Besides, my room is directly next to hers, and I like to shout whatever I feel when I'm making love. I couldn't do that. Storks or not, what I would yell wouldn't go down with Celia; she'd think I'd gone mad again or that I was in terrible pain."

"Why did you put her room next to yours?"

"I didn't!"

"Who did?"

"I thought you had."

"But I didn't take you to your room. How did you find the room you took?"

"My baggage was in there." She clapped a hand to her head. "Powell and Shaw, the foursquare new Englishmen! Those bunglers! They did it! They dropped the baggage in the first room they saw, and that was that."

"If you don't like this flat we can—"

"Darling, it isn't this wonderful flat on the only acceptable side of the best street of Geneva; it's simply, what are we going to do about Celia? We can't always outwit her. I don't have the strength or the imagination to dream up a new ruse every day to keep her busy. Besides, it would be rude."

Sian sat up, so fast that her breasts joggled deliciously. "The British Embassy! We must have an embassy at the League of Nations here, and if there is, they must have two acceptable young men—that's a fixed Foreign Office rule." She leaned across him in the bed to reach the telephone on the far table, and he kissed the underside of one breast as it flashed by.

"The British Embassy, please," Sian said in French into the telephone. She waited, "Hello? Is that the British Embassy? What is the name of your Ambassador? Sir Richard *Adler?* Oh, sheer heaven! Let me speak with him, please. This is the Marchioness of Shattock." She put her hand over the mouthpiece to speak to Francis. "I say, we are in luck.

Imagine! Dickie Adler!" Into the mouthpiece she said,
"Dickie? Oh, darling, how clever of you to be posted here.
How is Jane? Oh, isn't this *marvelous!* Celia and I will be
here for the summer, and she is looking very beautiful . . .
right behind Cologny . . . Haut-Crêt . . . it's called Les
Haubans. When can you come to dinner? . . . Yes, do
look." She beamed at Francis; all at once she knew there
would be no trouble about an orgasm when she disconnected. ". . . Friday will be perfect. And, Dickie? Do you
have two of the usual beautiful young men whom you can
bring along to sit on either side of Celia? . . . Oh, Dickie,
you are a darling. My love to Jane . . . Until Friday, then."

She put the telephone carefully back in its place, took
Francis in her arms, and began to ascend the north face of
one of the highest orgasms she had ever climbed. On reaching the summit, she greatly cheered a young watercolorist
painting in the garret directly above them by celebrating the
victorious ascent with outcries as exultant as those of a
Cunard liner.

They rested silently for a considerable time. At last Sian
spoke, very subdued. "But, my God, they aren't coming until
Friday. This is Monday." She rolled on her side to face him.
"How are we going to manage Tuesday, Wednesday, Thursday and Friday afternoons?"

He blinked with an enormous effort, "Dancing," he said.

"The dancing! Oh, darling, of course, the dancing. But we
must do it cleverly. We must have a chat with the dancing
master and insist that he give her one hour of theory. A
lecture on the philosophy, history and psychology of the
dance; then one hour of dancing. And she must be careful to
shower and to change so that she will not catch cold. What
with dressing, undressing, showering, toweling and dressing
again—plus the lectures *and* the dancing lessons—it should
use up three hours easily."

"I don't think they have showers in Switzerland."

"Nonsense."

Francis shrugged. "And I don't think she could dance
every day."

"Why not?"

"She would have to be a trained athlete. Anyway, if she went every day she might be tired of dancing by the end of the week."

"Dancing is a psychological *thing* with Celia! She could never grow tired of it."

"Three hours a day, five days a week is too much at the beginning."

"How often, then?"

"Three hours every other day."

Francis telephoned his voice teacher, who said he would make a few telephone calls. In twenty minutes he called back with the name and address of a dancing master of excellent reputation. Francis dropped Sian off at the dancing school on the grounds that it would be less suspicious if one of them were at home when Celia returned. He would send Powell to pick her up. "But this is exactly what I resent," Sian said. "Why must I have to deceive my own daughter in order to enjoy the identical natural act which made her existence possible in the first place?"

Francis felt a flash of fear that it would soon occur to Sian that the only solution to their quandary was marriage. Celia had to be tucked away somewhere for a few hours each day so that Sian could be kept appeased. Then he would have to invent ways to dispose of Sian for certain intervals so that he could win Celia. "If she studies dancing three days a week," he said, "we will ask the Ambassador to release one of his young men to take up the other afternoons—there are two of them for the duty after all—and we certainly should be able to forgo Sunday afternoons for her."

"Does she bore you, darling?"

"I didn't say any such thing."

"But you implied—"

"I meant only that one afternoon out of seven would be left over, and that—"

"Sunday in the country, darling! We will fill the house. That is what one does on Sunday in the country."

Seated on a swollen Victorian sofa, Sian waited in the small office of the dancing school in La Gradelle. The door opened, and a young man with shaggy black hair and eyebrows like fur awnings came into the room.

"Madam?"

"I am the Marchioness of Shattock."

"I am Duvalier."

"The dancing master?"

"I am the dancing master."

"What sort of dancing do you teach?"

"What do you wish to learn?"

"Not me. My daughter."

"A small child?"

"A girl of twenty."

"What has she studied?"

"Nothing yet. I wished to know if you are prepared to discuss the theory of the dance as a part of her instruction."

"Theory?"

"The history of dancing. Its philosophy. The disciplines and ideologies of great dancers of the past. The cultural conceptions of dance styles."

"She doesn't wish to learn how to dance?"

"Of course, but I want her to know the theory of the art as well." She was irritable and impatient to return to Francis. "Can you do it?"

Duvalier shrugged, "I have no objection."

"When could she start?"

"Do you wish private instruction for her?"

"Yes."

"At what time of day?"

"Oh, uh, three to, uh, five."

"She can begin on Wednesday, the day after tomorrow."

"I think—that is, I want the lessons to be three times a week."

"First I will see her. I will decide if she can learn to dance; then we will consider the schedule."

"Do your best to think in terms of Monday, Wednesday and Friday." She extended her hand and Duvalier shook it firmly. "One more thing," Sian said. "Do you have shower baths?"

His eyes widened and Duvalier smiled with enormous

pleasure. "You happen to be standing in the most modern dancing school in Europe, Madame," he replied. "This house may be the only house in Geneva, including all the hotels, which happens to have showers, because I, the master, believe in showers for the muscle tone. I have imported this shower at quite incredible cost from England."

"I am pleased."

"However, if your daughter is to have the dressing room with the shower there will be an extra cost of twenty-two per cent."

"I can see that you are an artist," Sian said. "Please bill me at Villa Les Haubans, Haut-Crêt."

"Thank you, madame."

In the Straker Squire, Francis sped back to the villa. Celia was painting. She faced the Alps, and her back and her long blond hair were all he could see as he hurried across the lawn. "How did you get back so early?" he called out to her.

She turned, smiling. "Shaw was watching either a pair of Pekingese or a small boat, and drove the car into a culvert. Luckily we were going quite slowly. He's still muddling it through, but I took a taxi here. Where is Mama?"

"I believe she's making the arrangements for your dancing studies."

"That's wonderful. I can hardly wait to begin."

"It's even more wonderful to be alone with you here."

"Alone? I suspect that about four servants are watching us at this moment."

"Do you mean that we can't ever—"

"Whatever *you* mean," Celia said calmly, "and whatever you want, can't be done here."

Francis sat down on a lawn chair near the easel.

"Move it back just a few feet," Celia said. "I think I'll try to paint your portrait." She took down the landscape she had begun and put a blank canvas on the easel.

Francis moved under the shade of the nearest tree. "Here?"

"Fine. Just look at me. At my face or my shoulder."

The sun warmed everything before Francis' eyes. It illuminated Celia's hair. She perched so lightly upon her stool that her bones seemed to him as hollow as a pelican's. She was flawless. If he weren't afraid of weeping he would laugh at the thought of the hundreds of times Sian had told him he possessed no feelings, that somehow he must learn the art. He seemed to have lost all power to stop himself from sliding down a steep hill at whose bottom he knew lay total darkness. Something about her was evoking a past he had never had. Perhaps she was something he had wanted long ago, and by losing her his feelings had been frozen until the renewed sight of her had melted them again. But there was no future for them, and there had been no past; there was only now and the brilliance of light which surrounded them. For the first time in his life Francis found himself living in the present.

"Celia, what are you going to do?"

"When?"

"With your life."

"I am going to dance."

"*Dance?*" If she had said she was going to knit or pluck petals from daisies for the rest of her life he could not have been more dismayed.

"That is all I ever wanted to do."

"Because of your foot?"

"I suppose so. It's an easy theory, at any rate, and so many people would be chagrined if that were not the explanation."

"You think it is not your foot?"

"Who knows? If it means anything, I suspect I want to dance because I was a prisoner for so long. Two feet would not have set me free. But if I could have danced, that would have freed me."

Though Francis followed her words, he was scarcely able to listen. Where could they find a meeting place? How could he reach her?

"I can't dance," he said. "I cannot even understand people who want to dance."

"I'm sorry."

"But I can talk about dancing. Does that bring us any closer?"

"It quiets my impatience—or it did. Perhaps now I am too close to dancing, and when I begin I may not be able to stop."

He stared at her, half afraid that she would run away, half afraid that she would not. Dancing. Why must there always be these elusive differences between people, when all that one of them was trying to convince the other was that the barrier of time between them did not matter? Could he learn to dance? He had mastered a dozen more difficult things, he told himself, and he had the iron determination to work as he had never worked before. But even if he could dance like Nijinsky, what about the rest? She knew less than nothing and he had taught himself too much. She would do everything by feeling, whereas he had dulled his feeling for everything but her by absorbing facts and rules. He had discarded what little he had been able to feel by training his memory to a point far beyond what this girl could ever learn, and in the process, had stunted himself so that he could never approach what she was able to feel. He felt like a boy with his arms outstretched to take the moon; the distance was too great between them. But if there was no place where their minds could meet, their bodies could touch, and in that way they could meet on common ground.

"I dream too," he said.

"Tell me."

"High places, honor, achievement. The male goals."

"Unreachable directly and so unlike an esthetic goal."

"For me, it has all been a most esthetic dance with a blindfold around my eyes. I've danced along the edges of icy cliffs and I've danced along greased ropes above yawning chasms. My life is a dance."

"Yes," Celia answered gravely. "Life must be a dance."

She would never be able to understand him, he was appalled to realize, because of the armor in which he had encased himself so securely that he could never get it off. He had welded all of it into place himself, piece by piece, and now it was so impenetrable that he could not remember what he had once been, beneath it.

A car came up the driveway and they turned to look. It was a taxi, and Sian stepped out of it. She seemed quite angry as she stalked toward them. "Damn you, Francis," she said. "You forgot to send the car for me."

He scrambled to his feet. "I am so sorry, Sian. I don't know how I could have forgotten."

"Shaw has disabled the car, Mama!" Celia said gleefully. "Isn't he a marvel? Today puts him equal in ineptitude to Powell."

"Oh, now I am really cross."

"And the moment Francis arrived I made him pose for his portrait. He didn't have a moment to send the car, if there had been a car to send."

At last Sian exploded her heavenly smile and held out a large package to Celia.

"What is it?"

"Leotards and slippers."

"Mama!"

"You will begin to dance on Wednesday afternoon at three o'clock."

"Oh, Mama!"

"The teacher is divine." She turned to Francis. "And, of course, the school does have a shower bath."

Chapter 26

 At the impromptu musicale that evening, the women were dismayed by Francis' singing.

"But you have an absolutely terrible voice," Sian told him.

"I have?"

"If you were dancing," Celia said, "you'd be hobbling."

"If you fence the way you sing, I can only say that it is a fortunate thing that we have moved into the era of the machine gun."

"But my voice teacher told me—"

"He must be a master criminal. Professor Moriarty may not have died at the Reichenbach Falls."

"You are not a natural singer, Francis," Celia explained, "and I don't think any teacher should be cruel enough to encourage you."

"Thank you very much," Francis replied. They were of the ancient peerage and they must know. "I really had no idea."

On Tuesday they drove completely around the lake in the

repaired car. Before departure Sian ordered Powell and
Shaw to empty their pockets; if they botched one thing that
day she would make them walk home. Before turning toward the far side of the lake they drove up to the Valais to
buy two cases of Fendant wine, but the man who sold it
advised them to drink it there. "The wine doesn't travel," he
said.

"Geneva is only sixty miles," Francis answered.

The man shrugged. They opened a bottle, and it was
delicious. They drove down to the lake again and had lunch
at Montreux, then returned to the villa by way of Lausanne
and Nyon. At home they opened another bottle of wine, and
Sian cursed the man for insisting that they taste the wine in
the highlands, for then they wouldn't have been aware of the
startling difference in taste.

After dinner they sat on the porch and sang three-part
harmony with fervor. The summer, which was not due for
over a month, seemed impatient to join them; the crickets
were celebrating the new greenness and the smell of spring
was heavy.

Everyone slept late on Wednesday. At lunch Francis
offered to drive Celia to dancing school, since he was going
to town to terminate the services of his voice teacher. Sian
left immediately after lunch to visit Dr. Boscawen at
Anieres, and as soon as she was out the door, Francis
suggested tensely that he and Celia set off a bit early so that
she would have time to store her things and familiarize
herself with the school.

In the two-seater Francis drove down the Haut-Crêt toward the city, but almost immediately he turned into a
walled lane called Chemin de Tirage which separated the
town's small cemetery into two parts. The lane was deserted
and very quiet.

"Why are we stopping?" Celia asked.

"I have to talk to you."

"But—"

"I can't go on any longer this way."

"I've been thinking about you too, Francis."

"I love you, Celia."

"Oh, Francis!" It was just like the books. She turned her face to him and he put his arms around her and kissed her. It was the first time she had ever been kissed, and though it lasted a long time, it did not seem long enough.

"That . . . was . . . so . . . exciting!" she gasped.

"Celia, we must be alone."

"We are alone."

"I mean *really* alone."

"Behind locked doors?"

He inhaled sharply. "Yes."

"Do you want to seduce me?"

"Celia!"

"Don't you want to be my lover?"

"I must be."

"But what about Mama?"

He shrugged in agony.

"I have thought about you so much," Celia said, "but perhaps I am drawn to you because Mama is in love with you." She grasped his coat lapel and gazed beseechingly up into his yellow eyes. "If we ever are alone the way you say, Francis, must you stop with Mama?"

"Stop?"

"Stop making love to her the way you want to make love to me? If that is so, I will not do it. You must continue with Mama the way you always have, and if you are in the practice of telling her that you love her, you must keep telling her that whether you mean it or not, just as you must say it to me whether you mean it or not."

"Mean it? Celia, I have never said that to anyone but you. I cannot live without you. Listen to me—hear these words— I know I sound like a lovestruck boy, but it is true."

"When I said I am drawn to you because Mama loves you, I want it to be entirely clear that if we should ever do what you want us to do, it would not be for any such silly reason as wanting to take revenge on her for having left me alone. I love Mama, and I understand why she had to do that. What I meant was that if Mama loves you, you must be a remarkable lover, because Mama must excel—she *must* excel."

"Will you come with me tomorrow?"

"Do you agree to continue with Mama?"

"Yes! Yes!" he said with some impatience.

"When will you be with her again?"

"I will not say."

"Now? This afternoon when I am dancing?"

"I tell you I refuse to talk about that, Celia."

"I could say that I wanted to dance every day. I could say that I had arranged to go again tomorrow, and then we could—"

"Yes. This time tomorrow," Francis said hoarsely. He kissed her again, and as she luxuriated in it she thought of all the men she'd had in her imagination, all of them characters in novels in which all girls, when they reached a certain age, an age far younger than her own, had wonderful lovers. Now she would too, and it was all right to let Francis make love to her simply because he *did* belong to Mama. She had to grope her way in learning to make love; she couldn't start out with some total stranger. For one thing she didn't even know any total strangers. And if Mama thought well enough of Francis to leave England for him, he must be perfect as a lover in every way, even if he was quite mad.

As Sian was driven through the beautiful, open fields behind Anieres she felt a pang of longing for those three years when she did not have to think, when she had been able to remain as patient as a vegetable and look out upon the lake. Many of her friends were still at the clinic, and she got out of the car as it entered the grounds and greeted them as she made her way toward the main door. She stopped and chatted with Mrs. Langley, who believed that she was dead and that the clinic was heaven; with the charming, nameless Austrian woman who had burned her children to death; with Mr. Flanson, who at will was able to go totally blind in either eye or in both together. Everyone was happy to see her and pleased and relieved that she had been able to return to safety from the outside world.

Sian and Dr. Boscawen sat on the tiny porch overlooking the lake and talked about Francis. "Is he steady?" the doctor asked.

"A rock."

"Good. But observe the rules."

"We are very careful. Celia knows as well what not to say."

"He can become homicidal again, of course," the doctor said gravely. "But the conditions which would bring it on are so remote that I hope I have done the right thing in allowing him to leave here and stay with you."

"In London he asked me to marry him."

"Do you want that?"

"More than anything else in the world. I love him."

"When will it happen?"

"I don't know. I really don't know."

"I suppose that everything is for the best. Do you believe that?"

"I do not."

"Do you believe that everything is for the worst?"

"I simply don't know whether it was better to have been widowed by the killing of the man I loved more than my own life, or whether it is worse to be hopelessly in love with a homicidal maniac. But at last I love a man who is alive. And no one really chooses the person with whom she falls in love."

"Ideally, we choose each other."

"Ideally?"

"Nature doesn't care if two people love, or if neither loves, or even if only one loves."

"You don't think Francis is capable of caring?"

The doctor shrugged. "Why do you say I think that?"

"If you had said it, I might agree with you were it not for the fact that my case is a rare exception. When one examines Francis' special madness, one sees how special and disgusting it is."

"How?"

"He is so insane that he believes he is superior. The lowborn are dirt to him. His only exception is one small social group on the planet—the British peerage. He knows he is superior to all Italian opera singers, all white American Protestants, all French generals, Buddhists, all members of the bar, all German poets and all of everyone else except the British peerage. He feels inferior to us—which is as revolting as his feeling of being superior to everyone else. But that special quality of his sickness makes me the exception. Oh, I grant you he could run off with some other lady peer after we get married, but I shall know how to screen him effectively from those. Right now he loves me in his fashion and I don't mind his terms one bit."

"Men are men," the doctor murmured. "If these weren't the terms, there would be something else." She smiled. "But if it turned out that Francis was incapable of truly loving you, what would you do?"

"Return to this place."

"You can say that so quickly? Have you thought about it?"

"I suppose I have."

"But you are not psychotic."

Sian sighed and stared bleakly out upon the lake. "What do you think I should do if I become convinced that Francis is incapable of loving me?"

"We are only conjecturing."

"Very well, let us conjecture."

"Why is the only alternative for a beautiful woman who has been crossed in love to hide herself away in a mental clinic?"

"Because I would do foolish and unseemly things if I stayed in the outside world, and because I wouldn't want to face living without . . . without . . ."

"Without a man?"

"Yes." Sian's voice faltered. "Without a man."

"But there are many men."

"I am forty years old. In forty years I have been able to find only two of them. I found them when I was relatively young, and I am becoming older every day. If I did find another man in the next twenty years, it would be too late for me."

"It isn't a statistical matter. Could you have foreseen that you would find your second man in a mental clinic?"

"Since I am rather set on this statistical view," Sian said, grinning suddenly, "you must admit that coming back here gives me a fifty per cent chance of finding my third. Lunatics can be quite fun, you know."

Celia entered the dancing school at La Gradelle as though it were her church. She was taken to a small private room with a bare couch, a chair, clothes hooks, a full-length mirror with an antique gilt frame, and a doorway to another room. That must be the room containing the shower which Mama keeps talking about, she thought with excitement. For all the talk about showers, Celia had never seen one. She went slowly into the tiled room and gasped.

The bathtub itself was adorned with exotic designs which might have been copied from the palace of a Pharaoh. The brightly polished brass fittings looked like the controls for the engines in the hold of a great battleship. Over the tub balanced a great carved mahogany hood which soared almost to the high ceiling. Its zinc-lined interior was covered with glistening, perforated porcelain so that strong sprays would shoot out from knees to chin while a torrent descended from overhead. Celia was eager to dance but she also looked forward to this magnificent shower afterward.

She dressed herself in the leotard and slippers, then tied her hair into a knot at the top of her head and secured it with a blue ribbon. She left the dressing room and floated down the stairs to a room which had three mirrored walls from floor to ceiling; a wooden bar at waist-high height running the length of the fourth wall; a row of benches at one end of the room and a piano at which a stout lady wearing a hat made of two stuffed doves was playing with her eyes closed. Twelve little girls in tutus were performing in unison, facing a tall, slender young man with a shock of black hair. As Celia closed the door behind her, moving shyly, not quite ready to be discovered, the young man turned to stare at her, then pointed imperiously to the benches. She sat down. She had forgotten Francis. She had forgotten her mother. She had lost interest in making love to Francis less than a day from now, though she had dreamed about love for so many years. Dancing was about to happen to her.

As she waited, staring raptly, she thought of Germans stamping and slapping, Russians squatting, leaping and spinning, Spaniards tapping, clicking and clacking. She thought of tiny brown women wearing silver bells near a silver sea in Java, and of Camargo and his *entrechat six*, and of Maria Taglioni, the first ballerina who had written: "In all my movements I remained straight, without strain; you could not hear me descend, because it was always my toe which struck first, the heel following gently to the ground. I adored all these steps in which I experienced an elevation which kept me almost unknown to the earth. Literally, I vibrated in the air."

She thought of the geometrical fancies of Carlo Blasis, the first great pedagogue of the ballet art, who at La Scala had taught the correlation of different parts of the body by planimetric terminology—curves and right angles—and not until the pupil had assimilated the lineal structure of the dance, was she allowed to begin to round the positions into plastic perfection. She deplored the self-serving arrogance of the English critic Chorley, who had regretted that the tips of Fanny Elssler's fingers had been too heavily rouged. She thought of Isadora Duncan dancing across the world, corsetless and barefoot, and of Pavlova inventing the tutu the better to show off her beautiful legs—

"Madamoiselle?"

Celia blinked. The tall slender young man was facing her, and the rest of the room was empty except for the lady at the piano.

"I am Duvalier. Your name, please?"

"I am Lady Celia Recknell."

"I may call you Milady?"

She nodded.

"You may call me Master."

"No. That is foreign to me."

He shrugged. "Then you will call me Duvalier." He smiled at her. "Where have you studied before?"

"I have never danced."

"I hope that it is not too late. Come." He took her hand and led her out onto the floor.

Powell and Shaw had to wait for almost an hour after the appointed time to bring Celia home that afternoon. She could hardly bear to leave and, in her innocence, she was almost as thrilled by her first shower bath as she had been with her first dancing lesson; when she entered the villa her cheeks were flushed and her eyes bright with life.

"My! Was it that good?" her mother asked.

"Better. Oh, I cannot tell you how much better! And I have asked to take lessons every day." Francis pursed his lips tightly to conceal his smile of smarmy satisfaction.

"But won't that be too much of a strain on your new foot, darling?" Sian asked.

"My new foot is made of steel, I think." As she spoke, it hurt her, throbbing dully, but in the rhythm of the piano accompaniment at the school. "Duvalier said it would be all right. He even said I might be a dancer."

The next afternoon Francis suggested that since he had to go into the city for his fencing lesson, he could drop Celia off at her school. The car rolled down the Haut-Crêt and made the same turn into the walled lane. As he kissed her Celia thought how much a matter of rote the movements of love-making were. When at last Francis came up for air, she said, "I am so sorry, Francis, but we won't be able to make love today."

"*Whaaaat?*"

"I really did enjoy the dancing so much yesterday, and I wasn't fibbing at all when I said that I'd arranged to take lessons every day."

"Celia, Celia—I haven't slept thinking about today! I've been in agony wanting you."

"I *am* sorry, Francis."

"Do you mean you are going to dance *every* day?"

"Not Sundays, of course. But I suspect I'll want to practice on Sundays."

"Are you saying that you don't want to make love with me?"

"Of course not. I want very much to make love with you. It's long past the time when I should have started making love, really, but—oh, Francis, I must dance first."

"But when? I tell you, I can't stand this! I can't go on like this!"

"I'm sure soon."

"Please don't talk to me as though I were some wretched, callow youth."

"But something will be sure to interrupt the dancing. The wonderful things don't last forever. And the moment that time comes, we will do everything you want."

C hapter 27

 The two young men Sir
Richard Adler brought to
dinner on Friday evening
were young indeed. Looking at them, Sian pictured anxious
parents pleading with Sir Richard to promise not to allow
them to pedal their tricycles too fast across the native quarter
in exotic Geneva. But, in fact, they merely looked very
young. Martin Battersby was thirty-one years old, looked
seventeen, and was the Commercial Attaché. John Montgomery, the Cultural Affairs Attaché, was a round-faced
twenty-eight, an enthusiastically distraught man who could
not stop wringing his hands even when holding a glass of
champagne. Each man detested the other and they com-
peted for Celia's attention fiercely.

Celia was made so happy by their snarling attentions, the
Ambassador realized that he could not possibly afford to
promote either young man; in their present posts they were
too valuable warriors in the combative arena of Geneva's
social life. All he had to do was to point them to their target

for the night; between them they would make any woman feel like Helen of Troy. Sir Richard actually hummed, for he was not an unmusical man, as he mentally framed the dispatch suggesting that young men be trained in competitive jealousy for the great social battles of diplomacy, and he saw Britain ruling the world through the women who ruled the men who attempted to prevent Britain from ruling the world. The dream flowered until he happened to glimpse Francis' face during an unguarded moment; experienced man that he was, he realized instantly such diplomacy would cause too many wars.

As he discussed the British-American War of 1812 with Lady Adler, Francis was feeling loathing for Battersby because of the man's repulsive habit of drinking whiskey from a champagne glass with his food. He felt mere revulsion for Montgomery, who droned on endlessly about gardening: "Gooseberries will grow on almost any soil that is well drained, but a few weeks before planting, try to remember to fork in one barrow load of indefectible organic matter to every eight square yards." Whatever Battersby's subject was, he whispered and leered it at Celia while Francis was obliged to explain to Lady Adler that the United States had indeed had provocation for its declaration of war.

"President Madison's message to Congress listed four major grounds," he said, hot with shame for Celia, who was rolling her eyes and hooting like a Klondike dance-hall girl. "The impressment of seamen, the violation of American neutral rights and territorial waters—

"But in your heart don't you feel that war is wrong?" Lady Adler asked. "Sir Richard and I feel in our hearts that the League of Nations stands for what is in the hearts of the better people everywhere—that there should be no more war."

The butler whispered to Francis that Cook had to see him, and with an anguished look at the noisy young people he rushed to the kitchen.

Mme. Kosta was a Hungarian who had been raised in the Grisons, two environments so disparate that she always reminded Francis of sweet-and-sour cooking and Yin-Yang philosophy.

"What is the matter?"

"The British Ambassador will not eat mango turnovers. It is something to do with India. Why didn't you tell me he would be here?"

"Madame Kosta, he is a diplomat. We will offer him some fruit and serve the others the mango turnovers."

"Please! There was a terrible incident at St. Moritz. He actually came into my kitchen. It was awful." She began to weep.

"No. Please don't, Madame Kosta. I agree. Very well, Shall we have puits d'amour? Sacristains? Would you enjoy making two lemon soufflés? All we need do is change the dish. What do you think, Madame Kosta?"

She nodded and blew her nose. The weight was lifted. He patted her and sped back to the table, expecting to find Celia doing the can-can, but the only new development was that John Montgomery had shifted from gooseberries. "I should like to point out," he was saying to Celia, "that succulents are not found in dry areas but in semi-deserts— which was how Geneva was beginning to look to me until tonight." He made the mistake of pausing for an instant so that the compliment could sink in, and Battersby raised his voice. "You must come aboard this little lake boat I've acquired, Lady Celia," he said. "Quite gay, actually. I snapped it up the moment I saw it. Never gave the chap a chance to change his mind."

They were such unmitigated asses, Francis raged. The alleged yachtsman, like Rudolf Rassendale with a mustache which could only have been left to him by a black sheep uncle, and the jolly gardener, a veal sausage of a man who had never needed to use a razor—

"Francis?" Sian called from across the table where she sat between Sir Richard and Don Jaime Arias, the same Spanish Ambassador whom they had met at Francis' first dinner party in Paris, who was now peering at him intently, checkbook open in front of him.

"Yes?" Francis answered distractedly.

"This incorrigible gambler on my left would like to play the game again. Will you please tell us who invented hats?"

Francis was annoyed by the diversion, but he answered

politely. "A Swiss named Guillaume Lear made the first hat in Paris in 1404."

"*Fantástico!*" Don Jaime muttered as he ripped his napkin in half under the table. He leaned over and whispered in Sian's ear. "What were worn before hats?" Sian asked Francis.

"Hoods. Charles the VII made hats fashionable in France in 1440, when he wore one lined with red velvet for his triumphal entry into Rouen."

"What doesn't this man know?" Don Jaime said as he scrawled out a check. Francis reflected bitterly that one thing he didn't know was whether this child was out to make a fool of him. Good God, both boobs were drinking whiskey now. Their breaths must be anesthetizing her. She would need fresh air badly soon.

"What a pity your country saw fit to turn its back on the League," Lady Adler said. On Francis' right, the Condesa de Aragon spoke directly into her soufflé, saying, "I do not like gardening," and this pleased Francis so much that he leaned across her back and tapped Montgomery on the arm. Reluctantly, the young man turned toward him.

"Here is a lady with fixed ideas on gardening," Francis said. Celia looked up and smiled, and his heart soared. Very soon the ladies would withdraw; there would follow twenty minutes of blather with port and these cretins, and then he'd be out like a shot into the other room to suggest that Celia stroll with him on the lawn for a bit of air.

But it was almost an hour later, while Battersby was performing his fourth card trick in the salon, before Francis could work himself to a place near Celia. In a low voice he invited her to share some very fresh air on the porch.

"But I can't," she protested, "Martin is doing his card tricks."

"Damn Martin," he said.

"Francis, I simply cannot."

He turned away from her in a tantrum of disappointment and stormed out onto the porch alone. He stared out at the lake, mixing one part of fury with two parts of dismay, stirring well and then adding a pinch of hopelessness. But when he heard the door open behind him his mood of wooden defeat turned to one of iron rage; he would make her pay for his suffering and he began disciplinary action by not bothering to turn to acknowledge her presence.

But it was Sian. "Are you all right, Francis?"

His rage melted into curdled self-pity. Despair filled him. He turned to her and forced a smile. "I may be liverish."

"Be careful of that. The French can't be entirely wrong, you know."

"About what?"

"Their preoccupation with the liver."

"Are our guests all enjoying themselves?" He moved a chair over for her and they sat down in the moonlight.

"Oh, yes."

"Good. I must say they are delightful people."

"Aren't they? Battersby is related to the Queen, you know."

Francis wheeled in his chair. "He isn't! How perfectly marvelous."

"It's a remote connection, of course, but he does live at Windsor when he's home, and those people are permitted to have such impressive notepaper. Everything is working out marvelously. He's taking Celia sailing tomorrow, and Montgomery has asked her to go flower-watching on the Saleve on Sunday. He seems to know everything about deadly nightshade." She sighed happily. "That will give us so much more time together—which makes me fonder of Celia."

Francis had to wait until the guests had left and Sian had disappeared into the kitchen to congratulate the staff, before settling things with Celia. He grabbed her by the shoulders and spun her around violently.

"Francis!"

"Damn you, Celia!"

"What have I done? Why are you so upset?"

"You know damned well what is the matter."

"You're jealous. Oh, Francis, I'm awestruck." She touched his cheek lightly with her fingertips. "Duvalier cannot teach me on Monday afternoon," she said. "Do you want to make love to me on Monday?"

Francis swayed. He felt so faint that he thought he was going to fall. At the sound of Sian's footsteps Celia went to the piano and riffled through some sheet music. "Have you ever heard of the Castles, Mama?" she asked as Sian came into the room. "The ballroom dancers?"

"Yes. I saw them during the War, I think. In London or some place."

"Duvalier saw them in Paris in 1912. He showed me some of their steps. It seems such a wonderful way to dance—so much less lonely than being a soloist and so much more feminine."

C hapter 28

Even to himself Francis seemed overcasual as he called up the stairway to announce that he was going into town if anyone wanted a ride. The instant he said it he could have choked himself with both hands; if Sian answered, how could he get out of the offer? In those seconds while he waited for a reply he decided that he could rush Sian into town, race back to the house with the excuse that he had forgotten something and then offer Celia a ride into town all over again. But suppose the car broke down as he was taking Sian in? Suppose she insisted on watching his fencing lesson? Just then Celia's voice, like an angel's, answered from above, "I'll be right down, Francis" and there was no response from Sian at all.

They drove into town silently, but neither of them was thinking of the afternoon ahead of them. Francis had detoured past the sexual act and was concentrating entirely on the problem of making Celia so dependent on him that when the moment came, i.e., when Mr. Link sent word that his peerage had been confirmed, he could ask her to marry him without any fear of refusal. It was easier to get married in Switzerland than in France. If he sent an anonymous letter to Mr. Morrie Cleave of the *Evening Standard* in Paris the story would be trumpeted all over London the next day. As he drove toward the rue des Granges flat he toyed with the idea of mentioning in the letter that the groom was the mysterious incognito "prince" whom the *Evening Standard* had uncovered in Paris almost nine months before. This would give the story more depth and a further touch of glamour. But once this marriage had been accepted by the police and the immigration authorities, and they had settled down in Ludlow Castle to entertain the cream of two continents, he would be recognized as a peer of the realm in his own right, as well as because of his wife's title. It was a better thing he was doing than if he had married Sian. Dear, darling, wonderful Sian. Celia had rounder dimensions—the daughter of a marquess, granddaughter of an earl, baroness in her own right descending through the female line, and if they could breed a daughter, then she would be a baroness in her own right and the daughter of an earl. Francis tingled all over as he felt the sensation again—for perhaps the thousandth time—of being presented to Their Majesties and chatting for a bit. He must study up on yachting and Saxe-Coburg. He would take a silent role until his English diction was perfected. It was coming along very well; he listened carefully whenever he spoke. In the past few weeks he rarely had heard American pronunciation flaw his speech, and he was certain that with a month or two of drilling by a dramatic coach, his accent would be almost as difficult to fathom as Sian's when she was speaking rapidly. Still, as a precaution, it would be best if during the first three or four evenings with Their Majesties, he remained soldier-silent but instantly responsive to their wishes.

The car flew along the broad quay toward the sweet city curving around the end of the lake and flanking the River Rhone just as it plunged downward to France. The water of the lake was apple-green and was capped with white under the wind and the angry sky. The small boats were on their way in because a storm was rising, but Francis, possessed by his own visions, was unaware of all of it, hardly aware that he was driving.

Celia was young and beautiful and wearing a tiara and a white silk gown and speaking such authentic English; she could do the chatting. Out of pride and a certain amount of coaching from him—which she would certainly accept without question—she would tell Their Majesties about his mysterious background and commanding parentage. It was entirely possible that just as the Vatican library was said to possess arcane secrets of alchemy and black magic, the Royal Family kept their own secret documents concerning the peers of their realm. With a raised eyebrow, by an understanding pat on the shoulder, by expanding his duties at the Court, they would let him know that they knew. In the beginning he might be invited to become a Gentleman Usher, privileged to make the King's bed. As he drove along the quay Francis regaled himself with the official directions for making the bed of the King of England: ". . . the Esquires to gather the sheet round together in their hand on either side of the bed, and go to the bed's head and strike down the same twice or thrice as they come down and shake the sheet of the feet; then lay it abroad the bed, then lay on the over fustian above; then take a pane of ermine and lay it above; then roll down the bed the space of an ell; yeomen take the pillows and beat them well with their hands and cast them up to the Esquires and let them lay on, as it pleaseth the King best . . ." He would be moved up through the ranks of courtiers discreetly, so as not to upset older peers, toward one of the Great Offices—perhaps Master Chamberlain, Master Marshal or Constable—to the place where he could serve best and most brilliantly at the court: Master Steward in charge of the Dispensary, the Baker, the Larder, the Cellars, the Spicery, the King's Kitchen, the Napery and the Ewery, the Squillery, the Wafery and the Scalding House.

He would serve them faithfully and well, Francis thought, as he turned the car into the rue des Granges and was comforted again by the sight of the even number on the building. Driving a Straker Squire to exactly the right flat in exactly the right part of town on exactly the right side of the best street for a lofty assignation gave him a sense of fulfillment, made him feel taller, and demonstrated his response to his sacred family trust.

As they drove Celia listened to the birds and watched the tiny white sails far out on the lake and dreamed that she was mounting broad steps to an altar at which she would at last celebrate her arrival at the station of womanhood. In all the novels she had ever read, the age at which the girl had been overcome by physical love did not matter. Some very young girls in a few of the books had had their first adventures with men older than Francis, and many of them were exactly her age. Which must be why she felt so right about everything— because of the time and because of her choice of lover to teach her and help her to develop into a loving and truly passionate and mature woman like Mama. By choosing, for this first important step, the man her darling mother had chosen, it seemed to Celia that every need had been met. It was true that with very rare exceptions, all the young women in the novels had been seduced by gentlemen. It was also true that their seductions had been far more precipitous (this seemed like such a long ride to the bed) and even more romantic (in a forest glen, while playing duets at the piano, immediately following the excitement of being rescued while riding a runaway horse). If today's assignation seemed more like that of two hardened sex fiends, this was only its superficial appearance. She could not, after all, allow Francis to sweep her off her feet while playing duets at home; there were so many servants even if Mama had not been there. And perhaps a hardened assignation by sex fiends was a perversely exciting extra way of thinking about what they were going to do.

She knew what they were going to do down to the last detail, but for the life of her she could not imagine what it would actually be like. One must get so . . . so self-conscious in those mad positions she had seen in those awful photographs. They made her think affectionately of Donen

Hall and of dear Kershaw, that ancient man who had been
the butler for as long as he had lived. Remembering Kershaw's vast collection of pornographic pictures and books,
which he had kept under lock and key in the piano bench
expressly intended for the scores of Mozart operas, she
smiled softly to herself. What did two people talk about
while assuming those grotesque positions in which their
bodies intertwined like knitted wool? So much of the time—
though not at *all* times—they were actually face to face; at
such close quarters it seemed impossible for the eyes to
focus, and whatever could one be expected to chat about at
such a moment? Francis must have undertaken prodigious
exercises, because in the demonstration photographs the
gentlemen apparently carried most of the weight of two
people. She wondered if that was why he had undertaken
fencing lessons, and gymnastics and weight-lifting in London. Was it all done at lightning speed? Was the inventive
and impossible-to-anticipate choreography of the bed executed in a continuous horizontal dance as it were? That must
be it. That would explain why neither the lady nor the
gentleman in Kershaw's pictures ever seemed to be chatting.
There was a world of concentrating to be done. They would
be too busy ringing the changes and readjusting to one, then
another, of the thirty-nine positions. One of the thirty-nine
pictures had to represent the starting point, but which one?
With much practice and patience and agility, each of the
positions could be managed. *But which was the opening
gambit and in which position was one required to end the
love-making?* Damn Kershaw, she thought as the car rolled
into rue des Granges; why hadn't he numbered those thirty-
nine pictures?

"What a perfectly beautiful apartment! Why, it must be
the hideaway of some South American war lord."

He seized her and kissed her hungrily, in fact she almost
choked. He pressed himself against her and seemed to wrap
his arms around her three times. She struggled and he knew
that she must be aflame with desire. "Francis! My word!" she
gasped when at last she was able to push him away. "What
has come over you?"

He took her by the wrist and pulled her across the wide salon to the master bedroom overlooking the Place Neuve far below. He undressed her very carefully, garment by garment, and kissed her all over as he did so. As though having memorized a musical score, he moaned tunefully as he slipped the petticoats off, one after another, until she sat naked before him, rather well kissed in a preliminary way. Celia found she was enjoying it all exceedingly and they did not seem to have come to the first position yet. Was she supposed to assume the first position? Was that her place in the ancient ritual? Would she humiliate him and herself? It was like a nightmare of appearing as the première ballerina in a great theater in which as she came out from the wings she simply forgot the entire choreography. She had often had such dreams. The prompter in the little box yelled, "Improvise! Improvise!" and she would fall into an Irish jig which Mungo had taught her at home. But how could one improvise at this?

Francis worked with the detachment of a dentist. He had anticipated all of the problems. Celia was a virgin, he was sure, because of her foot and her cast. The word play of Celia's foot having been in a cast tripped across his mind, but he erased it instantly. As a virgin she presented certain problems. That is, the first experience could be an unpleasant one, and if unpleasant, it was possible she would lose all interest in sex right at the start. If that happened, he would lose all power over her; it could even cost him her hand in marriage. Considering these stakes, Francis had abjured his fencing lessons for the last two weeks and during those hours had been taking lessons in deflowering. He had approached the matter sensibly. He had given the maître d'hôtel at the best hotel in town fifty francs and had asked him, man-to-man, for the name of the best bordello in the city. The maître d'hôtel had turned quite red and his hand involuntarily sought to hand back the money, but Francis had interrupted him sternly. "I will thank you," he had said in icy tones, "not to jump to vulgar conclusions. My interest in this business is hardly what you are thinking, and I will thank you to take that expression off your face at once."

The maître had apologized, but said that it was not his place to know about such things. This was the province of the chief concierge in a hotel for a man in Francis' position.

"Who is the man for the others?" Francis had asked, curious.

"The second concierge or the chief night concierge."

"You can't expect me to talk about a matter like this with a concierge whom I hardly know," Francis said testily. "You know me. You know how I dine, what I drink, how I live. You must talk about this to him, and then give me the information. After all, I certainly didn't plan to go to the place this evening."

Three days later Francis returned to the hotel for lunch. As always he ordered well and was exacting but fair. He sent suggestions about certain little improvements to the chef, and although he never got a reply, he knew these were appreciated. While he enjoyed coffee and calvados he fell into a reverie about the various honorary titles the Kings of England had conferred. He had decided that he was most taken with the office Charles I had conferred on Sir Thomas Brand "Embellisher of Letters to the Eastern Princess," when the maître d'hôtel appeared at his side and coughed lightly. Francis looked up.

"I have the information, sir."

"What information?"

"About the place?"

"Dammit, Louis, what place?"

The maître d'hôtel leaned over and murmured, "The brothel, sir."

Francis beamed his pleasure. He pulled out a wad of banknotes and pressed a hundred-franc note into Louis' hand. "I am pleased," he said. "You have done well. Call a cab, will you?"

"If you wish to go tonight, sir—"

"Tonight? I will go now."

The decision confused Louis, but with an effort he carried on.

Francis rather liked the atmosphere of the street and the small well-kept house in the Eaux-Vives section. He was ushered into a sitting room and then left alone. Within five minutes three sleepy-eyed young women of assorted sizes were seated in chairs around him. "Where is Madame?" he asked flatly, his eyes instructing the girls to leave at once. They departed, and after an unacceptably long wait a short, dark dumpy woman dressed in a shiny black dress with a white collar and cuffs entered the room and pursed her lips at him.

"Monsieur?"

Francis did not rise. "Please find us a room where we may chat quietly and share a bottle of champagne."

"We are not likely to be disturbed in this room at two o'clock in the afternoon, monsieur." Madame's lips somehow remained pursed while she spoke. "I will remind monsieur that this is a Swiss house. If monsieur, who has dismissed the girls, believes he can make certain unnatural arrangements, I feel it is my duty to tell him that this would not be possible."

"Damn Swiss brothels!" Francis cried out. "What kind of dirty minds do you have? Who has mentioned unnatural arrangements? I have come here prepared to pay for certain information—"

"Information?" She was aghast. "*Information?* You are a policeman?" She drew back in offense. "Out! Get out!"

Francis held up his hand, palm outward. "I have come here to seek certain sexual instruction," Francis said as soon as silence returned.

Madame at last unpursed and broke into a broad smile of understanding. "Instruction? Ah, instruction! But of course. Arlette! A bottle of Lanson 'oo to my private salon!"

When Celia had been carried to the bed, Francis stood before her, and staring down at her with what he hoped were burning eyes, undressed himself—rapidly at first, because after all she had seen men in bathing costume, then slowly, and breathing more and more heavily.

In spite of all of Kershaw's pictures, Celia gaped at what she saw. "Francis!" Involuntarily her hand touched her lower stomach. "Oh, my word, Francis!"

He lay beside her and set to work. He fondled and caressed and tongued and moaned and rubbed and nipped and bit and groaned. He talked. He lit spirit lamps and melted emolients and prepared his unguents while he carried out every stimulus known to gypsies, courtesans, scientists, the aristocracy and the upper, middle and lower classes upon her body, face, limbs, fingers and toes, palms and soles, and suddenly—just as a great storm can build from silence and dead air—Celia seemed to have recalled in their correct order every single tableau of Kershaw's pictures. She showed willing knowledge, though not yet mastery, of agilities and elevations, flights and *brisés;* as though she were the prima ballerina of a new art she moved swiftly, with eagerness and imagination, from *posé en tournant* to *jetés* and jigs, with rapid *flic-flacs* and throwing in an occasional *zapateado* from the flamenco. Nor did she seem to care, once aroused, that she did not know exactly the right things to say on such occasions; her improvisations of broken sound and speech suited each tableau precisely. Her *arques* took his responses and pinioned him; her limp *pas d'actions* had an extraordinary purity of line. At last she lost herself far, far above him in a final, ecstatic and unbelievably soaring *fouette saute* as she left the earth.

Chapter 29

 Sian had just finished her bath when Celia entered the room adjoining. The door between the rooms was open, but though Sian called out, Celia did not come in at once and when she did, seemed reluctant.

"Good afternoon, darling. Did you have a wonderful day?"

"Quite wonderful, Mama."

"But you are so pale."

Celia shrugged lightly but didn't answer.

"I am worried that too much dancing might exhaust you, dear."

"I don't think it will. Or if it does, only at first."

"You do seem happy."

"Oh, yes."

"Is what's-his-name—Duvalier—a considerate teacher? Did you learn a great deal today?"

"Yes, a tremendous amount."

"Why don't you rest now? I'll have something sent up to

you on a tray. Francis will make you something really special, and you can read and rest and get to bed early, just like an athlete in training. Which you are, in a way."

"Yes, Mama." Sian held her lightly and kissed her. "Phew!" Sian said, "Francis must have drenched himself in the eau de cologne today"—Celia stiffened under her hands—"because just riding with him in the car has you smelling like a barbershop."

"Mama?" Celia's voice trembled.

"Yes, dearest?"

"I never seem to tell you any more how much I love you. I must tell you now in case anything happens."

"Silly! What could happen?"

"Oh"—Celia's voice trailed off for a moment—"a car accident or drowning or anything."

"How cheerful of you! You must be very tired, but you are very dear to tell me that. I love you too, very much. Very, very much . . . in case anything happens." She laughed joyously. "Now have a warm bath and a nap and I'll lay on everything else."

Celia walked as naturally as she could with her stiffness and pain and turned on the bath taps. As she threw two extra handfuls of bath salts into the water and watched them dissolve, she realized those crystals were like the years of her life—in her palm at one moment and gone forever the next. She had never felt so *triste* before. It wasn't Mama or Mama's Francis, and it wasn't the guilt for what she had done to Mama because she couldn't feel guilt in that accusing way. But for a moment she imagined she knew what Eve had felt just after she had bitten into the apple of knowledge. She had found her body that afternoon, just as every book had said she would and should, but with it she had also found mortality. She undressed slowly and got into the tub. If her life were going to evaporate in the heat of time, she must make the most of it.

"This is luxury," Sian said. "Everyone's idea of luxury is different, and the ideas of the men who write the advertisements are the silliest. This is it: a flawless dinner alone for the first time in six months with the one man in the world you love."

"Celia isn't ill, is she?"

"No. Tired and very stiff. She actually hobbled when she walked, poor thing, and she looked exhausted. But the dancing is good for her, I am sure of that. You should have seen her eyes. But of course you saw when you drove her home."

"I didn't notice."

"You look rather well yourself tonight."

"It is you who looks divine. There cannot ever have been a more beautiful woman than you, Sian."

"How sensible of you to say that. Now, tell me all about the future."

"The future?"

"At the end of our last chapter, back in London. In a rather large bed in Farm Street you were saying—"

"Sian, I had no right to say that."

"I thought you had. But when will you think you have?"

"I won't wait until my peerage is confirmed by the House of Lords because Mr. Link tells me that it could take two or three years. But when he himself informs me that my claims are soundly based, then and only then will I tell you what I must tell you—what has to be, what has always been meant to be."

"My darling."

"Mr. Link is a scholar and perhaps so lost in his work that he forgets my impatience. I shall give him until August 1st; then he must tell me what he has discovered so far and what his conclusions are. I . . . I can't seem to think about anything else." His voice shook. "And I dream when I sleep, again and again, about a pretty, vivacious and very, very musical dark-haired woman whom I have never seen before but who must be my sister—or my mother as a girl—or an ancestor. I feel pulled behind a shooting star. I cannot always control my shaking hands or my shaking heart. Everything will change the day he tells me who I am. Things I never would have thought of doing under normal circumstances . . ." His yellow eyes were too bright and his forearms, not only his hands, trembled. "My parents would have cherished me were it not for a larger duty. I was left to lift myself up, and carry on for them, to honor their memory and the memory of all of my family before them by making the name shine, by fathering children of my own who will cause it to glow even brighter."

"Children?" Sian said. "That's odd. I had never thought of that. But why not? Of course, quite right. When they are forty I shall be over eighty."

"Forty is old to have children," Francis said.

"Not for you."

They ate with pleasure.

"I shall have many children, and you will train all our servants and cooks when you are not making love to me," Sian said, "and more truly than any fairy tale ever told, we shall live happily ever after."

Francis stared at her bleakly, and chewed on.

The following few weeks were prodigiously active for Francis. There were times when it seemed that the bed in the flat on the even-numbered side of rue des Granges was never cold. Somehow he managed his precise, dentist-like efficiencies with Sian on Tuesday and Thursday afternoons and Saturday mornings, and to attend to the growing needs of Celia on Monday and Friday afternoons and Wednesday mornings. This left little time for fencing. On the seventh day he rested. He repeated the phrase over and over again in the way that the words of a popular song can become glued to one's memory. "On the seventh day he rested" he would intone silently and repeatedly as he ministered his technique on each of them.

His patience with Mr. Link was boundless as well. He had heard nothing about either the final documentation or the claims, nor had he received the deed to the London house; there had been nothing since March. But he knew that Mr. Link, ever the professional, was a completely reliable man, and he was confident that almost any day the results would be received in the registered mail. But if he did not hear from Link by the first of August, then he would go after Mr. Link with a vengeance because he had been so lenient.

Jacques Crouch, the banker, had been a bore—a nagging, persistently old-womanish bore who never seemed to stop whining about the way the money was disappearing. But Francis liked him because he did appreciate good food and wine. And Crouch would stop his nattering the instant the proof arrived that Francis was an earl. Furthermore, for his loyalty Francis had decided to maintain a substantial account in the Swiss bank even if it meant transferring important family funds. In the meantime, he copulated, cooked and rested. The weather was unusually fine; it was a wonderful summer. The roses came up in abundance, and he and the gardener had every reason to believe that it would be a magnificent year for the hortensias, which had been moved out of the direct sunlight where last year's idiot had planted them.

He was in love. It was something which entered his mind the instant he awoke in the morning, regardless of whether it was Sian's day or Celia's day or his own day of rest. He knew that he must be a romantic in his heart because he could never have conceived that a marriage of convenience could have happened to him. Sian had helped him immeasurably, and he would always acknowledge her friendship. It was true that Celia's rank and beauty would help him, and of course that was convenient, but also he loved her. She loved sex; therefore she would have the very best sex. She loved dancing; therefore he would see that she had the finest dancing teachers in the world. The rest, all that was to be shared between them—Donen Hall, Ludlow Castle, his town house, her fecundity and their joint good health—all of it together would re-establish the dynasty which had temporarily lapsed when his mother and father had met and mated against the wishes of two great nations. Sian would come to understand why he had to choose Celia. He would be nothing less than direct, open and honest with her when the time came to say that he and Celia were to be married. He allowed himself to divert his thoughts for a moment to the question of whether two peers of their rank could be married in Westminster Abbey. The groom and the bride could approach by barge . . . August 1st was only one week away . . .

Now, where was he? Yes, he would be direct, open and

honest with Sian when the time came. She was a deeply passionate and stubborn woman, but she was also intelligent and she knew his problems as well or better than he knew them himself. If she insisted, they could carry on with a program of afternoon love-making which would be most satisfying to her. She would understand. He had to have heirs to carry on the line whose richness of noble blood could not be allowed to die out. She had said herself, several times, that she thought he might be the natural son of Queen Mary and Kaiser Wilhelm. That might well be. They could hardly have called him to their side, or allowed even their most trusted retainers to know the truth—at least not for many years after the conflict which had just ended. It was political dynamite. Wounds must be given time to heal. But he had to have sons ready to carry on the direct line of that mighty union, and if he were to breed, it had to be with a young, resilient woman. Sian would see that; Sian would understand. He loved Celia very much, but in many ways he loved Sian more. He loved her so, and yet he had to hurt her. What a rotten irony life was. But Sian knew him, and she would understand.

And Celia had to be told; she couldn't wait forever. Even in this short time she was so vastly accomplished at love-making that soon she would be strong enough to fly away. She was growing surer and more avid for life every day. What had to be done must be done soon.

Celia's responses to Francis had been shy and even a little uncomfortable at first, but she had been deeply excited and gradually she had flowered in the warmth of the secret sun inside her. When she understood what she felt, she marveled at the power of Francis and of her body to produce such enduring gratification. But then, in an exquisite irony of which she could not be aware, she began to want to give to another—someone, anyone—what Francis had given her: the intricate and extraordinary physics of sex which went far beyond any such mundane instincts as procreation. Francis' endless expertise and dazzling execution of pleasure upon pleasure was an adventure which she in turn must pass on to another so that he in turn could hand it on. Such pleasure was like a burning torch from the first fire on earth that was carried across mountains and deserts and seas around the world.

As Celia tried to sleep at night, still stirred by what Francis had churned up within her, she could think of nothing but other men on whom she must confer all these pleasures. But at first they were only the faceless men of the novels. The only men she knew were Francis, Martin Battersby and John Montgomery. It was discouraging. But there *was* one other man. She suddenly realized that she had been keeping him at the back of her mind until she had exhausted all other possibilities. If there was no other place to turn, that remaining man would be the one to whom she would offer her enthrallments. Beautiful Duvalier; lithe, long, graceful, muscled, thrilling Duvalier. Who deserved such a gift more than a dancer?

Through the summer, Celia worked hard at her dancing, never giving Duvalier any hint of her plan for him and cherishing it as she lived it over and over again in her mind. In June the course of the dancing changed. While they rested one day she showed him her collection of pictures of Vernon and Irene Castle, and of Maurice and Florence Walton, and Duvalier told her again that he had seen the Castles dance in Paris in 1912, ten years before. When he said that he had memorized every step they had made in the fox trot, the Castle Walk, the maxixe, the South American tango and the one-step, she pleaded with him to teach her. They danced so well together that he began to improvise and choreograph new steps and routines for them. They became more and more excited each time they danced, and when, a week later, Duvalier asked her if she would like to tour around the world with him, she sang her acceptance and said she would leave that very day with him if he gave the word. While they danced to a record on the gramophone in the mirrored room she put her face up to his. It seemed to him that even her eyes gave off heat. He kissed her. She held his face and kissed him back slowly and deliberately with the skill of an accomplished courtesan.

Ten minutes later Celia was teaching Duvalier all the wonders she had learned.

Because she was vaguely upset by Francis' growing impatience with Mr. Link and by his restlessness as he counted the days until the first of August, Sian went to Anieres to visit Dr. Boscawen on June 29th. Once again they sat on the small porch overlooking the lake and drank tea. It was a Monday afternoon, when Francis fenced and Celia was at dancing school, so there was leisure to sit in this peaceful place and talk about Francis with the only other person who knew him well.

Dr. Boscawen's diamonds sparkled as her long hands busied themselves with the tea. In a white silk dress more suitable for a day at Longchamps than a hospital visit, Sian wore a jade necklace to match her eyes. She looked more beautiful than anyone at the clinic could remember.

"You look so happy," Dr. Boscawen said.

"As indeed I am. Who could have imagined how happy I would be today if they had seen me a year ago?"

"Perhaps not I," the doctor answered.

"Nor I."

"You found the best medicine."

"Yes."

"How is Mr. Hillairet?"

"Quite fit."

"Calm?"

"Just about right, I would say."

"You are sure?"

"What are you thinking?"

"His banker came to see me. He was worried."

"Worried?"

"I am worried, too," Dr. Boscawen said sadly. "There is a pattern to these things. He is so important to you that I must tell you."

"Please."

"Francis spends his money at an incredible rate. In the beginning he was very conservative and, as an investor, quite brilliant. But since the breakdown which brought him

here—or to be correct, since he left here—he has been fling-
ing his money away as though he were an alchemist with an
endless supply of it." The doctor watched Sian carefully.
"It is a symptom which may be accompanied by other
symptoms."

"You are saying that he is still quite mad? But I know
that."

"What I am saying is that he is spending his fortune and
that at the current rate it will soon be gone."

Sian wasn't capable of understanding what was meant by
the phrase "spending one's fortune." One had money and one
used it as it was needed, just as one used one's motorcars or
one's houses. Vaguely she assumed that the money which
Francis held in the *Swiss* bank was being spent with prof-
ligacy; just as vaguely she assumed he had other banks in
different parts of the world, just as she and most of the
people she knew did. Hearing the concern in Dr. Boscawen's
voice, she concluded that what Francis was doing with his
Swiss account was bad because it foreshadowed other symptoms which had nothing to do with money.

"What did you tell the banker? I mean, what I am not sure
I understand is why the banker came to you about this at
all?"

"It was the banker who brought Francis here. He likes
Francis. He wanted to know whether I thought Francis
might be in need of commitment again and whether the
money should be impounded until such time as Francis
recovered his judgment. It was a proper, conservative thing
to have done, I am sure, and it was in Francis' interest."

"What did you decide?"

"I agreed. Francis may be at a dangerous time. These
things are always cyclical with him, and you should know
that and become as accustomed to it as the wife of a patient
who knows that her husband's temperature will rise and fall.
I agreed up to a point, that is. We analyzed Francis' ex-
penditures. There is the cost of the villa and of the servants
here—which is a rational expense. Gambling debts may not
be rational, but they are incurred by sane people, so I

discounted that. He had the heavy expense of buying the house in London, and . . ."

"A house in London? Please forgive me, Doctor; I seem to be conversing entirely in the form of questions."

"A few weeks ago a check cleared to the amount of twenty-one thousand pounds which was endorsed by the Jemma Jay Estate Agents. You didn't know?"

"No."

"He is barred from England, yet he bought this house. I thought that something had perhaps been worked out by the solicitors permitting him to return."

"No."

"Still, we can't say the purpose isn't rational. Many people buy properties they never see as an investment or for speculation."

"Not Francis." Sian bit her lower lip, then said, "He must have felt he needed the house to support his new position."

"The genealogist?"

"You know about Mr. Link?"

"Yes, and this part is not rational. I have seen the checks made out to Mr. Link. Francis has spent eleven thousand pounds in eight months for 'genealogical services.'"

"Eleven thousand pounds?" For the first time Sian was dismayed.

"Does Francis talk about Mr. Link?"

"All the time. He rarely talks about anything else. He has not heard from Mr. Link since March, and lately it has made him very restless and anxious. But he is certain that within a short time Mr. Link will have completed his researches establishing Francis' claims to an earldom."

"He is that certain?"

"Oh, he is dead certain. It is the keystone of his existence. Everything he plans and lives for depends upon it."

"And what do you think about it?"

"About Mr. Link or the earldom?"

"About Francis' chances of being admitted into the British peerage."

"Well, it's . . . it's"—Sian groped for another word and

couldn't find it—". . . it's mad. If Mr. Link has taken eleven thousand pounds from Francis by saying that there is a chance of establishing such a claim, then Mr. Link ought to be arrested and convicted."

"How can you be so sure? I have read about successful claims."

"No." Sian had to look away; her eyes closed and she breathed deeply as she waited for control. "Francis doesn't know what his name is. He doesn't know who his parents are. He doesn't know where he was born. All of Mr. Link's searches—if there were any—have been based upon a name of convenience which someone gave to Francis because he had to be called something. He will not stand up to it very well when Mr. Link tells him that the search has failed."

"Will he tell him that?"

"Link accepted the fees to make a search. He has to tell Francis something and show him extensive documentation, or else risk criminal charges. And Francis won't wait longer than August 1st. Three days from now he is going to demand that Mr. Link send him all the evidence. He has had nothing but talk so far, and if Mr. Link won't answer the telephone or mail, you may be sure Francis will send his solicitors after him because what Mr. Link has tempted him with is all that Francis wants in this world."

"Then it is a godsend that this Mr. Link is a crook."

Sian looked startled. Dr. Boscawen took the teacup out of Sian's hand and refilled it. "You love him. That is what counts because that is the whole reality here, the only reality."

Sian shut her eyes.

"Francis is deep in unreality. He will never be . . . normal. You know that; I know you know it and that you have decided to accept it."

"I love him."

"So . . . Francis can retrogress badly if Mr. Link tells him bad news. On the other hand, Francis can be held together—can perhaps be saved—if Mr. Link sends documentation stating that Francis does indeed have a legitimate claim to the peerage. There might be a long delay until such a claim is confirmed. How long?"

"A dozen years, perhaps. Even longer."

"Then you will have a dozen years. And he might get better in those dozen years and be able to take the final news with indifference. Mr. Link must tell him that he seems entitled to a peerage." Dr. Boscawen sighed heavily and sipped her tea while Sian watched her intently. "What are the alternatives?" the doctor continued. "Commitment to a mental clinic, protection of his property today, protection of his mind next week if Mr. Link tells him that his cause is hopeless. Mr. Hillairet is capable of worse violence than what happened in London. It could mean his lifetime in an institution."

Sian stood up. "I will handle Mr. Link and assure the outcome of his researches," she said. "May I use the telephone in your office?"

It was four o'clock in England when Sian reached her solicitor in London. She explained Link's culpability in minute detail. The solicitor asked if she wanted criminal charges brought against the man. No, she wanted the solicitor to see Mr. Link in person and immediately, to explain to him that criminal charges would be brought if Link did not arrange documentation to prove Francis' belief that he was a peer. In fact, she wanted it established within ten days by Mr. Link's undoubted professional skills that Francis was the true Earl of Willmott-Ludlow, and that he was to send a cable to Francis instantly, stating that the documentation of the claim was being completed and would be delivered by bonded messenger to Francis in Switzerland.

The solicitor was aghast at the thought that he was being asked to be a party to a forged peerage by a marchioness of the realm.

"Mr. Gitlin," Sian said firmly into the telephone. "What I have asked you to undertake will be supported by a medical certificate from the chief psychiatrist of the leading mental clinic in this part of Europe. The certificate will guarantee that this action is vital to save a man's sanity, and all

responsibility for the action will be assumed by the clinic.
On those grounds it is not too much to ask, is it, Mr. Gitlin?"
She did not wait for him to answer. "You will be acting for
me, as your firm has always acted for my family."

"Very well."

"It must be done today."

"It will be done today."

Chapter 30

Sian was so happy at the thought of what was in store for Francis that on reaching home she decided to telephone him at his *salle d'armes* and ask him to stay in town so that they could dine alone together. But the fencing master told her that not only was Francis not there but that he had discontinued his fencing lessons almost a month ago. Francis had said he was going to fence when he had left the house with Celia that afternoon. Perhaps he had decided to watch Celia dance; how nice it would be if Celia's future stepfather took a real interest in her career. But when she called the dancing school and Duvalier told her that Celia did not take dancing lessons on Monday or on Friday, she found she could hardly muster enough strength to put the telephone back on its cradle.

She sat quite still for a long time, remembering the smell of Francis' cologne on Celia's body, recalling the ambiguities of Celia's speech ever since and Francis' oblique contra-

dictory replies when she had talked to him about what was
in her heart, remembering with bitter shock his face and his
words, "Forty is old to have children." Ten minutes later she
called Powell and told him that they would be going into
town immediately. At her mirror she composed her face and
hair with cold, stiff fingers.

She entered the flat in the rue des Granges with her key;
moving quietly, she crossed the great salon and paused for
one terrified moment outside the bedroom door before opening it.

They were asleep. She stared at the bodies as though they
had been blackened by plague and emanated a miasma
which would destroy her. His head slept upon her daughter's naked breasts. Her legs were sprawled wantonly, and
the face which she should never have troubled to seek out
again at Donen Hall and pretended to love wore a faint
smile. She thought fleetingly of killing them, then returning
to the quiet room at Anieres forever. Then she saw it all for
the banality it was. To love him as much as she did was a
bore, she thought sadly, but to be so in love with such a bore
as this king of bores and to have to suffer the idiotic in-
congruity of this most conventional revenge by her daughter
was the greatest bore she had ever known. All the men of her
life—Colin, her brothers, Papa, now Francis—had deserted
her, but she was damned if she would suffer this last in-
dignity. She walked to the side of the bed where Francis lay
and with all the strength she could summon she brought her
fist downward to plunge it deep into Francis' stomach like a
driven sledgehammer. Francis' hoarse scream of agony
propelled Celia bolt upright, her eyes staring incredulously
into her mother's eyes. Gasping, Francis stared up at her
pitiless face in mortal fear. She did not look at him. Her eyes
held Celia's eyes. Celia did not speak. She could think only
that her mother was composed and deadly and beautiful:
white marble skin, hard and gleaming; bright red hair piled
atop green eyes which were slowly filling with tears. Celia
could not look away, and Sian felt a grudging pride for her;
the child understood consequences—cause and effect, crime
and punishment. She had bred a daughter who had the sort

of character she had always admired: no excuses, no explanations, no justifications.

Francis found voice enough to gasp, "For Christ's sake, Sian!"

"Why Christ's sake, Francis?" Sian shifted her gaze from Celia to his face. His eyes were wary but clear of guilt. She shuddered and wanted to cry out. His eyes did not acknowledge that he had maimed her forever, because they did not care if they had. She made herself address Celia. "Is this your revenge, Celia?"

Celia rolled away from Francis and stood up on the other side of the bed, naked.

"I have nothing to say, Mama. You have seen what it is."

"Did you get into bed with him out of love for him or out of hatred for me?"

"I love you, Mama."

"Cover yourself, please."

"Sian," Francis gasped. "I tried to tell you. Tomorrow, after I'd talked to Link I was going to tell you. It is my duty to marry Celia so that I can have sons. It had to be this way."

"Marry me?" Celia was confused by the announcement.

Francis' chin jutted skyward in his physical agony.

"Did you ever have any intention of marrying him, Celia?"

Celia saw what her mother thought she was concealing so well: that between them she and Francis had taken away something of great and abiding value, that it could be replaced by nothing but hopelessness, and that she and her mother could never return to the happiness they had been granted so wondrously and unexpectedly. It was the *consequence* of what Celia had chosen to do that she had not understood. She had worked and worked at the self-delusion that her mother loved Francis for the same reason she herself did. But it was not so. Her mother loved *everything* about this dull, silly man, and she would protect him for every hour that he would grant her his presence, no matter what he did to her. It was all quite disgusting, and the feeling of deep distaste showed on her face as she said, "I wouldn't marry him, Mama, if he were the only man left in the world." She scooped up clothing and shoes and left the room.

Francis was clutching himself and rocking from side to side like a small boat in a high sea, while raw sounds spilled out of his throat. "Use your powers, darling," Sian crooned. "Delude yourself that this has never happened. It's all you have. The more delusion, the less sanity; and the less sanity, the less we are able to love anything except delusion."

Chapter 31

 James Maitland was an American master of the complicated, tenuous and subtle art of massive organization, and he was far too busy a man to waste all forty-six days of a trip to Europe on anything as frivolous as a honeymoon. He knew what he wanted for the bank, and his seasoned, highly trained organization was directed how to get it. His dark-haired, lovely, vivacious wife, who was as knowledgable about music as he was about banking, knew what she wanted, and he was quick to see that both goals could be made to merge and effectively enhance each other. To the American and European newspaper-reading public, their wedding trip seemed kaleidoscopic, tumultuous and glittering. Everything seemed to happen to them simultaneously: state dinners with kings and queens and prime ministers; separate luncheons with finance and culture ministers; state operas, concerts and private viewings of great art; large grants given to music and painting, to the occasionally-starving, to public bond issues and to private education. These activities by Mr. and Mrs. Maitland were reported in newspapers in eight languages. Governmental Ministries of Finance, Interior, Agriculture and Culture saw to it that hundreds of functionaries smoothed the way before the visitors so that every move the happy couple made was quite effortless. Old decorations were renovated, new medals and orders were struck, crowds cheered, heads turned, all ears listened. Grandees of Spain sent Stacie to princesses in Italy, who pleaded with her to please receive duchesses in France. Stacie called on every single one of them because any one of them could be a special friend of Francis'. Money was scattered across the landscape so lavishly that the Maitlands' public popularity was enormous and their private appeal irresistible. The favor accorded to Mrs. Maitland was as great as that given to most crowned heads, and her preeminence as an international social leader, as a cultural high priestess, as an arbiter of fashion, art, entertaining, manners, elegance, poise and charm was spotlighted like a great state jewel for the world to admire. Through all the sound and the fury, James Maitland was able to do several hundreds of millions of dollars of sound loan business and to make over a half-billion dollars' worth of distress-priced investments on behalf of the bank—which was how both goals helped to serve each other. Wherever they went Stacie studied every crowd, listened intently to as many conversations as she could sort out, grimly confident that one of these fine days she would hear Francis' name spoken and that sooner or later she would confront him, looking far downward at him from her position so far above him.

In the limousine carrying them away from Milan, where they had both been decorated on the stage of la Scala by the Ministries of Finance and of Culture, en route to the private railroad car which waited to take them to Paris, Stacie said to her husband, "I'd give anything—ten years of my life—to see his arrogant face for just two minutes every morning for the next week while he reads the goddam newspapers, the son-of-a-bitch."

"The boys have been doing a good job," Jim said. "This is the best honeymoon a fellow ever had, and the best business trip I ever made."

"He must be ready to throw himself under a train," Stacie said with enormous pleasure. "What I'd give if I could only see the look on his silly face right now."

It was over three hours before Sian was able to move Francis. It had been necessary to send Powell out to find some ice. By the time they reached the villa at Haut-Crêt it was nine o'clock, but he no longer felt the need to vomit.

Sian helped him out on the porch to sit in the warm summer night overlooking the lake, while she went to look for Celia. But her daughter's room was empty. The closet was quite bare and her suitcases were gone. In her own room, on the pillow of her bed, Sian found the note.

Dearest Mama: By the time you get this I will have left Geneva to become a theatrical dancer with Duvalier. Do you remember the pictures of the Castles which I had at Donen Hall? That is how we will be dancing. We will call ourselves "The Duvaliers." He is a fine dancer. We will go to Paris first, I think, because he has many professional friends there. I have agreed to go with him on his assurance that we will go immediately to North and South America, and then to Asia or some other part of the world. I will write to Queen Street once a week so that you may know how I am faring. We will stay away from England for at least two years. Then I will come to see you after all that time, and perhaps we will be able to talk again. Please always remember the times when I told you how much I loved you "in case anything happened." Now everything has happened, and I love you even more, with devotion and admiration, and gratitude that you are my Mama.

I think of you at all hours but most of all—thank you, dearest, darling Mama—when I am dancing.

Celia

Francis sat on a rocking chair with his legs spread well apart, holding his stomach with both hands. Sitting beside him, Sian sang "The Death of Queen Adelaide" in a shrill, comic Cockney voice.

> "Old England may weep, her bright hopes are fled,
> The friend of the poor is no more,
> For Adelaide now is among the poor dead,
> And her loss we shall sadly deplore."

Summer had taken command of the lake. Sian felt a caressing peace; she was pervaded with a sense of having finished with all the negative part of her life and of having been allowed to begin all over again. She was aware of every mistake she could make with Francis, and of all the things he might do to them, but she would be safe in his arms for at least a while longer. They might be able to remain alone together, to keep the world away for the rest of their lives. A little ingenuity was required, that was all. Just a little ingenuity and they could be happy for the rest of their lives, because they were together.

> "For though noble her birth, and high was her station,
> Their wants she relieved without ostentation,
> But now she is gone, God Bless her!
> God bless her! God bless her!
> But now she is gone, God bless her!"

"You know some very odd songs," Francis said.

"How sweet of you! Would you like to hear 'Death of the Right Honorable Sir Robert Peel, Bart., M.P.'?"

"No, thank you. Adelaide must have been a fine woman. They named a city in Australia after her."

"I don't see the connection."

"Is Celia gone?"

"Yes."

"Where?"

"She is going to dance."

"Yes, of course."

"Francis, do you think I could be mystical?"

"If anyone is, you are."

"I have a conviction that you will have word from Mr. Link about your peerage very soon."

He turned to her eagerly. "You do?"

"I have always known that you were a peer. You have true nobility, true breeding, and you are a true aristocrat."

Francis' eyes became misty. "Thank you, Sian. That means so much to me. It means everything . . . thank you." He reached out blindly and took her hand. "If confirmation does come in a few days, how soon after that can we be married?"

She beamed at him and blushed. "As soon as the law allows, my darling."

"The law?"

"Posting the banns and whatever else the Swiss require."

The telephone in the salon rang. "I'll get it," Sian said. "The servants are all at the Post Office Ball in the village." She rose and crossed the porch, reached through the window and took up the telephone on the table just inside. "Hullo? . . . London calling Mr. Hillairet? . . . Who is it in London, please? Ah . . . yes . . . one moment, please." She turned away from the telephone, smiling at Francis. "It's Mr. Link, darling," she said happily.

Francis' face filled with light. His eyes opened wide with pleasurable anticipation, and he stood very tall when he rose.

"Hello? Link?" he said into the telephone as Sian returned to rock in her chair.

"Yes, this is Link. I am calling you from the airport at Croydon. I will leave the country and follow a rather elaborate travel pattern—to where, I cannot tell you."

"Well, I hope you have a delightful journey. What is the final news?"

"The news is that your Marchioness was a little late setting her dogs on me."

"I don't understand. I meant what is the news about my peerage?"

"There is no peerage, Mr. Hillairet. It was all a hoax, and the best part of it was that you hoaxed yourself. And there is no house in Gilbert Street. There never was a house, Mr. Hillairet— but I have your money."

Francis felt his body growing smaller and smaller. As he

shrunk he flattened into the shape of a sword, its edges as sharp as razors. He heard high-pitched, far-off singing sounds, and he knew these were the voices of his parents bidding him farewell, telling him that the dwarfs had won. The sounds grew fainter and fainter as he was propelled away from his parents forever with the speed of light.

". . . and this is merely a courtesy call, Mr. Hillairet, to thank you for being such a poor looney and to thank the Marchioness for giving me such ample warning. Ashes to ashes, Mr. Hillairet—you may now return to being the absolute nothing you have always been. A peer! You! Oh, you insignificant looney, what a delicious joke!" Francis could hear Mr. Link chuckling softly, and then the line was disconnected. He turned away from the telephone as taut as a strangling cord. The dwarfs were winning. They must not win. They had to be stopped so that he could get through the gates and race along the glorious road to the shining palace just over the hill where his mother waited and his father brooded.

He was amazingly short now. He was as small and as flat and as sharp as a sword.

"What did he say, darling? Francis! Francis, what happened?"

He moved toward her on his tiny feet. "All of this time you have been one of them," he said sadly. "The Trojan horse. You were the enemy within the gates. You are a dwarf!" he shouted, and sprang at her throat.

She went over sideways in the rocking chair, which overturned with her. Francis was on top of her, and as they hit the floor she twisted her body; this and the impact loosened his grip on her throat. She drove her knee upward into his groin, and as he screamed and loosed his hold she rolled away from him and was on her feet with the speed that terror brings, running across the porch and into the house. He lifted himself on all fours as she locked the door. By the time he had pulled himself to his feet by using the porch rail, she had rolled down the metal blinds between herself and the glass windows. When she had locked the door to the kitchen leading to the entry at the back of the house, she leaned haggardly against the back of a sofa and stared at the future and the mockery of her life.

Francis began to rattle the handle of the front door, feebly at first and then with growing power. Sian moved woodenly to the telephone, called the clinic and asked to be connected with Dr. Boscawen just as Francis kicked in a window, then rammed the blind with his shoulder.

The doctor heard the sound of breaking glass and the agony in Sian's voice; everything she had been dreading had happened at last.

"Has he—"

"He tried to kill me. I have him locked outside, on the porch."

"I will be there in fifteen minutes. My two extra attendants are at the ball in your village, but no matter. I can handle Mr. Hillairet; he responds well to sedation. If necessary, hide yourself until I get there." She disconnected.

Francis was banging steadily on the heavy oak door. Sian crossed the room slowly and slipped the chain lock into place. Then she took a deep breath and, weeping silently, opened the door the four inches the chain allowed.

"Is that you, Francis?"

The question startled him. He nodded at her, dazed. "Why are you out on the porch in your pajamas and robe? What has happened?"

"Is that Sian?"

"Yes, darling. It's me."

"Were you on the porch with me? Tonight? Some time ago?" His voice was hoarse and urgent.

"No, darling."

"But where were you?"

"I've been washing my hair. You remember."

"But weren't we on the porch together?"

"Tonight? No, darling. I've been upstairs washing my hair." Her face in the crack of the open door stared directly into Francis' dazed, confused eyes. "I heard you knock and I came down—just now."

He pushed at the door and the chain went taut. "The door won't open," he said.

"What a beautiful night." Sian was trembling. Her face was as white as chalk and her eyes were hidden in violet shadows. "Is that a full moon?"

"Is that you, Sian?"

"Yes, darling. See? It's me."

"The dwarfs have come back. They've done something very clever. They have driven Mr. Link out of England and have turned him against me by pretending to be you, and tonight on the porch they had one of their own people in the chair beside me—that close to me!—pretending to be you, and they almost brought it off."

Sian pushed her forehead against the back of the door, out of his sight. "Oh, Francis, my Francis," she keened softly.

"This means my parents must still be alive," Francis said, "or else they would not have bothered to come back to trap me."

"That would be wonderful, wouldn't it?"

"Sian! They're coming again! I can hear them! Save me, Sian!" He strained against the door, then began to pound on it. Each beat of his fist struck her heart and she could not bear his pain and fright. "Let me in. Oh, my God, let me in!"

Her shaking hand went to the chain. She inhaled sharply, then lifted her chin high, slid the bolt loose and opened the door wide. He rushed at her, slammed the door behind him, and put his arms around her tightly. She clung to him. "We're safe now," she whispered. "We're safe now."

When Dr. Boscawen came into the house she saw Francis lying on the sofa with his face pressed into its upholstery, his back to the room, and Sian weeping inconsolably on a straight-backed chair at the other side of the room. The doctor went directly to the kitchen, returned at once with a glass of water, sat beside Francis and touched his shoulder. He turned enough to see her. "You will take these pills, please, Mr. Hillairet," she said, holding his chin firmly and dropping three white pills in his open mouth. When he took the water from her and sipped it she rose at once and went to Sian. Francis spat the three pills into the space between the back of the sofa and the cushion on which his head was resting and lay very still, listening.

Dr. Boscawen insisted that Sian take one pill. "Your throat is badly bruised," she said. "But you are safe. It has come and gone."

"Everything has come and gone." Sian buried her face in her hands and sobbed brokenly.

"He has to be committed now. His money must be impounded, and other vestiges of him which you have known will be gone. He may be in a clinic for many years, and he will not in any way be the man you loved. Not any more. You cannot do any more for him, my dear."

Francis listened and planned. Dr. Boscawen had obviously been the ringleader all along. The pills, the confidence she inspired, the hypnosis. He had to escape. She would lock him up and their surgeons would sneak into the clinic in the night and he would be cut down and down, smaller and smaller. Sian was their innocent dupe, but their dupe nonetheless. It was all clear at last. He had to escape. Tonight would be the crucial time.

Sian's eyes were stone-dull as she stared at Francis' back. "I have never felt so sad," she said.

"What will you do now?" the doctor asked intently.

"I am going to live."

"In the world? Out in the world?"

"I am going home and wait for Celia," Sian said, and she stood up. "I am so tired. Will you help me, Doctor? Will you help me find my way to bed?" Dr. Boscawen took her arm and they walked toward the staircase.

"What a wonderful time of year to return to England," the doctor said. "I adore midsummer in London, and it is so pretty in the country. My husband was English, you know, and it doesn't seem long ago at all that we lived in Palace Gardens Terrace and the trees were simply ablaze with blossoms—"

As Dr. Boscawen's voice faded up the stairwell, Francis turned slowly. When he saw that he was alone in the room he sat up, then rose unsteadily but with tremendous will. He walked unsteadily across the salon to the back stairs, picking up speed with each second, and raced to his bedroom on the first floor in the far wing. He dressed rapidly, took a passport and his thick wallet from his desk drawer, then opened the window and dropped fifteen feet into the soft loam of a flower bed. He ran to the Straker Squire parked in the drive, and drove off into the darkness as silently as a shadow. He did not put the car's lights on until he was well down the road to the French frontier, four kilometers away, just beyond Chene-Bourg. He crossed the frontier without incident. Twenty-seven kilometers inside France he turned off the road, slumped over the wheel and fell into a deep sleep.

When Francis awoke it was eleven o'clock in the morning. He was stiff, but his head was clear and he felt very well. He drove to Bourg-en-Bresse, where he had a sumptuous lunch of an entire roast chicken. The fact that the Straker Squire had British license plates irritated him because he had thought for a brief moment of selling it. Instead, he abandoned it and took the next train to Paris. There he took a room in a small hotel in the 17th arrondissement, on the other side of the city from the station. He slept for fourteen hours and awoke in sunshine, fully alert and on his feet almost at the moment he opened his eyes. It was a hot day. The large room had five windows, and each window had an orange awning through which the sun filtered, giving the room an enriched glow as though he were standing inside a capsule of Vitamin C. He went at once to the writing desk and made a list.

1: Buy two shirts, three pairs of socks, small valise.

2: Cash on hand: twenty-six hundred and thirty-one Swiss francs.

3: Must accumulate enough money to retain expert genealogist. Will be quicker this time because I have family seat at Willmott-Ludlow as base. How accumulate? (a) list assets? (b) seek help from wealthy woman? (c) find employment?

4: Tell *no one* family background or plans. Dwarfs too well organized.

5: Buy comb and shaving things.

He telephoned to the concierge and asked him to send for a razor, a comb and some soap, then meticulously checked off item five. When he dressed he was amazed to find that he had no socks. He searched every corner of the room, looked in every drawer and closet. No socks. Was this a warning?

Should he change hotels? He called the concierge and asked him to send for a pair of black lisle socks, size eleven, then returned to the writing desk to list his assets.

I: *Assets*

(a) Racing Stable
(b) Two Rolls-Royces
(c) Bank Account—Graubendon-Zug, Suisse Coutts', London
(d) Lease on Farm Street flat has 61 years to run
(e) Furniture and objets d'art in Farm Street flat
(f) Claim against Mr. Link/Jemma Jay Estate Agents for Gilbert Street house payment
(g) Ten shares American Tel. & Tel.
(h) Cash on hand

II: *Debits*

Cannot liquidate any of these assets at present because the London solicitor, Mr. Gitlin, is obviously in the employ of Dwarfs. Cannot draw on Swiss bank account because M. Crouch untested re: Dwarf Position and could report to Dr. Boscawen, who then could trace me. Same ATT shares.

III: *Conclusion*

Must find highly remunerative work so that genealogist may be retained at once to establish *legal* right to peerage and re-entry into Britain when English assets may be recovered. What highly remunerative work? Banking does not pay enough.

Francis folded both lists carefully and put them inside his breast pocket. When the *chasseur* arrived with the order he tipped the boy fifty centimes. He shaved, combed and donned his new socks. How could he have forgotten to ask for a toothbrush? Again he called the concierge, and, at the latter's suggestion, added toothpaste to the list.

While waiting he pulled a chair up to the window and began to think. In an instant he had the solution. He would cook. In his wallet he had those treasured letters of recommendation from the Dowager Marchioness of Shattock and the Baroness Keys. As a cook he could earn twenty thousand dollars a year.

Working papers were out of the question. It would have to be a private establishment. Who? Where? As he saw it, he had three choices: the Princess Umbaratchini, the Raddatz sisters, and the Countess Kaya Smornya-Bakrescu. To work for the Raddatzes would mean working in Leipzig. Wrong climate. To work for the Countess meant Bucharest and an unrelenting emotional and physical strain which would certainly affect the quality of his work. Out. It would have to be the Princess. He called the concierge and asked him to please telephone the residence of the Princess Umbaratchini. A short time later she was on the phone, almost hysterical on hearing his voice.

"Bombola!" she yelled into the telephone. "Where are you? Come here. *Vieni, vieni, vieni!* Come to me!" He tried to interrupt, but she kept talking. "When you got here? How long? Tonight? We screw tonight?"

"Well, uh, I . . ."

"Tonight! Oh, you voice make-a me crazy."

"About, uh, ten?" He must dine alone. He had to conserve his funds.

"Tonight! Oh! Tonight we start and we screw for three days. Aieee! *Ciao, bombola!*" She disconnected.

He rang the doorbell at the Umbaratchini mansion at ten o'clock sharp, and seconds later was ushered into a drawing room where the princess and six people seemed to be waiting for him. She ran like a heron across the room and threw herself upon him, her jejune, waffling, soft mouth swallowing the lower half of his face. He knew four of the people from London. Two were Poles and two Austrian; the tallest Austrian had an excellent family name. He had never met Prince Umbaratchini, Giovanna's husband, or the prince's mistress, an American girl named Caroline Gounod, but he was proud to meet the prince, whose family was over fourteen hundred years old.

"I have heard so much about you from Giovanna," the prince said warmly, "that we felt we should stay to welcome you before the rest of us went off to dinner."

Giovanna, who already had her hand in Francis' pocket, said merrily, "Very well, you have met him. Good night, all. We shall be very busy." The ladies tittered and the men smiled. The prince beamed. He looked at his wristwatch.

"Yes, we must run," he said. "Good night, Mr. Hillairet."
Everyone wanted to shake his hand, and Miss Gounod
looked as though she might bite him on the thigh. Then
they were gone, and Francis reaped the whirlwind.

By noon on Friday, Giovanna agreed to go out for lunch.
It was a slow, lackadaisical meal. Her fires had been banked.
Over coffee and armagnac, he was able to talk to her calmly.

"Giovanna, I want a favor from you."

"Anything, dolling, anything."

"I would like you to hire me as your cook."

"What you say?"

"I am a very good cook; in fact, some of the very best
cooks in Europe have said that I am a great cook."

"Dolling, I don't doubt. But it is impossible."

"Why?"

"How could I sleep with my cook? It would disgrace
Umbie."

"Well, it isn't as though I'd be *only* your cook, is it? I
mean, I have met your husband socially, and we went to bed
very successfully long before I ever thought of cooking for
you. It isn't as though people would think you had found me
in the kitchen and seduced me."

"Baby-bombola, believe Giovanna. Women sleep with the
chauffeur. That is all right, that is accepted. But never the
cook. It is not done. Would you like to be chauffeur? I am
already tired of this chauffeur."

"I don't drive all that well, and I hardly know Paris at
all."

Giovanna shrugged.

"But, Giovanna, if I were the cook in your house we
wouldn't *have* to go to bed together . . ."

"Dolling, be sensible. Everyone in Paris knows we screw,
so who will believe if we don't screw? It would disgrace
Umbie. No. I don't care for myself, but I could not hurt
Umbie."

"You make it sound as though it is impossible for me to get
a job as a cook anywhere in Paris."

"With your reputation, yes, I agree. There are thirty-four
important Russian royals in Paris and they have to work as

taxi or doorman because no woman can sleep with her cook and they are human. No? Even with a butler. Margot Dunlop-Huynegin is taking a little bit now and then from her husband's valet, but of course she hates the husband and everyone knows that. It can't be done, sweet dolling love."

"I feel like a boor," Francis said. "I am sorry, Giovanna, I should have known. I shouldn't have put you in such a position. Please forgive me."

Francis went back to his hotel alone and remained there for two days, brooding. By Monday morning he was no further toward a solution, and was close to despair when Giovanna called with great excitement and a solution to his problems.

"Bambola! You can be a very rich cook!"

"No! Where? How?"

"We were with some very important people at a very important dinner last night, and the woman is looking for a great French *chef de cuisine*. I almost fainted. I thought of you, and when I think of you too quickly I can feel you and I almost faint. She is going at three o'clock this afternoon to the office where the people buy the cooks. You know? Madame Slavin in the Faubourg St. Honoré? The place—you know—I get my butlers there. So I called Madame Slavin and I tell her that the greatest *chef de cuisine* my family has ever known has just come back from London where he cook for that woman—you know—the English countess you was screwing with last year—and I tell her you are available. She begs with me to make you come to her at two o'clock. You will become fantastically rich, dolling."

Francis had a pleasant talk with Mme. Slavin, who appeared to be an excellent little woman. He agreed to an interview with the very, very important client at three o'clock, and promptly on the hour he was shown into the clients' room. He hesitated for the barest moment as he went through the doorway, because sitting in front of him was the small, lovely, dark-haired woman who had filled his dreams for more than a year. He had dreamed of her, but was she alive? Who could she be? Who was she?

"Madame Maitland," Mme. Slavin said, "I present to you

Monsieur François Hillairet, who is capable of speaking to you in French or in English, and who has the finest references as a *chef de cuisine* it has been my pleasure to examine for many years."

Stacie stared in shock at Francis. Her face had become so pale that the cosmetics glowed unhealthily. For a moment she was unable to speak or move.

"May Monsieur Hillairet sit, Madame Maitland?"

"Yes," Stacie whispered hoarsely. "Please leave us." Francis sat down as Mme. Slavin left the room. Stacie leaned forward and looked deeply into his bewildered yellow eyes. "Francis," she whispered, and the single word seemed to travel across a great distance of time and space and pain. But he misunderstood why she had spoken, and he began to tell of his qualifications for the post: of the dinners which had won him attention, of the great people he knew on both continents, of his repertoire of dishes. As he spoke, looking directly at her, Stacie finally comprehended that he really didn't know her. She was an exigent stranger and therefore a convenience to him, but those eyes which seemed baffled were only trying to remember if he had heard her name or seen her picture in some newspaper or listened to gossip about her. For the first time in her life she saw that he had always been mad. From the day she had met him he had been just as unable to accommodate reality as he was at this instant, and with this realization the precious past lost its value, and her mind turned it to dust and watched it blow away.

Everything had changed and yet nothing had changed. There was no meaning to life; one only did the best one could. By what she and Francis had done, they had become what they were meant to be, despite themselves. Here they were, and she wasn't unhappy any more. Here he was, and she didn't want him.

But this baffled, duped and empty man was a superb cook, and superb cooks were very hard to find. She interrupted his monologue. "You are engaged," she said as she rose to terminate the interview. "Madame Slavin will inform you of the details and give you your steamship ticket."

About the Author

Members of the Condon Cult will be relieved to learn that their peripatetic author, a member of the Jet Set since the days of the Lisbon Clipper, is currently preoccupied with blueprints for a house he is building on the Algarve coast of Portugal. In the past thirteen years he and his long-suffering wife have lived in Paris, Madrid, New York City, Mexico City and Geneva.

Mr. Condon's previous books (*The Oldest Confession, The Manchurian Candidate, Some Angry Angel, A Talent for Loving* and *An Infinity of Mirrors*) have been published in a total of sixteen languages and in Braille. *Any God Will Do* is his sixth novel; in between bouts with architects he is already at work on a seventh.